The Sea
of
Tears

Ironpass
Norther
Northwarden
Dencamp-on-the-Teeth
Kenting Rush
The Blackwood
Highcastle
Wolfram
Cavell Keep
EASTERN
KINGDOMS
Prank's Stone
THE
KINGDOM
Dolth
Rodez
Ran
The Straits of
Ilthros
Romney
Euper
Tiburn
THE
KINGDOM
OF
ROLDEM
Roldem
Sloop
Bas-Tyra
Sadara
yton
Silden
Cheam
Cross
Rillanon
Timons
The Sea of
Kingdoms
Grey Range
Deep Taunton
Mallow Haven
reen Reaches
The Peaks of Tranquility
Pointer's Head
Peaks
of
the
Quor
Jonril
EAT KESH
Kampari
es
Ishlang
Min
t
Mother
of
Waters
Dosra
Ithra
ara
Zacara
Caralién
DARK
HAVEN
Ishap's Deep
Kesh
esh
Surnom
Wasra
Grimstone Mountains
Overn Deep
Kimri
Tupa
Jalóme
Queral
The
Great
Sea
Guardians
Ahar
Hansulé
Ashunta
The Girdle of Kesh
Brijané
Teléman
The
Clasp
THE
DRAHALI
KAPUR
DESERT
The Belt
GON MERE
LESSER KESH
(KESHIAN CONFEDERACY)
Peaks
of
Torment
R.M. Askren 2007

A
KINGDOM
BESIEGED

A
KINGDOM
BESIEGED

BOOK ONE OF THE CHAOSWAR SAGA

RAYMOND E. FEIST

HARPER Voyager
An Imprint of HarperCollins*Publishers*

A KINGDOM BESIEGED. Copyright © 2011 by Raymond E. Feist. All rights reserved. Printed in the United States of America. No part of this book may be used or reproduced in any manner whatsoever without written permission except in the case of brief quotations embodied in critical articles and reviews. For information address HarperCollins Publishers, 10 East 53rd Street, New York, NY 10022.

HarperCollins books may be purchased for educational, business, or sales promotional use. For information please write: Special Markets Department, HarperCollins Publishers, 10 East 53rd Street, New York, NY 10022.

FIRST EDITION

Harper Voyager and design is a trademark of HCP LLC.

Designed by Jaime Putorti
Map designed by Ralph M. Askren, D.V.M.

Library of Congress Cataloging-in-Publication Data has been applied for.

ISBN 978-0-06-146839-1

11 12 13 14 15   OV/BVG   10 9 8 7 6 5 4 3 2 1

THIS ONE'S FOR JOHN AND TAMMY

CONTENTS

CONTENTS

ACKNOWLEDGMENTS

As is always the case, I must begin with thanks to the original mothers and fathers of Midkemia who generously gave me permission to use their playground; I trust I haven't abused it too much.

As always to Jonathan Matson, my thanks for being more than a business partner, but a friend of the very best kind, one who puts up with you with humor and affection just because that's the kind of person he is.

To the brilliant ladies at HarperCollins, on both sides of the pond, for making me look good.

I would also like to thank those whom I've come to know through the magic of modern social media: the mailing list and visitors to the website at Crydee.com, who have been around awhile; and new acquaintances on Facebook, MySpace, and Twitter, who have opened up a new avenue of communication between author and reader I wouldn't have dreamed of ten years ago. Thank you for your support and kind words; it means more than you can know.

Last, to my mother, who left us early this year, my constant thanks for being the first to believe I could do this and who painstakingly retyped every page of *Magician* so that when I sent it in for consideration it would "look professional." Not a day goes by I don't think of you, Mom.

Raymond E. Feist
San Diego, California
September 2010

A
KINGDOM
BESIEGED

CHILD

The skies shrieked.

Overhead, a storm of black energies shot out tendrils that reached forth and attached themselves to the first structure they encountered. The sound generated was almost as terrifying as the sight of everything they touched collapsing into rubble.

The inhabitants of the city fled in abject terror, ignoring the plight of others, even family or close friends. Above the onrushing tide of darkness loomed a figure, a thing of such massive size and monstrosity that it lay beyond comprehension.

The remaining King's Guardians did what they could to oppose the Darkness, but there was little they could achieve against such madness. A female fled through the streets amid the trampling throng. Fearful of what she might see, she chanced a quick glance behind her and clutched her child to her chest.

Other city residents huddled in doorways, given over to despair, waiting for the inevitability of their own destruction, weeping as they clung to one another, or staring toward the Centre, whence the Darkness was coming.

From the Time Before Time, legends about the Final End had persisted, but these stories were seen as nothing more than metaphors, cautionary tales with which the Elders might teach children so they could contribute usefully to the People during this particular Endurance.

It was said that some Elders had repeated the Endurance so many times that they remembered bits and pieces of previous incarnations and had begun to piece together the plan of everything in the world. It was even whispered that some had ventured into the realms of madness—known as the "Other Places" or "the Outside"—or even to the edge of the Void, and returned, but few credited such reports as anything other than tall tales.

The People rejoiced in their Existence and their Endurance, and when their personal end came they knew it was no more than an interruption of the Eternal Journey.

But what they faced now was the Final End, the termination of the Eternal Journey, and no words existed to express the terror and anguish that assailed them.

The female pushed through a knot of the People clustered at an intersection in the center of the city's Eastern Canton. Some had come to seek the Sunrise Gate but, having come here, did not seem to know what to do next.

Nothing in the history of the People had prepared them for the Darkness.

The mother looked down at her child, who clutched her robe with delicate claws, her black eyes enormous in the still-tiny face. "My child," she whispered, and although the screams and cries from those surrounding them drowned out the sound, the child saw her mother's lips move and understood. She smiled at her mother, showing rapidly growing fangs. Her baby skin had already sloughed off and her first set of scales were visible. If she could feed her, her mother thought, she would grow quickly and would be better able to flee.

"But flee where?"

East.

Out of the gate to the Quartz Mountains and through the Valley of Flame, then on to the Kingdom's boundary. It was rumored that others had found safety in the Kingdom of Ma'har, to the south, where age-old enmities had been put aside in the face of the common terror.

The mother elbowed her way through the press, sensing more than seeing that a fight had erupted to the north. Ancient perceptions, buried under civilized training, rose to the surface to aid her and the child. Along with them rose ancient hungers, appetites for the flesh of something more substantial than the lesser animals the King had decreed would form their sustenance. Soon the People would become like the Mad Ones, struggling for survival by devouring one another. She sensed that several threats were converging, threats that would soon turn into feeding frenzies, and she knew that to be caught up in one of those would be her doom or the child's, or both.

She chanced a brief look back and as she had suspected, claws were being wielded and fangs were dripping blood. A feeding frenzy would soon sweep through this area of the city and even with her child's life in the balance, she could easily be caught up in it. Neither of them had fed in a very long time.

A few Guardians not detailed to delay the onslaught were quickly intervening, their flaming swords rising and falling, dispatching not only those involved in the nascent frenzy but also those unfortunate enough to be slow in departing.

She turned and fled.

Once, like so many who lived in the city, she had marveled at the splendor of the King and his Guardians. They were magnificent in their armor, their terrible beauty a source of fear and breeding lust. It was forbidden for a Guardian to breed, but that didn't still a young female's desire when they flew by, their massive red wings unfurled, eyes blazing as they sought out any source of discord that might break the King's peace.

Now, she wondered how anyone could gaze back at the all-consuming Darkness and imagine any part of the realm enjoying the King's peace.

She hurried on to join a press of frightened citizens making their way through the Sunrise Gate, the eastern entrance to the King's city. The jostling and bumping threatened to turn into fights, and fights would turn into frenzies. She felt her fear and rage rising. Glancing down at the child, she found its eyes studying her face. It seemed to see more, know more, than a baby should.

The streets running eastward were becoming ever more crowded as others sought to put as much distance as possible between themselves and the coming Final End. She turned down a back alley, running past two males who appeared to be on the verge of conflict, the energy generated by one's mounting rage acting like a beacon to others nearby. Within minutes another melee would erupt, drawing the attention of the Guardians; and then yet more lives would be lost.

Part of her wondered, as she ducked around a corner, if there was any point in trying to maintain order in the face of the Final End, anyway, especially now that the King was gone. Those Guardians left behind were attempting to keep the peace, but to what end?

Everyone lived and died by the King's edict: his word was law, which was how it was and always had been.

Thus had the Kingdom of Dahun flourished through many Endurances, and Existence was as it should be. The People thrived, at peace with the other kingdoms, safe from the predations of the Savage Ones and the Mad Ones beyond.

But now he was gone.

She found herself assailed by a rising hopelessness, an alien emotion for which she had no name. Suddenly she wondered why she should go on, whether there was anything to gain by it. And then her child stirred against her, and she knew the answer.

The child was hungry. And so was she.

She spoke her own name, "Lair'ss," as if she wished her child to remember it. *So much left undone,* she thought as she hurried on.

With the King gone no one could say what would become of the People now that the Final End was approaching, but she was determined to see her child to safety or die trying.

When she reached the wall, she saw the stairs to the ramparts were empty, so she climbed to get a better view of the gate. As she had feared, riots were under way everywhere as terrified people tried to leave, but the remaining Guardians at the gate held them back. No one could leave the city without the King's writ; and the King was gone. She paused, fearful and undecided.

She turned and looked down on the city of her birth: Das'taas. It had been a place of terrifying majesty, and although it was never truly at rest, it had gradually achieved a state of equipoise, a state almost approaching tranquillity. While the People would never be without their impulses toward bloody violence and destruction, the King and his Guardians had managed to keep it to a minimum, even though there were many with ancient memories that stretched back to the Time Before Time, when the People had lived like the Savages and the Mad Ones, when every individual had been spawned in the birth pits, creatures of frantic need and limited power. Strength had been earned, and the price had been bloody. Child had eaten child, and the victor had emerged stronger, smarter, and more cunning. The subsequent battles were never ending.

Then Dahun had arisen, as had Maarg, Simote, and others, each carving out their empires. Of all these rulers, Dahun had moved farthest from the madness and savagery that marked the People. But his most bitter enemy, Maarg, had been more like the Mad Ones during his rule. Dahun had instituted laws and created the Guardians, and the majesty of the People had reached its highest expression, seeking to evolve them in a way unknown before. In the end, Maarg had created a realm in which the chaos of the Mad Ones had been contained, channeled, and used to build a meritocracy, in which merit was defined by strength, cunning, and the ability to recruit allies, vassals, and protectors.

All this Lair'ss knew: her memories, and those of others, flowed through her as she looked at the city, trying to decide what she should do. She crouched to prevent her child and herself from being seen against the sky by those below. Where were the flyers? she wondered.

The child stirred, hunger making her fractious. Lair'ss slapped her lightly, just enough to communicate danger but not hard enough to hurt, and the child fell quiet instantly, understanding the warning.

The role of parent was not natural to the People. Yet for generations Dahun had demanded pairs meet, mate, and then rear children. The days of crawling out of the birth pits were behind them, and each parent was required to teach a child as well as provide for it. Letting the child die or giving in to rage and killing it brought harsh punishment. Like all of her clan and class, Lair'ss did not fully understand all she had been taught. She had spent most of her youth dreaming of murder and male mates until she had been paired with Dagri. Then she had learned a skill, becoming a mender of garments, working long hours in a room with other females.

Each night she would return to her mate, but he had perished opposing the Final End that was now upon them. Now, she felt an unfamiliar pang at the thought of him; she hadn't particularly liked Dagri when Dahun's Masjester had paired them. Still, he had become familiar, and the child seemed to find him agreeable. He had been a vassal of a rising servant of the King and had gained rank and some prestige. He was young and powerful, and the matings had been fun and always rewarding. She had even felt some delight when giving him the news that she would bear a child, which had been an unexpectedly pleasant experience. She was not sure why, but she had found joy in knowing he wanted that child.

Now she felt an emptiness inside her when she thought of Dagri. He had left with the King's army to fight against Maarg, and neither the King nor Dagri had returned. She had often wondered what had happened. Had he died in battle surrounded by comrades and enemies? The image that came to her brought her both sadness and pride. Or was he lost in some distant land, with no way of returning? That image made her grieve.

Yet despite everything coming to ruin around her, she still felt it was her duty to Dagri to care for his child. She glanced down at it now, large enough that its weight was a burden on her arm, and saw those dark eyes regarding her again. What was it thinking? Did it think?

She shook her head, knowing the answer. Of course it thought. She had killed for it and seen it eat, making it stronger and smarter. Even now the child responded to her quiet words or touch, as Lair'ss wished. If anything, the child was cunning enough that if she could feed it one or two more times, it would become more of an ally in this flight and less of a hindrance.

Lair'ss knew it was time. With everything falling apart, the stricture against preying on others of the People would no longer be obeyed. She was certain others had already taken to the old ways, and as a result potential enemies, those who would devour her and the child, were growing more powerful and arising at every hand.

She peered in all directions until she saw a furtive figure hiding in the shadows below. A small being, it trembled at being discovered.

In a swift series of moves, Lair'ss put down the child, giving it a warning poke to keep it quiet, leaped from the rampart to the stairs halfway down, and was upon the hiding figure before it knew it. After delivering a quick stunning blow, she carried the limp being up to her child.

No sooner had the unconscious figure been lain on the stones than the child threw herself with astonishing energy upon it. The shock of the attack roused the tiny creature, but Lair'ss was ready for it. A long talon slashed its throat.

Fighting back her own hunger, the mother watched her daughter feed. She could swear she saw the child grow before her eyes. The need to push the child aside and feed upon the creature herself was almost overwhelming, but her mind was still relatively free of animal rage, and she knew it was crucial that the child grow quickly. She would be too large to carry now, but after this feast, she should grow large enough that she should be able to keep pace with her mother.

Ignoring her own hunger pangs, Lair'ss watched as the corpse was consumed—bone, sinew, hair, and skin—until nothing was left but the simple robe and sandals it wore. Lair'ss's brow furrowed. In her haste she had not noticed the design of the robes. The dead creature was an Archivist, a keeper of knowledge.

Now her daughter looked at her, her gaze narrowing for an instant. Then she spoke her first words. "Thank you, Mother. That was . . . enlightening."

"You can talk . . . ?" said Lair'ss, stating the obvious.

"This one . . . lacked strength or magic . . . but he had knowledge." The child spoke each word carefully, as if trying them out and judging them before uttering a syllable. Then she rose up on slightly unsteady feet; the growth she had gained from her feasting had changed her balance and she needed a few minutes to adjust. Then she looked at her mother and added, "A great deal of knowledge."

Lair'ss knew fear then. Before her eyes, in a matter of minutes, her daughter had ceased being a mewling infant and was now a young adult, one with memories and knowledge belonging to the most guarded caste of the King's court, the Archivists.

The child's face was now almost on a level with the larger female who sat huddled against the inner wall. "I am ready, Mother," she said.

Lair'ss accepted that. Her child now had knowledge.

The child glanced around to see if they were still hidden. Then she declared, "I know a way." She turned and moved downward; unquestioning, Lair'ss followed.

They struggled though the jagged rocks. Over the city wall, down the gullies that ages of wind and rain had carved out along the roadside and through the marshes. Flaming jets of gas had barred their way, but the child knew the route to take. From the moment she had devoured the Archivist, she had become a being unlike any Lair'ss had known.

At one point they huddled beneath an outcrop of rocks as a solitary flyer hovered overhead, seeking prey below. The child would be an easy target, and if Lair'ss's strength became any more depleted, she would be no match for the winged predator.

In the quiet of early morning, as the nocturnal predators were sweeping the mountains one last time before returning to their lairs, the child looked into her mother's face, barely visible in the faint light from the stars above and the tiny moon nearing the western horizon. Softly she said, "I know things, Mother."

Weak from hunger, Lair'ss replied, "Yes, I understand."

"Do you?" The child took her mother's face gently between her hands. "The Archivist's . . . knowledge, but not his memories, are mine. I know things, but other things are empty, holes in my mind." She tilted her head to one side, her eyes fastened on her mother's features. "Tell me."

"What, Daughter?"

"Tell me those things I do not know."

"I do not understand."

The child gazed out from under the sheltering rock at the setting moon. "What is that?" she said, pointing to the faint light on the western horizon.

"That is Das'taas, or what is left of it," said her mother weakly. "It was our home."

"Why did we leave?"

"The Darkness came and our Lord Dahun was gone and no one knew how to fight it."

"Darkness?" asked Child.

Lair'ss was so weak now that she sensed this might be her last conversation with her daughter. "I know little, but this much is what is known. The Darkness came from the Centre."

The child tilted her head as if remembering something. "Ah, yes, the Centre. The Ancient Heart."

"I do not know it by that name, but the Old Kingdoms, Despaira, Paingor, Mournhome, Abandos, and the others held sway since the first days after the Time Before Time. Our Lord Dahun paid tribute to the Old Kingdoms, and we stood as a bulwark against the Savages." Lair'ss inclined her head behind them. "There, to the east, where we go now. But we were told a bad thing happened."

"What, Mother?"

"I do not know," Lair'ss said wearily. "So much of what has happened is a mystery." She stared out toward the distant city. "I have been told we once lived like the Savages, spawning in pits, fighting for survival from the first moment. Each death returned us to the pits, and the struggle was endless.

"I have been told that the Kings brought order and taught us how to live a new way, how to build as well as destroy, how to care for one another without constant killing. We were told these were good things."

"Why?"

"Again, I do not know," she said with a long sigh. "But what the King wills is law."

The younger female was quiet for a while as the sun to the east grew brighter. Finally she asked, "Where do we go?" prodded Child.

After a moment, her mother answered, "To the east, toward the lands of the Savages and the Mad Ones."

"Why?" asked Child.

"Because there is nowhere else to go," answered her mother softly.

A smile crossed the child's lips and she said, "No, there is another place to go." Suddenly she lunged forward and her fangs closed around her mother's throat, and with one pull, she tore it open. Blood fountained and she drank deeply as the light faded from her mother's eyes.

Thoughts came with the feeding, not her own, but those of the being whose life she ended.

A time of calm, with a male, by the name of Dagri, who was her father. He had vanished with the King.

Images flashed, some understandable and some not, places, faces, struggles and quiet. And some of the holes in her knowledge were filled in as the more abstract knowledge she had gained from the Archivist blended with her mother's experiences.

There are been a stable time, a time of Dahun's dominion. Then word had come of a struggle to the west. Dahun's kingdom was not one of the Old Kingdoms, but one of the Second Kingdoms, those that ringed the five original Kingdoms.

Then had been a war, not here, but in some other place, against a king named Maarg, and her father and others had gone with Dahun to fight him. No one had returned, leaving only the city Guardians and those who knew magic to face the Darkness when it appeared. No one knew what had become of the Old Kingdoms.

Bits and pieces of knowledge of those times and places seemed to float around the periphery of her thoughts, almost understood, tantalizingly so, but still not coherent. She knew one thing, though: if she were to survive, she needed more knowledge and power.

She regarded what was left of her mother's body, then consumed what was left. She kept feeling odd sensations as she did so and tried to put a name to them, but couldn't. In a strange way, she regretted the need to feed on the female who had brought her into this world, but her abstract knowledge of her race's breeding history made it difficult to understand why she would feel a bond with this female more than any other. She paused; the Archivist thought of their collective society as "the race," but her mother had been taught to consider herself a member of "the People." Child understood that this was a distinction, but why it was important eluded her.

She crawled out from under the overhang, peering about for any threat. In the distance she saw a group of flyers frantically beating toward her, so she ducked back under the overhang until she was certain they had passed. Peering to the west, she saw a dark spot on the horizon. From the knowledge she had inherited from her feeding she knew it to be something fundamentally wrong, and a radical and terrible change in the order of her world, yet it remained abstract to her. She had no feelings about that.

Feelings?

She paused. Strange sensations in the pit of her stomach and rising up into her chest and throat visited her, but she had no name for them. For an instant she wondered if she was in danger from them, like poison or exposure to dangerous magics.

Something tickled the edge of her consciousness. She paused and considered this unfathomable material. From the knowledge she had gained from the Archivist, she understood that memories were either there or not. To have memories from those devoured, yet be unable to reach them was unheard of; so this must be something else.

But if it was something else, then what was it?

Still not enough knowledge, she thought, and certainly not enough power. She must hunt. She must grow stronger, more powerful.

There was a stirring above, and suddenly another flyer dropped out of the evening sky. Without thought, she reached out a hand, but not in the clawed defensive position. Instead, her palm faced the attacker and a searing bolt of energy shot from it and slicked cleanly through his neck, severing the head, which dropped at her feet as the body crashed into the rocks a few feet away.

Child felt only mild hunger but knew she needed more food to become more powerful than she was.

She hunkered down to begin eating the flyer's head. "Magic," she said softly to herself. But she had not encountered a spellcaster, let alone devoured one. Even more softly she pondered, "Now where did that come from?"

Then she set about eating the creature's brain.

1

HUNT

The horses reared.

The two young riders kept them under control, their long hours of training used to good effect in the face of the unexpected attack. From the brush behind them came the shouts of the men-at-arms and the baying of the dogs, signaling that relief would be there in minutes. Until then, the two youthful hunters were on their own. The two riders had come through an upland scrub of gorse and heather, growing in a swath of sandy soil that had been denuded of trees in ages past.

Searching for wild boar or stag, the brothers from Crydee had stumbled upon something both unexpected and terrifying: a sleeping wyvern.

First cousin to a dragon, the green-scaled beast was far from its usual mountainous hunting grounds and had been asleep in a deep gully masked from their approach by tall ferns and brush.

Now, disturbed from its rest, the angry beast rose up, snapping its wings wide to take to the sky.

"What?" shouted Brendan to his elder brother.

"Don't let it get away!" replied Martin.

"Why? We can't eat it!"

"No, but think of the trophy on the wall!"

With a grunt of resignation, the younger brother dropped his boar spear, threw his leg over his horse's neck, and dropped to the ground, nimbly removing his bow from his shoulder as he did so. His horse, usually a well-trained mare, was all too happy to run off as fast as possible from the large predator. Brendan drew a broad-tipped arrow from his quiver, nocked his bow, and drew and fired in a matter of seconds.

The arrow flew truly, striking the emerald creature squarely at the joint of shoulder and wing, and it faltered. Slowly, the wing drooped limply.

Martin leaped off his horse, gripping his boar spear tightly, and his horse sped off after Brendan's mount. The injured wyvern snarled and reared up and inhaled deeply, making a strange clucking sound.

"Oh, damn!" said Brendan.

"Down!" shouted his brother, diving to the right.

Brendan leaped to the left as a searing blast of flame cut through the air where he had been standing only a moment before. He could feel the hair on his head singe as the flames missed him by bare inches. He kept rolling, unable to see the wyvern, though he could hear it roar and smell the acrid smoke and blackened soil as it attacked wildly.

Having clutched the spear to his chest, along the same axis as his body so that he could come swiftly to his feet, Martin launched himself upright. The wyvern seemed momentarily confused by having two antagonists moving in different directions. Then it fixed its eyes on Brendan and started to suck in more air. From what Martin knew of wyvern behavior, his brother was about to be targeted again with another blast of flames. He cast the spear despairingly, but the range was too far: it fell agonizingly close, but short of the creature.

Suddenly, miraculously, an arrow sliced through the space between the brothers, taking the wyvern in the throat. The creature gagged, choked, and staggered backward, then shuddered and began to thrash in pain. Reprieved, the brothers raced forward. Martin retrieved his spear and impaled the creature upon it, while Brendan took careful aim and loosed an arrow into the exposed joint between the wyvern's neck and torso, straight at the creature's heart. It thrashed for another long moment, then fell still in death.

Looking to see the author of the saving shot, the brothers saw a young woman in leather breeches, tunic, and knee-high riding boots standing a little way away from them. She wore a short rider's cape thrown back over her left shoulder for quick access to the quiver slung across her back. Her bow was a double recurved, compact and easy to shoot from horseback or on foot, evolved from an ancient Tsurani design, but no weapon for a beginner. Only the traditional hunter's longbow had more power and range.

Brendan's face lit up at the sight of her. "Lady Bethany, a pleasure as always." He shouldered his own bow and wiped perspiration from his brow and grinned as he glanced over at his brother and saw how Martin attempted to rein in his expression of annoyance and replace it with a neutral expression.

Born a year apart, the two brothers might as well have been twins. Unlike their older brother, Hal, who looked like their father, being broad of shoulder and chest, dark of hair, and six inches above six feet in height, these two brothers took after their mother. Their hair was a lighter brown, their eyes were blue rather than dark brown, and they were lithe in movement, slender of frame, and four inches shorter than both their father and Hal. They had a whipcord strength and resilience rather than brute power.

Bethany's dark red hair fell to her shoulders, and her face was elegant and finely formed. Her smile carried a hint of something akin to condescension as she walked in measured steps, leading her horse toward the fallen beast. "You looked as if you could use a little assistance," she said with barely veiled humor. Like the brothers she stood on the verge of adulthood, glorious in her youth and taking it for granted. She would be nineteen years old at the next Midsummer Feast, as would Martin. The three of them had been friends since babyhood. Her father was Robert, Earl of Carse, vassal to their father, Lord Henry, Duke of Crydee. She was the tallest woman in either Carse or Crydee at six feet.

Martin frowned. "I thought you said you found hunting a bore?"

"I find most things a bore," she said with a laugh. "I changed my mind about hunting and decided to catch up with you louts."

Noise from behind her indicated that the rest of the Duke's hunting party was closing in. A moment later, three horses burst through the underbrush and the riders reined in as they regarded the three young hunters and the dead wyvern.

The rider in the middle was Duke Henry, known as Harry, since his father had also been named Henry. He grinned at the sight of his two boys and the daughter of his friend standing without injury over the fallen monster. His face was sunburned and weathered, making him look older than his forty-nine years, his dark beard showing shots of grey. "What do you think of that, Robert?" he asked the rider on his right.

Robert, Earl of Carse, reined in. His blond hair had turned grey at an early age, so it looked nearly white in the midafternoon sun. Like his companion, his face was sunburned and weather-beaten. That his daughter was as good an archer as any man in the west pleased him. "I think my daughter's arrow did the honors," he answered. Then his expression darkened. "But riding unattended from the castle was the pinnacle of foolishness!"

The woodlands around Crydee had been pacified for generations, but they were still not without risk. He took a deep breath of resignation; Bethany was his only child and had been much indulged. As a result she was willful and impetuous at times, much to his despair.

Bethany smiled at her father's ire; she had been a nettle as often as a balm. Growing up, she had developed a combative nature. "I grew bored with the chatter of the ladies of Crydee." She smiled and nodded at the Duke. "No offense is intended, my lord, but I have only so much interest in needlework and cooking, to my mother's chagrin. My limit was reached, so I decided some sport was needed." She glanced at the fallen creature. "Though this sport did end abruptly."

"Ha!" said the Duke, and he laughed. "So one should wish, Lady Bethany. A wounded wyvern is a dangerous beast. Most would give the creature a wide berth."

The trackers and beaters and dogs had arrived, and Huntmaster Rodney motioned for the beast to be secured.

Brendan said, "We all took a hand in killing the wyvern, Father, but I'll concede honors to Bethany. Her arrow spared me a scorching, I'll avow."

Martin nodded in agreement, as if who claimed the kill was of no importance to him.

"What do you intend to do with it?" asked Robert. "You can't eat it."

The brothers glanced at the repeat of the oft-repeated joke. The nobility in the east might hunt the big predators for sport, but along the Far Coast they were nothing more than a nuisance, a menace to herds and farms. Years of controlling the population of big cats, packs of dogs and wolves, and dragon kin such as the wyverns had kept their incursion into the lowlands a rare occurrence. Most of the Duke's hunting was for giant boar—as it was today—elk up in the foothills, deer in the forest, and giant bears.

"I think its head on the wall would make a wonderful trophy for my room, Father," said Bethany, shouldering her bow.

Lord Robert glanced at his host, who shook his head, barely containing his mirth. "Not one for finery?" asked the Duke.

"Silks and oils, gowns and shoes are lost on my Bethany."

Turning back to his only child, he said, "It will hang in the trophy hall in the keep, not your quarters."

Martin cleaned off the head of his boar spear in the tall grass, then handed it to one of the men-at-arms.

Brendan grinned. "Remembering her attire at the last Midsummer Feast of Banapis, I don't think finery is entirely lost on her."

Even the usually dour Martin was forced to smile at this. "It seems you took note."

Now it was Bethany's turn to look slightly annoyed, and the color rose in her fair cheeks. It was a poorly kept secret that everyone expected the Earl's daughter eventually to become the next Duchess of Crydee when Henry's eldest son, Hal, became Duke. The politics of the Kingdom required all such alliances to be approved by the King, but as the Duke and his family were distant kin to the Royal House of conDoin, it kept things simpler if no strong alliances were formed between those nobles on the Far Coast and the powerful noble houses in the distant Eastern Realm.

"How fares young Hal?" asked Robert of his host.

Harry's expression revealed his pride in his eldest. "Very well, according to his last missive." The younger Henry was away at the university on the island kingdom of Roldem. "His teachers grade him well, his presence in the royal court does honor to our house, and he only loses a little when he gambles. He writes that he intends to enter the Tournament of Champions."

"Bold," said Robert, watching as the three youngsters retrieved their respective horses and mounted up. "The best swordsmen in the world vie for the title Champion of the Masters' Court."

"He's a fair hand with the blade," offered Martin as he rode over to his father. Martin often understated things, sometimes from a dry sense of humor, at other times from a skeptical view of the world. He was always reserved in his praise or condemnation, rarely smiled or displayed displeasure, keeping his own counsel on most matters.

Brendan could barely contain his delight. "He's the finest blade in the west. Only Martin here can press Hal. According to family lore, he's a match for our ancestor, Prince Arutha."

Brendan was the youngest, seemingly set loose in the world with but one purpose, to plague his siblings. He had been a happy baby and a rambunctious child, always striving to keep up with his older brothers. There was rarely a circumstance that found him unsmiling or unable to wrench humor out of the situation.

"A legendary name," said the Earl with a polite nod.

"Now, if he could only learn to master the bow . . ." Brendan added with an evil grin. Martin had never been well suited to the weapon and had shunned it for the sword.

Robert saw the brothers eyeing each other. He had known all three sons of the Duke since they were born and was used to their constant rivalry. Should this discussion continue, he knew it would become an argument with Martin growing more frustrated by the moment, to Brendan's evil delight.

Sensing that his sons were on the verge of another of their many confrontations, the Duke shouted, "Bearers, bring the head of the beast to the keep. We'll make a trophy of its head for Lady Bethany!"

Her father's scowl caused a grin to return to the girl's face.

The Duke continued. "And you two"—he pointed at first Martin then Brendan—"behave yourselves or I'll have you riding night patrol along the eastern border."

Both boys knew their father wasn't joking as each had had to endure more than one night with the garrison's night patrols, wending their way through treacherous forests in the bitterly cold dark. "Yes, Father," they replied, almost in unison.

The Huntmaster set his bearers to work, while the nobility started the ride back to Crydee Keep.

21

As they made their way among the boles of the forest, seeking the game trail that would lead them back to the road to Crydee, Bethany said in a falsely sweet tone, "Too bad you boys didn't find a boar."

Both brothers exchanged looks, and for a rare moment, Brendan's sour expression matched Martin's.

Supper was festive despite the furious storm building outside. The mood was abetted by a roaring fire in the great hall, ample wine, and a sense of safety from the fury of the elements. The banter around the table was predictable; the two families were close and the meals shared uncountable.

Formal seating had been abandoned years before, as the two wives, the Duchess Caralin and the Countess Marriann, had quickly become like sisters, and had talked across their two husbands until the Duke had decided that comfort outweighed protocol.

So the Earl Robert sat in the seat tradition gave to host's wife, while she sat in his. The two men could chat, as could their wives, and harmony was ensured.

The Duke's two sons sat to the right of the Earl, while Lady Bethany sat to her mother's left. After most of the meal had been consumed, Brendan elbowed his brother lightly. "What is it?"

"What is what?" said Martin, his brow furrowed as if irritated by the question.

Martin's dour expression made Brendan's grin broaden, as if he sensed another opportunity to vex his brother. "Either you're dying to overhear Mother's conversation with Countess Marriann, or there's something on the end of Bethany's nose."

Martin had indeed been inclining his head in that direction as his brother spoke, but his gaze returned with a snap to his brother. His expression was one Brendan had seen only rarely, a deep and threatening look that warned the youngest brother that this time he had stepped too far over the line. Those previous experiences usually resulted in Brendan running very fast for his mother's protection when he was very young, or his father or his brother Hal's when older.

But rather than erupt in the rage that followed that particular black look, Martin simply lowered his voice and said, "You saw nothing."

His tone was so filled with controlled anger and menace that Brendan could only nod.

Sensing something between his sons, Duke Harry said, "If this storm gets worse, we'll have a lot of work to do in the town for quite a few days." He looked at Martin. "I'll want you to take a patrol to the north and northeast, to see how the villagers fare." Then he said to Brendan, "And you're old enough to lead one as well. To the south and southeast."

"I can see to those villages on my way home, Your Grace," said Earl Robert.

"Linger a few days more," said Harry. With a warm smile he glanced to where his wife sat in animated conversation with the Countess and added, "They do so miss each other."

"True," said the Earl. "We do seem to have less time for visits."

Leaning over, Harry asked, "You have closer ties with kin in the east. What do you hear?"

The Earl knew exactly what the Duke referred to. "Little. It is as if people are suddenly cautious to the point of silence."

Almost since the creation of the Western Realm of the Kingdom there had been rivalry between west and east. Everything east of the small city of Malac's Cross was viewed as "the real Kingdom of the Isles" to the majority of citizens and the ruling Congress of Lords. The west was often seen as a drain on national resources, since much of it was empty and mountainous or, worse, inhabited by nonhumans, dwarves, elves, trolls, goblins, and the Brotherhood of the Dark Path. Administration costs were high relative to the amount of revenue generated for the Crown, and there was almost no political advantage to be had from serving in the west. Real military and political advancement came from serving in the Eastern Realm. Hunting down raiding bands of goblins or trolls was not a path to promotion; fighting against Keshian raiders or border skirmishes against the Eastern Kingdoms was.

"I count on you for something more dependable than what comes through Krondor," said the Duke. "Your family is new to the Far Coast, while my house . . ." He let the sentence trail off.

The history of House conDoin in Crydee was well known. A brother to the King had conquered the Far Coast, once Great Kesh's most far-flung frontier, and annexed it to the Kingdom, almost doubling the breadth of the nation in less than five years. Liking the area where he had ended up after his struggles, he had persuaded his brother to give him the Far Coast and built the very keep in which they now dined, Crydee.

Carse, the Earl's home, was actually the more critical trading and commerce center, being blessed with a far better harbor and sitting squarely at the heart of the coast, with all farming, mining, and foresting materials bound for export eventually finding their way to Carse's docks.

Earl Robert's father had been given the office of earl by Henry's grandfather, with the King's blessing, when the previous earl had died without issue. As no estate on the Far Coast was considered desirable enough for any eastern noble, the award went unchallenged. More than once Lord Henry had considered that he, Earl Robert, and Morris, Earl of Tulan, were almost an autonomous little kingdom unto themselves. The taxes paid to the Crown were modest, reduced by half by what the Prince in Krondor took, but the requirements were meager as well, so for the most part the Far Coast was ignored.

"One hears rumors," said Robert, leaning over. "The King's health is poor, according to one cousin I consider reliable. It's said that healing priests are required frequently for maladies that would be counted mild in most men his age."

Henry sighed as he sat back, lifted his goblet of wine, and took a sip. "Patrick was the last true conDoin king, in my judgment. Those who have come after are like his wife, vindictive and manipulative, always plotting: true eastern rulers." He set down his wine. "Mark you well, if the King dies without male issue, we may be sucked into conflict."

Robert's expression clouded. "Civil war, Harry?"

Henry shook his head. "No, but a political struggle in the Congress that could keep the throne vacant for a long time. And if that happens . . ." He shrugged.

"A regent. Who do you think the Congress would be likely to appoint?"

"There's the rub," said Henry. "You'd have to ask your eastern kin. I haven't the foggiest."

The Duke retrieved his freshly filled cup and drank slowly as he reflected. What he had said about the last "true" king was a dangerous remark should any but the most trusted of friends, like Robert of Carse, overhear it.

The conDoins were the longest line of rulers in the history of the Kingdom of the Isles. There had been petty kings on the Island of Rillanon before the rise of this dynasty, but it had been a conDoin who had first planted the banner of the Isles on the mainland and conquered Bas-Tyra. It had been con-Doin kings who had forged a nation to rival Great Kesh to the south and kept the pesky Eastern Kingdoms in control and forged a close relationship with the island kingdom of Roldem.

Robert noticed his friend's thoughtful expression. "What?"

"Roldem."

"What of Roldem?"

Henry leaned over, as if cautious of being overheard, even here in the heart of his own demesne. "Without an acknowledged heir, there are many claimants to the throne."

Robert waved aside the remark. "Your family has more distant cousins than a hive has bees, but there are only a few of royal blood."

"There are three princes—"

"Seven," interrupted Robert. "You and your three sons are of the blood royal."

Henry grimaced. "By the grace of our ancestor, we've renounced claim to the inheritance of anything but Crydee."

"Martin Longbow may have, to avoid a civil war with his brothers, but that was then. This is now. There are many in the Congress who would consider you a worthy claimant to the throne should the need arise. They would rally to you."

"You speak boldly, Robert. Many might say you tread the edge of treason, but I have no interest, for myself or my sons. Back to the truths of the moment: there are three nephews who would vie for the Crown. Oliver, the King's nephew, is closest in blood, but from the King's sister's marriage to Prince Michael of Semrick, and that makes him a foreigner in the eyes of many. Montgomery, Earl of Rillanon, and Duke Chadwick of Ran are both cousins to the King, though distant."

Robert sat back and let out a long sigh. "It's a shame King Gregory wasn't the lady's man his father was. Patrick left a litter of bastards along the way before he married. Still, he has managed to sire one son." The Earl paused, then added, "Prince Oliver's a good lad, and you're right, he has as much conDoin blood in him as any, and he's betrothed to the Duke of Bas-Tyra's second daughter, Grace. Since the Tsurani war the houses of Bas-Tyra and conDoin have stood close, more than a hundred years as one."

"That's a powerful faction," agreed the Duke. "But Gregory has yet to name Oliver as his heir. The lad is approaching his twentieth year, and Gregory is not likely to produce another son, no matter how hard he and that girl he married try." Both men chuckled. After the unexpected death of the Queen, the King had chosen to marry a girl barely a year older than his son. She was the daughter of a minor court noble, who had been raised up in rank by the auspicious marriage. The girl's only grace was her stunning beauty, and it was reported she kept the King very happy, but other than that, she seemed a simple soul.

Rumors abounded that the King's health was not as it should be. Given his age, barely fifty years, and his short rule, only five years since the death of his father, the potential for instability in the Kingdom was higher than it had been in a century.

"Montgomery is not a factor," Robert continued. "He's a creature of the court and is likely to emerge as a candidate only as a compromise short of war, but he has no standing, no factions behind him, nothing. He's just there."

"But he is the King's sister's second son, and as close by blood as anyone after Oliver."

"It is regrettable that his older brother didn't live. Now, he was a young man of talent."

Henry nodded and said nothing. The death of Montgomery's elder brother Alexander had always been something viewed with suspicion. No one gave voice to the thought, but his death in a raid by Ceresian pirates had seemed both pointless and convenient. The pirates had raided an estate that was heavily fortified yet contained little of worth. Some trinkets had been looted, but the only notable thing had been the death of the King's nephew, who was at that time the leading contender for the title of heir to the throne. Fortunately, Oliver had been born soon after and the question of inheritance seemed to subside.

"Do you think Edward is a factor?" asked Robert.

"No. He's a prince in name only." Henry laughed. "And he might make a good king, because he desperately does not want the position. He rules in Krondor only as a favor to the King's late father. Patrick and Edward were as brothers. He looks upon Gregory as a nephew, and he'll stay there until relieved. He will certainly retire to his estates in the east when Oliver comes west."

"So if no heir is named by the King, and the King passes, who will the Congress support?" asked Henry. "That is the question."

Robert let out a long breath as if in exasperation. "Only the gods know, I suspect. And Sir William Alcorn."

Henry gave a wry chuckle. "Our oddly mysterious Sir William."

Both men fell silent as they considered the man just named. A common soldier by all accounts, from the city of Rillanon, an islander born, he had risen quickly to the rank of Knight-Captain and had been promoted to the King's personal guard.

But when the King was a young man and sent by his father to study at the University of Roldem, Knight-Captain William had been named head of the then Prince Gregory's personal retinue and had returned two years later as Sir William Alcorn, newly appointed personal adviser to the heir to the throne. Now five years later he was adviser to the King of Isles.

"He seems to favor no faction."

"Or he plays off one side against the other, securing his own position."

Robert sighed. "It is rumored he is now the most powerful man in the Kingdom, despite his overt displays of modesty and humility. The King hangs upon his every word, which means no few of the lords of the Congress do as well."

"How the truth is seen often defines the truth," observed Henry. "If he is feared for power, how much power he truly has to wield is immaterial, for the fear is still real. And how does Lord Jamison take his position as First Adviser being usurped?"

Robert shrugged. "He's still a power, but he's aging. His son James the third is able, but it's his grandson, yet another James . . . Jim's the one to keep an eye on."

The Earl nodded. Both men had met Jim Dasher in his guise as Lord Jamison, grandson to the Duke of Rillanon.

"What is known about Alcorn?" posed Earl Robert. "He rose through the ranks, hardly the first man of common birth to do that—Duke James's grandfather was a common street lad, a thief even by some recounting. But this Sir William holds no specific title—it is said he refuses them, though even the office of Duke of Rillanon might be his for the asking once Lord James steps down."

Henry shook his head ruefully. "The current Duke might object; I think he sees the office going to his son or grandson. And Lord James is still a man with whom to reckon. He holds together the Congress of Lords, truth to tell."

"Well," said Earl Robert, "it is of little concern for us on the Far Coast, it's true." Then he smiled, "Yet it is always interesting."

"You're a more political animal than I, Robert. But to say it is of little concern is to assume things will go forward as they have in the past, and that may not be so. There's a difference between the Crown ignoring us and abandoning us. It's when I consider that possible bleak future I'm glad to have friends such as you and Morris here in the west."

"Ever your loyal vassal, my friend."

At that moment a soldier, drenched to the skin, hurried into the keep, approached the Duke's table, and bowed. "My lord, a ship is making for the harbor." He sounded out of breath.

The Duke stood. "In this weather?"

"We have tried to warn them off with red flash powder in the lighthouse, but they've ignored us and are coming straight in!"

The Duke looked to Robert. As one they said, "Reinman!"

Henry said, "Only that madman would run before the gale and think to not end up with his ship a half mile inland. Let's go up to the tower." He motioned for Robert to follow, but by then the boys and Bethany had also stood up.

"Father," said Martin. "You'll never see anything from up there!"

"If it's Reinman and he doesn't bring that ship to heel in this gale, we'll have plenty to see," Henry answered. He moved out of the great hall toward the stairs that led to the tallest tower in the fore of the keep. It was called the Magician's Tower, for once the Duke's ancestor, Lord Borric, had given it over to a magician and his apprentice. Now vacant, it still afforded the best view of the western vista.

Servants hurried to bring oiled cloaks for the Duke's court. As Henry and Robert reached the top of the tower, a page barely able to catch his breath overtook them and handed each man a heavy hooded cloak of canvas soaked in seal oil. Moments later the two rulers were atop the tower, faces into the biting rain, attempting to see what they could in the darkness.

As the others gathered behind them, Earl Robert shouted over the wind, "Can you see anything?"

Henry pointed. "Look!"

The town of Crydee was shuttered fast against the storm, but light could be glimpsed leaking around the edges of shutters, through cracks in door frames, and from the lanterns of those who hurried toward the docks. The alarm was sounding, and it carried faintly to those atop Crydee Keep's tallest tower.

In the distance the glow from Longpoint Lighthouse could barely be seen, faintly red from the powder that had been tossed on the beacon to warn ships off attempting to enter the harbor.

In a severe storm, ships would make for headland seven miles up the coast and heave to behind the shelter of some tall bluffs. In a storm like this, the wise choice could be to keep sailing along the coast and circle back when the winds lessened, or to drop anchor and turn the bow into the gale.

But this captain was no ordinary seaman; rather, as Lord Henry had observed, he was something of a madman. Considered the finest captain in the King's Western Fleet, he was always the first to be sent after pirates and on dangerous missions.

"It must be something important to make Reinman chance coming in tonight!" shouted Martin from behind his father.

"The fool!" replied Robert. "He'll crash into the docks!"

In the rain and gloom, the ship raced past the lighthouse

like an eerie shadow, a skeleton thing of grey and black lit by the yellow-and-white reflections of torches along the break-water leading out to the lighthouse. As the vessel entered the harbor every door and window of every shop along the wharf was thrown open despite the rain, as onlookers gaped in wonder at the mad captain who drove his ship to destruction.

Suddenly, a bloom of light appeared around the ship, expanding bubblelike into a sphere of almost daylight brilliance. Within the dome of brilliance they could easily see the ship's crew frantically chopping at the rigging with hand axes so the sails quickly fell away.

"Damn!" said the Duke quietly.

2

WARNING

The wind howled.

Captain Jason Reinman bellowed to be heard above the noise. "Cut 'em loose, damn ya!"

The crew had been ordered aloft during the mad dash toward the harbor of Crydee in preparation for this desperate act.

"Hard to starboard!" he shouted, and two men wrestling with the long handle on the rudder shoved with all their strength toward the left, to bring the balky ship around in the opposite direction.

The *Royal Messenger*'s timbers groaned in protest as the ship fought against stresses she was not designed to withstand. Turning to the man seated on the deck next to him, Captain Reinman shouted, "Hold! Just a few more minutes!"

The man squatted on the decks, his eyes closed and his face a mask of concentration as he fought to stay upright on the tossing deck. Reinman's sunburned face turned upward, and he saw with satisfaction that the sails had all been cut loose and were now littering the decks. He'd refit in Crydee and what sail he'd lost the Duke could replace for him. The ropes would be mended and should any of his men have been overly zealous with the axes, the spars would be repaired.

The sound of the storm died away: the bubble of light was a tiny pool of calm in the middle of the storm-tossed harbor. "Don't you fail me, you magic-wielding sot! You're not allowed to pass out until we are at the docks!" If the man at whom Reinman was shouting heard him he gave no indication, seemingly intent on keeping himself sitting upright.

The ship came about in the relative calm of the bubble of magic, and Reinman shouted, "Get the fenders over the side! As soon as this shell is down, the gale will slam us into the docks. I don't want to sail home on a pile of kindling!" To the men aloft, he said, "Grab hold and hang on, it's going to be rough!"

As the large padded fenders went over the side to protect the ship from the dock wall, the magic bubble collapsed, and as the captain had predicted, the sudden gale slammed the hull against the pilings. But the fenders did their work and although there was the sound of wood cracking, both the dock and the ship held intact.

Then the ship rolled and the grinding sound of wood on wood was almost painfully loud, and the three masts came down toward the cobbles of the harborside road at alarming speed. Men aloft held on for their lives, shouting in alarm.

But just as it seemed the ship would roll on its side and smash the yards into the ground, the movement stopped. For a pregnant moment the spars hovered mere feet above the stones, then they started to travel back the way they came. Men's voices rose again in alarm as they realized they might be suddenly pitched off in the other direction.

"Hang on!" shouted the captain as he gripped the railing that had almost been overhead a moment before. Glancing around, he noticed that his companion on the poop deck was nowhere to be seen. "Drunken fool!" he shouted at the spot recently vacated and then returned his attention to not being flung over the side of his ship.

As the ship rolled back, more creaking signaled the continuation of the elements' assault on the vessel he loved dearly. He silently damned the need for such reckless behavior and vowed that should the ship be rendered salvage, he would see to it that Lord James Dasher Jamison paid for a new one out of his own pocket—though having secret access to the King's treasury, he would barely miss the sum.

The ship was upright for a moment, then continued on its recoil, but the force of the wind and sea kept it from rolling very far. Captain Reinman let go of the railing and shouted, "Make fast! Any man not already dead get this ship securely lashed. Any man dead will answer to me!"

He hurried to the fore railing and looked around. The ship was in better shape than he had any right to expect, but not as pretty as he would have liked. But it did not seem that the main timbers had been compromised, so he thought a few days of carpentry and paint would make her as good as new.

He took a brief moment to congratulate himself on the insane entrance into Crydee Harbor and then shouted, "Anyone seen that drunken magician?"

One of the deckhands shouted, "Oh, was that's what that was, sir? I think he went over the side when we heeled back." Suddenly realizing what he said, the sailor shouted, "Man overboard!"

Half a dozen sailors hurried to the rail, and one pointed, "There!"

Two men went over the sides despite the dangerous chop in the water and the risk of being swept into the side of the ship or, worse, under the docks in what had to be a clutter of debris.

The object of their search, a slender man with a usually unruly thatch of black hair that was now plastered to his skull, sputtered and coughed as one sailor dragged him to the surface and held his head above water. The second sailor helped pull him to the side of the ship where two other sailors clung tightly to ropes despite the slashing winds.

Drenched, miserable, and wretched, the man in the soaked robes looked at the captain and said, "We there?"

"More or less," said Reinman with a grin. "Mr. Williams!"

The first mate appeared in front of his captain. "Aye, sir."

"Get below and see how much work needs to be done. I didn't hear anything to make me believe we have any serious damage. Don't tell me I'm wrong, if you please."

The first mate saluted and turned away. Like the captain, the first mate knew the ship as well as he knew the face of his wife and children. He suspected that the groaning of wood and snapping of lines would mean repair, but nothing major. He'd heard the sound of a keelson cracking in a storm, and it was a sound he'd never forget.

Captain Reinman ordered, "Run out the gangway!"

The crew nearest to the docks hurried to obey. Unlike passenger ships with their fancy gangways with steps and rails, this was a merely a wide board of hardwood that managed to reach the docks without bowing so much it wouldn't support a man carrying cargo.

No sooner had it touched the dock than Reinman was down it, his leather boots sliding along the plank as much as walking it. As he expected, by the time he stood on the dock, a company of horsemen was riding to meet him.

Duke Henry, Earl Robert, and half a dozen men-at-arms reined in.

"Miserable night for a ride, Your Grace," said the captain with a grin, ignoring the pelting rain. Standing in the storm, water coursing off his head and shoulders, the redheaded seaman looked as if he was almost enjoying the experience.

"Hell of a landing," said Duke Henry. "It must be something urgent to make you pull a stunt like that."

"You could say," he glanced around, "though it will keep for another few minutes until we can be alone. Strict instructions: for your ears only."

The Duke nodded. He motioned to one of his escorts. "Give the captain your horse and follow on foot."

The soldier did as ordered and handed the reins to Reinman. The captain mounted a little clumsily, as riding was not his first occupation, but once in the saddle he seemed comfortable enough.

"To the keep!" said the Duke over the wind's howl, and they turned back and started up the main street of Crydee Town, the boulevard that would take them to shelter and a roaring fire.

Still dripping wet, Captain Reinman accepted a heavy towel and began mopping his face, but he waved away a servant bearing a change of clothes. "In a minute," he said, then to the Duke. "A word, my lord."

They stood in the entrance to the keep with the Duchess, Countess, and the three children waiting for an explanation for the mad display they had just witnessed. Both Martin and Brendan had started to speak at once, but the captain's words cut them short.

Somewhat surprised by Reinman's more than usually abrupt manner, the Duke nodded to the others to return to the great hall, indicating that he and the captain would join them. The two men moved to a corner of the entry hall and the Duke said, "Now, what is so important you'll risk wrecking the King's fastest ship to tell me a day early?"

"Orders from the Crown, my lord. You're to begin muster."

The Duke's face remained impassive, but the skin around his eyes tightened. "It's war, then?"

"Not yet, but soon, perhaps. Lord Sutherland and the Duke of Ran both say the frontier is quiet, but rumors have it Kesh is moving in the south and you're to be ready to support Yabon or even Krondor if the need arises."

Henry considered. War along the Far Coast had occurred only twice in the history of the Kingdom: the original conquest when the land was wrested from Kesh, and then the Tsurani invasion. The people of the Far Coast had known peace for a century and had almost nothing to do with Kesh, save for the occasional trader looking for exotic goods.

But east of the Straits of Darkness it was another matter. The border between the two giant nations had long borne witness to skirmishes and incursions as one side or the other sought advantage. The last time a major assault on the Kingdom had occurred had been on the heels of the invasion by the forces of the Emerald Queen. With the entire west in rubble, Kesh had moved against Krondor, only to be sent home with its tail between legs by the power of the sorcerer Pug. He had scolded both sides against such wasteful recklessness and thus had earned the enmity of the Crown. Yet his lesson had held, as there had been little by way of conflict between the two giant nations for almost fifty years. The occasional border clash in the Vale of Dreams was not unusual, but this was the first hint of any major military action against the Kingdom by the Empire of Great Kesh.

Henry said, "They expect a move against Krondor?"

Reinman shrugged. "What the King's council expects, I have no idea. If Kesh moves against Krondor, Yabon will have to move south in support, and you no doubt will be sent east to support Yabon. But that's just speculation. All I know is that I have my orders from the mouth of Lord Jamison."

"Richard or James?"

"James."

Henry let out a long sigh. Richard was the Prince's Knight-Marshal, second cousin to James, who was a lot closer to the Crown in Rillanon. If the message came from him, it really did mean war was coming. "So Jim was in Krondor?"

"The man seems to be everywhere," said Reinman, mopping his head one more time with the towel. "I don't know how he does it, but I hear from this bloke or that that he was seen a week ago in Rillanon, then I see him in Krondor, and unless he's sprouted wings and flown I don't know how he could do that short of killing a string of horses and not sleeping for a week."

"He has his ways, obviously," said the Duke. "Change into something dry and come into the hall. Dinner's still on the table and I'm sure the boys will pester you with questions once I tell everyone what's going on."

"You're going to tell everyone?"

"Remember where you are, Captain. This is Crydee. If there's been a Keshian spy around here in the last ten years, he was lost and wandering far from anywhere he should be.

"And I must instruct Earl Robert as well as send messages down to Tulan so Earl Morris can begin his muster." He smiled. "After the entrance you made, if you think I could tell my wife that this is a matter of state . . . well, you don't remember my wife very well."

With a grin the captain said, "Well, yes, there is that."

"Besides, my boys are old enough that they need to learn some warcraft, and while I'm loath to see them fight this young, they are conDoins."

"Aye, my lord, there is that as well."

The Duke led Reinman into the hall where the others waited expectantly. He motioned for the servants to depart, then quickly recounted the very simple but vital order from the Crown.

Earl Robert shook his head. "Muster. It's a bad time of year, my lord. Spring planting begins in a few weeks."

"I know, but wars are inconvenient at any time of the year. Still, we can muster levies in stages. One man in three to report as soon as word reaches, outfit and train and return to the village in two weeks or three, the next man, then the last, and by the time we reach full muster, the planting should be in."

"If the rain stops," added Martin with a sour expression. "The ground won't be ready for most crops for a week if it stops tomorrow, Father."

"Farmer, are you?" asked Reinman with a grin.

Brendan returned the grin while Martin tried to suppress a chuckle. "Father believes in the old virtues. We were forced to work at every apprenticeship in the duchy for a week or two as we grew up, the better to understand the lives of our subjects."

"The King's subjects," corrected his father. "The citizens of the duchy are ours to protect, but they belong to no man, not even the King, though they are charged to obey him. As are we. Such is the tradition of the Great Freedom, upon which our nation is founded."

"So I've been told," said Brendan, rolling his eyes.

Martin changed the subject: "Captain, how did you manage that . . . event, in the harbor, with the light bubble in the midst of the storm?"

"Ah!" said Reinman, obviously delighted. "That was my weather witch."

"Weather witch?" asked the Duke.

"Well, he's not really a witch, I'll grant you, but 'weather magician' doesn't roll off the tongue quite as neatly. Besides, it annoys him."

"Who is he?"

"Bellard, by name," answered the captain. "One of the lot from Stardock. He was up with the elves north of here for a couple of years, learning weather magic from their spellweavers." He nodded in thanks as a mug of steaming mulled wine was presented to him by a servant. He sipped at this for a moment, then put down the mug and said, "Quite good at it, too, save for one problem."

"What would that be?" asked Earl Robert.

"He drinks."

"Ah, a drunkard," said Martin.

"Well, not really," said the captain. "He was having the devils trying to learn the magic, and got tipsy at one of the moon festivals or sun festivals or flower festivals or whatever it is the elves use as an excuse to get drunk and carry on, so they did, and apparently not wishing to offend his hosts, he did as well. Then the fun began. As I hear the story, after several cups of wine, he caused quite a little tempest in the middle of the forest. Took a few of the spellweavers a bit of time to make things right.

"So Bellard discovered that because he's a human, not an elf, or at least that's what he thinks, he has to be drunk to make the magic work."

"Ah!" said Brendan in obvious delight. "He must love that!"

"Actually, quite the opposite. Turns out the other thing Bellard discovered at that festival was he didn't care for strong drink. We have to hold him down and pour the grog down his gullet if we need his craft."

Everyone was wide-eyed at that, and indeed Brendan and his father were both openmouthed as well. Then the room erupted into laughter. Even the captain chuckled. "He fair hates it, really. But he drinks and does a masterful job, as you could see tonight, creating that bubble of calm in the middle of the storm. He pushed us along with a steady wind for three days, once, on a run from Rillanon around the southern nations up to Krondor—when we would have been becalmed for goodness knows how many days. Had the grandfather of all thumping heads for days after that and a sour stomach to put a man off food for life."

"Why does he do it?" asked Lady Bethany. "Surely there are other magics he's more suited to?"

"I don't know," said Reinman with a laugh. "Perhaps it's because I told him he was pressed into service on the Prince's writ and had no choice?"

"You didn't?" said the Duke. "The press was outlawed after the war with the Tsurani."

"Yes," said Reinman with an evil barking laugh, "but he doesn't know that."

Laughter burst out again, though Brendan and the ladies all looked pained at the amusement at such duplicity. Reinman said, "In the end, he will be well rewarded. His service to the Crown will not be taken for granted."

Martin said, "What of Hal?"

"Yes," added Brendan, "should he be recalled?"

"As to that," replied Reinman before the Duke could answer, "for the time being, the Prince would appreciate it if we kept word of the Western Muster from eastern ears."

Henry waved the captain to a chair and held up his hand. Martin was standing closest to the door, so he opened it and motioned the servants waiting outside to enter. "Serve us, then leave us," the Duke told his staff.

The servants hurried to make sure everyone at the table was supplied with more food and drink, then left.

"Sending the servants away?" asked Robert.

"They gossip, and while I trust all in this household, a stray word to a merchant, or a visiting seaman would be unfortunate . . ." He paused. "Now, Jason, what aren't you telling us?"

Reinman smiled. "Just rumors. Before I left Rillanon last it was being said the King was ill, again."

Henry sat back. "Cousin Gregory was never the man his father was," he said softly. "And with no sons . . ."

"He would save a lot of trouble naming Oliver as his heir," said Robert.

Reinman sat back. "Prince Edward would appreciate that," he observed dryly. "The Prince of Krondor can hardly wait for the King to name another to the post and let him retire back to 'civilization' as he likes to call the capital." Reinman shrugged. "As capitals go, Krondor's not such a bad place, though it does lack a certain grandeur. Edward lives in deathly fear that somehow he's going to make a terrible mistake one day and end up King." They all laughed.

"Eddie was always a caretaker appointment," said Henry thoughtfully. "He has no political support and no ambition. I think if the Congress rallied and named him King after Gregory, he'd find a way to reject the crown and run off to his estates. He has a lavish villa on a small island off Roldem."

Robert added, "Where it is said his wife spends most of her time"—he glanced at the ladies—"reviewing the household guard."

The Duchess raised an eyebrow. "Who are reputed to all be very handsome, very young and . . . very tall."

Countess Marriann and Lady Bethany both laughed out loud at the remarks, while the two boys exchanged glances before Brendan's eyes widened and he said, "Oh!"

"Marriages of state are not always what they might be," said his mother, as if that was all that needed to be added.

Reinman seemed uncomfortable. "You were speaking of Hal," he said. "How is he doing at that school in Roldem?"

"That school in Roldem" was the royal university, the finest educational facility in the world. It had been created originally for Roldem's nobility and royalty as a place where they could study art, music, history, and the natural sciences, as well as magic and military skills. But over the years it had attracted the best from every surrounding kingdom and the Empire, until it had become almost a necessity for any young man of rank seeking to advance.

"No one from the Far Coast has attended before," said Henry, "but Hal seems to be enjoying it, or at least so his letters suggest."

"He's entering the Masters' Court Championship," said Brendan to the captain.

"That's a feather in his cap if he wins," said Reinman.

Henry glanced at a shuttered window, as if he could somehow see the still-pouring rain outside. "Given the distance, it's about midday in Roldem. He may be competing now, if he hasn't already been eliminated."

The swordsman lunged while the crowed watched in silent admiration as the combatants parried furiously. They were evenly matched, and this was the first of three bouts to name the new Champion of the Masters' Court.

The dark-haired youth from the Far Coast of the Kingdom had been an unexpected challenger who had been discounted by the betting touts in the early rounds. As he rose rapidly, vanquishing his first three opponents easily, the betting had shifted quickly, until now he was considered an even bet to emerge as the new champion.

His opponent had been the favorite, a blond youth of roughly the same age.

Henry conDoin, the eldest son of Duke Henry of Crydee, parried, riposted, then feinted left and lunged right. "Touché!" cried out the Master of the Court.

The crowd erupted in appreciative applause.

The two combatants exchanged bows and retired to separate corners of the huge dueling hall that was the heart of the Masters' Court in Roldem City.

The blond youth returned to stand by his father. "He's very good."

Talwin Hawkins, the thirty-second Champion of the Masters' Court, nodded, then smiled at his son. "Almost as good as you. You'll have to be a little more focused. Even though you watched him, you didn't expect him to be this quick. Now he can take risks, because he only needs one touch to win. You need two."

Ty Hawkins turned a slightly sour expression on his father. He knew he was right, for young Tyrone Hawkins, the twenty-five-year-old son of a former champion, had been such a dominating force in the Masters' Court as a student that he had entered the competition a heavy favorite. That reputation had aided him in easily disposing of all his early opponents, and he had become a little too self-confident in his father's estimation.

"He favors a triple combination," Tal said to his son. Looking into the young man's face, he considered how much he resembled his mother, Teal, and how deeply Tal had come to love him, even though he wasn't his true father. Large blue eyes and a dusting of freckles gave a boyish countenance to a strong young face, with a smile that made him charming to the ladies. "If you can recognize it as he begins," he went on, "you can get under his second feint and reach him."

"And if I don't recognize it, he'll win the match," Ty said wryly.

Returning the lad's crooked smile, Tal said, "Worse things happen."

"True," said Ty. "Nobody dies here . . . usually."

That got him a dark look from his father, for part of the lore of the Masters' Court was the attempt on his father's life by two opponents that had ended in the first intentional bloodshed in the Court in a hundred and fifty years.

Waiting for the second round of the final bout to be signaled, both young men regarded their surroundings. Ty had been to the training floor countless times, but it was Henry's first visit to the court; indeed it was his first visit to Roldem. He had seen this hall for the first time when he was allowed his four practice bouts against the instructors only two days ago.

Yet for both young men the grandeur of the vast hall was still daunting. Large carved wooden columns surrounded a massive wooden floor that had been polished to a gleam like metal, like burnished copper. Intricate patterns had been worked into the floor. These served a function beyond aesthetics, for each pattern defined a dueling area, from the confined, narrow dueling path for rapier fencing, to the larger octagon for longer blades.

This was the reason the Masters' Court existed.

More than two centuries earlier, the King of Roldem had commanded a tourney to name the greatest swordsman in the world. Contestants of all rank—noble and common—had traveled from as far away as the southernmost province of the Empire of Great Kesh, the distant Free Cities of Natal, and all points in between. The prize had been fabled: a golden broadsword studded with gems. It was a prize unmatched in the Kingdom's history.

For two weeks the contest had continued, until a local noble, Count Versi Dango, had triumphed. To the King's astonishment, the Count had announced he would reject the prize so that the King might use the sword to pay for the construction of an academy dedicated to the art of the blade, and there hold this recurring contest, thus creating the Masters' Court.

The King had ordered the construction of this school, covering an entire city block in the heart of the island kingdom's capital, and over the years it had been rebuilt and refined until it now resembled a palace as much as a school. When it was finished, another tourney was held, and Count Dango had successfully defended his reputation as premier swordsman in the world. Every five years swordsmen gathered to compete for the title of Champion of the Masters' Court. Four times Dango had prevailed as the ultimate victor, until a wound had prevented him from competing further.

Now, the instructor who was Master of the Court signaled for the two combatants to return. Both young men assumed their positions as the Master held out his arm between them. They approached and raised their blades; the Master took hold of the points, brought them together, then stepped back crying, "Fence!"

Instantly Ty launched a wicked overhand lunge that almost struck home, driving Henry back a step. Then Ty recovered and took a step forward, his sword extended, his left hand resting on his hip, not raised in the air for balance as most fencers favored. His father had taught him there was little advantage in doing this unless one overbalanced, since holding the hand aloft robbed you of energy; this was not a severe problem on the fencing floor, but one that could get you killed in a battle.

Henry took a slight hopping step and started a circular motion with his blade, and Ty knew he was about to try that same triple move that had cost him a touch. Instead of pulling back on the second feint, Ty extended his arm, gaining right of way, and made an extraordinary low lunge, which struck Henry less than an inch above his belt, but still it was a clean strike. Even before the Master could announce it, Henry shouted, "Touché!"

Both combatants stood at attention for a moment, saluted each other, then turned to their respective ends of the floor. Henry came over to where his trainer, Swordmaster Phillip, waited. "He saw that one coming," said the old warrior.

Henry nodded and removed the basket helmet worn during these combats. Slightly out of breath, he said, "I was foolish to try the same move twice. He cozened me into trying that with his high lunge. Made me think he was desperate." He took the offered towel and wiped his face. "So now we come down to one touch for the championship."

"Too bad your father isn't here. Win or lose this last touch, you've done your family proud, Hal."

Henry nodded. "Better than I expected, really."

"Your many-greats-uncle Arutha was reputed to be a wicked swordsman. Seems you've inherited that skill."

With a tired grin, Henry said, "Good thing, 'cause I'm nothing like the bowman my great-great-grandfather Martin was."

"Or your grandfather, or your father," said the Swordmaster dryly.

Realizing the rare compliments were over, Henry returned his mask and said, "Or my little brother."

"Or that lad who works at the blacksmith's."

"So what you're saying is, I should win this."

"That's the general idea."

The two combatants returned to the fencing floor and the waiting Master of the Court. He held out his hand, and the two young men raised their swords. He gripped the two padded points then removed his hand suddenly, shouting, "Fence!"

Back and forth fought the two young swordsmen, equal in gifts and guile. They measured, attacked, regrouped, and defended in an instant. The life of a match such as this was measured in seconds, yet everyone in the audience was not anxious for it to conclude. And they were not to be disappointed.

Across the floor, advance and retreat, to and fro, the two young swordsmen battled. Experienced warriors like Tal Hawkins and Swordmaster Phillip recognized that the two duelists were evenly matched: Ty possessed slightly better technique, but Henry was just a touch quicker. The winner would be decided by whoever made the first mistake, either in concentration, mistiming, or succumbing to fatigue.

With a rhythm of its own, the contest moved in a furious staccato, punctuated by brief pauses as the two combatants took a moment to assess each other.

Then Ty launched a furious high-line attack, driving Henry back toward his own end of the floor. If he could be forced to step across his own end line, he would lose on a fault.

"Oh . . ." said Swordmaster Phillip as his finest student retreated in a way that looked as if he was losing control. But before he could accept that his pupil was about to be defeated by a clever attack, a remarkable thing happened.

Ty thrust at the highest point a legal touch was permitted—the tunic just below the face guard—a move that should have caused Henry to move either to his right or his left, as he had no room behind him. Either step would have taken him off line and out of the prescribed area, causing him to forfeit the match, or to lose his balance.

But Henry simply kept his left foot firmly planted a scant fraction of an inch before the end line, twisted his body and slid his right leg forward, allowing the tip of Ty's foil to cut through the air just above his canvas tunic. As he slid forward, Henry extended his arm and found Ty running right up against his foil tip.

The crowd gasped as the two combatants froze in tableau. For the briefest second there was no sound in the room, then the Master of Ceremonies shouted, "Judges?"

Four judges, one at each corner of the combat area, were required to signal a valid touch. The two closest to Henry's end of the floor looked at each other, each unsure of what he had just seen. Henry now sat on the floor, in a full split, one leg straight ahead and one behind, while Ty held his position, his body bowing Henry's blade. "This is really uncomfortable," Hal said just loud enough that those nearby could hear.

"Embarrassing, really," said Ty.

The Master signaled for the two judges to join him and said, "Contestants, return to your positions."

Ty held out his left hand and Henry took it, letting his opponent pull him to his feet. "That looked painful," said Ty as he removed his helmet.

Removing his own helmet, Henry brushed his dark brown hair aside and winced. "You have no idea."

As Henry reached him, Swordmaster Phillip said, "I've never seen a move like that before. What was it?"

"Desperation," said Henry. Taking the offered towel, he dried his face. "He really is better than I am, you know that?"

"Yes," said Phillip softly, "but not by much. And not enough for you not to contest. He may win, but so may you."

"What's taking the judges so long?"

"My guess is they're arguing about right of way. Tyron was still extended, so you had no right of way, even though he ran right up on your sword point. I'd rule it a nontouch and make you do it over again."

"I don't think I can," said Henry with a wince. "I think I'm going to need to see a healer if I ever want to have children."

"Probably just a muscle. Rest for a while and it will heal."

"I can feel my left leg is not what it should be, Swordmaster. It feels weaker than it ought to and if I push off, even a little, it hurts like demon fire."

Phillip stepped back. "Try to lunge."

Henry attempted a lunge just to Phillip's right and lost his balance. Phillip caught him before he could collapse to the floor. He patted the young man on the shoulder affectionately, then said in a loud voice, "Masters of the Court!"

The three masters who had been taking council in the hall turned as one and the seniormost said, "What is it?"

"We must withdraw."

There was an audible groan of disappointment through the hall from the spectators as the Master of Ceremonies said, "Why do you withdraw?"

"My young master is injured and unable to continue."

Ty and his father crossed the floor. As they neared the judges, Ty said, "I can wait if young Lord Henry needs time to recover. An hour if needed, or perhaps tomorrow?"

Henry was limping visibly now. He shook his head. "No, good sir. I cannot continue and," he said with a wince, "I suspect I will not be at my best for a while." He smiled at his opponent. "Well won, young Hawkins." Lowering his voice he added, "You probably would have won in any event. You really are the best I have met."

"Fairly said," returned Ty, "and no one has ever pressed me as hard as you." He looked at the three judges, who nodded.

The Master of Ceremonies proclaimed, "As young Lord conDoin cannot continue we judge this match concluded. Hail the Champion of the Masters' Court, Tyrone Hawkins!"

The crowd was obviously disappointed at the lack of a resolution by combat, but after a hesitant start, they cheered loudly. Even if the final touch was absent, the tourney had provided days of entertainment, and the champion was without a doubt an exceptional swordsman.

When the applause died down, Ty said quietly, "This will come as a great relief to the King's Master of Ceremonies, for to postpone the great gala would put the man into an apoplexy."

Henry glanced over at the royal box where the King and his family had been watching the finals and saw a visible expression of relief on the face of the Master of Ceremonies as he moved to stand before the King.

"Time to get your prize," Tal Hawkins told his son. To Henry he said, "Please, you must let me send a healer friend: he can get you right in a day or two. Those groin injuries are more than annoying, I know. If not treated quickly, they can linger for months, years even."

Hal nodded his acceptance of the offer.

The two finalists and their companions were escorted to the royal box where they bowed before the King of Roldem. King Carole was an aging man with grey hair, but he still looked alert and happy. Next to him sat his wife, Queen Gertrude, and to her side stood their youngest son, Prince Grandprey, who was only a few years older than the two combatants and was dressed in the uniform of a general of the Royal Army; and his sister, the Princess Stephané, resplendent in a gown of softly folded yellow silk, which spread gracefully out to the floor. Her shoulders were bare and her somewhat daring décolletage was hidden by a sheer shoulder wrap of the same hue. Her choice of colors made a dramatic contrast to her chestnut hair and striking brown eyes.

Henry tried not to blush as he looked away from her, then he noticed Ty Hawkins was staring boldly at the King's daughter. And Hal instantly decided he disliked the victor of the contest.

On the King's right side stood Crown Prince Constantine, the Heir Apparent to the throne, and the middle son, Prince Albér, the Heir Presumptive. Henry and Tyrone both bowed before the royal family.

The Master of Ceremonies said, "Your Majesties, Your Highnesses, the victor and vanquished of today's final match. Lord Henry of Crydee, approach."

As the first among those who were defeated by the winner, Hal was awarded a miniature silver sword. As he knelt to receive the gift from the hand of the Crown Prince, the King said, "Shame to end this way lad; you've acquitted yourself admirably. Still, second is nothing to be ashamed of. Maybe you'll have better luck in the next tourney."

"Your Majesty is gracious," said Hal, accepting the sword and with some discomfort returning to stand next to Swordmaster Phillip.

"We'll send a healer over to your quarters at the university and have that . . . leg seen to. You must be ready for tomorrow's gala," said the King.

"I thank Your Majesty," said Hal, bowing.

"Tyrone Hawkins of Olasko," intoned the Master of Ceremonies.

Ty knelt and the King said, "Young Hawkins. I gave the King's prize to your father many years ago." He gave Tal a rueful smile. "That was a day we'll never forget."

The bout had ended in the death of two of Tal's opponents: a trained swordsman from Kesh who had come with one purpose, to kill the young swordsman, and a lieutenant in the army of Olasko who had been among those responsible for the death of most of Tal's people.

The King said, "So concludes this contest, and we shall gather in five years to see if young Hawkins can continue his family's achievements. I bid you, good lords, ladies, and gentlemen, a fair day and will welcome many of you to our gala tomorrow night."

Everyone who had been seated rose when the King stood and led his wife and family from the Hall of the Masters' Court. As Ty turned to find Hal staring at him with a narrowed gaze, a man wended his way though the press of folk leaving the building to come stand before Tal.

But it was Hal who spoke first, "Lord Jamison!"

James Dasher Jamison, Baron of the Prince's Court in Krondor, nodded at the young nobleman and then to Ty and his father. "Well, Jim," said Tal Hawkins, "this is an unexpected pleasure."

Lord Jamison, also known as Jim Dasher to some, glanced around the room and said, "Unexpected, I warrant, but hardly a pleasure." Lowering his voice a little, he added, "We need to speak in private, Hawkins." Then he turned to

Hal and said, "Don't wander too far, Hal. I need to speak with you as well."

Moving a short distance away from the throng surrounding the victor, Jim said, "Tal, I need to ask you a favor."

"What?" replied Hawkins. His relationship with Jim Dasher and everyone else associated with the Conclave of Shadows had been a mixed one at best. They had saved his life as a child but exacted a high price in service, and even now, after he had been formally released from their service, they still were a presence in his life. He knew he owed all that he was to them, but there was no tender affection in his sense of obligation.

"I need you to keep a close watch on young conDoin over there."

"Why?"

"Something's coming. I will tell you more tonight, in private."

"Very well, but how am I to keep watch over him while he's at the university living in the students' dormitory?"

"We don't let him return there." Jim glanced over his shoulder at the two young swordsmen and their admirers. "Invite him to dine with your family at the River House tonight, and I'll chance by afterward to have words with you both. Yes, that would serve."

"Very well, again," said Hawkins, nodding his head once, then moving past the dark-eyed Kingdom noble.

Jim Dasher glanced around the room, trying to discern who might be observing him. If Kesh had agents in the room—which was almost certain—they would be very good at their jobs, which meant that he stood scant chance of identifying them. Still, a moment to scan the room was little price to pay against the slight chance an agent might make a mistake and reveal himself.

Or herself, he amended as he caught sight of a young woman staring at him, then averting her eyes a moment later. Jim resisted an impulse to sigh; irrespective of her true intent, she had wished to be noticed, and notice her he had. If she was only an ambitious status seeker, singling out the slightly older, but still very eligible nobleman from the Kingdom for a possible profitable liaison, or a Keshian spy, he had to find out.

Relaxing his expression and attempting to appear merely an interested spectator in the day's events, he appeared to meander through the crowd, but he made a straight path toward this woman.

A brief distraction arrived in the form of Lord Carrington, a minor court baron attached to the Kingdom's delegation to Roldem, a fussy, officious man with an inflated sense of his ability at diplomacy and a strong appetite for gossip. "Lord Jamison!" he exclaimed, taking Jim's hand for a brief, limp squeeze.

"My lord," said Jim, trying not to take his eyes off the beautiful brunette he felt certain was a Keshian spy.

"Pity young Lord Henry didn't continue," said Carrington. "Had a bit of gold wagered on him and it would have done wonders for the Isles to have a champion in the Masters' Court. Still," he said, glancing over his shoulder to where Ty and Hal still talked to the onlookers, "I suppose it's the next best, what with Hawkins over there claiming some title or another in the west, even though he now resides in Olasko."

Sensing a potentially long conversation, Jim said, "I've known Talwin Hawkins for years, my lord Baron. His title is not 'claimed' but his own."

"Oh?" Like every other member of the King's court in Rillanon, Carrington wasn't entirely certain what Jim did for the Crown, but he knew it was important and, besides, his grandfather was still Duke of Rillanon. "I see."

"Somehow I don't think you do," said Jim under his breath, then loudly spoke up. "Excuse my, my lord, I must speak to someone over there."

Before the portly courtier could reply, Jim was away from him and heading straight toward a large pillar next to which the object of his attention had paused. The woman glanced at

Jim, and a small, almost flirtatious smile crossed her lips. Jim wondered if perhaps he had misjudged the woman: perhaps she wasn't an agent of the Empire but merely a young woman with her eye on a man of position and wealth.

He reached the pillar a moment after she had passed behind it, and she was nowhere to be seen.

"I'll be damned," Jim muttered, glancing around. He was very good at keeping watch on someone in a crowd, even across a busy market in a big city, but for the moment, he seemed to have met his match. She was better.

3

MYSTERIES

Dinner had been festive.

At Tal Hawkins's request, Hal and Phillip had dined at the River House, a restaurant located in one of the richer districts in the city. Named after the original establishment Hawkins had opened in the city of Olasko years earlier, it enjoyed much the same success and reputation as the original. The food was splendid, the most important personages in the Kingdom came to dine there, and not being a tavern or inn, the dining room was not crowded with travelers, merchants, and foreigners. In other words, the establishment appealed to the worst in Roldemish elitism and snobbery.

To Hal's surprise, a healer had arrived before the meal and had used some impressive magic to heal the groin injury and now he was beginning to wish he had agreed to a one-day postponement. He found himself drawn to Ty, though he still was fairly sure he disliked him after the way he had looked at the Princess. Hal was working himself into a fair state of youthful jealousy over a girl he hadn't even spoken with, despite the fact it was a foregone conclusion he was to marry Lady Bethany of Carse.

Jim had acted as host at dinner, despite the invitation coming from Tal. At first Hal and Phillip had been a little surprised, but after the first course of wine and food arrived, all questions of who had made the invitation were put aside. For Hal and Phillip, this was the finest meal they had ever had.

At the halfway point, Hal said, "I feel fit to burst, my lord Hawkins, yet I can't wait to see what your next culinary surprise is."

"Not 'my lord,' just Tal."

Jim smiled. "Our host is being modest. He holds the title of Court Baron in the Kingdom, though he abides in Olasko now and has a few commendations from Roldem." For years an independent duchy, Olasko had become part of the Kingdom of Roldem as part of a treaty settlement after the last independent duke, Kaspar, had been deposed. Tal had played a major hand in that and as a result was highly regarded in Roldem. He still resided in Olasko, but kept quarters in the River House.

"Still," said Tal, "I fear my patents are . . ."—he glanced at Jim—"not of sufficient import to deserve the honorific." In fact, both men knew that the original role played by Tal, that of an obscure Kingdom noble, was a charade. Born of a tribal people high in the mountains called the High Fastness, which bordered Olasko to the west, he had been one of the few survivors of a brutal war waged on his nation. Fate and circumstance, and the invisible hand of the Conclave of Shadows, had led him around the world and had gained him fame and wealth, but it had come at a bitter price. Finally, he said, "Just Tal is fine."

"Where did you learn to fence?" Ty asked Hal. "I didn't expect such skill from someone from . . ." He paused as if trying to pick his next words carefully. The Far Coast of the Kingdom might as well have been on another world to those who lived around the Sea of Kingdoms.

Hal grinned. "The rustic west?" he supplied.

Swordmaster Phillip shrugged. "It's true, but there are

several lads I've trained who would be no shame to the Duchy of Crydee had they come in his stead."

"It's not all broadswords and heater shields," said Hal. "Our family's tradition is to train in a variety of weapons. The Far Coast is heavily wooded, with few places for battles on open land, so we train as we must to defend our homes."

"Interesting," said Tal. "I know from experience that terrain is critical, and those who do not know how to fight where they find themselves are at a disadvantage." He was thinking of his mountainous homeland and how different warfare was there compared to the more civilized regions of the Eastern Kingdoms where there were roads and rivers to transport armies and their necessities.

"We have a good number of archers," said Hal. "Both bondsmen and franklins, most of whom are skilled hunters with the longbow."

At that Tal smiled.

"You know the bow?" asked Phillip.

As wine was poured by the servants, Talwin began to shake his head, but it was Jim who answered. "He can take a rider out of his seat at a hundred yards."

Tal's eyes narrowed. That story was only known to a few, and up until this minute he would have bet every gold coin he had that Jim Dasher had never heard the tale of his hunting down the mercenary named Raven.

After being silent for a brief second, Tal said, "Could once, but I fear my skills have declined with age."

Suddenly Swordmaster Phillip was animated. "You know, speaking of riders, there's this new sort of bow, Keshian originally, a double recurved laminated with ox horn instead of heartwood. Have you seen it?"

Jim caught Tal's eye, and Hawkins said, "Yes, but perhaps we can discuss archery another time, Swordmaster." He had noticed that the last of the other diners had departed. "We are alone, Jim."

"The servants?"

"All with me for years and trusted. If Roldem or Kesh has an agent in my employee, Pug's got some magic-users who cannot do their jobs."

"Good enough," said Jim. He turned first to Hal, then Tal, and said, "I have sought you out to bring you warnings, both of you."

"What?" asked the young western lord, under the influence of a little too much wine, but not quite drunk.

Jim held up his hand to silence him. "On instructions from the Prince of Krondor, the call has been sent to your father for the Western Muster."

Phillip was half out of his seat at hearing that. "I must return to Crydee at once!"

"Please, sit," said Jim. "You can't find a ship until morning to get you to Salador, so abide a few moments longer."

"Why the muster?" Tal asked. "I would not have thought the west was at much risk."

"The Prince, at the King's direction, is being cautious. All forces in the west—the Principality, the Southern Marches, Yabon, and Crydee—are to muster." Jim sat back obviously unhappy. "It's what we don't know that has us worried." Glancing at Hawkins, he said, "Our western friends are probably not too current with the gossip from the Imperial Keshian Court."

Hal said, "I suspect you're not talking ladies' fashions, as from what I hear, they hardly wear enough clothing to worry about such a thing." Seeing that his humor was falling flat, he sat back in his chair and said, "Sorry," to Ty's obvious amusement.

Tal shook his head. "Just that there's a growing faction within their ruling body, the Gallery of Lords and Masters, between some of the Trueblood, especially among the Master of the Chariots and some generals of the Inner Legion."

Phillip said, "If I know my history, it's only about twenty years since the last time that alliance nearly plunged the Empire into civil war."

Jim paused for a moment, before saying, "Correct. Tal, what else is being gossiped about in the halls of power?" He was uncertain how much either man knew (and he was certain both boys were ignorant of) the true nature of the events Phillip referred to. An evil sorcerer by the name of Leso Varen had taken possession of the old Emperor's body and almost destroyed the heart of Great Kesh. The story made public had been that Pug and other members of the Academy of Magicians at Stardock had hunted down a rogue spellcaster who had attempted to destroy the royal family.

Tal continued, "Most of what we hear seems to be the usual Keshian politics. The envoys to the Court of Roldem are much as you'd expect: Truebloods with ties to the Imperial Family, loyal beyond question to the Emperor, so what we hear over dinner is fairly much what you'd expect from those worthies." He looked at Jim. "Emperor Sezioti feels a debt to Pug and the Conclave, as well as having a much kinder perspective on the Kingdom for the aid that saved his family from Leso Varen."

"He does," said Jim. "However, not so many in the Gallery of Lords and Masters feel as the Imperials do. Remember, it's been more than twenty years since Sezioti took the throne, and while his brother Dangai still commands the Inner Legions, outside the Imperials there are many of the Trueblood who seek to expand their power."

"But war with the Kingdom?" asked Hal. "It makes no sense."

"On the surface," said Jim. "But there are two things that make me itch." He held up one finger. "A common enemy defuses internal conflict, and while the Emperor and his brother may feel some debt to the Kingdom for events long past, we've had more than enough bloodshed along the border, especially in the Vale of Dreams, to overwhelm those happier reminiscences." He held up a second finger. "They smell weakness. The Kingdom has never been more vulnerable."

Tal let out a long sigh. "The King."

"Yes, the King. Gregory is weak. And while his father, Patrick, was hardly that, he was imprudent. He let his well-known temper bring him to insult Kesh on more than one occasion. So we've lacked a prudent ruler for many years.

"Edward is a fine administrator, but the west has been almost forgotten in a generation, and . . ." He sat back.

"What?" asked Hal, now alarmed. "You don't expect Kesh to attack Crydee, certainly?"

"We must prepare for all eventualities," said Jim.

Hal was suddenly focused, all hint of intoxication gone. "The muster will be kept close to home and no companies sent east until Krondor is threatened. Should we be attacked, Yabon will answer our call for reinforcements and Crydee's forces will be sent to Yabon. Kesh would be foolish to sail up from Elarial and attack Tulan or Carse."

"You've a good military mind there, young Henry," said Jim. "But logic in war is often knowing things your enemy does not."

"We must be prepared," said Phillip, frowning. He had reached his limit of understanding. He might be a fine soldier and a decent tactician, but complex strategy was beyond his area of expertise.

"What makes you think Kesh might strike in the west?" asked Tal.

Choosing his words carefully, for only a handful of men in the Kingdom really understood his true role in the affairs of the Kingdom, Jim said, "I am led to believe there are large mobilizations of forces in the south, including garrisons in the Keshian Confederacy." The Confederacy was a large region of tribal lands, city states, and loose alliances dominated and controlled by Kesh for centuries, though they had never been fully pacified.

"Can they draw forces from the garrisons in the Confederacy?"

"Normally, no," answered Jim. An expression of concern crossed his face for a moment before it became unreadable once more.

"The nations of the Confederacy are constantly in one of two conditions: open rebellion against the Empire, or planning the next rebellion. Those legions are vital for the stability of the southern third of the Empire. Without them, the Confederates would sweep north and occupy as much Imperial land as possible."

Ty glanced at his father then asked Jim, "Why? I mean, if the Empire pulls its forces out of the Confederacy, wouldn't the people in the Confederacy just . . . let them go away?"

Jim forced a smile. "Not much Keshian history in your education, eh?" He turned serious again. "If you were to ride through that region, Ty, you'd find yourself in a miserable land."

He put his hands together and formed a circle, thumbs pointing upward, an inch apart. "Imagine this is the Confederacy. Across the top of the circle lie two ranges of mountains forming the Girdle of Kesh: the western, longer half is called the Belt." He wiggled his right thumb. "The shorter, eastern half is the Clasp." He wiggled his left thumb. "There are two towns on the north of the Girdle, Lockpoint and Teléman. Neither is rightly a town, more like very large garrisons with civilians to support them. Their task is to keep murderous hordes of very angry Confederates from sweeping north through the only major pass between the Belt and the Clasp.

"To the east of what passes for arable land is the Drahali-Kapur Desert. To the west the Dragon Mere swamplands, and south an arid, rolling plain leading to more mountains, swamps, and woodlands aptly named the Forest of the Lost, because no one who's ever ventured in there has come back to tell us what's in there. As for the plains, they're hardly useful: thin topsoil and little water, except when it's storm season and everything is under three feet of water for a month.

"In short, the people who reside in the Confederacy would prefer to live just about anywhere else in the world but on their own land. But, and here you see the perverse nature of humankind in fullest flower, they'll happily kill one another over who gets to squat on which miserable piece of land. There's one town on a rocky peninsula called Brijané, home to the Brijaner sea raiders. The Imperial treasury pays them handsomely not to build ships to transport people north from the Confederacy. And they pretty much hate everyone else down there, especially the Ashunta horsemen.

"But the one thing that keeps the mountain people from killing the flatlanders, the flatlanders from killing the swamp raiders, and everyone from killing the desert men is a universal hatred of the Empire. That's what binds them together."

Jim looked off into the distance for a moment, thinking, then said, "No, I cannot begin to imagine how Kesh could strip her southern garrisons for a war in the north. Yet . . ."

"Doesn't the King have agents in Kesh?" Hal asked.

Jim glanced at Tal and then said, "It is rumored so." He shrugged. "But information is scant and unreliable."

"Well, then," said Hal. "We'll just have to be ready for whatever Kesh brings." He didn't sound like a young man exhibiting false bravado, but rather a thoughtful future leader of men.

Jim studied him for a moment, then glanced around. "It's getting late and I must get to bed soon, for there's a full day of diplomatic nonsense I must endure before tomorrow's gala." Everyone stood, and Jim said, "Hal, if I might request something."

"Sir?"

"Do not return to the university tonight. With the hour late and stirrings of trouble in the air, I would sleep better knowing you are safe. You may be distant kin to His Majesty, but you are still kin and I would feel a personal responsibility should anything happen to you while I was in this city."

Tal said, "We have extra rooms for those rare occasions when a patron is not safe to go home. The bedding is fresh. Ty, show our two guests to their rooms."

"You can travel to the university in the morning," said Jim, "as you must look your best tomorrow evening." To Phillip, he said, "Feel free to return to your duke, tomorrow, Swordmaster. Until certain matters here in Roldem are resolved, I will personally undertake to look after young Lord Henry's well-being. Rest assured, and please let his father know this is the case."

"I will, sir. Then goodnight, gentlemen," said Swordmaster Phillip.

Ty led the two guests upstairs. When they were out of earshot, Tal said, "What's really going on down there, Jim?"

While not close, the two men knew each other well enough that Tal knew Jim was very high up in the King's court, a much more important man than his rank indicated. He also knew Jim was in charge of the King's intelligence service. And each knew the other had served the Conclave in the past.

"I don't know, Tal, and that's the gods' truth. What has me concerned is that all my reports from north of the Girdle are routine: everything in the Empire itself is calm. But all my agents south of the Girdle have gone silent."

"Silent?"

"I haven't had a report from anyone in the Confederacy in three months. The two men I've dispatched to see why have yet to return or report."

"Now I understand your worry."

"There's something going on down there, and there are strange reports coming from the Imperial Court. There's a faction of the Gallery of Lords and Masters that is almost outright calling for war against the Kingdoms."

"Kingdoms?"

"Roldem as well as the Isles."

"Are they mad? Roldem's fleet alongside the Isles would sweep every Imperial ship from the ocean. The Quegans would love an excuse to sack Durbin and Elarial in the west."

"They are not mad," said Jim, tapping his cheek absently as if goading himself to think. "But if it's true, this makes no sense."

"What else?" asked Tal.

"You don't miss much, do you?"

"My people are taught at a very early age to be observant, and the Conclave put me through some rigorous training." With a small smile he said, "Why do you think I get so few invitations to play cards?" Then his features became solemn once more. "You hid it well, but there's something you didn't tell young Lord Henry."

"The Prince is worried as to what might occur should Crydee be ordered to reinforce Krondor. It's a small enough army—the smallest in the west—and there's a lot of territory to protect."

"Protect?" Tal's gaze narrowed. "If the attack is on Krondor, you don't expect a simultaneous assault on the Far Coast, surely?"

"Not from Kesh."

"Then from whom?"

Jim shook his head. "Just suffice it to say the Prince is not sanguine about Crydee's neighbors."

For a moment, Tal was confused. "The Free Cities . . . ?" Then comprehension dawned. "The *elves*?"

"The Star Elves, in particular. We've had a long and peaceful relationship with those in Elvandar, but these newcomers . . ." Jim fell silent. After a long moment he went on, "I don't know what to tell you. They've made no hostile act, yet they are aloof; and we get reports now and again of people wandering near their borders disappearing, never to be seen again. They've come to some sort of understanding with the dwarves to their south, but as I understand it, friendship is hardly the word. They are an unknown quantity, and unknowns make me very nervous."

"What do you hear from Pug?"

"Nothing," said Jim. "If the Conclave has heard rumors of war, they are not sharing them with me. Besides, Pug has always said he will not become involved in matters of national conflict again."

Talwin was silent as he thought about this, then said, "He might if such a war would weaken us enough to be unable to withstand another assault . . . like the Dasati."

Both men fell silent. An entire world, Kelewan, had been destroyed in a barely repulsed attack by powerful forces from another plane of reality. And for more than ten years all members of the Conclave, active or not, had been asked to keep their ears open for any news of demon activity.

Jim said, "Perhaps I should presume to remind him of that?"

"Perhaps," agreed Tal, "you should. I wonder what Pug is up to these days?"

Pug looked around the cave. Magnus held his hand aloft, using magic to create a bright light on the palm of his hand, which he moved around the room like a lantern. "We're too late," he said.

"Yes," said Amirantha. "What happened here happened more than a year ago."

Amirantha's companion, the old warrior Brandos, knelt, complaining, "Ah. My knees aren't what they once were." He peered at the stones around the broken remnants of a wooden table. "Fair tore this place apart, it did."

Looking at the Demon Master, Pug asked, "What do you think happened?"

Amirantha, Warlock of the Satumbria, considered the question. He was garbed in plainer fashion than he had effected when Pug had first met him. He was still vain enough to trim his beard daily and make sure his flowing dark hair was combed, but his florid robes with their golden and silver threading lay in a clothes chest at the old castle on Sorcerer's Isle that served as the headquarters for the Conclave of Shadows. Unlike the mummery he had employed to flummox local nobles and convince them to pay him gold to chase away the very demons he summoned, his work with the Conclave had involved real danger and traveling under harsh conditions. Now he wore simple tunics and trousers and rugged leather boots.

After thinking about the question for a moment, Amirantha said, "I think the object of our search conducted his last summoning here." He pointed to a distant corner, and Magnus turned his hand in that direction, throwing light upon it.

The tall, white-haired magician, Pug's sole surviving child, moved closer until they could see clearly what Amirantha had noticed. Outlined more darkly than the rock against which it lay was the form of a man, crouching. Brandos ran his hand over the surface of the cave wall. "It's as if he was turned to ash and pounded into the rock itself."

The old fighter had been with Amirantha for most of his life, having been a boy when the Warlock had taken him under his care. Now looking older than his mentor, he turned to face Pug and the others. "I've seen this before, but I can't remember where."

"I do," said Amirantha. "Years ago, when you were a child, it happened at one of the very first summonings you were party to, remember?" When it became clear that Brandos didn't, he prompted, "The cat?"

"Oh!" responded Brandos as comprehension dawned. "Yes, the cat!"

Amirantha said, "When Brandos was a child and came to live with me, I thought having a boy along would make me look even more credible as I came to rid a town or village of a demon. After all, what sort of mountebank would lovingly care for a child?"

"Your kind," said Brandos with a rueful smile.

"The cat?" prompted Pug.

"Yes, the cat. It's a long tale, but the part that applies here is that my friend, when he was a boy, managed to interrupt one of my summonings at the worst possible moment. He was annoying a cat we had around the house and it fled into my chamber . . . well, instead of the tractable creature I expected, one showed up I'd never seen before or since. A massive winged monster that spewed fire of an incredible heat."

"Nearly burned the entire house down," added Brandos. Pug and Magnus could tell the story had been told enough times that it had become one of those family lore events that was treasured as much for the entertainment value as it had caused outrage and consternation at the time it had happened.

"Unfortunately for the cat, but fortunately for me, the creature's attention seemed drawn to movement. I was motionless, in the midst of my summoning, while the cat was scampering, stopping only long enough to hiss at the demon.

"The demon made short work of it, and I was able to banish it back to the demon realm, but not before, as Brandos said, a rather large fire had broken out in my chambers.

"When we went back the next day to see what might be salvaged, the outline of the cat could clearly be seen against the wall, much as you see here."

"Another accident?" asked Pug, his brow furrowing. "Or another attempt by those behind the Demon War to destroy anyone who might eventually oppose them?"

Looking around the cave, Amirantha said, "We can only speculate."

Pug's frustration was surfacing. Since the advent of demon incursions into Midkemia, and especially after the events several years earlier at the abandoned Keshian fortress above the Valley of Lost Men, he was blocked at every turn as he attempted to understand what was threatening his world. Something unprecedented was occurring in the demon realm, which Pug and his companions referred to as the Fifth Circle, and while evidence of that upheaval and its potential danger to Midkemia was scant and infrequent, Pug knew that even though the Demon King Dahun had been destroyed attempting to enter this realm, they were still far from safe.

In fact, one topic of conversation revisited on a regular basis with the Warlock was what could cause a powerful

Demon Lord to flee from that realm into this one; not coming at the head of an army as had happened in the past, to conquer and destroy, but sneaking in disguised as a human, seeking to find a safe place to hide.

To hide from what?

That was always the question they were left with.

With a last look around the cave, Pug said, "Magnus?"

Understanding his father's wishes, the younger magician motioned for the others to stand close to him and a moment later they were all back in the large entrance hall on Sorcerer's Island.

It was early spring, and the weather was still cold and damp. "Have you ever considered rebuilding that lovely villa?" Brandos asked lightly.

Pug shot him a sharp glance. The remnants of the sprawling estate that had housed his school of magic had been the scene of his worst defeat at the hands of those seeking to destroy the Conclave, and it had cost him the lives of his wife, son, and daughter-in-law, as well as more than two dozen students. The charred timbers and stones still standing were being quickly overgrown with vines and wild grasses. In not too many more years it would be difficult for anyone chancing on the site to recognize it as the once-proud home of a thriving community.

Without further comment Pug turned and walked away to speak with Jason, the magician who acted as the castle's reeve, the man who was responsible for the fortification and those living within it while Pug and Magnus were absent.

Brandos glanced at Magnus, who shrugged slightly. If the white-haired magician understood his father's reason for keeping the villa abandoned, he wasn't sharing it. At first it had simply been a matter of expediency, in case enemies were spying on them, suggesting that the Conclave had been destroyed and that only a few refugees were left huddling for safety in the old castle on the bluffs overlooking the Bitter Sea. Which, Brandos conceded silently to himself, wasn't that far from the truth.

But the Conclave had endured, even thrived, though it was now scattered across the entire span of the world, with pockets of research and teaching located in isolated spots, while many who worked for the organization did so in the hearts of power, in various courts and capitals.

Amirantha watched Magnus follow his father and turned to his old companion. "You still have a knack for it, don't you?"

"Apparently," said Brandos. He let out a long sigh. "I've seen it before and I know you have. He's hanging on by sheer will and there's no joy in him."

Amirantha took a moment, then looked around. "Could there be any joy here?"

Both men knew the answer already. They had supped with others from the Conclave here many times, a warm fire in the hearth, chatting about this and that, but on none of those occasions had there been anything close to a sense of celebration. When a child was born, it was somewhere else. When the great holidays of Midwinter Day or Midsummer Day, the Planting Celebration, or the Harvest Festival came along, they were largely ignored save perhaps for a minor remark.

Of all in the Conclave, only a handful resided permanently here in the castle. Among those who stayed were Amirantha, Brandos, and Brandos's wife, Samantha; Jason, the castle's caretaker; Rose, his wife and a magician in her own right; and a very young apprentice, Maloc. And of course Pug and Magnus. There were always one or two others coming and going, but those eight composed the whole of the household of the castle.

Brandos said, "We've seen a lot here, but there's more to this than just a man having trouble moving on after the death of his wife and son."

Amirantha motioned for Brandos to follow him up the stairs leading to the tower room put aside for him. They passed the door into Brandos and Samantha's quarters, and the old fighter stopped briefly to put away his sword and shield and change out of his shirt. Then he followed his adopted father up to the topmost room.

Brandos said, "We could go back to Gashen Tor. Samantha misses the women from the village." The village was called Talumba, and it was situated two days east of the city of Maharta, now the capital of the Kingdom of Muboya. For an idle moment Amirantha wondered how Kaspar of Olasko was faring; he was the First Minister to the Maharaja of Muboya and had returned to serve his lord and master when they had finished with the Demon Gate business five years earlier.

"No," said Amirantha. "But take Samantha and go for a visit. I think it would do both of you some good."

"What about you?" asked Brandos, scrutinizing his foster father for any sign of distress or sadness. The mood throughout this place tended toward melancholy, and the Warlock was already a man given to dark introspection if given half a chance.

"Actually, Gulamendis has invited me to visit him at E'bar."

Gulamendis was another Demon Master, one of the Taredhel, or Star Elves, and he and Amirantha had become friends, or as friendly as one of those arrogant creatures could be with a human. Their affinity stemmed from a ravenous curiosity about all things demon, and Gulamendis has spent close to a year in residence here before returning to the city built in the Grey Tower Mountains by his people.

"Well, say hello for me," said Brandos. "Now, how do we get to Gashen Tor? Do you have one of those orb things, or is it a long sea voyage?"

"I'll ask Jason if he has one to lend."

"He may say no," answered Brandos. "Seems they're breaking down, and none of the artificers, even of Tsurani descent up in LaMut, know how to fix them or make new ones."

Amirantha frowned. "I would have thought after all these years Pug would have seen to that."

A voice from the door said, "I know a great deal, Amirantha, but I don't know everything."

Brandos hadn't heard the magician come up the stairs, and he stepped aside to let him into the room.

"No disrespect intended, Pug."

"I know," said Pug. "I overheard a bit. So you're going to visit the elves in E'bar?"

"Overdue," said Amirantha. He motioned for Pug to take the chair by the small desk, while he sat on his bed. "We're at something of a dead end. I'm not entirely sure what specifically you're seeking, but each piece of information your agents turn up leads us to a dead end."

"Very dead, sometimes," said Brandos. Seeing his humor fall flat, he said, "I think I'll go tell Samantha to pack up and we'll talk about a visit home."

"Ask Magnus to take you and arrange a signal to fetch you back. You were right about the Tsurani orbs: we're down to a scant few and need them for more pressing use."

"I understand. Thanks for lending us Magnus," said Brandos as he departed.

Amirantha watched him go. Then he looked over at the magician. "Pug, I don't claim to know you well, but it has been over five years now. And I do know what a driven man looks like. I even share your sense of alarm over what we've discovered up to this point, but I detect an urgency in you that doesn't seem entirely born out of what we know. What is it you're not telling me?"

Pug's face was immobile, though his eyes searched the Warlock's face. "A time is coming, soon, when I will tell you things you will wish I had never told you." Then he got to his feet, turned away, and hurried down the tower stairs.

Amirantha was left alone to reflect on this. He had a nasty feeling that what Pug had just said was almost certainly true.

4

JOURNEY

Amirantha was astonished.

He had been unprepared for the magnificence of the Star Elves' city, E'bar. Although less than three years had elapsed since it had been completed, the city was anything but unfinished or roughly hewn; it showed grace and beauty far beyond even the most impressive human achievements in Rillanon, the Jeweled City, capital of the Kingdom of the Isles, or the Upper City in the city of Kesh, home of the Imperial Family and the Truebloods.

Here were few of the massive stone-and-wood constructions of humans; here, stone had been sculptured in a fashion far beyond any mortal mason's ability. Amirantha roughly understood the concept: geomancers willed stone into a fluid state, then sculpted it. Human geomancers were rare, though some did exist, but their craft was crude compared to what Amirantha saw before him.

The entire wall around the city appeared seamless, as if crafted from a single stone of mountainous size. Gates to the north and south and smaller portals to the east and west appeared to have organically grown within the wall as it was formed, and the Warlock thought this might not have been far from the truth. Even the gates themselves were of stone, though how they were engineered to swing freely upon unseen hinges was beyond his ability to even guess at. Even the background tingle of magic he felt when Pug or Magnus used their powers was missing. There was a far more subtle sense of the otherworldly to this place, something he had experienced in a much more disturbing fashion when dealing with certain demons. That alone would have fascinated him, but it was merely one of a million details that strove to capture his thoughts.

Everywhere there was color, subtle but vivid. Columns of pale sand and rose edged in white or silver rose to support graceful arches above streets. Even the streets were paved with alternating squares of bright ochre and grey, with light purple grouting in between. Window shades were of the finest silk, many-layered to block unwelcome gazes yet allow light to enter. And the gold! Everywhere gold glistened in the sunlight, decorating the poles from which flew bright banners and pennons. Gold adorned doors and windows and ran as trim along rooflines. It was astonishing.

"I'm gawking, aren't I?" he asked his host.

Gulamendis, Demon Master of the Taredhel, smiled. "More than one visitor to E'bar looks as you do now. You'll get accustomed to it." Glancing around to see if he was being overheard, he added, "Truth to tell, we are a vain people. And I suspect my people look much that way when they visit Elvandar."

"Do many of you journey to pay homage to the Queen?"

"More than the Lord Regent likes." He paused, awkward. "Come, let us refresh ourselves. You will pay a courtesy call on the Lord Regent later today, but before that we must speak of many things."

The elf's tone was almost conversational, but Amirantha had spent enough time with Gulamendis to know that his host was troubled and that many things were best not discussed in the open. Amirantha had arrived at the eastern portal and had not been allowed to step into E'bar until Gulamendis arrived to escort him. The Warlock had the distinct feeling that had his host not put in an appearance, he might have found it difficult to depart in peace. The two Sentinels looked like seasoned, hardened fighters, not the sort of city watch or constable one tended to find on the gates of a human city.

In the distance a baby's crying could be heard briefly until it was calmed by its mother. "I understand babies are a rarity among your kind," Amirantha said.

Gulamendis looked at him with one raised eyebrow. "Really. Who told you that?"

"Perhaps I misunderstood."

"If you are thinking of the other races of the Edhel, perhaps. But the Taredhel are a fecund race. I know little of our distant kin, but we enjoy our children."

Amirantha had the sense that he had stumbled across something significant but couldn't quite put his finger on what it was. He decided to wait until such a time as he could speak with Pug, who knew as much about the elves as any human living.

They reached Gulamendis's quarters, and the elf beckoned for his guest to enter.

As quarters went, the Warlock had lived in far worse, but somehow he had expected a little more, given the opulence and splendor he had seen elsewhere in this city. The walls were bare, with no decoration of any sort, and the only furniture was simple: a bed, a table, a chair that Gulamendis offered his guest while he sat on the bed, and a pair of chests. The one other thing that caught his eye was a small case of scrolls and books. Otherwise, it looked more like a monk's quarters than a scholar's.

"Where do you eat?" asked Amirantha.

"We have a large kitchen in the square. We all take turns helping, cooking, cleaning. Should I choose a mate, larger quarters will be found for me, and once children arrive, larger still." He smiled. "There's little chance of that, I suspect."

"Really?" The Warlock knew very little about the Star Elves, but he had a vague sense that the elf with whom he spoke was not well regarded.

"I will say, though, these are better quarters than the last the Lord Regent allotted me."

Amirantha frowned.

"I was housed for weeks in an iron cage in the Lord Regent's compound while my brother was exploring this world, as a hostage against his good behavior."

"Sounds uncomfortable."

With a small, bitter laugh, the Demon Master said, "It was. So, we invited you years ago, and now you appear. Why?"

"To the point," agreed Amirantha. "Pug and I have been chasing every tale of demon or summoner since we witnessed"—he paused as Gulamendis held up his hand, palm outward, cautioning him against specifics—"what we witnessed. So far we have found little that is useful: empty huts, abandoned homes, deserted caves. Or we find signs of conflict and destruction. Not one demon summoner we had working for our . . ."—he glanced around—"friends, has survived."

At the choice of words, Gulamendis queried, "Survived?"

"Someone, it appears, is hunting down Demon Masters and demon summoners," said Amirantha quietly. "And it appears a fair number of demons have come into the world and broken wards and killed their summoners."

"They'd be powerful," said Gulamendis thoughtfully.

"But where are they?"

Gulamendis was silent for more than a minute as he pondered the question. Finally he said, "How many do you estimate?"

"More than a dozen."

"Ah." He smiled as he looked at his human friend. "Now I see the reason for the visit. Does Pug know?"

"He knows there are more than a dozen demons loose in this realm. He doesn't know the significance of that fact."

"Demons hiding." Gulamendis appeared amused by the revelation. "It hardly bears contemplation, does it?"

The Warlock was forced to agree. "Nothing like this has occurred before."

"That we are aware of, you mean."

Amirantha, Warlock of the Satumbria, let out a long sigh. "Because if this is true, one must ask, how many others are there we know nothing of, and—"

"Why are they here?" finished the elf.

Child studied the terrain below. It had been a week since she had devoured her mother, and she had fed only three times since. Most of the energy consumed had gone to replenish her already-depleted strength, but she had gained a little size and power. She didn't question how she knew what she knew: what she had inherited from those she ate, and what was from her own experience. She didn't care. She had to survive. That was all she needed to know; everything else was academic.

A group of three small creatures huddled below an over-hanging rock, much as she and her mother had a week before, waiting for dark apparently in the hope that they could find better shelter. She wondered why they weren't concerned by night predators. She knew the night predators to be even more dangerous than those who hunted in the day.

This piece of knowledge wasn't something she had in-herited; this was from experience. There had been a bitter fight the night after she had consumed her mother. The night hunter had been upon her before she had even known she was under attack. Only a slight misjudgment on his part had saved her, for rather than snap her neck the hunter had bitten deep into her shoulder. She used the scant instant she had gained to reach up with her left hand and use her claws to good effect. She had forced him to release his bite, then spun while yanking his head back until it had been *her* fangs ripping out *his* throat.

She had gained a great deal of knowledge on how to hunt in these mountains from him. And her night vision was now exceptional. She had used her new abilities to good advantage, but even so, the amount of prey was scant. Now she looked down upon a possible feast.

It depended on how able these three were likely to be at protecting themselves. She had learned almost at forfeit of her life that there was a gulf between knowledge and experience. By consuming the Archivist's knowledge, she knew a great deal more than any her age among the People should know, but as far as experience was concerned she still was a child. *The* Child, as she thought of herself.

But although she lacked experience, she possessed cunning. She was sure she could master all three of these pitiful fugitives if she planned . . . *Planned?* she thought. Until that moment her existence had been mostly in the moment, with some part of her consciousness knowing she needed to move east, to get away from the advancing Darkness. She wished she could trap a flyer, for if she could consume one, she might gain the blessing of flight; her essence was still forming, and with flight she would be able to hunt better, move faster, and reconnoiter more efficiently. Unfortunately, flyers had been rare, and when she had seen them, they had been far too high to attract their attention. Besides, she had considered at last, any flyer bold enough to attack her directly would probably be both experienced and powerful.

Glancing around, she saw the shadows deepen, dark maroon and purple shades slipping into black, while the brilliance of the red, yellow, and orange rocks faded to grey before her eyes. There was something tickling at the edge of her mind, a pleasant feeling at witnessing this otherwise prosaic event. After a moment she connected it to a concept; it was nice to look at; it was . . . pretty? Yes, that was the concept. It made her feel better to look at something pretty.

She waited, and when the sun was low in the west, the three fugitives came out from their hiding place. She instantly recognized the robes of the last to emerge: another Archivist. She smiled. Scampering above them for a dozen yards, she leaped upon the first in line, breaking his neck before he could react, then wheeled and ripped out the throat of the second.

The Archivist crouched, seeing the futility of running from a more powerful opponent, and backed away. What was he doing? she wondered. Then she laughed. "You think that if hunger has driven me to a frenzy, I may devour these two while you make your escape?"

The Archivist said, "Yes, that would be logical."

She tapped the side of her head. "I know things, too. I have devoured one of your class."

The Archivist stood, drawing himself up to his full height. He was about the size she had been days before; now she towered over him by two heads. "Why do you not attack?"

She moved toward him purposefully. "Tell me about the difference between knowledge and experience."

"Knowledge is abstracted," he answered, "learned from any number of sources. Experience is that which we encounter in our own right, as life brings it, and from which we process knowledge that can be gained no other way."

"Which is better?"

"Knowledge," said the Archivist without hesitation. "Experience is limited, while knowledge can be gained from many other beings' experiences."

"But knowledge without experience . . ." she began.

He finished, " . . . limits how well that knowledge can be applied."

"What is missing?"

"You need a teacher."

She smiled. "Yes. If you teach me, I will let you live; more, I will hunt for you."

Seeing the powerful young female before him, the Archivist knew there was only one answer that would enable him to live beyond the few seconds. "I will teach you. I am Belog."

"I am Child. Come, eat with me."

Seeing nothing odd in it, the Archivist joined his new student in feasting on the two servants who had moments before been his companions. He considered that although he had not devoured a companion since his youth, it was, after all, the way of the People.

No matter how civilized King Dahun might have tried to make them, they were at heart the same as the Savage Ones or the Mad Ones. At their core they were all demons.

5

COURT

The heralds blew their trumpets.

The entire court turned and bowed as the King of Roldem entered, escorting his wife to their twin thrones at the far end of the great hall of the palace.

The hall was bedecked in the royal colors, large banners of powder blue with golden trim, featuring the dolphin crest of the royal house. The King's personal guard likewise wore tabards of the same colors, but the rest of the evening's finery was a riot of different hues.

In years past, the fashion of the court had gone through a phase Jim Dasher thought of as "drab"—muted grey and black attire for the men and deep, dark colors for the women's gowns. But this season those who decided such things had decreed that bright festive colors would be the choice. Jim felt a little odd in a brilliant green tunic and yellow leggings. He prayed that trousers would return to fashion soon; he disliked tights.

His black boots were ankle high and the most valued item he wore; despite their fashionable appearance they were durable and versatile, just as useful for clambering over rooftops without slipping as for slogging through the sewers, since they could be cleaned with a simple wipe of a cloth.

Jim hadn't clambered over a rooftop or slogged through a sewer for a few years, but some habits were hard to break. He glanced around the room.

Young Lord Henry stood next to Ty Hawkins, while Talwin Hawkins was in conversation with a minor Keshian noble. Jim made a note to ask Tal what the Keshian had wanted to speak of. He knew that war was almost certainly coming, and he knew that every agent of Kesh in the Kingdom Sea region would be gathering every scrap of information out there, as were his own agents, some fifteen of which were currently on this island.

Jim kept his frustration buried: to the casual onlooker he would be another minor Kingdom noble come to the court of Roldem for personal or political gain, but one hardly worth more than a cursory examination despite his famous grandfather. At this point in his career, Jim knew he was known to his enemies, who were many, and appeared transparent to those who weren't. This was as he wished it, for as long as the pretense was kept up, no harm would come to him when he appeared openly at court. It was when he vanished from sight and emerged among the shadows that murder would begin.

Jim moved among the crowd, making his way slowly toward the throne. He could expect to be presented to the King in about an hour, some time just before the Champion of the Masters' Court was presented.

He studied young Ty Hawkins, involved in an animated conversation with Henry conDoin. The King of the Isles's distant cousin listened with a smile as his opponent of the previous day told a tale.

It was on young men such as these the fate of the Kingdom of the Isles, and perhaps all of Triagia, would turn, Jim knew. Capable young men who were free of the corruption of politics and greed.

Ty was problematic, because his father was a Kingdom noble in name only. That fiction had been created by the Conclave to employ Tal as a weapon for the Conclave's service, and it gave him entrance to certain venues in the Kingdom of the Isles, just as his rank as past Champion of the Masters' Court gave it to him here in Roldem, but Talwin Hawkins was a grudging servant of the Conclave at best and no servant at all at worst. Still, keeping him at least as an ally would serve, if the son could be captured, thought Jim. And if the need arose, Jim had the power to make that false patent of nobility a real one. Not that Tal needed it, as he was becoming rich beyond the dreams of the mountain boy he had once been, but it might prove useful to turn his son into a Kingdom noble some day. In Roldem they would both have status as Champions of the Masters' Court, but neither would achieve rank. And as Jim knew rank, as well as privilege, had its uses.

Now it was Henry's turn to tell a tale. Jim had no doubt both stories were being inflated to bolster the young men's standing; they stood like two young roosters with their chests puffed out, seeing who could crow loudest at daybreak. One day they'd be bitter rivals or like brothers, and only fate would determine which it would be.

Jim looked away from the throne and felt his heart sink. Making a beeline for him was the Kingdom of the Isles's ambassador to Roldem, His Excellency Lord John Ravenscar; and on his arm was none other than the Lady Franciezka Sorboz.

"My lord," said the ambassador, fixing Jim with a skeptical look. "I was unaware you were in Roldem," he said. It was customary for Kingdom nobles to make themselves known to the ambassador upon arriving on the island.

"Apologies, Your Excellency," said Jim. "The press of business caused me to be remiss in my duty."

"You know the Lady Franciezka, I believe," said the ambassador. The sight of the portly bureaucrat, resplendent in a maroon silk surcoat, white ruffled suit, and white leggings made Jim wish even more fervently for the return of men's trousers to this court, for he looked like nothing more than a fat-bellied, spindly-legged turkey in those hose.

Franciezka, on the other hand, looked magnificent in whatever she wore, Jim knew from experience. She also looked magnificent wearing nothing at all, which Jim also knew from experience. They had been lovers on several occasions, and she had tried to kill him twice, for purely professional reasons. She was one of the King of Roldem's deadliest agents and ran the equivalent of Jim's intelligence service, the Secret Police of Roldem.

She had the face of a girl ten years younger, a fact that had enabled her to disguise herself as a child when needed; she could look the part of a girl of fifteen or less or a crone of eighty years. She had a slender body bordering on the boyish, except for a round backside that Jim had always had a weakness for, but he knew her body to be as strong as a rapier's blade, deadly despite being slight.

Pale blond hair that was almost white in the day's sunlight framed delicate features. Large blue eyes turned upon him as she said, "Why, Lord James, I'm almost as aggrieved as the ambassador at your not letting me know you were in the city."

She wore a brilliant yellow gown with green silk trim set with pearls of white and black, and a series of gold-threaded tassels hung at the hem, sweeping the floor as she moved. Like the other ladies' gowns this evening, her décolletage was cut low, the bodice was lifted, and the waist cinched. Jim wondered how women breathed in these outfits. The skirt flared out slightly to the sides and behind, with a daring slit up the front to knee height.

Jim felt some pleasure in noting that the color of their clothing was complementary.

With a smile, Jim said, "I find that surprising, my lady. I would have assumed someone you knew might have mentioned I was in town."

"Oh, you underestimate how hard you can be to find, at times, my lord," she said, batting her long fair lashes in an almost theatrical way that seemed to captivate Lord Ravenscar and annoy Jim in equal measure.

Jim found himself wondering what Franciezka was after. She was not one given to idle banter or social small talk unless it was part of a ploy. She was an important figure at the royal court of Roldem, but few knew her real role. She was a minor lady-in-waiting to the Princess Stephané, a tutor-cum-surrogate elder sister. Certainly, Queen Gertrude couldn't have found a better instructor to show the younger woman how to spot men of bad intent from across the room. But this was the sort of event Franciezka was usually more than content to avoid.

That gave Jim pause for a moment to glance toward the thrones. Three sons and a daughter and all ripe for state marriage. The two older princes, Constantine and Albér, were in attendance, both wearing the uniforms of the Roldem navy, Constantine an admiral and his younger brother a captain. Grandprey wore the dress uniform of an army general, and it was considered by most that he was the most able commander among the three. Some day his brother would be king and Grandy, as he was known, would be his Lord Marshall, while Albér would command the fleet as Grand Admiral.

Constantine was the prize, for his wife would some day be queen, but after him came Stephané. As the King's youngest and only daughter, she commanded a special place in her father's heart, and he would wed her carefully as much for her happiness as his kingdom's security. No lesser prince of Kesh or an Eastern Kingdom minor noble would take her leagues away from her parents. She would probably end up married to a noble of Roldem, possibly a Kingdom noble, but one who would live here, close to the palace, for that was the King's pleasure.

"Those two boys don't have a clue, do they?" asked Franciezka.

"My lady?" asked Lord Ravenscar.

Jim smiled, knowing exactly what she meant. "No, but it's their night—particularly Ty's, though Henry having been forced to withdraw due to injury makes it his night as well. Let them dream of a beautiful princess for one night."

And Jim was forced to admit the Princess had become a true beauty, which surprised many. Her mother had been judged a handsome woman in her youth, but never a head turner. She had been the Grand Duchess of Maladon to the north. The Duchy of Maladon and Semrick had strong ties to the Isles, but her father had wished for strong ties to Roldem. So the marriage had been arranged. The King and Queen had come to care deeply for each other and were temperamentally well suited as a couple.

Roldem's position in the Sea of Kingdoms made it a unique power. Its navy wasn't as large as Kesh's or that of the Kingdom of the Isles, but it was the best, ship for ship. The royal court of Roldem had seen to that, employing the finest and most innovative shipwrights and shipfitters in the world. Like the navy, the army of Roldem was a crack outfit, man for man the equal of any, though far smaller than either of its more powerful neighbors.

Roldem's power derived from its history: it was the first of the truly great courts on the continent of Triagia, exporting a great deal of its culture to the Kingdom of the Isles and the Eastern Kingdoms. Even Great Kesh, although an older nation, didn't reach the heights of art and science that Roldem had for years after consolidating its far-flung empire.

And Roldem's position had been enhanced when it moved in a combined assault on the Duchy of Olasko to thwart the evil plans of the mad necromancer Leso Varen, resulting in the overthrow of Kaspar, Duke of Olasko. The installation of Duke Varen Rodoski, a cousin of Roldem's king, brought Olasko into Roldem as its biggest duchy. While the Kingdom of the Isles muttered about this, Jim knew it was the only outcome that could have kept peace in the region. Besides, it made Roldem a better ally for the Isles in the fight that was surely coming.

Franciezka laughed. "I suppose there's no harm in dreaming, is there, my lord?"

Lord Ravenscar looked completely lost as to exactly what they were talking about. "I . . . ah, of course," he agreed.

"Come, Excellency," said Franciezka, "let us have a cup of wine and you can tell me the court gossip from Rillanon."

Obviously glad to have her to himself, Lord Ravenscar bowed slightly to Lord James, than began to lead the lovely woman away. Franciezka let a green silken handkerchief slip out of her hand. It fluttered to the ground at Jim's feet. At a carefully judged moment, she turned and said, "Oh, dear. A moment, Your Excellency." She turned back before the ambassador could see what was happening to retrieve the handkerchief that Jim had just picked up. Smiling, she said softly, "My town house. Midnight. Come alone and don't be seen."

Jim handed over the dropped kerchief without a word. As he watched her retreat from him, he wondered whether this would be a social or a political call. Either way, he conceded, it would prove interesting.

Jim reached the thrones just as the two combatants were bowing and backing away. He had misjudged his status and had been presented after the two finalists in the Masters' Court, not before them, and arrived just as the herald was announcing, "Earl Murroy, Envoy Plenipotentiary without portfolio from His Majesty, the King of Isles, Lord James Jamison, Baron of the Prince's Court."

The last title was the reason Ravenscar and others who served as resident ambassadors disliked Jim so much; he had the King's authority—really, his grandfather, the Duke of Rillanon's—to do pretty much as he saw fit when it came to any political situation on the Sea of Kingdoms. It tended to eclipse their sun just a bit.

Jim moved forward, bowed before the entire royal family, and muttered his wishes for their good health and long life. He nodded with a smile as the King muttered something pleasant in return, then departed.

As he did so, he noticed some familiar figures also approaching: four young men, two escorting young women. The two who escorted the women were as unlike as two men could be. One was slender, with dark hair and eyes and the quick moves of an athletic fencer. The other was redheaded, broad of shoulder and looked like a brawler. He grinned widely at the sight of Jim Dasher. "Jim! We didn't know you were here."

Jim made his greetings, first to the ladies who returned his genuine smile. Of all the people in Roldem he genuinely enjoyed spending time with, he now was in the presence of the majority. "A moment," said the redheaded man. "Matters of court protocol."

The herald announced, "Your Majesties, the Earl Servan and the Countess Lauretta." The dark-haired man bowed. "Uncle, Aunt, to your good health."

The King smiled. "It is good to have you in court, as always, Nephew."

As they moved away, the herald sang out, "Sir Jonathan Killaroo and the Lady Adella." They were greeted and moved on. The two single men were introduced as "Sir Tad," and "Sir Zane," and after they had made their obeisances, the group continued with Jim in tow to a large buffet where food was being portioned out to the guests.

Sir Jonathan spoke softly in his wife's ear, then kissed her cheek and moved off to speak to Jim in relative privacy. "Any word?" asked Jim.

"Nothing," said Jommy, which was the name by which the onetime street tough from the distant continent of Novindus was known to his friends. "The Conclave's agents are just as silent as your own."

The relationship between Jim Dasher and the Conclave of Shadows had been a long but strained one, and often it was the bond of friendship these two men shared that kept it from fraying any further. The four young men had served with Jim in a struggle against a demon cult known as the Black Caps, and the shedding of blood together had left them close.

Glancing around, Jim noticed Servan's gaze had wandered to where the two of them spoke. "How are you getting along with Servan these days?"

Jommy laughed. "He's got a good heart, and in another life we'd be brothers, but I don't think he'll ever forgive me for marrying his sister."

"She seems happy enough."

"She should. She's expecting our third."

Jim clapped Jommy on the shoulder. "Congratulations!"

Servan heard the word and saw the two men smiling and turned away with a rueful smile of his own, shaking his head as if asking silently by what cruel fate the gods had decided his sister should fall in love with such a lout.

Jommy said, "We need to get those two married off." He indicated with a nod Tad and Zane.

"I thought Zane . . . wasn't he betrothed?"

"Almost. But he has a wandering eye, that one."

"And Tad's too mindful of his duty." A moment of sadness passed over his face. "You three are as close to family . . ." He let the thought go unfinished.

Jommy's eyes scanned the room, never for an instant forgetting they might be overheard if he wasn't cautious. "I know. Have you spoken with Pug recently?"

"Not in a while," Jim kept his voice down despite the chatter of voices filling the hall. "He's out chasing demons and seems almost obsessed with it."

Neither man needed to remind the other it was a demon that had killed Pug's wife, Miranda. And it was the servant of the Demon King Dahun who had destroyed the home in which Pug's youngest son and his wife had died.

Jim said, "Well, let's turn to happier thoughts. Why don't we conspire to meet: you, me, Tad, and Zane, at the River House tomorrow? If your wife doesn't object, just us boys?"

"I'd like that," said Jommy. "She won't mind. It's why I married her: who else would put up with a fool like me?" His face openly showed a profound gratitude for her existence. He glanced over to where she was in conversation with a knot of ladies, and as if she felt his gaze, she turned and looked right at her husband. She smiled and with a slight inclination of her head asked silently how long he would be.

Jommy shook his head slightly, then nodded. He turned back to Jim. "She's feeling neglected." With a grin he added, "I'd best be back to her before she thinks we're plotting over here."

As his broad-shouldered friend walked back to his wife, Jim thought: *Plotting indeed.*

Jim Dasher crouched atop the roof of Lady Franciezka Sorboz's town house, feeling the cold ocean night air in his knees. He was definitely getting too old to be out in the field, or at least playing Jimmy the Hand meets a Nighthawk.

That story was family lore, and it reminded Jim that there were certain feats attributed to his ancestor he found somehow incredible. The falling off the roof and catching himself without dislocating his shoulders while the Nighthawk overbalanced and fell to his death . . . Jim glanced down. Dislocated shoulders certainly, then falling all the way to the cobbles, to die in agony. Then again, when Jimmy had accomplished that legendary feat he was but a lad of thirteen or fourteen years— no one was quite sure at what age he had come to Prince Arutha's attention—and everyone knew boys had incredible flexibility in their joints.

He would give half his fortune for the flexibility and resilience he had possessed at twenty-four years, let alone fourteen. Sitting and sliding to the eaves overhanging the balcony to Franciezka's bedroom was far less dashing, but as no one was watching, Jim really didn't care. He was tired and cold, his joints creaky and stiff. Although he welcomed Franciezka's company for either pleasure or business, he still thought getting to see her unobserved was perhaps more trouble than it was worth.

He lowered himself down off the eaves and dropped lightly to the balcony. As he had expected, the door inside had been left unlatched. He entered the bedroom.

Franciezka sat at a writing table, wearing a comfortable-looking lounging robe. "On time, as always," she said with a smile.

"You're not trying to kill me this time, then?" He sat on the bed opposite her.

She turned and handed him a large document. "Not this time. For better or worse it seems we're allies again."

He read the two pages and then reread them. She remained silent while he did so. When he had finished, he said, "Is he certain?"

"Does he sound uncertain?"

"No," said Jim. He let out a long sigh, half relief, half irritation.

"Are any of your agents reporting anything like that?"

"None of my agents are reporting anything. All my agents south of the Girdle have gone silent."

"Not good," she said, looking distressed at the news. "Hallon is my only agent who's managed to get anything out of that region."

He tapped the document that named the author.

"Everyone else has gone silent, too."

"Hazara-Khan."

"Yes," she nodded at the name of the man who was almost certainly the head of the Keshian Intelligence Corps.

"I like him a great deal, personally, but he can be a murderous bastard when he wants."

She stretched. "As can we all."

"If he's killing our agents, war is certain," said Jim, suddenly feeling older than his age.

Her sigh matched his mood, and for the briefest instant he felt a slight twinge inside and shut it out as quickly as he could. It was one of the gods' little jokes that the perfect woman in his life was the one he could never have.

His shoulders sagged as he returned the document he had just read to her. "Six hundred ships?"

"That's Hallon's best estimate, and he's one of my best." Franciezka rose, crossed to sit next to him, and put her hand over his. "And if what he heard at the docks was correct, three hundred of them have already left Hansulé and are sailing past the Forest of the Lost. This isn't another minor prince of Kesh deciding to make a name for himself grabbing land in the Vale of Dreams, Jim."

"No," he said, falling back on to the bed. Staring at the canopy overhead he let out another long sigh. "This has all the earmarks of an invasion."

"But why the west?" she asked. "Kesh has shown no interest in reclaiming Queg, the Free Cities, or the Far Coast since it abandoned them."

"I do not know," said Jim, looking up at her. "You know, you have an incredible face," he added, sitting up. "Would you consider for just a moment grabbing all the gold you've squirreled away over the years while I do the same, then running away with me to some tiny island miles from here where we can settle down with trusted servants and have some children?"

"I've been considering it since the moment I met you, Lord James Jamison, agent of the King, Jim Dasher, thief of Krondor and leader of the Mockers. But we both know that can never happen." A moment of sadness passed across her face, then she brightened. "Besides, can you imagine what a murderous little crew our children would turn out to be?"

For a brief instant, he appeared to want to say something, then he smiled. He kissed her on the cheek and said, "Goodnight."

She feigned a pout. "And I thought you were going to stay."

"So did I," he admitted with honest regret. "When you're not trying to kill me, there's no one I'd rather spend my time with."

"Flatterer," she said, theatrically batting her lashes. "I'm pleased that we're going to be on the same side when the bloodletting begins."

"Apparently it's already begun. I'll instruct key agents to ensure you get copies of all the information we get; as Hazara-Khan is shredding our networks, we need to share intelligence. You know where to send me copies of what you find."

"Of course I do. What are you planning?"

"If my agents are dead, I've got to get down there and see for myself what is happening."

She removed her ring and tossed it to him, and he caught it in midair.

"Look for Hallon. You'll find him at your usual haunts, the seedier dockside taverns in Hansulé. Rough-looking fellow, dark hair, facial scars—"

"You've just described half the men in that city."

"Tattoo of a dagger on his left forearm. He'll recognize that signet and help if he can."

"Thank you, Lady Franciezka Sorboz, lady-in-waiting to the Princess, also Frankie the Razor, Madam Francis . . ." He stopped naming her aliases. "I really do thank you, Franciezka," he said in earnest.

"We're allies now," she replied in a serious tone. "The half of the fleet that didn't leave Hansulé is almost certainly heading this way. The combined fleets of Roldem and the Isles should be able to deal with the Keshians, but at no small cost. And if they're also marching an army this way . . ." She let the thought go unfinished.

Jim nodded. He tossed the signet into the air, then let it fall into the palm of his hand. Without another word he was out the door and over the balcony.

"And don't get yourself killed, Jim," Franciezka said after him.

Lying back on the bed, she stared up at the canopy and repeated, "Don't get yourself killed."

Supper was far more pleasant than Jim had anticipated. Jommy, Tad, and Zane were the closest thing to friends he had. As Jim Dasher, thief and confidence trickster from Krondor, he had served with them when they were young soldiers training under Kaspar of Olasko for special service. They were still in special services, to the Conclave of Shadows, though they all three currently enjoyed court rank in Roldem, as a result of that special service. All had gained the rank of Court Knight, and each had secured small estates in Olasko, though they all maintained apartments on Roldem Island.

Jommy was married to the King's niece, which gave him an additional entrée to the court. His brother-in-law, Servan, was Franciezka's most important agent at court, though almost no one knew this; indeed, Jim had only chanced upon that information by dint of luck and being very good at his job. Jim wondered absently if Jommy had any idea who his brother-in-law really was, and if he might benefit from Jim telling him.

Tad and Zane had been rough-and-tumble village boys who had been raised by Pug's youngest son, Caleb. As such they stood in a unique position, for they were his foster grandchildren. Jommy was in a fashion as well, though there were no ties of birth or marriage.

Both were still unwed, but for entirely different reasons. Tad fell in love with every woman of quality he met, to the detriment of his winning a heart. He was too easy. Zane, on the other hand, was a womanizer with a bad reputation in most social circles; this had the double effect of keeping serious women away while making him even more attractive to young women who seemed not to know better. Not a handsome pair, Tad was showing early grey, as sandy-haired people often do, and Zane had an intense darkness about him with a merry glint in his eyes. Although not particularly striking, he had learned how to talk women into all manner of things against their own personal best interest.

Talwin Hawkins was another matter. He was an occasional ally of the Conclave, and a former servant, but by dint of his earlier service he had been cast free of any obligation to the Conclave by Pug. Jim had occasionally wondered how wise that had been, but reminded himself that as much as he would have loved to have had the River House restaurants in both Roldem and Olasko as listening posts for intelligence, willing servants were far more reliable than those pressed to duty. And in a crisis, he believed he could count on Tal to stand alongside the Conclave. It was not in his nature to stand aside or serve evil.

That left the boys: Ty knew a little of his father's role in destroying those who had nearly obliterated his people, the Orosini of the Mountains, a tribal people who were slowly reclaiming their heritage. Many like Tal and his wife, Teal, had spent too many years in cities, years that had blunted their interest and ability to live the old life. It was a life of which Ty knew nothing.

Jim turned to see Hal smiling at a joke Tad had made and thought, *There's a prince without a principality.* He had grown up with conDoin kings, as had every other citizen of the Kingdom of the Isles. They were the founding dynasty; they had united the tribes on the Island of Rillanon and spread their banner to the mainland, eventually conquering enough territory to create a nation to rival Great Kesh on this continent.

But it was a dynasty at its end, Jim feared. The vigor was gone, the energy and drive that had given the line a rebirth after the short unhappy reign of Rodric IV. His successor, Hal's great-great-uncle, Lyam I, had been a great king, a charismatic leader who had inspired love and loyalty in his people after twelve brutal years of war with the invading Tsurani.

Tragedy had kept Lyam from having a son, so the crown went to Borric II, his nephew, who proved as apt and able a ruler as his uncle. Borric's twin brother, Prince Erland, had been as able in his role as his brother, and between the two of them the Kingdom of the Isles had been well served.

But Borric's son Patrick had been the last of the able rulers, and Patrick's son Gregory had no heir. For the third time since the conDoins took the crown of the Isles, there had been a chance for multiple claimants to the throne. The last time civil war had been stemmed by Hal's ancestor Martin renouncing the crown for himself and his heirs. But the time before that a great deal of blood had been shed before Borric I took the head of Jon the Pretender.

And the last thing Jim wished to contemplate was a kingdom divided on the eve of what he was certain was going to be a major war with Great Kesh.

"Lost in thought?" asked Tal.

Jim smiled. "Yes." He glanced around the table, then said, "Tal, could we have the room?"

Tal nodded. The other dinner guests had left an hour before and with a quick word to the serving staff, who hurried to the kitchen, the room was empty save for Jim and his guests.

"Not to belabor the point, but I'm certain war is coming," said Jim. He held up his hand before questions could be asked. "I will sum up. There are factions within the Imperial Keshian Army, specifically within the Inner Legion, who are calling for expansion."

Tad interrupted. "The Vale of Dreams?"

"Traditionally that's always been their first target. The Vale is the lushest farmland on Triagia and because of the constant warfare, sparsely populated. A colony of Keshian or Kingdom farmers there could double the region's output of farm goods within two years, tenfold in five."

Hal was silent, but he knew he had suddenly been propelled into something far more important than a pleasant social evening.

"But this is something massive. On a far greater scale, perhaps, than we've ever seen. A fleet of perhaps as many as three hundred ships departed Hansulé recently, sailing south."

Jommy looked confused. "South? Are they sailing to Novindus?"

"My best guess is around the southern coast between the Lost Forest and the Island of Snakes and then up to Injune or Elarial. From there . . . ?" He shrugged.

"If they mean to take the Vale," said Tad, "they could be supported out of Durbin. They'd need a fleet that big to keep the Quegans from getting involved as well as keeping the Kingdom's Western Fleet in Port Vykor busy."

"They could go anywhere." He looked at Hal and said, "Including the Far Coast. The Prince of Krondor has called the Western Muster."

Hal, Ty, and Tal knew this from two nights before, but Tad, Zane, and Jommy all looked surprised. "War footing on the Far Coast?" asked Jommy. "Is it that dire?"

"I think so." Jim pushed himself back from the table. "And I need to travel, so to the end of this night, let me add this." He looked at Tal. "While I'm gone, I would appreciate it if you would agree to aid these other three in their charge." Both men knew Jim wasn't speaking of any political loyalties, but rather Tad, Zane, and Jommy's responsibility to the Conclave of Shadows. "I know your relationship to our mutual friends is complicated, but I trust you implicitly."

"I'll do what I can," said Hawkins, and Jim knew that was as good as a promise.

"Gentlemen," he said to the three foster brothers, "I leave this to you. You've never failed me or the Crowns of Isles or Roldem, and I expect you won't now."

Hal looked confused. "I'm not sure I understand. I'm not even sure why you asked me here."

Jim moved around the table and put his hand on Hal's shoulder. "These four men—and young Ty there—are going to take my place while I'm gone. In my absence you're to consider them your protectors."

"We will do whatever is needed," said Zane.

"Yes," agreed Tad.

"I don't understand. What is 'whatever is needed'?" asked Hal.

It was young Ty who answered. "Too much wine? You're a little slow today, Hal. They're going to keep you alive when Kesh sends assassins to kill you."

6

MUSTER

Men shouted orders.

Brendan and Martin sat their mounts beside their father, watching and learning as much as if they were also on the muster field. In the distance the archers were shooting at the butts, large piles of loosely packed earth with a target before it. Unlike the King's army, the Western Muster had no company of fletchers planing arrows, flocks of geese to cull for the arrow flights, or a score of blacksmiths turning out steel arrowheads. Each man of the muster would be given a freshly made longbow and a score of arrows; and when he was home, he'd be obliged to practice for an hour a morning on the butt he'd build alongside his hut, home, or barn. Should a man return with less than eighteen arrows intact, he would be fined a copper coin for each additional replacement beyond two.

Such was the state of military economy in the Western Realm of the Kingdom.

As soon as Reinman and his drunken weather magician had left Crydee, the Duke had begun the muster. This group was the second of three that would train here. It was difficult for the frontier duchy, for there were farmsteads scattered along the entirety of the Far Coast.

Martin looked over at the makeshift workshed where two experienced bowyers, with the help of their apprentices, showed five young men how to turn thick yew branches into bow staves. He remembered his own time in the shed and remembered the other woods that could be used: ash, some oaks, and elm, but yew wood was the finest. He recalled the delight he had felt when he had turned his first branch into a stave and the elder bowyer had studied it and proclaimed it well done, seeing how Martin had shaped it with the heartwood at the grip and along the rear spine, the sapwood in front, an ideal natural lamination that was the best a simple bow could be.

It was ironic, though Martin found no humor in it, that as much as he had enjoyed making that bow, he had been a terrible archer. Not really terrible, he amended as he gave himself some credit, but average. His younger brother and even Bethany were better archers. Having equaled his elder brother, Hal, didn't placate the dour young man; Hal was the finest swordsman in Crydee, perhaps in the world if he won the Masters' Court. Martin disliked constantly being second to others, though there was no one else in Crydee besides Hal who could best him.

Glancing to where Lady Bethany approached beside her father, he realized he was frowning and forced himself to a smile.

"Robert!" the Duke said. "I didn't expect you back so soon. Lady Bethany, always a pleasure. Robert, did your wife not travel with you?"

"She's not one for long rides," said Earl Robert. "And I felt the need to come along quickly with some news."

Duke Henry said, "Boys, keep the men at it. They're lagging in the afternoon heat. No stopping until the supper bell rings."

His sons indicated they would and watched as their father and Lord Robert rode off a short distance. Bethany rode up and turned her horse so that she was alongside Martin's. "Well, I guess you didn't expect to see me again so soon?"

Brendan's eyes narrowed slightly. She had her head cocked as if she were looking past Martin at him, but her eyes were trained on Martin's face, while he seemed intent on overseeing a sloppy drill of swordsmen banging away with practice swords against one another's shields. Despite being made of wood, the swords and shields were actually heavier than their metal counterparts so that when the footmen went to battle, the equipment would be lighter than what had become familiar to them. The same was true of the heavy pikemen and spearmen running with their weapons across a distant field.

After a second too long, Martin glanced at her and said, "What? Oh, yes. Always a pleasure to see you, Bethany." But then something caught his eye and he shouted, "You, there!" He put his heels to his horse's sides and moved out, circling around the dueling footmen, then dismounted. Taking one man's place, he took his sword and shield and demonstrated how the combat practice was supposed to be conducted. A sergeant of the castle guard saw the young lord dismount and came over to see what was happening.

Martin threw himself into the drill and delivered two ringing blows that soon had his opponent stumbling backward.

"What do you think that's about?" asked Bethany.

Brendan glanced her way and said, "I have no idea."

Bethany started back to where her father and the Duke were finishing their private chat. As the youngest son watched her go, he saw her turn again to stare at Martin. With a sigh, he said to himself, "Then again, maybe I do."

The evening meal was a mixture of light banter interspersed with moments of quiet as everyone seemed caught up in their own thoughts. Martin and Bethany appeared to make a point of ignoring each other, and Brendan was troubled by it.

The four of them had been raised together for as long as Brendan could remember. It was always assumed that some day Bethany would wed Hal, but Brendan now realized that was only an assumption, one that his father or mother had never spoken of; and right now he knew one thing, though he wasn't sure he fully understood it. Something had changed between Bethany and Martin on her last visit. Without words, their feelings for each other had shifted. Martin had said nothing to his brother; not that he would, for Martin most among the family always kept his own counsel. But Bethany was also distant, chatting with his mother and managing somehow to avoid all the male members of the household as well as her own father.

He was currently lost in conversation with Brendan's father, who had as yet to tell his sons why Earl Robert had appeared unexpectedly. Brendan balanced his youthful impatience with the knowledge that his father would tell him what he needed to know when he saw fit. Realizing there was no further reason to remain at the table, he said, "Father?"

"Yes?"

"It's been a long day. If you permit, I'd like to turn in early."

A little surprised by his usually rambunctious youngest's request, the Duke waved permission and Brendan nodded to the others at the table and departed. A sudden sinking feeling in the pit of his stomach told him that no matter what else, little good could come out of what was passing between Martin and Bethany. With a fatigued sigh, he pushed open the door to his quarters and threw himself down on his simple bed. Rolling over, he stared at the stones of the ceiling and thought, *Perhaps the war will distract the two of them.*

After the guests had retired, Duchess Caralin turned to her husband. "Bed?"

Duke Henry sat on a divan, a recent addition to the old castle's private quarters. The room had been used since the castle's construction as an informal meeting room, and the

Duke had also decided it was an ideal place for his family to spend time together; Henry found it far more convivial than the drafty great hall. He looked up from his musing and smiled. "No, a while longer I think. I have much to think about."

Caralin tilted her head to regard her husband. They had spent nearly thirty years together and at times she knew him better than she knew herself, yet at moments like this she didn't have a clue as to what he was thinking. "Robert's news must have been very troubling."

Henry's eyes widened and he sat up a bit straighter. "Oh, that. No, that's not it at all." He motioned for her to return to the divan, and as she sat down he said, "I'm sorry. I should have mentioned that to you and the boys. Robert wanted to share some information about our neighbors to the east, the elves in E'bar."

"Oh," she said, her brow furrowing a little. "I thought it had to do with the coming war."

"It may, truth to tell," said her husband. "I hope not. I asked Robert to send a messenger to their Lord Regent informing him of the possibilities of conflict in the area. I had Robert stress that it likely would be nothing of import, just a precautionary warning.

"The messenger rode for three days to the gates of their city and was stopped. According to Robert, whatever passes for a sentry officer with these elves refused to let him into the city, took the message, and turned the rider away."

"Well, he got the message then, didn't he, this Lord Regent?"

"Yes, but that's not the point, dear. Nor is the poor treatment of the messenger. Elven manners are not our own. We have always been on good terms with the Elf Queen and her court to the north, but these newcomers are a different stripe of cat, I'm afraid. No, it's what the officer *said* to the messenger."

"What was that?"

"Any human who trespasses on the land of the Taredhel—as they call themselves—would be 'dealt with.'"

"That sounds unfriendly."

"Yes," he agreed with a slowly released breath, sounding fatigued. "If the Keshians come and these elves remain neutral, that's one thing. If they close their borders entirely—"

"Anyone fleeing eastward will be trespassing on their territory."

"As always, you grasp the heart of the matter."

Softly, as if not to be overheard, she said, "Do you think... we may have to flee?"

"No, no," he said, hugging her for reassurance. "I'm just trying to anticipate every possibility, my love." He kissed her cheek, then smiled as he looked into her eyes. "The Keshians moving against the Far Coast? Why would they do that?" He stood and put out his hand, and she took it, and rose. "There's nothing here they could possibly desire. Forests? Farms? They have ample forests and farms in the Empire of Great Kesh. No, they'll almost certainly move against the Vale of Dreams again. And the Prince of Krondor will order Lord Sutherland and the Knight-Marshal of the West to drive them back, and when the dust settles, the old lines will be drawn again, with a jot of difference here, a smidgen of change there."

Gripping his arm and walking closely at his side, Caralin said, "I hope you're right."

Silently he nodded, knowing he probably was, but prepared for being utterly wrong. As many married couples do, they conspired to walk together silently, not needing to say another word.

Pug sat behind his desk, as he had for countless days since coming to the island. But unlike most days, his mind refused to grapple with the problems before him. Instead it kept returning to Brandos's question about rebuilding the villa.

He had no good reason for considering it. He found himself unable even to imagine beginning the work. He knew that with a small group of skilled craftsmen from the mainland, and some magic provided by Magnus and himself, the villa could be resurrected in months, rather than the years it had probably taken the original inhabitants of this island.

Yet something in him became angry at the very thought of rebuilding his home. It was as if even to think about it was to diminish the loss he still felt.

After Miranda had died, his otherwise steely resolve had wavered. He had revisited that last moment of her life countless times, seeing it over and over again in his mind. *If I had been a moment quicker,* he thought to himself, *or if I had seen the demon move an instant earlier . . .* He knew the futility of this sort of thinking. He was more than a hundred years old and had watched many people die unfortunate deaths—far more than had passed on in the fullness of their years—yet this death haunted him.

Yes, she had been his wife, and he had loved her. . .

Pug sat back and sighed. He reached for the pot of tea that had been sitting on his desk all morning and found it empty. He could ring a bell and someone would bring him a new pot. He looked at the mess his desk had become and realized he could ring that same bell and someone would sort out all the clutter. He then found himself laughing slightly, realizing he would spend more time searching for where one of his earnest young pupils had put things than he would just cleaning up the clutter himself.

First, tea.

Pug made his way down the long circular stairs from his office, in the tower atop the one opposite Amirantha's. He wondered how the Warlock was getting on with his visit to E'bar and was certain he and Gulamendis were furiously comparing notes. He hoped the visit would produce something more tangible than the numerous dead ends they'd encountered.

After the bloody mess that had been the Gates of Darkness down in the Valley of Lost Men in northern Kesh, Pug had asked every contact he had around the globe—and there were many—to spread the word that there was wealth, safety, or both for any demon summoner who wished it; all the Conclave wanted was more information.

Reaching the bottom of the tower, Pug was forced to admit the results had been less than spectacular. Those few magic-users who had made their way to Sorcerer's Isle had proven to be charlatans, of limited knowledge and skill, ignorant of anything larger than their own narrow experience. A few had added one or two facts to Pug's knowledge, but only to corroborate what he had suspected to be the case before they arrived: there were upheavals on an unimagined scale in progress in the demon realm.

Amirantha had also been trying to make sense of the ancient volume of demon lore they had retrieved from the island of Queg. He had done a fair job of divining what was nonsense, what was a metaphorical approximation of reality, and what could be called "facts." Though Pug was beginning to think the demon realm's very nature made "facts" somewhat mutable.

As he entered the great room, Pug caught sight of his son. "Magnus."

Magnus turned and regarded him. After a brief second he said, "Something's up. What?"

"Let's rebuild the villa."

The younger magician hesitated for a moment. Then he nodded. "I think that's a good idea." Looking at the empty teapot in his father's hand he said, "May I join you?"

"Always."

The kitchen was empty, but the fire still burned in the metal stove constructed within the roasting hearth. Pug filled the pot with water from a large bucket, then rinsed it out, and refilled it. He put it down in front of the fire on the hot metal plate and waited for it to boil.

"What caused you to change your mind?" asked Magnus.

"It's time." So much of what he fought against was a dark despair that arose from a bargain struck with Lims-Kragma, the Death Goddess, when he had been given three choices: to end his life at the hands of the demon Jakan; to take up the burden of becoming an avatar of the God of Magic, hastening his return to Midkemia; or to come back and finish the struggle, but at a price. The price was to watch everyone he loved die before him. So far that had included a son, adopted daughter, then another son and his wife. Of his bloodline, only Magnus remained. There were the three foster grandsons, Jommy, Tad, and Zane . . . Pug was forced to admit he had let his fear of the curse allow him to become estranged from his great-grandsons, Jimmy and Dash Jamison. Although they were not blood relatives (they were his adopted daughter's children), they still were dear to him. And there was Jim Dasher, Jimmy Jamison's grandson. Pug sighed; he liked the complex, dangerous man, mostly because there were moments when he glimpsed his many-great-grandfather, Jimmy the Hand, in him; but if there was any spark of affection, it had not been fanned into a flame. He liked Jim, but he hardly loved him.

Over the years Pug had become adept at steeling himself against feelings that might cause him to betray his higher calling, to protect this world and everyone else on it. Yet those feelings were there—hidden, buried even—but there nevertheless.

As they waited for the kettle to boil, Magnus said, "Who should oversee the rebuilding?"

"I will, I think," said his father. "I know every beam and stone of that place as well as or better than anyone else." He smiled. "I lived there longer than anyone else."

Magnus returned the smile. "It's good to see you . . . this way, Father."

"Losing your mother and brother was hard on you, too, Magnus. I lost sight of that in my own grief, I'm sorry to say."

Magnus was silent for a moment. His face reminded Pug of Miranda's. It was longer than his father's, with higher cheekbones; but his eyes were from some mysterious ancestor unknown to Pug. They were as blue as frozen ice and could gaze right through a person. He said softly, "I have never been a man to measure my sorrows against another's sorrows, Father. I thought you would not as well."

"I just mean that becoming lost in my own misery, I perhaps didn't give as much attention to your pain, that is all." Pug lowered his eyes. "It's a poor father who turns his back on his son's hurt, no matter how grown the son."

Magnus nodded. "We are both the sort to retreat into ourselves at times like that. There is no fault in this; it's a matter of our nature." With a slight smile he said, "Besides, I'm too big for you to pick up so I can cry on your shoulder."

Pug was forced to laugh. "It's been a few years since I did that, hasn't it?"

The water reached a simmer and Magnus fetched the pot. He put it down on the table and said, "What now?"

Pug looked at his son and picked up the pot. "Now, I've got a mess of an office to deal with; tomorrow we begin rebuilding."

Magnus impulsively reached out and hugged his father, then said, "Good."

Pug left the kitchen while his son sat back down at the table. After a moment, Magnus let out a long sigh and allowed himself a short time to reflect. As tears welled up in his eyes he wiped them away and stood up. There was a great deal of work to be done, and it would not wait because some wounds would not heal. And perhaps the work would help the healing. Still, deep within was a sense that even after all the years since his mother's and brother's deaths, there was no hope of those wounds healing, but perhaps time might deaden them.

The lookout shouted "Sails in sight!," and the captain called for men aloft. As much as he hated being barefoot in the cold, Jim Dasher, freebooting merchant sailor out of Hansulé, endured it. Jim knew enough of the barmen, whores, and dockworkers to convince anyone he was Jaman Rufiki. His dark hair but fair skin made him look like a Sea of Kingdom's man, which fit with his false life story: born in Pointer's Head, whence he had first shipped out, then spent years along the Great Sea, from Ithra down to Brijané.

He had used his transportation orb to arrive in Queral unseen, where he was met by his agents. No one south of that city had reported in the last three months, and he suspected his safe houses in the south of the Empire might have been compromised. He didn't wish to risk appearing in a room full of murderers in Hansulé, so he arrived at the nearest city where he knew he'd be safe, purchased as fast a horse as he could, and rode it nearly to death getting to Hansulé.

There he had found what Franciezka's agents had reported to her: a massive fleet at anchor, nearly two hundred ships. He wondered if another hundred had departed since her agents had last reported or if their report had been inaccurate. One night in the local taverns had given him his answer: the initial three hundred had departed southward, as reported, and another hundred had left just the week before, also heading south.

Jim had been left to ponder what madness had gripped the Imperial Keshian Court. Peace had benefited both nations since the ill-fated attempt by Kesh to lay siege to Krondor after the Serpent War. The west from the Far Coast to Krondor had been in shambles after the Emerald Queen's invasion had driven the Armies of the West back to Nightmare Ridge where at last they had been thrown back.

Pug had forced an armistice down the throats of both sides, effectively severing all ties with the Kingdom, but saving it nevertheless. Now after years of rebuilding, the Kingdom was as strong in the west as it had been before the Emerald Queen's invasion of the Bitter Sea. War now made no sense whatsoever.

There must be something I'm not seeing, Jim thought as he climbed the rigging. As much as he hated sailors' work, he was good enough at it that he aroused no suspicion. Getting this berth had been more difficult than anticipated, since the Imperial Keshian Army was involved. They had guards standing at every recruitment position at the docks, and Jim had no doubt agents of the Imperial Intelligence Corps were as well. His current opposite number was the young and very talented Kaseem abu Hazara-Khan, the latest in a line of very wily desert men from the Jal-Pur entrusted with the safety of the Empire.

Jim had liked his father a great deal, but he had come to an untimely demise, one Jim was certain was not natural. All Jim knew was he had had no hand in it, a fact he had made sure to impress on Kaseem. Even to this day, two years later, Jim had no inkling of who had managed to kill the cleverest man he had ever opposed. Even if he had wanted him dead—which he had on more than one occasion—he was uncertain how he might manage it. And without vanity, Jim knew if he couldn't think of a way, no one else should be able to, either.

Jim didn't know Kaseem well; he was difficult to read and he had never seen him face-to-face, as he had his father. In Jim's line of work, one learned of one's opponents by how they operated their networks and conducted the spy trade—and how many bodies littered the way. The Hazara-Khans, going back to the founder of the Imperial Keshian Intelligence Corps, Abdur Rachman Memo Hazara-Khan, had been adept at keeping bloodshed to a minimum while confounding the Kingdom as often as they could. Jim was merely the latest head of the King's spy network to curse the day the Hazara-Khans first drew breath.

Jim knew one thing: all intelligence went through Kaseem abu Hazara-Khan, and if he could have an hour with him, Jim might learn why the greatest empire in the world's history had decided to attack the second- and third-most-powerful nations together. For to attack the Isles was to attack Roldem: they were too closely allied for the Kingdom of Roldem to back away graciously from the conflict and play the part of neutral party or honest broker.

Jim reefed sails along with the other seamen, his feet planted firmly on the ropes below the yard. He looked up and saw the ship was slowly being brought into a harborage on the north side of a massive island. *The Island of Snakes,* he thought. *Why would we be stopping here?*

As he secured the sails he did a rough calculation. About thirty or more ships were at anchor, a few warships, but mostly merchant vessels, the majority being coast huggers like the one he served on. Jim knew that as soon as he signed on the *Suja* he was not heading around the world. There had been no deepwater ships in the flotilla in Hansulé when he had arrived. He just didn't know if they would be heading north or south. As soon as they weighed anchor, he had known they'd be following the two fleets that had departed before them.

Gossip had it that the first fleet had consisted mostly of warships with a few support vessels. He assumed they would enter the Bitter Sea and sweep away any Quegan galleys foolish enough to come south or any privateers sailing out of Durbin. Their target had to be the Kingdom's fleet at Port Vykor. If they came in and hit them fast, they could set up defenses in that captured city and keep the Armies of the West from moving to support the Kingdom town of Landreth on the north shore of the Sea of Dreams. If they could hold it for a month, the Vale of Dreams would effectively be Kesh's for years to come.

But why stop at a deserted island? They were sufficiently provisioned for the journey up to Elarial, which was a large city with deepwater facilities for refitting and outfitting ships. It was the logical place to replenish supplies. So why were they here?

Jim finished his work as the anchor was dropped, and word was passed for the day watch to go below to the mess. He headed down the companionway and fell in line to get his meal. He ate without thinking about what was in the bowl and drank the weak, watery ale that was his portion for the day.

Above his head he could hear activity on deck and wondered who was working if the day watch and night watch were both below. Unlike deepwater ships on long voyages, there was no midwatch. Once sails were set along the coast and the business of keeping the ship in good order was in hand, there were ample moments for rest on either watch.

When the meal was over, most men fell into bunks, as was their habit, but Jim went up on deck to see if he could make any sense of what was taking place. He reached the top of the companionway and ducked down as he came out, just in case the captain or first officer was concerned about such a trespass.

No one was watching the exit from below. The *Suja* was a two-master, both lanteen rigged, and was well suited to work the coasts. Her company was small, no more than thirty men, so Jim had little trouble staying out of view.

In the distance he could see boats ferrying cargo from the island to the ships anchored closer to the shore. The captain glanced down from the poop deck and noticed Jim, but said nothing, turning his attention back to the land. Jim took that to mean there was no prohibition about being on deck.

Whoever had been unloading on deck had made quick work of it. A bundle of what looked to be small crates were lashed down near the forecastle, under a canvas cover. Jim moved to the railing and looked down to see the longboat that had brought the cargo pulling away. Those on deck must have gone over the side just moments before Jim had come up on deck.

In the longboat were four sailors rowing easily, since the large craft was empty. In the stern was a hooded figure with his hand on the tiller and when Jim noticed the hand, his heart almost leaped into his throat.

Sticking out of the sleeve of a deep red robe was a green-scaled hand ending in black talons. There was only one race on this world it could belong to.

Pantathians!

7

TRAVELER

Child screamed.

The flyer had come out of the noonday sun and struck hard enough to stun her for a moment. Only by ducking her chin and twisting to the left did she manage to avoid having her throat ripped out from behind, though she took a deep gash to her shoulder. She swung her elbow viciously, catching the flyer on the side of the head.

It was all she needed.

Before the flyer regained his senses, she had her fangs in his throat and had bitten down hard and deep enough to end his life. Thoughts and images came flooding into her, as was always the case with a kill, and she felt herself grow again. She was now physically the match of any but the most powerful Demon Lords: the flyer only survived for as long as it did because of surprise and her momentary disorientation. She realized this might continue to be a problem, for she did not appear to be as powerful as she was. It was her magic and knowledge that had given her an advantage over the vast majority of individual demons she encountered, and she was wise enough to avoid groups too powerful to destroy.

She had grown in size and was as physically mature as she was likely to get through natural means. She was, by the standards of their race, a particularly striking female. Gender was often a matter of choice among demonkind, and some like Belog were male in only the most superficial sense of the term.

For striking she was, tall and lithe, with curving hips and long legs. She had a flat stomach despite her ravenous appetite, and she had developed a round, if small, bosom. Her neck was long, but what was most striking were her features; she had kept her small fangs, but otherwise her face was almost human in her features, as if she was inclined to become a succubus of the First Realm. Belog wondered if perhaps in her previous existence she had been such, for she had shown only passing interest in them, yet had seemed almost single-minded in her curiosity about the demon realm.

She paused as she drank in the essence of the flyer and realized she had to exert her will. She felt a strong desire to transform herself into a flyer. She didn't hesitate. Flying would have given her speed and the ability to hunt, but she would lose strength, and as she sensed her power growing, she decided it was better to guard her strength rather than waste it by transforming herself into a creature of lesser might.

She knew that should she choose, she could direct her future growth to choosing wings. But to be a flyer of her size would require mastery of magic, a topic she returned to frequently, so it was a possibility, just not now.

She motioned to Belog to come out from behind the rocks where he hid, waiting to see the outcome of the attack, knowing that had the flyer been victorious, Belog would have attempted to steal away while the flyer feasted upon her.

They were in the middle of a vast plateau riven with gullies, valleys with dead ends, deep crevasses that forced them to double back and pick their way across the baked red landscape. It was torturous travel, but they kept moving.

The air hung heavy with dust and the smell of sulfur, metallic hints of copper and iron, and the stench of decay. Plumes of hot gases erupted around them, yellowish foul geysers and fumaroles. Hellish was the only word to describe it, a fact she found oddly amusing, but she wasn't entirely sure why.

She beckoned for Belog to consume what she had left. As he ate, she asked, "Why are the flyers so slight?"

"Creatures that fly have hollow bones, though the bone wall is sturdy. They must be light so their wings can lift them. The muscles that drive the wings are powerful, though." He stopped to bite deep into the dead flyer's haunch. There was still enough energy left within the flesh to sustain him for a few more days. She was being generous in how much she provided. Or calculating; it was the nature of demons that the first sacrifice to hunger was intelligence, yet her desire for knowledge was equal to her hunger for flesh. She was not only keeping him alive, she was keeping him useful.

He swallowed, then said, "Some flyers can lift their own weight, but they tend to be smaller than this. It is a limited choice."

"I came to that conclusion just now. Why give up power?"

"Speed and vision—each is a different sort of power. You can see threats coming from farther away; you can outrun pursuit. You can soar high above the struggle." He shrugged as if to indicate he was offering reasons, not making a judgment. "But you have to sacrifice strength."

"I have seen . . ." She stopped. "No, I have another's memories of massive flyers, carrying weapons and wearing armor."

"Such creatures fly by more than the strength of their wings. They use magic to keep aloft. They are very powerful, lords, princes, and kings."

"Why?"

Belog had come to understand that this was Child's usual method of inquiry, following a thread of discussion till she found out what she wanted to know.

"In the Time Before Time, when we were all like Savages," he began. He had discovered after several beatings at her hands that she had a preference for old lore; so perhaps the first Archivist she had devoured had a preference for ancient history. "A great chieftain arose among the first of the People. His name was Aelor. He ruled the inner kingdoms and brought order out of chaos. He decreed that we live on a great disc, at the center of which he established the first settlements. Five original kingdoms, each ruled by their own king, followed by others, and all were known as the First Kingdoms. Around those kingdoms arose the Second Kingdoms, then the Savage Lands and beyond that, Madness."

He could see that she was growing impatient, having heard this before. "In service to those kings, some were granted protection as vassals to their lords. Some among those were given great power as their reward, including magic."

At the mention of magic, he could see her attention grow rapt, and he knew he had made the right choice. "Tell me more about magic," she said.

Belog had come to recognize her moods, and when she exhibited a keen interest for a subject, he could not gloss over anything, no matter how tedious he might find the discussion. In his experience, she was unique, and how she came to be this way was a mystery. She came from a class of demon that for lack of a better conceptual term would be labeled "laborer" or "servant," and not worth much consideration by any being of power. Her mother was a menial, and her father a worker in support of the King's army who had gone off to wage war against the minions of Maarg, when things as Belog knew them had begun to unravel.

He continued, "Magic is the name for a system of controlling power that spans the divide between the tangible and the intangible. By the force of will, the keen intellect of the mind, and the ability to discipline oneself, a person can practice 'magic,' as it is called."

"Can you do magic?" she asked, ardently curious.

115

"No, that wasn't permitted. Our lord Dahun saw clearly in his mind that there needed to be a distinct demarcation between classes, lest one being grow too powerful and overturn the balance of things."

She laughed, the first time she had felt the impulse and the first time he had heard one of his race do so out of mere amusement. "Lest one being grow too powerful and challenge his might!" She fixed Belog with a sharp eye. "I know more by the day, my teacher. Perhaps some day I will know as much as you."

"A day to be welcomed, as a teacher, for you know your student has learned all you have to offer, but one to be feared as well."

"Because without my need for you, you become another meal?" she asked with what could only have been a mocking tone.

"Because one fears the loss of such inspiring company," he replied.

She cocked her head to one side, then chuckled. "I believe that is called flattery."

His eyes widened. "You do indeed possess great knowledge, Child. I have never spoken to you of such a thing. It is not a concept widely known to our race. Only the class of succubae, the seducers and drainers of life, are adept at it. They use it to gull lesser beings." She gazed at him with fascination. "It is something weaker beings employ, a convention of false praise in exchange for favorable regard from a more powerful being. It is a tool of seduction, so . . ."

"Magic," she interrupted. "I would learn it."

He took a deep breath. "Then we must seek another, and this may prove difficult, Child. We must find a magic-user powerful enough to be useful to us, but not so powerful as to destroy us all. Our lord Dahun was jealous in his allocation of magic and controlled carefully who was allowed to use it."

"I believe magic-users exist among the Savages."

He was quiet again. He was often surprised at the knowledge she already possessed. Finally, he conceded her point. "Yes, but there is an additional risk. The Savages are more like animals than rational beings. They exist in the old ways, slaughtering one another for position. King Maarg allowed his realm to retain many savage customs, and he was anathema to Lord Dahun. It was Maarg whom Dahun went to destroy when last our lord left us."

"I think our lord left because of *that,*" Child said pointing to the east.

Belog didn't need to be told what "that" was, for he knew she meant the dark wave of destruction that oozed and flowed out of the Centre, devouring all it touched.

"The Darkness," he said quietly. "But if so, why the show of arms and might? Why march against Maarg? Why not"— he made a gesture with his flattened hand—"just slip away?"

Child cocked her head to one side. He had come to recognize this meant she was grappling with a problem. "I do not know," she said at the last. "I should think, though, that for a king of Dahun's majesty, it would be difficult to slip anywhere, unnoticed." She smiled. "Perhaps he needed a diversion?"

He marveled again at the complexity of her mind. Had the horror from the Centre not come upon them, this one would have been culled early and evaluated. Either she would have been placed in an area of critical need and educated or she would have been killed as potentially dangerous. She was a remarkable child. He wondered if she had been someone remarkable before her last death, and if this new order imposed by Dahun, with matings and child rearing encouraged rather than simply letting offspring spawn in the crèches and fend for themselves, might have done something to her mind.

For among the People, as soon as life returned after death, the faster one fed and the quicker one grew, the more of one's previous life-memories endured. Belog was old for his race; he was more than a century past his prime, which was unheard of before the coming of Dahun. He knew he had been very young when the Demon King had taken power, but his memories were fading into the dim mists of the past.

"Perhaps, but that is for another time and place to ponder. If you want to learn magic, we must make a plan."

Her smile broadened to a grin. "I love to plan. I am very pleased I didn't eat you, Belog."

"As I am, Child."

They were now close to the road east, forced to hug its verge by the exigencies of the landscape and marauding bands of demons. A large band of very small demons scurried along the verge on the other side of the broad road, while Child and Belog watched from behind a rock on a rise. "So many," she observed, and Belog couldn't tell if she spoke out of hunger or simply idle curiosity. Hers was easily the most inquisitive mind he had ever encountered.

"Tell me about armies," Child said suddenly.

Belog was surprised. "In what respect?"

"Why do they exist?" Her voice betrayed a note of frustration he had become familiar with, as if she expected him to know her moods and desires without asking.

"No matter how powerful a lord or king, there are others out there of equal or greater power. Armies are expressions of a . . ." He stopped, as if groping for the proper words. "A need for respite in the struggle, I think would be the best way to put it."

"I don't understand," Child said, slightly petulantly. "What is this 'respite'?"

"We are by nature a race that struggles," he began as they walked across the broken land that signaled the edge of the Kingdom of Dahun and the beginning of what had once been the Kingdom of Maarg. "Ever since the Time Before Time, we have been born, have killed and eaten, or been killed and eaten, and we have been reborn. If we are fortunate, life experiences give us purpose and direction and we endure for a time.

"Some rise to great power, and many serve willingly in exchange for protection and privilege. Dahun had many generals, many counselors, many who were given the duty to administer his realm."

"Armies, Belog, tell me of armies."

"Other kings, rivals, also have their demesnes and as individuals struggle and contest with one another. Armies are a threat; if you attack me, I will defend myself, or if you annoy me, I will attack you. Maarg controlled a great kingdom, but he was afraid of Dahun and worried about the other kings in the savage realms. Other kings of the Second Kingdoms contended with Dahun, and with one another—alliances shifted constantly—and sometimes armies were unleashed, and wars were fought. But for long periods of time, armies were held in check. Large armies at the ready deter others from attacking."

"Ah," said Child, as if she understood. "The larger the army, the longer the respite."

"To a point. Armies require a great deal of support: food, weapons, a place for them to sleep."

"Explain?" demanded Child.

They walked down a widening gully until they came to three branching gullies, directing them uphill again. Belog knew that once this must have been a large pond or small lake with three feeding rivers. He spoke quickly of logistics and keeping an army fit and ready to fight. Of the need for support so that soldiers did not fall to killing one another in the old, savage way.

When she tired of the detail, she would interrupt with another question. "Tell me about war and victory and defeat," she instructed.

He turned his narrative skills to best effect and launched into a long discourse on the nature of organized struggle while they climbed up the long slope toward the mountains beyond. Although there was much about this relationship he found tedious, his constant lecturing was honing the skills of his trade. He was required by Child's endless questions to reach into his memory for facts and thoughts untouched in years.

As an Archivist he had been given the responsibility to help with the cataloging and organization of whatever knowledge came to King Dahun: books, scrolls, devices, anything and everything that might prove useful to their Demon Lord. The Archivists had become the closest thing to a brotherhood seen in the demon realm, for every night when they sat in their shared quarters, they would tell one another of those things they had encountered during the day.

Belog had been among the first in his guild and possessed more knowledge than all but a few among them. He had a particular bent for associations, so he saw how knowledge discovered and shared by one might relate to knowledge discovered by another, in a way that was not immediately apparent to others. If any demon in the guild had been considered "senior" or of highest rank, it was probably Belog, though those in his calling had never made much of an issue of this. By nature they were as close to being gentle as a demon could be.

Cresting the ridge, Child said, "Where do we go now, Teacher?"

He was secretly pleased to be called this, but answered, "It depends on where you wish to go."

She fixed him with a look that told him she was unhappy with that reply, but he was growing in certainty that it would take a situation of crisis proportions for her to kill him. If there was such a thing as affection in their race, these two had chanced upon it.

"I was not mocking you, Child," he said, taking a moment's rest upon a rock. The long trek was taking its toll. He knew his intelligence was beginning to decline. It would take weeks, perhaps as much as a month of not eating, but eventually he would devolve to a near-animal state and attack Child, even though it would be death for him to do so.

He gazed up into her face and was again astonished at how she was evolving, becoming finer featured and even more alluring. She must have been a succubus in her previous incarnation; he was almost certain of it now. From the way she was beginning to appear, he was sure she had spent a great deal of time on the mortal planes. Softly he said, "I think you have already decided where we are going, Child."

She smiled and then laughed aloud. It was a musical, beautiful sound. Then her expression turned somber. She pointed to the east. "How long before *the Darkness* gets here?"

"I do not know, Child. It appears to keep growing no matter what is done; fire, steel, magic have been brought against it, yet it happily embraces whatever it touches. A sharpened steel arrow, a falling shard of masonry, the cowering figure of a child, all are welcomed to oblivion by its touch. It is relentless, but unhurried." He paused and calculated. "I judge a few years, maybe five."

"But it will come?"

"If we have learned anything of the Darkness, it is that it is inevitable."

"Then we cannot stop," she said. "If we travel for another five years, then in ten it will overtake us. Nothing can stop it."

"The Darkness dissolves everything it touches, and even the stones scream in pain as they are rendered into nothing, yet the Darkness itself is silent, making no sound whatever. It is without substance, yet it consumes all. Yet no matter how much it consumes, it remains without substance. Nothing appeases it, nothing stops it. It just is."

"What do you think it wants?" asked Child, still staring into the distance.

"I cannot pretend to know," said the old teacher with a sigh. "It is something of a speculation in itself that the Darkness may even be capable of wanting, which would require awareness. Does the wind want anything? Or the rain that falls? Or the fire that burns? Does the sand want as we tread upon it?"

Fixing Belog with a strange expression, Child said, "The wind wants balance, the rain wants to seep as far down as possible, and the fire wants to breathe and grow." Then she smiled a tiny smile and added, "I must confess I have no idea what the sand wants."

He was silent for a long while as he considered her words, then said, "Yet those are mere explanations of their nature and their reason for existence, not any concession to will and consciousness."

"Perhaps," she said with a shrug. "I will not be here when the Darkness arrives, no matter how far I must travel."

"Where will you go?" asked Belog.

"Tell me of Dahun's war on Maarg in the mortal realm," she demanded.

He was surprised by the question, and a little annoyed that she had ignored his. Yet it was clear it was time to start moving again, heading into the now-ravaged former Kingdom of Maarg, looking for only she knew what, and along the way he would be expected to educate and, to a lesser degree, entertain her. And Child would hunt for and feed him.

As existences went, outside the comfort of working on behalf of the King with the other Archivists, this wasn't a particularly unpleasant one, save for all the walking, he amended silently.

As they continued, he told of the summoning of all the King's forces, how his army was marshaled and every magic at his disposal was used to transport them to a world in the mortal realm, where the armies of Maarg, along with Sebran, Chatak, and other kings of the Second Kingdoms as well as chieftains and warlords of the Savage Lands had been fighting with a race known as the Star Elves. They were physically weak, mortal beings, but they had been cunning and used powerful magic effectively. Their soldiers could not stand against the combined might of five demon armies, but each demon had faced a dozen swords, and the demon legion had paid a price for their victories. More than a million demons had been returned to the breeding crèches, it was estimated, and had the demons been mortal, the war would have been over. But each time a demon died, it returned to the world of its birth, and quickly it was fed and nurtured to fighting strength, then returned to the struggle.

Then Dahun had struck, when Maarg's force had inexplicably turned on their own allies, and Dahun had descended on the remnants, and in the end had fought his way across the mortal realm.

Then nothing more had been heard from the great Demon King or his generals. His army and all his retainers had vanished, as if they had never lived.

And Dahun's kingdom had been left to defend itself against the Darkness.

She began asking questions, and he attempted to answer them as best he could.

"Why are all rulers male?" she asked at one point.

"They aren't. All kings are male. Female rulers are called queens."

She nodded and said nothing, and they went on their way, leaving behind a horror even two demons could not understand.

8

SAILOR

The storm roiled.

The *Suja* slammed through heavy combers as it rounded the headlands before making the long run into Caralyan Bay. The crew had proven as ignorant as Jim expected, dock dregs hired at the last minute against the presence of someone such as himself, a Kingdom spy. All they knew was that every ship in Kesh seemed to have been gathered at Hansulé and all of them needed able-bodied sailors.

Jim knew where the ship was by the simple expedient of being able to calculate speed and position in his head. It had been something of a surprise when he had overheard an officer ask the captain where they were headed and he had discovered they were bound for Caralyan and not the deepwater harbor at Elarial.

Still, at the moment, Jim was too busy keeping a grip on wet sheets while reefing sails to wonder about the logic behind that choice. It was the dead of night, and the only way Jim and the other men aloft could find their way around the rigging was by the light of a single shuttered oil lantern on each mast and by touch. The ropes were rough enough that he could keep a grip on them with his toes and haul in canvas. But it was the most dangerous task a sailor had to face, working aloft in a gale at night.

Jim was certain that when the storm broke, several ships would be lost along the way. The storm had blown for over a day now, and the only good of it was that they would reach their destination two days ahead of schedule.

Jim lashed the sails furiously and then made his way to the relative safety of the mast. There he clambered down to the top of the shroud and from there scampered down to the deck. The captain was apparently happy with the timing of things, since the storm seemed to be lessening and he would run for another hour on those sails left up.

Jim made his way below to the relative dryness and warmth of the crew deck. The deck was almost empty as most of the watch was still aloft. Jim went to the hammock he had claimed when he had first gone below and ran his hand absently over the edge closest to the ship's bulkhead. A satisfying lump greeted his passing touch: his concealed transport orb snuggled away in the fabric where the support rope was sewn into place. He threw himself into the canvas, content to dry off as best he could in the cold, damp air. There had been a supply of rough linen rags to dry off with when the storm began, but they were now in a heap by the companionway, soaked and probably growing a heroic infection of mildew, Jim thought. Still, what he would give for one hot dry towel right now.

On the other hand, he could still be aloft. He didn't have to feign fatigue. He knew two or three others would come stumbling below in minutes as more top-riggers were sent below. He wanted them to find a soundly sleeping sailor, not someone to engage in idle chatter. Had they any information worth gleaning, he'd have been happy to be gossiping like a woman at market, but as he knew as much about this voyage as they did, he'd rather sleep.

Of all the roles Jim had undertaken during his career, he despised being a sailor above all others. He'd rather wrangle angry camels across the summer heat of the Jal-Pur Desert or fight his way out of a bandit fortress than spend one more night aboard this ship.

Yet duty called. He had to know what this fleet was about, for while he lacked specificity, he had no doubt whatever the truth turned out to be it was ill news for the Kingdom. As he let sleep take him, he wondered not for the first time what role the Pantathian Serpent Priests had in all this.

Sleep was brief as the order for all hands on deck came at dawn. Jim arose amid the usual grumbling of the men, adding a brief invective directed toward whatever lunatic had decreed this expedition, in keeping with his character, then headed up on deck.

Rather than be sent aloft to unfurl sails, he was directed toward the bow where a gang manned the capstan that lowered the anchor. It was a grey dawn, but the storm had blown out, leaving them on a choppy sea of slate and metallic green, under a hazy sky. But what had Jim's attention was that they were being directed toward a spot near shore, where the ship would drop anchor.

As he expected, those not aloft already were told to man the lee side and watch for rocks. He went to the railing and glanced over, seeing nothing but deep choppy water and the occasional foam cap. He glanced toward shore and saw they were less than a quarter of a mile off the breakers. He calculated they were still a half-day's sail from the city, and he wondered just how many ships had already arrived.

As the dawn grew lighter and the weather became more clement, he got his answer: more ships than he had dreamed possible. As if to endorse his worst fear, a squadron of Brijaner longships hove into view, moving to a location somehow communicated to them by whoever was in charge of this impossible fleet.

Glancing around to ensure no one was watching, Jim scrambled up a shroud to the mainmast, then quickly climbed to the top spar and looked toward the distant port. They were still far enough away that there was no sign of land where he knew the city would be. They were anchored in a vast curving bay, only serving as decent harborage up in the top of the arch, where the mass of land to the north sheltered it from the worst weather coming in from the northwest. At least now Jim understood why they were here instead of up at Elarial. This many ships would clog even the vast entrance to that harbor.

Then another certainty struck him: Kaseem abu Hazara-Khan must have spotted his agents in Caralyan and was having them shadowed. No ship in this flotilla would be close enough to the city to be observed, unless by magic, or by one of Jim's agents hiring a boat for a lovely day's sailing.

With a sinking feeling in the pit of his stomach, he slithered down a sheet and dropped nimbly to the deck. He had wondered why all his agents south of here had gone silent, and those from here and to the north were untouched. Now he realized that Hazara-Khan didn't care. Whatever he was planning, it would be in full play before word of this massive fleet reached the Kingdom.

Jim knew two things: he had to find out where this massive navy was heading, the Far Coast or Krondor; then he had to get off this ship and return to Krondor. He calculated. Logic dictated that the Empire of Great Kesh was going to attempt to reclaim all the land lost hundreds of years ago in one crushing assault. If those Brijaner longships were the first through the Straits of Darkness and could provide a screen against Quegan raiders, the rest of this fleet could make straight along the southern coast of the Bitter Sea and launch a three-pronged assault on Land's End, Port Vykor, and Krondor.

Calvary could be on its way north from the Keshian cities of Jonril and Nar Ayab to come at the Vale of Dreams from the southeast, while the garrison of Durbin would be in support of the Keshian forces already in Shamata. Kesh would control the Vale within a week: Land's End would fall in days, and if the King's Western Fleet was caught at anchor at Port Vykor, Kesh would control the Bitter Sea.

If he were conducting this assault, he would set a blockade of Krondor and then a raid up to Sarth, ensuring that help from Yabon would not be forthcoming. The forces on the Far Coast would be insignificant, and if brought east through the passes in the Grey Towers, they'd be backed up behind those forces from Yabon halted north of Sarth.

Then Jim stopped. The only part of this that made no sense whatsoever is what Hazara-Khan would do in the south. He did not need to see the Keshian general's orders and plans to know that every garrison south of the Overn Deep had been marshaled and was now aboard these ships. By conventional logic, hordes of very angry tribesmen should be pouring though the Girdle of Kesh into the lush farmlands of the southern Empire.

Is this where the Pantathians played a part? he wondered. For something had to convince them to keep the peace without the heel of Kesh's boot on their necks.

Suddenly Jim was as near panic as he was inclined to get. He had discovered everything possible to discover on this ship, but getting off was problematic. He could use his secret orb to return to his office in Krondor, which was his plan as soon as he knew more. The problem was in learning more. He was anchored near enough off the coast that swimming through breakers to reach the beach was not a terrible danger. But once on the coast, then what? He would have more than twenty miles on foot before he reached any portion of the bay that would give him any more useful information, or faster transportation, and he would still have no idea what the plan was. There had to be another way.

He moved without thought at the order of the first mate, to start smartening up some lines and cleaning the decks. That meant the captain planned on staying awhile. Jim resisted an urge to vent his frustration vocally and instead settled for a repeat of the same thought: there had to be another way.

Two uneventful days went by, which didn't mean Jim had time to dwell upon his current position; a ship at sea, even one at anchor, required a great deal of attention, and as the *Suja* was shorthanded—as apparently was every other vessel in the fleet—watches were half day on, half day off, though the "off" was a matter of definition. After meals on the crew deck, there were sails to mend, ropes to splice, as well as wandering through the guts of the ship with a lantern investigating leaks and ensuring the storm hadn't damaged the masts or the keelson. Jim elected to do the hull inspection, hoping to find some cargo or other indication of what this ship's role was to be, but he was frustrated to the point of madness in discovering the hold was empty. There was cargo on deck, he knew, crates brought aboard by the Pantathians, but they were lashed down under heavy canvas and there was always someone on deck; he stood no chance of being able to investigate the contents.

The third morning, ships began to weigh anchor, the Brijaner longships among the first. Jim took a deep breath to still his impatience; they were the logical first-strike flotilla, as they could outmaneuver any Quegan galley in the Bitter Sea and would most likely run a screen so that heavier Keshian war galleys could come in behind and strike straight for Port Vykor.

More than once Jim itched to grab his teleportation orb and get to Krondor, but he knew he was at the point at which the warning he would bring would be scant days before Kingdom picket ships west of Land's End caught sight of the foreign sails. A week's extra preparation would mean little against this onslaught.

Then came the order for the *Suja* to raise anchor and lower sails. But the trim was for maneuvering, and the order was to make way toward the city of Caralyan, not head out to sea. Jim got aloft with the top gang and unfurled sails and then got busy trimming them. They were sailing a close reach into a turn that would put a following breeze behind them as the wind was from the south this day, and it would be easy to pick up too much speed if the captain wanted a slow approach. Given the clutter of ships ahead, Jim was certain the captain wanted a very slow, cautious approach. As they neared the harbor, Jim could scarcely believe his eyes, for there were still more than a hundred ships standing off, as cargo barges and small service boats ran back and forth from land; they were not just coming out of the harbor itself, but from along the beaches beyond.

The order was given to drop anchor and reef sails, every man stood to, and the ship came to rest less than a quarter of a mile from a long beach. In the distance he could make out the smudge on the horizon he knew was the city of Caralyan, or at least the smoke from its chimneys. He had never cared for this city, finding it a second-rate port and rarely worth watching, but he had an agent there, anyway.

A longboat came toward the ship, and the first mate shouted orders to get cargo nets ready. Jim manned the boom with two other men, and another half-dozen sailors pushed aside the main hatchway and scrambled below to receive cargo.

The net was lowered and Jim waited on the hoist until the signal was given. He and two other men turned the heavy crank, and the winch turned as the net rose into view.

Jim almost let go as a very disturbed-looking cow stared at him. There was another one snug in a sling beside the first, and it was lowing piteously. Jim was no expert on animal husbandry, but he had traveled through enough farmland to recognize dairy cattle.

Livestock keeps longer than slaughtered meat, so bringing cattle, sheep, or even pigs, which are notoriously hard to herd, along behind an army was not unheard of, especially if good hunting wasn't anticipated. But dairy cattle?

Then his eyes widened even more as men, women, and children climbed aboard and suddenly Jim understood exactly what was going on. He glanced around to see that everyone else was intent on their job and started gauging when he might get away to his hammock and activate his transport orb; for he now knew exactly what some insane group of Keshian nobles had decided to do.

This wasn't a mere military adventure. It was more than just an all-out assault on the Western Realm of the Kingdom of the Isles, or even a bid to claim all of the Vale of Dreams after years of border skirmishes.

Before him were men and women from half a dozen dissimilar places: desert people from Drahali-Kapur, swamp dwellers from the Dragon Mere and E'Ramere, Ashunta horsemen, and Isalani famers, all from the Keshian Confederation.

Kesh wasn't guarding its borders from the Confederates desperate for better land in the southern Empire. The Empire was bringing Confederates to the Far Coast and meant to give them Kingdom land.

This wasn't just another war; it was a wholesale invasion and colonization. They didn't intend to conquer those lands and rule a fractious population; they were going to displace that population with people who would gratefully obey Imperial law so they could hold on to their new, treasured homes.

Jim glanced around and saw more ships unfurling sails to begin their voyage to the north. Without knowing the exact number of ships, he could only estimate, but at the very least the Empire of Great Kesh was bringing more than twenty thousand farmers, herdsmen, and craftsmen to the Far Coast, roughly three times the entire population of Kingdom citizens. And the majority of fighting-age men had been mustered and were probably now halfway to Krondor.

Jim fought the sense of nausea that rose in his gullet.

Jim watched as the last of the "cargo" came aboard. The men among the colonists had moved into like groups, keeping as much distance away from traditional enemies as the confined space below permitted.

He was climbing rigging behind the poop deck when he heard the captain shout, "We're ready. Stand by to weigh anchor!"

Glancing around, Jim saw something over by the next ship that made him pause. As more and more colonists had been boarding the ships, he had considered how Great Kesh was going to seize the Far Coast. It had been a question he could not answer beyond some vague concept of a massive advantage in numbers.

Compared with the Confederacy, the Far Coast was teeming with riches. But it was still sparsely populated after more than a hundred and fifty years. Two huge wars in the last hundred years had devastated the Western Realm, and the population had been low to begin with. The only city of any size was Carse, though Crydee was still capital of the duchy, and those population centers, along with Tulan in the south, were relatively stable, having grown by barely more than a tenth since the invasion of the west by the army of the Emerald Queen.

He could see why Kesh might want to reclaim the Far Coast after all these years; moving a large portion of the population of the Confederacy made sense. It would pacify a large portion of the rebellious Confederates by thinning out the population and reducing the competition for precious natural resources among those who remained. And it would quickly establish a thriving colony on the Far Coast that could exploit the region far more efficiently than the Kingdom had heretofore, providing a quickly profitable revenue source, but still keeping taxes low for those new colonists.

Jim almost admired the audacity of the plan, the sheer scope of it. What a stunning triumph it would be for whatever faction of generals and nobles in the Gallery of Lords and Masters was behind this! But then his admiration fell short when he considered it was his kingdom that was being carved up to make this dream a reality.

What he saw on the next ship suddenly brought the entire plan together. Slavers. The next ship was boarding a party of at least fifty members of Kesh's Slavers' Guild.

Outlawed in the Kingdom for nearly two centuries, slavery was still an institution in Kesh. More than one Keshian slave had died trying to reach safety in the Kingdom, but few could get across the frontier.

The sick feeling returned to the pit of Jim's stomach. Now he knew how Kesh's invading colonists would deal with those they displaced. He had imagined them being run up into the hills to find their way to the east and the haven of Yabon, or the Free Cities, or perhaps seeking sanctuary with the dwarves or the elves up in Elvandar.

Two problems solved at once, thought Jim as he started back down the ropes, as if he had an important task besides scuttling up to the yards and unfurling sails. First the villagers and townspeople would not have to be considered as a potential liability; boys displaced from their homes would not grow up to be outlaws and bandits in the woodlands and forests of the Far Coast, and some of the expense of this massive invasion would be underwritten by a vast influx of new bodies for the trading blocs in every city in the Empire.

For one brief second Jim felt overwhelmed. Who could have devised this insane plan, one so overreaching that it might even work? No one he knew among the rulers of Great Kesh hated the Kingdom enough or was covetous enough to . . .

Then it hit him. There was one common weakness shared by both the Kingdom of the Isles and the Empire of Great Kesh; both were currently ruled by unsure men with no apparent heirs. With the crown in play, a great many political promises could be made irrespective of the likelihood of those promises being kept. When the conditions of a promise were, "When I gain the crown . . . ," those involved knew both the price of failure and the scope of the riches that might be attached to success.

Jim hit the deck and scampered below, heading straight for his bunk. He found his tiny sphere and quickly removed it from the fabric of his hammock. He slid the tiny lever that enabled him to select one of three destinations and then the second lever to activate it.

Nothing happened.

Jim barely contained a primitive scream of frustration as he repeatedly tried the device on all of its settings. It had simply stopped working. He knew the Tsurani devices were old, and many had failed, but he had taken the one he judged most likely to work and had guessed wrong.

He was so caught up in this unexpected change in his plans that he was unaware of the man coming up behind him until the last possible instant. Jim spun and crouched, ready to fight for his life. But he was an instant too late. As a club struck him on the side of the head, a blinding explosion of light was followed by blackness.

Jim's head pounded as if he had been on a seven-day drinking spree, and his jaw throbbed. He blinked as he opened his eyes and tried to focus.

He wasn't on the ship.

He could sense a difference in the air. It was dry and warm where it had been cool and damp. He was in the desert. Or near it.

He looked around and found himself in a large room. He was tied to a heavy wooden chair. A quick personal inventory told him he had not been abused beyond the blow that had rendered him unconscious. From the ringing in his ears he judged that a good thing; another blow like the first one and he might not be waking up now. Two more and it was certain he would never wake up at all.

He felt the man stirring before he heard a sound or saw movement, then realized someone was in the corner watching him from the shadows. It was only a moment before he heard a voice say, "Ah, at last. Light."

From behind Jim someone else lit a lantern and Jim at last could make out his companion in the room. A dark-skinned man with a fashionably trimmed beard stood up slowly. He wore rich robes in the fashion of the people of the Jal-Pur and he smiled. He was young, more than twenty years Jim's junior, but Jim knew he was already a man to fear.

"Kaseem abu Hazara-Khan," Jim said and found his voice came out as little more than a whisper.

With a wave of his hand, the Keshian said, "Water. Quickly. And untie his hands."

Two men appeared from the corners behind him, one cutting the ropes around Jim's wrists, and the other putting a cup of cool water to Jim's lips. Jim's hands were shaking when they came up to grip the cup and he drank greedily. When he finished, he spoke and his voice was stronger. "How long?"

"Two days. I'm sorry to say my agent was a bit more enthusiastic in fetching you here than I had instructed. He shall be punished." He stood looking down on Jim. "Lord James Dasher Jamison, it is good to see you again. Or should I be calling you 'Jim Dasher'? From your current attire, I'm uncertain. Or would you prefer, 'Jimmyhand,' or 'Quick Jim'?"

"What do you want, Kaseem?" said Jim. As the unnamed head of Keshian Intelligence, like his father and grandfathers before him, the young Keshian had played the role of minor court noble in the Imperial Court of Kesh, never for a minute revealing his knowledge of Jim's position. It was an amiable fiction they both observed. To be dropping all pretense meant something significant.

After a long pause Kaseem said, "What makes you think I want anything?"

Jim sighed. "Fine. If I must play. For you to have a man on that ship means you were following me since Hansulé. You're a powerful man, but even you can't have an agent on *every* single ship in that fleet.

"For your man to drop his role as a sailor and bring me in before I escape to return to the Kingdom means either you want me dead or you want something from me, and as I am not dead, I assume it's the latter. So what do you want, Kaseem?" he asked for the third time.

"Ah, Jim," said the Keshian noble. "You and I have a problem."

"Which is?"

Coming to kneel beside Jim, the young Keshian desert man put his hand on Jim's shoulder in an apparently friendly fashion. "Our two governments seem suddenly to be populated by madmen, and as ironic as the gods can be at times, nothing like this has happened in my lifetime. This is the long and short of it: you are the only man I can trust to help end this insane war, and I am the only man you can trust."

There were many things Jim thought he might hear from his opposite number, but this hadn't once occurred to him as a possibility.

9

CONCLAVE

Pug cast his spell.

Without any apparent physical effort, he gestured and a wall frame rose off the ground, where the carpenters had laid it, and hovered in the air for a moment. Two workers grabbed it by the ends, and Pug moved sixty feet of wall into place without difficulty where it was quickly attached at the base by large iron spikes driven into the foundation stones. Straps of iron were then attached at the corners to link it to the already-standing rear wall of the main house.

"Thank you, Pug," said the chief builder.

"You're welcome, Shane." He liked the rough-mannered stonemason who would now oversee the placing of each stone against the frame. The interior would be plastered and when they were finished there would once again be a Villa Beata on Sorcerer's Isle.

Pug turned to see his son directing the disposition of a huge pallet of stones. Two younger magicians, Herbert and Lillian, were using their abilities to lift and steer the stones that Shane would use to face the building. Pug's decision was not to rebuild the villa to its original specification, but to build it more to his own personal taste and to change a few things he hadn't cared for over the years he had resided on the island.

For one thing, he was not rebuilding the ancient communal bath. It had proved to be a waste of resources for it was rarely used, and when it was, it was hard to keep the hot water hot and the cold water cold because of the younger magicians' seemingly uncontrollable impulses in playing pranks on one another. Some of the cultures from which his students hailed had a strict segregation of the sexes while others did not, and one person's modesty was another's oddly amusing behavior.

Thinking of a group of sisters who had been students years before, he also remembered that some of them found the baths an ideal place to hold parties that quickly got out of hand. He was certain at various times both his sons had found themselves in a steaming bath with an assortment of playful companions. Thinking of Caleb caused Pug to pause for a moment, but there was no use indulging in maudlin thoughts. Letting go of the sadness, he forced himself to remember a happy moment with Caleb and Marie, Caleb's wife, then turned his attention back to the work at hand.

He would install bathing rooms in every dormitory: if students wanted to frolic nude, they could do so on the other side of the island; there was ample water in the lake.

A voice from the top of the ridge caused Pug to turn. A young student was waving down at the building site, shouting something Pug could not understand, but his behavior implied it was of some urgency.

Pug used his magic to suddenly appear next to the youngster who stumbled back a step. "What is it, Phillip?"

"Ships!" answered the student. "Jack sent me to tell you that many ships are passing to the south."

"Thank you," said Pug and vanished.

A moment later he stood atop the highest tower of the Black Castle, above two windows that conveniently flickered an evil blue light should any ship pass within sight at night, both to alert anyone in the castle and as a warning for seafarers not to come ashore. It was part of the entire charade surrounding the person of the "Black Sorcerer," a creation of Pug's father-in-law, Macros the Black, and one continued after his departure by Pug. It protected the privacy of those on the island: anyone who ignored it was either someone welcome on the island, or someone subjected to less subtle means of dissuasion.

The young magician there turned without surprise and said, "I make it at least a dozen sails." Jack was slender, with sandy-colored hair and piercing blue eyes. Pug also knew those eyes were capable of seeing quite a bit farther than most, a natural ability of magic that was as yet untrained. Pug took advantage of that by putting the young man on lookout duty at least once a week.

"I haven't your eyes," said Pug with a smile. He formed a circle with his hands, spoke a soft incantation, and suddenly the air in the circle shimmered. The image of the distant horizon within that circle suddenly shifted, seeming to jump toward Pug as he willed the very air to bend, magnifying the image.

"I've never seen ships like those," said Jack.

"Not on this sea, no," said Pug. The ships were square rigged, fast in a following breeze, most carrying only a single mast, with one or two larger vessels possessing a second mast with a lanteen-rigged sail. The shorter ships had four rowers a side and the longer ships eight, so it was clear the rowing would only be for short periods of maneuvering, not for long travel. On the bow of each ship was a colorful figure: a dragon, an eagle, or a hawk, each with a carved woman's head in miniature just below, painted in bright hues. "They're Keshian."

"I've never seen their like in Durbin," said Jack.

"Those are Brijaner longships, from the eastern shores of the Empire of Great Kesh. The Brijaners are raiders, but this is too far from home for them to be operating without the Empire's approval. Something is going on." He waved his hands and the image vanished.

"I see sails farther to the south," said Jack, peering as if he could will himself to see farther than the limits of his sight.

Pug said, "I'll go take a look." And he disappeared.

An instant later Pug stood in midair, using his arts to keep him aloft. He was so high that if a lookout on the topmast of one of the ships below glanced up, he'd appear like nothing more than a bird soaring aloft.

Pug lingered long enough only to apprise himself of what was under way, then he returned to the villa construction site.

Magnus said, "Father?"

"Send word, I want everyone back here as soon as possible for a meeting of the Conclave."

"Everyone?" Since the attack on the island during which his wife, Miranda, had died, Pug had never requested more than two or three members of the Conclave be present at any one time. The mad magician Leso Varen had somehow managed to circumvent the island's many magical defenses, and Pug had become almost obsessed with never allowing his most important lieutenants to gather and become a single target again.

"Everyone," Pug repeated.

Magnus didn't hesitate, using his considerable skills to transport himself in an instant to his father's study in the Black Castle. A device had been constructed that could be used to summon any or all members of the Conclave of Shadows's inner circle, those men and women upon whom the organization effectively rested. The device was a large sphere with runic markings around it, each attuned to a member of the inner circle. By depressing the mark associated with that member, the indicated person would receive an unmistakable sensation, a feeling akin to an itch that couldn't be scratched, annoying enough to awaken any but the soundest sleeper. It would last for ten seconds and then repeat in half an hour and would continue until the member arrived on the island. Pug used the irritation the device caused to drive home the point that these devices he provided were precious and needed to be closely guarded. The idea of having to travel from the other side of the world by conventional means with the recurring itch was a strong goad.

Almost immediately members of the inner council began to arrive. Magnus could feel the magical energies even as far away from the meeting cave as he was. He transported himself to a position just outside and walked into the large cavern set within the hillside on the north side of the island.

Pug was already there, along with Jason, the magician who acted as Pug's reeve when he and Magnus were both absent from the island, and the first of the thirty-three summoned members of the Conclave.

Grand Master Creegan of the Order of the Shield of the Weak, the martial order of the Temple of Dala, shook his head ruefully. "I trust this is important. I was about to begin a meeting with the senior members of my order when the call arrived. I can put them off for a few hours, but even the authority of my office has limits."

"Understood," said Pug, shaking his hand.

The arrivals continued for a full twenty minutes. The last to make it through were those on the other side of the world, who had been asleep when the call came, several of whom still looked barely awake. A quick head count showed they were all present save two, and Pug began. "We can't wait. I'm sorry to convene this meeting so abruptly, but something has occurred and we need to address it at once."

The cave had remained unchanged since they had first been introduced to it by Gathis, the odd, goblinlike servant of Macros the Black. Like so many things associated with Macros, two things remained a mystery: the whereabouts of Gathis who had simply vanished one day, leaving Pug alone in charge of the island; and the true nature of the cave.

At first it appeared to be little more than a deep depression in the side of the hill, but when you turned a corner inside it, the cavern presented itself. In a semicircle along the walls was a ledge of stone that provided a natural seating area, allowing the members to sit in relative comfort. And in the center of the cavern rose a pillar of stone, on top of which rested a statue to Sarig, the lost God of Magic. Over the years the aspect of the bust had changed by mysterious means so that it represented men, women, and other beings who were somehow at that moment an avatar of the god.

Pug could never quite fathom if there was something truly significant about the statue, or if it was merely some manifestation of Macros's love of the theatrical.

A still-sleepy magician named Jerome hurried in, obviously having just got dressed after bathing, his wet hair still plastered to his skull. "Sorry," he said, nodding in greeting.

That left just one member missing. Glancing around the cave, Pug said questioningly, "Sandreena?"

It was Grand Master Creegan who replied. "There is no reason I can imagine that would keep her from answering the call. She must be incapacitated somehow."

Magnus said, "Or the device failed."

Pug sighed and nodded. The ancient Tsurani transportation orbs were becoming a problem. Translocation or teleportation was one of the more difficult feats, even for practiced magicians. Magnus was unparalleled in his ability to travel anywhere he had visited before, as well as certain places he had never seen on the basis of unique features well described to him. Pug could travel easily to any place he could see, or knew, and Magnus had helped him master greater range. But only a handful of magicians could match even Pug's more limited abilities, and many of the agents of the Conclave, like Grand Master Creegan, were not magicians.

Pug whispered to Magnus, "If it's the device, make sure to turn off the summons. I can't have her itching every half hour." He paused. "Unless you'd like to face her and her mace when she finally does get here?"

Magnus vanished and in a moment he was back. "Taken care of, Father."

Pug said, "And Amirantha?"

Magnus said, "Despite his residency here for the last few years, you've never formally invited him into the Conclave, so he doesn't have means to return in a hurry. I'll have to fetch him from the elven city."

Pug said, "Later. I'd rather not disturb him while he's at E'bar." His gaze traveled around the assembled members of the Conclave. Then he took a deep breath and announced, "Apparently a very large war is erupting between the Empire of Great Kesh and the Kingdom of the Isles."

Everyone in the room appeared surprised, yet there was little evidence of shock. One magician, by the name of Brandtly, whom Pug had serving as a liaison with Stardock, said, "We've heard rumors, and some of the Keshian magicians at Stardock have been absent of late, but rumors of war in the Vale are constant."

Grand Master Creegan asked, "You've had no word from agents in either court?"

"We don't properly have an agent in the court in Rillanon," Pug said, "though we enjoy a special relationship with their intelligence service." Most in the room knew of Pug's treatment of the future King of Isles, Prince Patrick of Krondor, at the end of the war with the Emerald Queen, when Kesh had tried to press its advantage against the Kingdom's weakened defenses in the west. Pug had ended the war but had publicly embarrassed the hot-tempered young monarch. Since then relations between the Conclave and the Kingdom had been strained at best, hostile at worst. "If James Jamison had heard anything that had any bearing on this, I can't imagine he wouldn't share that intelligence with us. He more than anyone in the King's service has a sense of what is at stake, what dangers are still out there." His hand waved vaguely toward the cave entrance, but everyone knew he meant those unknown beings behind the onslaught of demons against this realm. "It may have been years since our enemies last assaulted us, but they will come again, there is no doubt. And we will need every force at our disposal to oppose them. We cannot permit this war. Two devastated armies will not do; two plundered populations will not do." His voice rose. "Two severely weakened nations will not do.

"None of our friends in the court of the Emperor have hinted at such an undertaking. We've had reports detailing debates within the Chamber of Lords and Masters, some calling for a more aggressive policy toward the Kingdom, especially regarding the Vale of Dreams. But no warnings, no alarms, nothing." Pug let out a long breath. "This is no mad adventure conducted by dissidents or a breakaway faction in the Empire. For something of this scale, the Emperor himself had to give approval, or at least be in no position to object."

Pug looked at Creegan. "Had the temples any warning?"

"No, just the usual: some members of the Congress of Lords urging a more belligerent posture toward Kesh, and closer ties with Roldem." He stopped. "Usually, those in favor of adventure turn their eyes to the Eastern Kingdoms, seeking to expand in that direction. War with Kesh is never anyone's notion of a good idea." He paused, then added, "But we haven't received any reports from our temples or shrines in the south of Kesh for over a month now. And Sandreena was investigating some reports of . . ."

"What?" prompted Pug.

"Just some things that sounded to her as if the Black Caps might have returned."

The Black Caps were a group of murderers and thugs attached to those who had been in the service of Belasco, the mad magician who had attempted to bring the Demon King Dahun into this realm and had been possessed by him for his trouble. In the end, both the magician and the Demon Lord had been destroyed, but many of those serving them had escaped into the wilds of Kesh. Any rumor of their reemergence would have attracted Sandreena's attention, as she had more run-ins with them than anyone else.

"You didn't think this worthy of a mention?" asked Magnus.

"I would have once she returned," said Creegan. Members of the Conclave were not merely Pug's agents, but powerful men and women in their own right, and many bristled at the idea they had to defend their choices within their own areas of influence.

Pug held up his hand, forestalling any argument. "I trust each of you to let me know what's critical."

He looked from face to face, almost as if trying to read their thoughts, then seized upon something Creegan had said. "Sandreena ventured to the south of Great Kesh?"

"Yes, somewhere below the Girdle," said the Grand Master.

"Have any of you received reports from your agents south of the Girdle recently?"

Glances were exchanged, and finally a woman named Veronica said, "No. But then it's not unusual to not hear from them for months. There is very little that happens in the Confederacy that has any particular bearing on our interests, save the occasional magician who is found and recruited for the Academy or your island."

Pug nodded. "If our enemies know us as well as I think they do, where better to stage a massive operation against us than somewhere we just choose to ignore?"

Daniel, a highly placed warrior in the martial order known as the Hammer, stood up. The Hammer was a disavowed sect putatively associated with the Temple of Tith-Onanka. In fact, they were close to being a mercenary army, tolerated on both sides of the border between Kesh and the Kingdom. They answered only to their leader, the Knight-Marshal of the order, and it had taken years for Pug to place an agent within their ranks: like other martial orders associated with the temples, they were wary of spies and had magical means by which they could ferret them out. "How big was the fleet you saw, Pug?" Daniel asked.

"I counted over one hundred ships making for Port Vykor or Krondor."

"If they're sending that many ships into the Bitter Sea, they have other fleets as well. They'll not leave their coasts unprotected from pirates, raiders, retaliation, or other disasters. Moreover, the combined fleets of Roldem and Isles in the Sea of Kingdoms need to be met with a show of strength." Daniel paused, thinking. "To muster such a fleet south of the Girdle and then sail up to the Straits of Darkness and into the Bitter Sea within a few weeks to catch the Kingdom unawares . . ." He stopped. "What I'm trying to say is the execution may have only taken weeks, but the planning . . . that's been months, perhaps years. Food, weapons, drinking water: it's a massive cargo! It all has to be moved somewhere out of the way, somewhere they have a reasonable expectation of privacy." Daniel looked around the room as if looking for someone to argue against his point. No one did.

"South of the Girdle would be an obvious choice," said Magnus. "We presume, perhaps wrongly, that the Empire is primarily in a position to pacify, not to be used as a staging area."

"Ah, but there's more than simply hauling a few casks of water, some loaves of bread, hogsheads of hard cheese and dried beef and leaving them on a beach for ships to pick up," continued Daniel. "Moving goods through the market sets up ripples." He looked at the tall, white-haired magician. "You're smarter than most, Magnus, but like all of us you're ignorant about one thing or another.

"I'm in logistics, and that's how I made my way into the Hammer, feeding the bastards." He laughed. "The point is, if I wander into a city and buy up enough food for a thousand men, prices go up, others can't find what they're seeking, and word goes out to the world that that city needs whatever it is I bought. Shippers then scramble, buying whatever they think they can quickly get to market where I am, and that creates more demand farther away." He wiggled his fingers. "Ripples, you see? Like a rock in a pond. The thing is: with this bastard of a fleet sailing around there are no ripples."

Pug nodded. "Which means goods are being supplied from outside the normal channels of supply. From somewhere we have no informants." He waved his hand and an image appeared in the air. "This is a likeness of map I found years ago in Macros's library, of the southern half of the Empire. From what I've learned since I found it, the borders are fluid, the clans and nations variable, and little can be fixed beyond the location of a few big towns on the coast."

"It looks as if it's mainly desert, swamps, and mountains," said Daniel. "And I know what little farmland is down there is old, worn out and dry. The Confederates are always looking for an excuse to push north. And any large supply of food there would be eaten, not warehoused."

Magnus pointed. "What about that large island to the south?"

"That's the Island of Snakes," said Daniel. "No one lives there. The north side's a cold, forlorn place, and that's the good side. The southern half is close enough to the pole you get winter most of the year, and summer's nothing to call warm and inviting."

Pug was silent for a moment. Then he said, "Snakes? Snakes don't live in cold, barren places. I've never seen snakes where there's snow on the ground for much of the year."

"Who drew the map?" asked Creegan.

"Macros himself," said Pug, making it vanish with a wave of his hand. "He often took old scraps of things he found, pieced them together like puzzles, then annotated them. I've taken to annotating his annotations," he added with a rueful smile, "where I know he made a mistake."

"Maybe 'snakes' is a mistranslation," said Daniel. "Or maybe it referred to snakelike rivers, or some other thing."

"Or maybe it's a place where cold-weather snakes exist," countered Pug. "Still, whatever the reason for the odd name, that's where I'd be warehousing my foodstuffs and weapons."

"I'd have my ships sail out of the Keshian ports," Daniel continued, "for they'd only need a normal supply of provisions, then run down there to pick up whatever else I needed. Then I could make the long run along the southern coast, up the western coast into the Bitter Sea, then on to Krondor. The currents along the western coast of Kesh are from the south, so it's a fast run. Keeps the need for provisions for the crews and soldiers to a minimum.

"Still," said Daniel, "you'd think if they were stockpiling goods and food and weapons down there, we'd have had some sort of hint over the last year or so."

"Those weapons must be coming from somewhere, Father," agreed Magnus. "One would assume that should Kesh's armorers and weaponmakers be increasing production lately, some attention might be paid by one of our agents, or one of the Kingdom's."

Daniel agreed. "There would be a demand for raw materials, Pug. More iron from the mines, more ships carrying it to the foundries, more coal for the forges, more leather, more wood, all that someone, somewhere would surely have noticed."

"Maybe they did," said Pug absently.

Everyone stared at him.

At last, he said, "Over the years our enemies may have proved mad by our standards, but they have also proved to be cunning. Leso Varen almost captured and controlled two nations, Olasko and Great Kesh itself, working essentially alone both times. Belasco managed to bring a small demon army into our realm before we were able to close off that gate.

"What if it's just been going on long enough that we never noticed an increase in the demand for weapons and other necessary equipment?" He looked at Daniel. "Where does the Hammer buy its swords?"

Daniel shook his head as if caught by surprise. "Ah . . . places. We have swordmakers in several cities we regularly do business with. Some of the brothers of the order are gifted craftsman, so we manage most of the repairs ourselves."

So if one of your sources were suddenly to start making twelve swords instead of ten . . . ?"

"I think I understand," said Daniel with dawning comprehension. "If a swordmaker in Elarial was given an order for fifty new blades by the Hammer but produced fifty-five and sent the extra five along in a shipment of other goods somewhere else . . . who would notice?"

"Yes," said Pug. "But let us not dwell on how, but rather who and where."

"Well, that damn snake place seems a likely where," said Daniel.

"Yes," agreed Pug. "And if that is the place, then we'll soon know who."

"You're sending someone?" asked Magnus.

"No," said Pug. "This time I'm going myself."

"Really?" Magnus sounded shocked.

"I've been sitting on this island feeling pity for myself far too long, son." He flashed a smile Magnus hadn't seen in years. "It's time for me to get out and do some of the hard work myself. Besides, it's a part of this world I've never visited before. It should be interesting."

Ruefully, Magnus said, "Let's hope it's not *too* interesting."

10

REVERSAL

Sandreena sprinted.

Not for the first time in her life she was thankful for the rigorous training her order had inflicted on her. Her ability to move suddenly and rapidly while wearing heavy mail armor, holding a sword and shield, had saved her life more than once.

Her opponent was obviously unprepared for just how fast she closed the distance, and when she drove her shoulder into him, he flew backward as if struck by a battering ram. The man was wearing a buff-colored coat over jack armor—a rough suede vest over a thick, quilted singlet—effective for arrows that didn't strike full on and glancing blows from swords. For a fully armored Sergeant Knight-Adamant slamming into him, he might as well be naked. He lay sprawled out for a moment, then tried to move, but collapsed backward with a groan of pain, his eyes going in and out of focus.

Sandreena gave him a quick glance and decided she might have broken a few ribs as well as having stunned him. Leveling her sword at his throat, she waited until he either passed out or regained consciousness.

He passed out. She sighed as she put up her sword. She looked around to make sure he had been alone, but if he had had confederates, they were making good their escape. She knelt to check that the man wasn't shamming. A firm poke into ribs that were at the very least bruised if not broken brought no response. She knew he was not engaging in any sort of mummery. It was a lucky thing for her assailant that she had been leading her horse up the trail; had she been on horseback, she'd have ridden him down and he'd be in even worse shape.

She took one minute to circle around the ambush spot: it was hard to believe this idiot would have taken on a Knight-Adamant of the Order of the Shield of the Weak alone. She saw he was armed with a short bow that might have caused her injury if he had been a good enough archer to strike at one of the tiny openings in her armor. It was highly unlikely though: the loop chain she wore would keep all but the sharpest broad-head arrows launched by the most powerful longbows from doing anything more than irritate her. He didn't even have a sword, just a dirk and a buckler, which told her he was first and foremost an archer, since it was the shield of choice among bowmen. Some of the really practiced archers could fire their bows while wearing a buckler on their forearms, already in place if the bow needed to be dropped in hand-to-hand combat.

Sandreena sat on a rock next to the unconscious attacker and took a long breath. It had been a hard day. In fact, it had been a hard month.

The Grand Master of her order had given her free rein to hunt down any remnants of a group known to her as the Black Caps. Five years earlier they had almost killed her, but that wasn't her only reason for wanting to ferret out any last enclave of the murdering scum.

A mixture of fanatic believers and hired mercenaries who had come under the control of the mad magician Belasco, they had aided in the summoning of a Demon King, Dahun, into this realm. Only the quick action of Pug and his Conclave along with Sandreena and her former lover, Amirantha the Warlock, had blocked their plan.

But rather than any sense of triumph, everyone had come away with a sense of foreboding. For every answer they had uncovered, they had been left with more questions.

Hours of long discussion had followed the events in the abandoned fortress in that portion of Kesh known as the Valley of Lost Men between Amirantha and another demon summoner, an elf named Gulamendis, Pug and Magnus, and the other magic-users. They examined all manner of theories as to what was occurring in the demon realm that would cause a Demon King to attempt to possess a human and enter the world of Midkemia undetected. They even consulted, and pored over endlessly, a book they had purloined from the archives of the island kingdom of Queg.

Sandreena's experience with demons was far more prosaic. She saw a demon; she killed it. Or, using her clerical magic, banished it back to whence it came. Even so, she recognized there were bigger problems in play now, and she was content to let the Grand Master, the Demon Masters, and the magicians worry about that, content for her task to be out in the world seeking information for them.

She just wished it didn't always involve this much tedium.

Rumors had surfaced lately that a group of men was gathering near the southeastern foothills of the Peaks of the Quor. They sounded a great deal like the thugs who had almost killed her in her first encounter with them. Beaten, raped, then thrown off a cliff onto the rocks below, she had survived only by the Goddess's mercy. In her final battle at the Demon Gate, she had taken an additional measure of revenge against those murderous dogs.

She regarded her unconscious companion and vowed that if he was another of those bastards, he'd soon be joining them, even though her order had strictures on what was and was not acceptable behavior in a Knight-Adamant, and murder out of hand, even if it was labeled "execution," was not permitted. She knew she'd dispatch any member of that gang without hesitation, then petition the Goddess for forgiveness later.

She had been frustrated to find the rumors unfounded, but one small item of information had caught her attention: a demand for more fish than usual from traders heading south. The local fishing villages along that rocky stretch of coast had sold off excess catch for years to passing traders. Salted properly, the fish was standard fare on long-haul shipping out of the deepwater ports heading across the sea to Novindus, or south around the landmass, to the western coast of the Empire or even up to the Bitter Sea.

But a chance remark in a tavern from a fisherman about how his newfound wealth would allow him to buy a second boat so his sons could expand the family trade got her to wondering, and after some investigation, she'd uncovered a pattern: everyone along the long, usually impoverished, coast of the peninsula below the Peaks of the Quor was enjoying unprecedented prosperity. Her interest was doubly piqued when she found a village making weapons. The local smith had been an armorer for the Empire until his army service of twenty years was over, and he had retired to this forlorn coast in the hope of some quiet. He had made his living fashioning iron fittings for wagons and making and repairing farm tools, and hardware for fishing boats. Then had come an order for a dozen short swords, of the fashion employed by Kesh's army of Dog Soldiers.

She had tracked that shipment down to Hansulé where she found an incredible number of ships coming and going. She continued to pick up rumors, and by the time she'd been in that city for a week, she was certain something important was coming together. She had reported to the local shrine of Dala in the city, asking for word to be passed back to her order in Rillanon, then she continued nosing around.

Another shipment heading south caught her notice. It was a very odd mix of farm equipment and livestock gear, traces, halters, wagon reins, and other leather goods. It was heading south. Kesh did little trading with the people in the subject regions of the Keshian Confederacy, and the annual tribute from the south barely covered the expense of collecting it. Only enough trade goods headed south to keep the region pacified, but it was a trickle.

Until recently. Now it was a flood.

After a week of watching, listening, and occasionally taking off her armor and arms, donning the trappings of her earlier trade as a brothel denizen, she had amassed enough information from enough different sources to come to the conclusion that her first instincts were correct, and something big was under way.

Ships were now coming in to Hansulé, and not just coasters. Deepwater vessels were anchored off the coast, and warships of all sorts were coming by in squadrons. And those that departed all went south.

So she did, too.

Now she found herself in very cold hill country just a few miles from the southern coast of Triagia. The Confederacy was unlike anywhere she had visited before. South of the Girdle of Kesh she had been viewed with suspicion, even hostility, in the villages and towns where she had stopped. Only her heavy arms and obvious ability to use them, as well as her clear identification with a temple order, kept the harassment to a minimum.

There was only one minor Temple of Dala in this region, where even those monks and priests viewed her arrival with some concern. No Knight-Adamant of the Order of the Shield of the Weak had visited that temple within the memory of the oldest member of the order.

She asked that messages be sent back to the mother temple in Rillanon. The head priest was polite but vague. She had a suspicion that Grand Master Creegan would be reading her report a few years after whatever mystery she was chasing was found, identified, and resolved.

She was thankful the Conclave had other agents throughout Kesh, for she was sure something this big would attract notice. It would be a tragedy if Pug and the others were solely dependent on her for intelligence.

She kept an eye on the unconscious man before her as she recounted her travels. First to one town, then another, as a pattern began to emerge. Empty hovels on farmsteads, towns with half the buildings abandoned, tiny villages deserted. There had been no signs of sickness, no plague, no famine, though food was always scarce in this region. Sandreena had seen such places after war, but there was no sign of any destruction. It was as if people had just picked up their belongings and left. It was early autumn south of the equator, and rain was falling frequently. The trails were muddy and washed out, but she could see signs of movement, many people on foot, wagons, and livestock, all moving south.

Where were they going?

She had been following such a trail when she had reached a village an hour's ride to the north of where she sat now. As she had cared for her horse, she had seen half a dozen heavily laden wagons followed by one obviously occupied by a family: father and mother, three children, and a dog that happily ran after the wagon but didn't trouble the horses. The children were fractious, the women looked haggard, and the men suspicious.

Sandreena had fed and watered her mount, had a quick bite and a mug of bitter ale at what passed for a tavern in this area, then set off after them.

She had been keeping her distance, falling back out of sight, then trotting forward to the top of a rise or turn in the road to ensure she didn't lose them.

Then came that irritating itch that meant she was being summoned to a meeting of the Conclave. She weighed her choice of actions and decided that her duty lay first in finding the reason for all the troublesome things she had witnessed. She was loath to quit when she was so close to uncovering the truth. So she had turned off the little orb, placed it in her boot, and returned her attention to the wagons ahead. She was catching up with them when her ambusher had surprised her with an arrow that had sped past her head, missing her face by less than an inch.

The man on the ground began to stir. Sandreena got up from the rock. When the man's eyes opened, he found Sandreena's sword point at his throat.

"Oi," he said as his eyes focused on the lethal blade. "Let's have none of that now, sister." He was speaking the local Keshian dialect, Lower Delkian.

She tilted her head slightly as she stepped back and said, "Slowly."

He got gingerly to his feet, obviously still dazed. "Can't say as I expected you to charge," he said. He grinned and said, "Right near did me in."

"Bodie," she said.

His eyebrows rose and he switched to the King's Tongue. "Good ear." To her it sounded like *Gud ar.* "Not too many in these parts would catch the accent."

"Hard not to miss that mangling of the King's Tongue, or any other language apparently."

He leaned forward, hands on his knees. "Bit wobbly, still," he said. "You clopped me a good one to the side of me head."

"You're fortunate that's all you got. I'm usually less forgiving with people trying to kill me."

"Kill you?" he said and laughed, then winced at the pain that brought him "Sister, if I'd wanted to kill you, you'd have not seen the arrow in your throat. I'm hardly modest when it comes to my bow skills. I've not met my better with one."

"Hardly modest, indeed." She looked at him. Slender, about her age, perhaps, dark hair that was little more than a shaggy thatch, a few days' growth of beard and clothes that were not *quite* filthy. Glancing at the bow on the ground, she saw that it was perfectly maintained. "If you weren't trying to kill me, what were you doing?"

"Trying to slow you down a bit, that's all. Man up in Darmin," which was the town where she had begun following the wagons, "paid me some coin to follow some wagons for an hour, then slow down anyone who might be following. Didn't say a thing about killing, else I'd have asked for a lot more." He glanced at the angle of the sun and said, "Looks like I was gone an hour or so."

"About that."

"Well," he said with a broad smile, "seems like I've stalled you long enough, sister, so I'll be on my way now."

"Wait a minute," said Sandreena. To emphasize the point, she extended her sword blade, making a barrier between them.

"Yes?"

"You expect me to let you walk away?"

"Can't see why not, sister. Spent an arrow to get your attention and took a fair beating in exchange; seems a fair bargain, all things considered."

"I'll be the judge of that."

The man lost his smile. "Look, you've had your bit of fun. Unless you're breaking vows, I know you Dala lot don't shed blood at whim. So unless you see me beating up some little boys and take their side, I think we're done here."

He took a step forward and found the flat of Sandreena's blade hard against his chest.

His smile returned. "Then again, maybe we're not. What can I do for you?"

"Start with a name."

"Ned. From Bodie, as you sussed."

"You're a very long way from home."

"It's a fact," he admitted, glancing around. He moved toward the rock where Sandreena had waited for him to regain consciousness and sat down. "Travel a bit here and there. I'm a hired bow, as you can tell, and I heard there was a fair bit of work down here, so I came."

"What did you hear?"

"Stuff and nonsense from what I can tell," said the mercenary. "I did some work up in the Vale of Dreams, but that's too much like bloody warfare, if you get my meaning. I'd rather take on less frantic work: caravan guard, watchman at a tavern, something where mostly I just need to be a bigger bully than the bully I'm tossing out, don't you see?"

"Thug for hire."

"Something like that." He gave a noncommittal shrug. "So what's it going to be?"

"Who hired you to slow me down? And were they clear no killing was involved?"

"Well, truth to tell," began Ned, and then Sandreena pressed her sword hard against his chest. "Well, I took it to mean it was up to me as to what I was doing, don't you see? I mean, a bag of coppers is fair enough wages for a little show-and-tell on the highway—" She smacked him with the blade.

"Ow!" he said a little too theatrically. She knew he might have a little bruise, but his buff coat and gambeson quilt blunted the impact. "Well, he may have thought he was entitled to a bit more than he got." He shrugged. "Can't see if it matters, one way or the other. I mean, he said 'slow her down' so that's what I did. You've wasted a good hour or more here, right?"

"Right," she agreed. She stepped forward, and with her left fist struck him hard enough to send him backward off the kick in his bruised ribs. A loud grunt of pain and a choked-off sob, then a long, ragged intake of breath told her she had caused him some serious pain. "Now, again, who paid you?"

On hands and knees, head down, he looked as if he might pass out. Quietly he croaked out, "Honestly, sister, I don't know. A bloke. Just a bloke. He bought me a drink, chatted me up, asked my trade, then offered me a job. That's all. Look," he added, pulling a small purse from under his belt, "count it. It's fifty coppers. A miserable half silver, and for what? Getting my ribs stave in?"

She kicked him again. And he collapsed with a groan and curled his knees to his chest.

"Who hired you?"

"I swear by any god you wish to name," he almost whispered through the pain, "I don't know. He never said his name and I didn't ask."

Sandreena had an instinct about these things. Kneeling, she grabbed him by the hair and yanked his head up. Putting her sword against his throat, she said, "One last time. His name?" She pushed a little and the edge of the blade dug into Ned's throat, painfully she was certain.

"Nazir," Ned whispered. "He never told me his name, that's the gods' truth, but I overheard one of his men call him Nazir."

"Men? How many?"

"Three. There were others," he said as she released his hair and stood up. "Maybe another two or three outside the inn. When they left, it sounded like a large band of men. I didn't follow because I was to wait for you. He gave me a good enough description, not that I needed it. No one ever sees a Knight-Adamant of any order down here." He tried to smile, but it was obvious his face hurt where she had struck him. "Certainly not a beauty like you, sister."

"Horse?"

He hiked his thumb over his shoulder.

"Good. Get it and don't make me chase you."

"Wouldn't think of it." He got to his feet slowly, wincing as he walked. It was clear the beating she had just administered had taken its toll.

As Sandreena turned to get her own horse, Ned stooped to pick up his bow. Suddenly in a fluid move he had an arrow out of his hip quiver and nocked on the string. "Sister!" he shouted.

She turned to see him draw and quickly crouched and raised her shield.

"Little knot in that tree behind your horse!" He let fly the arrow. The shaft whizzed past Sandreena's ear, then she heard the thunk as it hit wood. Turning, she saw there were two knots in the bole of an old oak about a dozen yards behind her, and in the smaller of the two the arrow had struck dead center.

"Wasn't joking, sister. If I had wanted you dead, you'd be dead. Even beaten, I'm the best archer I know. Now, I'll get me horse."

She watched his retreating back, unsure of what to make of him. Bodie was a long way from here, up on the southern coast of the Sea of Kingdoms, near Timons. It was frontier country, with a rough and ready population of fishermen, miners, and workers of all stripes, and it had a fair reputation for fighting men.

Ned appeared typical of the brawlers she knew from the docks of that town; it was impossible to mimic how those men mangled the King's Tongue, with their contractions and missing *h*'s at the start of words and missing *r*'s at the end. But there was something about his manner that was different. He was smarter than he let on, she thought. It was not a foolish man who allowed a potential adversary to underestimate him. And with the speed and accuracy with which he had put that arrow into the place on the tree he had called, she knew he could just as easily have put one in her throat, as he had boasted. Now she wondered how much damage she had really inflicted on him and how much of his current condition was feigned.

So what to do? she wondered silently as he returned leading a nicely-cared-for bay gelding. She mounted her grey mare, and the two horses made greeting noises. She gestured down the road. "Let's go see why that man wanted me slowed down, and you can tell me all you know about him as we ride."

"Not much to say, sister. He was a dark-haired fellow, medium build, wore a heavy cloak. Spoke the local tongue with an accent; northern Keshian I'd say. Seemed to know who you were, though."

"Really?"

"Well, he asked if I'd seen a Knight-Adamant of the Order of Dala and I said I'd seen you take your grey into the stable. But later he mentioned you by name, if that's Sandreena."

"It is," she confirmed.

"Anyway, sister, I take this Nazir bloke for a smuggler, except he wasn't trying to slow down Imperial Customs, but a Knight-Adamant, and last I paid attention, you lot don't care who's not paying the Emperor's customs fees, so I figure it's got to be something else. He don't look like no slaver, but you never can tell, and freeing poor villagers is something more to your calling, I'm thinking.

"But in the end it's all guesswork, isn't it?"

Sandreena said nothing. He could be leading her into a trap, but why all the theater if that was so? He could have taken her out of her saddle with a fowling blunt arrow, of that she was certain, or at least distracted her long enough for others to have dragged her from the saddle. She knew she would have inflicted a fair degree of damage on anyone doing so, but three or four men could have swarmed her down.

So maybe Ned was telling the truth and the only thing his employer, this Nazir, wished was for her not to overtake them before they concluded whatever business brought them to this distant, forlorn shore.

The grey of the overcast clouds matched her mood.

They rode along quietly for half an hour, until Sandreena could smell the sea air and hear the distant pounding surf. The rolling woodlands had started to thin and as they came out from between two stands of trees, Sandreena could see sails on the horizon. A pair of longboats in the distance was rowing toward one remaining ship, while half a dozen wagons stood empty on the beach. They were on a rocky bluff a mere dozen feet above the sand, in the middle of a notch cut into its face by weather and obvious traffic. It was clearly the way down to the beach.

"Where are they going?" she asked Ned, not taking her eyes off the ship. If their sudden arrival had disturbed anyone still on the beach, there was no sign of it.

"Don't have a notion." He turned his horse in a lazy circle away from hers. "You'll have to ask him."

"Who?" she said, then her head whipped around as men came out of the trees behind them, a pair on each side with bows trained on her, while two others hurried forward with their weapons at the ready. For a brief instant she contemplated fighting, then she saw four horsemen coming up the road. More than a dozen men quickly surrounded her.

The man Ned had described as Nazir approached with the men on horseback. "Good. She's unharmed."

"As you requested," said Ned. He grinned at Sandreena. "Sorry, sister, but I told you the truth. He paid me to slow you down, not kill you. I didn't mention the part where he paid me to bring you here, though." He rubbed his bruised cheek and winced. "You made me earn my pay, that's a fact." Turning to the robed man, he said, "Now, my gold."

The man reached into his robe and nodded once. Suddenly an arrow shot from behind them took Ned through the neck, the head protruding from his throat. His eyes widened briefly and his fingers touched the arrow as if he could scarcely believe what was happening to him. Then his eyes lost focus and he tumbled out of his saddle.

The robed man rode up next to Sandreena. "He was not one of us. Cooperate and you will live. If you don't, you will end up in the dust like him." His men quickly rid Sandreena of her weapons and shield, but allowed her to remain on her horse.

"Come," said the leader of this band. "We have a fair distance to ride yet and much to do."

Without another word, Sandreena was led away. Remembering the summons that morning, she hoped that her lack of reply would mean that Pug was sending someone to find her, for she had no doubt into whose hands she had fallen.

These murderers were Black Caps.

11

SIEGE

The lookout shouted.

"Ships off the headlands!"

A village boy named Jerrod turned and knelt before a small brazier, blowing furiously on the coals for a second, before plunging an oil-soaked straw torch into the hot coals, whereupon the flames almost exploded in his face. He rushed to a giant wicker construction, a bundle of reeds, grasses, and wood, on top of which a pile of inflammable tinder was piled, and tossed the torch in as he had been shown. As he had been warned, the volatile bundle roared into flames within seconds. The mix was designed to burn bright and produce voluminous black smoke so that it could be seen by day or night. The heat it gave off was enormous, and the boy backed away.

"It's done!" Jerrod shouted.

The lookout, named Percy, came scampering down from his rocky perch shouting, "Come on! Our job is done!"

It was late afternoon and a fresh breeze was blowing. The smoke rose and scattered, yet the two boys knew another lookout up the coast would see it and another lad would start his fire, and that one in turn would be seen at the castle above

Crydee. It would take the two boys the better part of a day to reach the closest outpost, a garrison camp ten miles up the King's Highway, for neither could ride, and even if they could, horses could not be spared for them.

A series of signal fires had been erected along the coast by order of the Duke of Crydee. Earlier fires had told the garrison that ships had been sighted along the coast, heading north from first Tulan, then Carse. Only one report from Carse had got through to the castle from Earl Robert, reporting that he and his men were attempting to repulse an onslaught of Keshian soldiers.

The report had arrived with Lord Robert's wife, Marri-ann, and his daughter, Bethany, who was not happy to have been sent away from Carse.

Now Bethany stood on the tower at Castle Crydee and asked Martin, "What will you do?"

"It's already done," said the Duke's middle son. "Fast riders were dispatched to overtake Father. He's halfway to Yabon by now, but if we can hold out for a week or so, he should arrive in time to relieve us."

Without a thought, she slipped her arm through his as if in need of reassurance. "How many men do you have?"

"Father left me a hundred."

She shivered and leaned into him, as if seeking warmth, even though it was a balmy night. "Is that enough?"

"Should be." He patted her hand where it rested on his arm. "If my studies are any guide, they'll need to bring more than a thousand men to storm the castle and even then it'll be touch and go. We've tested the defenses."

"The Tsurani siege?"

"Yes. When Father left, I made a point of studying the writings about that siege." He looked at her calmly. "Did you know Prince Arutha was a year younger than I am now when he took command, after Swordmaster Fannon was wounded?"

She didn't recognize the names, but she did recognize Martin's determination to take charge of the situation and protect the town.

As if reading her mind, he said, "It's time to bring in the town."

Turning to a point overlooking the inner courtyard, Martin saw the man he sought. "Sergeant Ruther!"

Looking up, the sergeant saw the Duke's son atop the tower and shouted back, "Sir?"

"Sound the alarm, and get the townspeople up here. Have them bring all the food they can carry."

Sergeant Ruther snapped off a salute and turned to two soldiers by the gate. "You heard the young lord! Get going!" The sergeant was a short man with a protruding lower jaw and a mean squint, which made him the object of fear among the garrison. He also had a deep abiding affection for his men that he kept well hidden. He was near retirement age, portly with a belly hanging over his belt, but no one in the garrison doubted he was still a hard man to kill.

The soldiers exchanged glances. "Yes, Sergeant!" they cried in unison, then trotted out of the gate toward the town.

The townspeople had already been alerted that there might be a call to the castle, so Martin hoped they'd have prepared in some fashion for this. But he knew there would surely be some panic and that many would not have understood it was not only necessary to bring foodstuffs and clothing for their time inside the city's walls, but also to deny the invaders as much comfort as possible. Orders had gone out that any food left behind should be fouled, but he suspected people would have spent too much time trying to hide valuables the invaders would likely find anyway. Martin knew that the farmers would scatter their herds and flocks rather than put them down in the hope that after the siege some could be reclaimed. At least if the Keshians had to forage to find them, that would be a distraction, Martin thought. He felt Bethany pressing closely to him and turned.

"You should go to your mother," he said softly.

"She's with your mother."

"I know, but the family quarters are the safest part of the castle."

"There's no hurry," Bethany said softly, drawing still closer. "How long?"

"From the headlands, they'll be at the mouth of the harbor in three or four hours. Then it depends on how prepared they are to come ashore and if they expect much resistance." He was silent for a moment, and she studied his face.

Of the three brothers Martin had always been the most difficult to read, which was why she had always found him the most interesting. He was not the hale-fellow-well-met that his brother Hal was, nor was he like Brendan, an impish prankster. Martin was the thoughtful brother. He was often cross with her, which she found amusing, as she knew it hid his true feelings. She had decided more than a year ago how she felt about him, but decided he would get no help from her in untangling his own feelings toward her.

He sensed her studying him and turned. "What?"

"I find it fascinating how much alike you and Brendan appear, yet in reality you are hardly alike at all."

He gave her one of his rare half smiles. "Beth, you've known us all your life, and you're only now noticing I'm not like that little menace?"

"I just find it a bit odd, really," she said, turning her eyes back on the town below. Already the sound of alarm was being raised, and shouts and cries echoed up to where they stood.

Martin gently disengaged her arm from his, his mood turning serious. "You found an odd time to think about this. Come on, I have much to do and I would feel a great deal better if I knew you were safe."

As he started to turn away, she moved forward and kissed him impulsively, long and deep. He tensed for a moment, then returned the embrace. When she pulled back, she could see a glistening in his eyes.

"We've let too many things go unsaid for too long," she whispered. "When your father returns, I want you to speak to him."

"About what?" Martin said, speaking softly as if he feared being overheard.

Her face clouded over and her eyes narrowed. "About us, you fool!"

His lips quirked. "What about us?"

Her eyes widened, and then she saw the smile. "You right bastard!" she said, then she kissed him again.

"I know. It's just that—"

"Everyone expects me to marry Hal," she interrupted. "I know. But no one's asked me, and no one's asked Hal. He's always treated me like a little sister. But you . . ." She kissed him a third time. "You've always been able to . . . somehow get under my skin, to make me think when I didn't want to and to endure my . . . bad behavior, with good grace."

Letting out a long sigh, Martin said, "As much as I adore you, and obviously I have done a poor job of hiding that, may I say"—his voice rose to a near shout—"you've picked an impossible moment to profess your love!" He laughed. "But you never were one for choosing the proper moment, were you?" He kissed her before she could answer and then added, "Very well, I'll speak to Father when this is over."

He glanced down at the town as the clamor of voices and the sounds of fear and panic rose. "But now I have to go calm the people whose care has been given over to me. We both have rank and privilege, so it is time we both showed we deserve them."

Gently he turned her around, and with a slight pressure on her arm indicated it was time to go down the stairs into a much darker and grimmer time than either had ever experienced.

The ships hove to at the mouth of the harbor at sundown. Martin watched as the last of the townspeople crowded into the yard below. When the last was through, he signaled for the gates to be closed. Sergeant Ruther, standing beside him with his arms crossed, said, "Now we dig in." Martin glanced at him and the sergeant added, "Sir."

Martin shook his head. "It's all right, Sergeant. I'm new to this."

"We're all new at this, sir. My father was a baby the last time this castle was attacked."

"Still, we've had our fair share of tussles."

"Yes, sir, but meaning no disrespect, a bunch of bandits or a raiding party of trolls is one thing. We're about to make the acquaintance of some Keshian Dog Soldiers. Not the same thing."

"Dog Soldiers? What should we expect?"

"Can't rightly say. Not one man in Crydee has faced them, and all I know is what I was told when I was a young soldier."

"Which was?" asked Martin, genuinely curious.

"Old Sergeant Mason, who was here when I was a recruit, he told me he spent time down in Landreth serving with a company of Borderers, under Lord Sutherland's command. It was a quick rise to glory, he said, else he'd never have earned promotion. Anyway, he said that most of the time they crossed swords with rogue mercenary companies or outlaws, but there was this one time they ran afoul of a company of Keshians.

"The way he told it made me think it was the toughest fight of his life, and he'd seen a few. What he said was 'they just keep coming.' They have no respect for life, not yours, not their own.

"Kesh is a funny place, from what I've been told. Trueblood women running around nearly naked and no one minds, the rest being not much better than cattle to them Truebloods. But they're hunters, you see, and don't think much of warriors."

"I don't follow," admitted Martin.

"See, the thing is, you can only rise so high not being a Trueblood, and as they don't give much glory to fighting men anyway, it makes for a vicious army. They don't do it for glory, you see. They're called Dog Soldiers for two reasons, according to Sergeant Mason: first is they're kept penned up like mad dogs and only unleashed on Kesh's enemies. Otherwise they don't mix with other people: they've got their own fortresses, their own families, grow their own crops, and make their own weapons. They're loyal to their masters, like dogs. The other is that they bring dogs along on long marches so they can eat them. Though I have my doubts about that bit."

Martin said nothing, then repeated, "They just keep coming."

"That's what Mason said. They won't give quarter and they don't ask for any. They just keep coming until you kill enough of them they get tired and run off. Or die to the last, I guess." He paused. "It's about honor, not glory. They're a brotherhood, a clan, something like that, and they die for one another."

Martin felt the pit of his stomach grow cold and found his knuckles turning white as he heard the gates to the castle slam shut. He willed himself to relax, then saw something that made him smile.

Despite promising to stay with their mothers, Lady Bethany was down in the courtyard, organizing the townspeople and assigning areas of the large bailey to families, sending all livestock around to the rear of the castle.

"She's something, that one," Ruther said with a smile.

Martin returned the smile. "That she is."

"Well, sir, if you're not needing me, there are things to do."

"You are dismissed, Sergeant," said Martin.

Alone on the top of the castle's outer gatehouse, looking down at organization slowly emerging from chaos, Martin took a deep breath. He reminded himself that he was a year older than Prince Arutha had been at the start of his legendary career. Then he muttered, "Of course he had Swordmaster Fannon and Great-Grandfather with him, and my Swordmaster is in Roldem with my brother, and my younger brother is riding with Father."

He felt terribly alone, yet despite wishing Bethany away and safe, he was thankful to his bones that she was here.

And he would do whatever was needed to keep her safe.

The night dragged on. By midnight those remaining outside the central keep huddled under makeshift shelters of wood and blankets, gathered around campfires, or under the few military tents Sergeant Ruther found abandoned in one corner of the castle's armory.

Many of the townspeople had been crowded into the keep itself; storage had been shifted around, and the extra space thus made was filled to overflowing. Families with small children had been given priority and had the safest rooms deep within the keep; women with older daughters had been packed into the outer rooms and towers.

Every man capable of bearing arms, between the ages of fourteen and seventy, was issued a weapon. Sergeant Ruther took it upon himself, in the Swordmaster's absence, to determine which detail each man was given, which was fine with Martin.

The young commander of the garrison had spent most of the night watching for signs of the Keshians coming ashore. It was now clear that they were not attempting a night landing and would wait for dawn.

"You should get some sleep." The voice was his mother's.

Martin turned and said, "What about you, Mother?"

She smiled. "There's still much to do. Usually we prepare food for the town only twice a year, at Banapis and Midwinter. Now we must cook what we can every day."

"We'll manage. Father will return soon."

"Not soon enough." She sighed. "What are your plans?"

"Simple enough. We see what they bring in the morning and then we determine the best way to hold them until Father returns with the garrison."

"What about . . . ?"

"What?"

"I . . . I've never been through a war."

"None of us have," said Martin, patting her hand. "It's going to be fine, Mother. We have provisions and enough trained soldiers alongside the townsmen that we can repulse up to ten times the number of defenders. If they have less than two thousand soldiers and heavy siege machines, we will hold."

"I just . . ." She sighed again. "I just wish your Father was here, and your brothers."

"As do I," said Martin, feeling the burden settle fully on his shoulders. "Now, why don't you get some sleep and I'll try to do the same."

She smiled at her son, turned, and started down the stairs with him behind.

If the Keshians came before dawn, someone would rouse him. He felt out on his feet and that was before even one arrow had been unleashed, or one sword drawn in anger.

Martin was awakened by a loud knock on the door. He had fallen asleep in his clothing, only removing his boots. He got up fast. "What?"

"Sergeant Ruther said to wake you, sir," came the answer from other side of the door.

"On my way!" shouted Martin, slipping into his boots.

The morning was foggy, as was typical for this time of the year. The sun hadn't yet risen from behind the distant Grey Tower Mountains to burn off the marine moisture in the air. An hour after the sun cleared the peaks behind, the town below would be in bright sunlight, but for now it was shrouded in dense mist.

Martin was no longer content to watch from his high perch over the castle's main entrance, above the keep's portcullis that marked the last defense, but was now on the wall above the main gate, as close to the town as he could get.

The original keep built by the first Duke of Crydee had been a stand-alone building, without an outer wall. It had been surrounded by a moat, which was long since filled in, and the barbican with its double iron portcullis and killing ground between them had been attached to the main entrance to the keep. The outbuildings and outer wall had been added years later, the latter having no barbican, just a simple wooden gate. As stout as it was, and for all the punishment the defenders might inflict on those below, Martin knew that eventually it would fall and everyone within the bailey between the wall and keep would be in peril.

Sergeant Ruther said without preamble, "They're down there in the town, moving cautiously from the sound of things, perhaps expecting traps."

"Pity we didn't have time to leave some," said Martin.

"There's only so much you can do on short notice, sir. If we'd had some means of knowing they were coming before they hit Carse, we might have convinced some of that lot"— he used his chin to indicate the hundreds now camped in the bailey below—"to come in a few days early and let us rig a welcome for the Keshians. But you do what you can, as they say."

Martin could only nod.

Slowly the sounds of men, wagons, and horses moving through the town grew louder. "Siege engines?" asked Martin, feeling a sudden tightness in his chest and stomach.

"Take a lot to knock these walls down, sir." Ruther pointed down to the main gate, which had been reinforced during the night with a bracework of heavy timbers.

"Well, let's see what they're bringing in."

Slowly the haze lifted, then suddenly a gust of wind cleared away the morning fog and presented Martin and the other onlookers atop the walls with a clear view of what they faced.

"Damn me!" the sergeant swore.

"Indeed," said Martin softly, not sure he was making sense of what he saw.

A company of soldiers stood arrayed across the entire approach to the town from the castle, just out of arrow flight from any but the stoutest longbow. Martin took in their garb: a traditional Keshian metal helm with a chain metal neck piece hanging behind, a sharply pointed spear tip at the crown (effective at discouraging an enemy from dropping on them from above, he thought); a chain coat; and heavy woolen trousers tucked into calf-high boots so that the fabric belled out. A leather vest was drawn over that, cinched at the waist by a heavy leather belt with an iron buckle. The combination of leather over mail would be very effective against arrows, slowing down a broad-head enough that the chain would catch it, earning the target no more than a nasty cut rather than certain death.

Each man carried a scimitar—the traditional curved sword—and a round buckler. Every fourth man also carried a short bow slung over his shoulder.

"I see no siege engines," Martin said.

"But look what else they brought."

Behind the line of solders a flood of people could be seen coming up from the docks and going into the buildings. Men, women, and children, several who seemed to be scuffling over some scavenged item or another, and among them moved what could only be wardens or marshals, breaking up fights and commanding them to go here or there.

A runner came up the steps from below, out of breath. "Word from the tower, sir."

"What?" said Martin, not taking his eyes off the scene below.

"A large company has broken off and is taking the north road, but . . ."

"But what?"

"They don't look like infantry or cavalry, sir."

Martin's curiosity was piqued. "What do they look like?"

"Well, sir, like farmers coming to market, or rather it would if they were going the other way. I mean, it looks like they're herding cattle and sheep up the road."

"Heading to the farms, crofts, and pastures," said the sergeant. "Well, now, isn't that a kiss from granny?"

Martin frowned. "I don't understand."

"Look what they're bringing up."

What appeared to be a company of engineers was hurrying up the road, while horsemen drove the milling men, women, and children out of the street, making way. They were carrying building materials unlike anything Martin had seen before.

The line of infantry parted, letting the engineers through, and then Martin saw what they were putting together. "It's a barricade."

"The bastards just walk in and took the town, sir. Now they're telling us to sit here and rot, or sally forth and drive them to the harbor."

"They're not going to attack?" asked Martin, now completely confused.

"Why should they? They'll just sit and let us starve."

In the distance a great rumbling could be heard. The sergeant turned to the young runner. "Joey, back up you go and find out what that is, then come back, straightaway, there's a good lad."

The boy ran off and Ruther said, "Well, it's clear whatever else they have in mind, they mean to stay. They brought a whole damn town with them."

After a few minutes Joey returned. "They're unloading some big machines by the docks. Kelton says they look like trebuchets."

Kelton was the soldier Ruther had put up in the tower because he had the sharpest eyes in the garrison.

"Well, if that's what he says they are, then that's what they are. Maybe they're not going to try to starve us out after all. But at least they're in no hurry to attack."

That worried Martin more than anything else. They would have to assume that the moment they were spotted, the call for reinforcements would go out, and reinforcements would be on their way. Why weren't they in a hurry?

The day wore on, and those in the castle watched in fascination. The fortification on the eastern edge of the town was quickly made secure, and at sunset a daunting wall rose up that had been bolstered with sandbags brought up from the shore. Now there was a six-foot breastwork with a firing platform behind, where arches could fire upon anyone venturing from the castle.

"If we had sortied this morning . . ." Martin clenched his fists, the frustration of not knowing what the enemy's next move would be taking its toll.

"We would have run into who knows what, sir," finished the sergeant. "We can only see that lot. Who knows how many more soldiers they have unloaded down by the docks, or still waiting aboard ship? They don't seem worried about us."

"Which is why I am concerned," countered Martin. "It's as if—"

"Sir!" came the shout. "A white flag!"

Martin looked in the indicated direction and saw what must be a Keshian officer approaching under a flag of truce. He came up to the gate and looked up at the faces there. "I seek parley!" he shouted. "Who is in charge here?"

"I am!" Martin shouted back. "I am Martin conDoin . . ." He hesitated, then added, "Prince Martin of Crydee." He was entitled to the honorific, though no one in his family had used it since Prince Arutha had left Crydee to take up the office of Prince of Krondor. His brother, Martin's namesake, had insisted only the title of duke be conferred upon him, a tradition followed for three generations after.

"Greetings, Highness," replied the officer. "I am Hartun Gorves, Captain of the Fourth Legion, Third Regiment, servant of His Most Honored Majesty, the Emperor of Great Kesh, blessings be upon him. My lord and master bids you depart this land, peacefully, and safe conduct to the east will be guaranteed. He reminds you these lands are Keshian, ancient Bosania, taken from the Empire most violently and without cause by your ancestor.

"He bids you depart and swears that he will treat harshly any of his servants who would trouble you. Take with you your possessions and goods, livestock and chattels, but begone at once, otherwise I am instructed to deal with you in the most severe manner."

Martin stood uncertain for a long moment. Of all the things he had expected to hear, the simple demand that he and everyone in the duchy pick up and move wasn't one of them. That Kesh meant to occupy this land was now beyond doubt: this was no simple raiding expedition, for booty or political gain; they sought to reclaim land that had not been part of the Empire in over two centuries, yet were treating the Kingdom's expansion as if it had occurred but a few weeks prior.

At last Martin said, "You're joking."

The officer bowed. "Most assuredly not, fair prince. I and two of my officers would be willing hostages in your travels. Once you reach the borders of the land called Yabon, we will leave your company, and you may deal with the garrison there."

"Garrison?" shouted Ruther. "What does that mean?"

"By the time you reach Yabon, it will once again be Keshian, as will the so-called Free Cities and that abomination known as Queg. The garrison at Yabon will escort you to the border at Questor's View and then on to Krondor. From there you will be free to continue on to the borders of the Kingdom and cross without harassment."

"Borders of the Kingdom!" echoed the sergeant furiously. Martin put his hand on his arm, and the old soldier fell silent.

"And where is this border?" asked Martin.

"Darkmoor. That was your traditional frontier and that is where it is again, for all lands west of there are now Keshian. Once you reach Darkmoor, you will once more be on Kingdom soil. The Empire is reclaiming its realm, from Crydee to Krondor, Yabon and LaMut. Even as we speak the armies of Great Kesh are marching and our navies are sweeping through the Bitter Sea. You are now trespassing on Keshian soil, my prince," declared Captain Gorves. "You have two days to make ready for your departure or I shall bring horrors upon you and your people that no man should have to contemplate. It is a simple choice; leave or die."

With that he turned and walked away, leaving a stunned Martin unable to speak.

12

ESCAPE

Jim Dasher ran.

Four armed men were following him and his guide, and he knew that if they were overtaken, he was certainly a dead man. Whoever was hunting him had proved to be relentless. They were dashing through the alleys and streets of Ranom, a miserable little trading port at the foot of the Trollhome Mountains in Western Kesh. The plan had been to get to a ship waiting in the harbor and then sail to Durbin, as close to the border as a Keshian freighter could travel. Getting from Durbin to the Kingdom's closest city, Land's End, was Jim's problem. Jim silently cursed Kaseem's agent aboard the ship where he was captured; instead of merely removing the Tsurani transportation orb that Jim had hidden, he had prodded it with a dagger point, thinking it some sort of tiny multilevered lockbox, and his meddling had rendered it inoperable. Now the only way back to behind the Kingdom's lines was by his own wits.

His guide made a motion with his head, indicating a turn to the left, and they both darted down an alleyway. The guide suddenly leaped for a low overhanging roof and, by the time

Jim could follow his lead, was hanging from roof beams in deep shadows under the roof's eaves, just a foot above a tall man's head. Jim knew exactly what was being said without words. They couldn't outrun the assassins, so their only choice was to get behind them.

A moment later the four men came down the street, and not for the first time Jim was disturbed by how silently they moved. These were men who resembled the legendary Nighthawks, a cult of demon-worshipping assassins detailed in memoirs by his great-great-grandfather James, the first Jamison, the legendary Jimmy the Hand of the Mockers.

There was a rueful sense of fate that visited Jim as he clung precariously to the eaves, waiting for his pursuers to run underneath him.

As a boy his father, the second James, had raised him to be a servant of the Crown, as he was, but his uncle Dasher, after whom he was also named, and Great-Uncle Dashel used to regale the young Jim with stories of his namesake, the first James. As a child Jim had insisted for a time on being called "Jimmyhand," and the moniker had stuck. More than once he had employed it to good use, in his guise as Jim Dasher, simple thief and pickpocket in the Mockers. But more than once he had also decided that somewhere along the way he had got caught up in his own myth, and that without realizing it, he was competing with the ghost of a dead forbear. But, good gods, Nighthawks?

If they were indeed a resurgence of that long-believed-dead clan of murderers, things were even more dire than he thought. It was believed the Nighthawks had finally been obliterated by Eric Von Darkmoor's special attack unit, the Prince's Own, in the long-abandoned Cavell Keep, some ten years ago. Silently, Jim thought of them as cockroaches: you thought you'd killed them all, but they kept showing up.

The same thought had passed through his mind after seeing the Pantathian Serpent Priest in that longboat. Every report he had read indicated they had been obliterated years ago and the birthing crèche in their underground lair in Novindus destroyed. Another nest of cockroaches, apparently.

The pursuers ran quietly underneath, and Jim held his breath, praying they would not notice they were passing scant inches below their quarry, or they would be able simply to impale him and his companion as easily as spearing fruit on tree branch with a pointed stick. Jim felt more than heard his companion let himself lightly down to the ground. Jim followed, his shoulders and hips burning from the exertion of holding himself in place. *I am getting too old for this nonsense,* he thought. His father and grandfather were both putting pressure on him to marry and start a more mundane life in the King's service, and he was getting to be convinced that was a really fine idea. Not for the first time he considered asking Franciezka to quit her post with the Crown of Roldem and run off to some tiny island where they could eat, sleep, and make love.

The guide motioned and Jim followed, running silently through the dark streets of the city. Ducking through a maze of alleys, they reached an unmarked door, and the guide opened it.

Jim followed him inside without hesitation and closed the door behind him. "We shall be safe here," said the guide.

"Not for long."

"Yes, they will double back, but unless they can track by magic, they'll have a hundred doors to investigate." He caught his breath and added, "The sun will rise in an hour. We can attempt to get down to the docks in the throng going to work. Rest now. I will go and seek help to get you out of the port. If I am not back by dawn, it means I have been captured or am dead; make your way to the docks as best you can and seek out a boat called the *Mialaba,* the name of a woman from the captain's homeland. He is a man named Nefu. He can be trusted. Tell him you need to find a ship for Durbin and he will get you safely there. Latch the door behind me."

Jim waved a tired hand, indicating that he understood, and the guide slipped out of the door. Jim latched it and sat down heavily on a large, tied bundle of cloth.

When he looked around, he saw he was in the back room of some sort of enterprise, a tailor's shop by the look of it. Whoever owned it was absent, and Jim was certain the shop must be one of Kaseem's safe houses in this town.

He settled in, determined to sort through the strange events he'd endured since awakening in Ranom. For several hours, Kaseem abu Hazara-Khan had detailed to Jim what had occurred in his nation to bring this war on so suddenly and unexpectedly.

It had begun, according to the desert man, with the unexpected rise in the Gallery of Lords and Masters by a few members of the nobility who were close friends with a Keshian prince by the name of Harfum, a distant nephew of the Emperor. This sort of nepotism and cronyism was nothing new in the Empire, and as long as it didn't get too obvious and abusive, no one cared about it. The only thing Keshian nobility cared about was keeping their own rank and privileges. The offices granted these men were minor: supervising taxes in a distant province, overseeing the garrisons along the southern border with the Confederacy, supervising the building of ships, levying duties on goods transported by caravan. Nothing in these appointments signaled building a power base or creating a faction within the Gallery of Lords and Masters so no one objected.

Then came rumors about a caravan carrying certain goods being diverted at the request of the newly appointed minister for that district, or a shipbuilding request that seemed to originate in some vague office attached to the Imperial Navy, but with no one quite sure who was authorizing that purchase. It seemed that Prince Harfum's friends were always somewhere around when things turned odd, but Kaseem could not establish a clear pattern or find compelling evidence to present to his master, the Imperial Chancellor, or to the Emperor himself.

Also the corruption that was common to Kesh's bureaucracy hid much of what was going on, since bribes were paid for falsified cargo manifests, and caravan freight was signed off without inspection. Bolts of cloth turned out to have sharp, hard edges; urns were filled with herbs that had steel broad-heads attached, and pottery was made from steel with nose and cheek guards. Bows were smuggled as trade goods; swords, shields, and armor as raw timber. Iron ore intended for the Imperial Armory at one city was diverted to a retired swordmaker's forge in a different city. When a hundred horses were requisitioned for a garrison, eighty would arrive and a notation on a document would explain away the discrepancy. Mules, oxen, horses, dried foodstuff, crates for food, water barrels, and casks—all the necessities to put an army on the march—slowly wended their way through the Empire, always heading south. And it had been going on for more than two years, before the spymaster of Kesh even had an inkling.

By the time Kaseem had sensed something was amiss—his agents began to vanish, or mysteriously file reports that made little sense at the time—and he realized his network of intelligence operatives had been compromised, it was much too late.

As Kaseem had made ready to leave the city of Kesh to investigate what he feared to be the case—high treason running rampant in the government—the attacks had begun. The first attempt had been by one of his most trusted agents, the man he had put in charge of the entire network in the city of Kesh and the surrounding region of the Overn Deep. That meant he could trust no one in the city of Kesh. Three times armed men had almost killed Kaseem as he made his escape, but he wasn't considered the wiliest man in Great Kesh without reason.

Kaseem had taken a fast horse and headed west toward Caralyan rather than north to his home in the Jal-Pur. Every road from the city of Kesh directly leading to the Jal-Pur would be watched by those trying to kill him, so his intention had been to sail around into the Bitter Sea, then to the port of Ranom. From here he would ride to his father's camp, at one of many desert oases, where he knew he would be safe.

It was only by the strangest chance that one of the agents Kaseem had detailed to watch for Kingdom spies had noticed Jim. He had contrived to join the same ship's company as a common sailor set to keep an eye on Jim. That "sailor" was now Jim's guide here in Ranom; he was named Destan and was a man Jim would have been happy to have in his service. Jim was very good at not being noticed when he so chose, so the fact that Destan had spotted something to make him suspicious must make him a very valuable asset to Kaseem.

Destan had been detailed to Hansulé to keep an eye on the insanity of mobilization that had gripped the Empire, to ascertain where all the arms and supply were heading, so it was, for him, a happy coincidence that Jim was signing on as a sailor on the same fleet. When he caught sight of Jim checking a lump in his hammock, he had managed to ferret out the tiny Tsurani sphere. But then he had prodded at it with a dagger, trying to open it, and had only succeeded in breaking it. But that was of secondary importance; at that point he knew that Jim was someone to whom his master would most certainly wish to speak.

When Jim had tried to escape, Destan had struck him from behind, an effective enough means to render him docile, and carried him up on deck while everyone else was busy. Since he had Jim wrapped in canvas, he looked like just another sailor moving something important from one place to another. He had dumped Jim in a sail locker and came back half an hour later to drug him.

Jim had awakened here in Ranom. He was uncertain how he had got there from Caralyan so fast, but decided that Kaseem must have his own supply of Tsurani devices, or some other magical equivalent, a magician in his service who could transport others as Magnus could, perhaps. When Jim had broached the subject, Kaseem had been noncommittal: if he possessed such a device, he wasn't offering one to Jim Dasher to get back to the Kingdom.

Kaseem had problems of his own, it was clear to see, and Jim was touched by his willingness to help one of his most dangerous opponents. For a brief instant he considered it ironic that Franciezka and Kaseem were the two people most likely to have him killed, ultimately, yet in them he had found kindred souls. Not for the first time he considered he had chosen a very strange trade in life.

In the hours during which Kaseem abu Hazara-Khan had told Jim his tale, a pattern had emerged, but he had remained silent and kept listening. Kaseem had explained in detail how his own network of agents had been compromised from within, as well as effectively countered and blunted by outside forces. He admitted that he had spent so much of his time watching the kingdoms of Isles and Roldem or the Southern Confederacy that he had neglected his own nation's internal politics, assuming that the traditional Keshian blood sport known as "government" would continue as it had over the centuries.

Someone had taken advantage of that; and from the scope of the betrayal, Kaseem was certain this usurpation of his network had been under way for perhaps as long as five years.

Jim's first question was to consider who would benefit from a massive war between the Kingdom and Kesh. Logically, no one. He had become enough of a pragmatist that he conceded a little criminal activity was inevitable, though he had tried to keep his Mockers from cutting too many throats, and then only those who more or less deserved it. He believed there would always be some military adventure, but that it needed to be kept in check because the Kingdom had other enemies to confront. But Kesh had no Brotherhood of the Dark Path and their goblin allies on their northern border, and a rapidly growing city of odd, very powerful elves who did not appear to be particularly friendly.

The Eastern Kingdoms were closer to the Isles than Kesh,

and there had constantly been border squabbles since the Isles had once been just one of a group of petty kingdoms in the Sea of Kingdoms. So it was the Isles that kept a fractious group of neighbors in check; though Roldem's presence in Olasko lately had stabilized things to a point at which reports from Jim's agents in Miskalon, Salmater, and Far Lorin were rendered mundane to the point of tedium.

On the whole, Jim considered war a waste of resources, especially human ability and talent, and tried to keep the Kingdom out of them. War represented a failure of intelligence and diplomacy and caused far more trouble than it solved.

There were just wars; the Tsurani invasion over a century before and the invasion of the Emerald Queen's army in his grandfather's time had both been defensive wars that had to be waged to the last drop of blood.

But this . . . ?

As far as Jim could tell, this was a needless launching of the most massive war seen on Midkemia since the onslaught of the Emerald Queen's army, and that war had devastated an entire continent and brought ruin to half of the Kingdom. It had been the last time Kesh had sought to move against the Kingdom, seeing it weak and vulnerable after the destruction of Krondor.

But since the magician Pug had forced both sides to peace . . .

Pug? Jim sighed. He had a difficult relationship with the magician and his Conclave of Shadows, but at least Pug was trustworthy. And by dint of his being the adoptive father of Jim's great-great-grandmother, a distant relative.

Something on this scale needed to be discussed with Pug. But given where Jim currently sat, his ability to reach Sorcerer's Isle was somewhat problematic, being far to the northeast and in the middle of what was likely to be a war zone involving three navies: Kesh, the Kingdom, and the Kingdom of Queg. One more time he silently cursed Destan for disabling the orb; one of the previously established destinations in that device had been Pug's island. Now not only was he forced to remove himself from what was verging on becoming a death trap, he had to find his way to an even more difficult destination.

He debated several choices, including stealing a horse and making the ride to Durbin. The majority of arms and men would be moving by sea, but that didn't preclude overland units making their way to support the garrison at Shamata, and a single rider on a dusty road across an arid desert would certainly bring attention.

No, his best choice was by sea. If his guide didn't appear soon, Jim would find the *Mialaba* and a man named Nefu.

Time passed slowly, and Destan didn't return. Finally Jim saw light beneath the door and heard enough street noise to conclude that morning was upon him.

He opened the door cautiously and peered out. In the street just beyond the alley he could see men and women hurrying along as the workday started. Like Durbin, this hot-weather city's business started early, eased off during the hottest part of the day, then resumed in the late afternoon and continued deep into the evening. This would be Jim's best opportunity to get to the docks and find Nefu.

He considered his appearance. He was still wearing his sailor's garb and knew he would be instantly recognized if any of the men who had chased him caught a glimpse. He stepped back inside and closed the door. The tailor's shop would soon be visited by its owner and workers, no doubt, so he had best come up with whatever disguise he could cobble together as quickly as possible.

He opened the door opposite the one leading to the alley and found a room in which clients were probably greeted and where the cutting and sewing were done. Half a dozen garments were on display, and one caught Jim's eye. It was a robe, the sort preferred by the desert tribes of the Jal-Pur, worn open in front but that could be closed and secured with a large sash, and a matching cloth head cover. Jim had spent

enough time in the desert to know that punishing cold nights
and stinging sandstorms required a well-made covering. This
had the look of a merchant's robes, but not robes a wealthy
merchant would wear. If this garment was ready for a client
who had paid in advance, its disappearance would quickly
be noticed. If it was stock ready to be bought by someone
who happened by, perhaps not as soon. He checked swiftly
through the other garments and discarded them as not being
useful and then made a decision.

He removed his shirt, a simple white linen top with an
open collar and quarter-length sleeves, and chose a more
finely fashioned red shirt that would go nicely with the deep
indigo of the robe. The grey flannel trousers he wore would
have to suffice.

In his belt he had the coin purse returned to him by
Kaseem, and he counted out a few coins, estimating the price
he would have got with haggling, and left half again as much,
placing it where the shopkeeper would find it. He hoped the
silver coins would convince the man that someone had sold
the garments but neglected to put away the coins; or at least
give the man less reason to call the city watch. Since the local
watchmen were as corrupt and unreliable as they were in any
other port city in the Empire, Jim felt he stood a reasonable
chance of being out of the city before the alarm was raised.

He slipped on the shirt and robe, then moved back
through the storage room and again peered out of the door.
The tempo of the city was quickening as he slipped out into
the alley. He walked purposefully to the corner and entered
the flow of traffic. As he made his way toward the docks, he
looked around and found what he sought next, a bootmaker.
The shop was just opening as he entered and the proprietor
greeted him. "Sir, what service can we offer you?"

"Boots," Jim said in the language of the desert men.

The bootmaker looked confused for a moment, then Jim
repeated the word in Keshian, heavily accented to sound as if
he was not terribly fluent.

"I make the finest boots in the Empire," claimed the man, speaking loudly and slowly as if it would make it easier for Jim to understand him. He indicated that Jim should sit on a bench and he would measure him.

Jim said, "No, boots now."

The man was apologetic. "I have no boots already made, sir. Each man's foot is of a different size, so I need a week or so to measure, cut leather, and fashion it; you understand?"

Jim pointed to six pairs of boots on a shelf behind the man. "What of those?"

"Those are awaiting their purchasers," said the bootmaker, but a calculating look crossed his face. "Perhaps . . ."

Jim dropped his leather purse on the counter. The noise the coins made was unambiguous.

"Let me see the size . . ."

Ten minutes later Jim left the shop wearing black leather boots that were almost a perfect fit; they were a tiny bit short in the toes, but, being leather, they would stretch if he wore them long enough.

Another stop at a weapons merchant and he was striding down the street looking as much like a desert rider of the Jal-Pur as he could manage given the circumstances. He spoke the language fluently and without accent and knew enough about the region to deceive most people who didn't know him on sight. His headgear was worn in the fashion of the Jal-Pur, the nose and mouth cover left to hang loosely to one side, so it could be pulled up in seconds if a sandstorm suddenly blew up. It was just enough to hide his features without looking as if he was trying to hide them.

That was what he was concerned about. The four assassins had not only known him, one knew him well: Amed Dabu Asam, who until he had tried to kill Jim had been his most trusted agent in the region.

They had come mere hours after Destan had conveyed Jim to Kaseem's safe house, and it was by the barest chance they had been alerted to someone being just outside the door, a bare creak of wood where someone misstepped ever so slightly, a creak that had meant the difference between life and death as Jim, Destan, and Kaseem had all been crouched in a secret room with weapons ready where a moment before they would have been taken unawares.

The revelation that Amed was no longer to be trusted had cast an even darker shadow over the events unfolding around them. Jim had sighed. "If Amed is a traitor, there is no one in my organization I can fully trust."

Kaseem had answered, "I know the feeling. Some of the men who tried to kill me had served my father before me."

The two leaders of the rival intelligence services had vowed to return to their respective capital cities to ferret out the traitors. Both had also vowed that all activity previously directed at each other would be put aside until the real architect of this mad war and multiple betrayals had been uncovered.

Kaseem needed to reach his people's camp and appear to be digging in for a long siege: he had a cousin who looked remarkably like him, and with a few minor alterations to his appearance, any spies or traitors who might be nearby would glimpse the fugitive prince of the desert. While his cousin kept his eyes focused on the desert, Kaseem would slip away in disguise to the city of Kesh looking nothing like himself.

As for Jim, he had to reach Sorcerer's Isle and speak with Pug.

He reached the docks without incident and hesitated for a moment. There were at least two hundred boats and ships at the quays or at anchor in the harbor, a higher number than was usual for this port, but given the circumstances in the Bitter Sea these days, Jim assumed some of them were there because their owners had no desire to sail waters crowded with three hostile navies.

Since little cargo was coming ashore or being ferried out to a waiting ship, the dock was crowded with stevedores looking for work. As he walked past, a few looked at him expectantly, thinking Jim was perhaps a ship owner or agent.

He glanced about and then saw a band of street boys congregating around a vendor's fruit cart near one of the major streets that intersected with the docks, no doubt waiting for their opportunity to purloin a rich pear or savory plum when the seller wasn't looking. Scant chance of that as the man had one eye fixed on the ragged crew while he shouted the quality of his wares to all and sundry.

Jim discreetly held up a copper coin until one of the boys took notice. He glanced to see if any of his compatriots had noticed and seeing they hadn't, he scampered over to stand in front of Jim, just far enough away that he could leap out of arm's reach if Jim attempted to harm him. But all Jim said was, "*Mialaba?*"

The boy pointed silently to the end of the dock and Jim flipped the coin to him and moved quickly away. The far end of the harbor was occupied by boats of various sizes, but no cargo vessels. All appeared to be short haulers. Ferries and shallow launches waited to take cargo and passengers out to ships at anchor, while a few fishing vessels in from nearby villages were unloading the previous day's catch.

Jim moved with urgency, but not so quickly as to call attention to himself. He was experiencing what he called his "bump of trouble," a name inherited from his ancestor, the first Jimmy: a sense of impending danger. It had been annoying him the entire time he had been in this city.

As he worked his way down the dock he saw at last a small two-masted lugger. A sailor was repairing ropes on the bow and Jim called up, "*Mialaba?*"

"Yes," said the sailor barely looking up.

"Nefu?"

The man stood up and moved to the back of the boat, then returned a moment later with a second man, who said, "You looking for me?"

"If your name is Nefu."

"It is." He was a barrel-chested man of at least fifty summers, with a balding head surrounded by a fringe of hair so white James assumed he must have been fair haired when he was younger, red or blond. His skin was weather-beaten and worn, and he looked as if he should be holding down a chair in the corner of some dockside alehouse. But his eyes were like blue daggers as they looked at Jim, and Jim had no doubt those "old" arms and legs were coils of power from years of hard work and, if he worked for Kaseem, no doubt years of hard fighting.

"We have a mutual friend. He said to seek you out."

"Who would that be?" asked Nefu as his deckhand tried to look as if he wasn't listening to every word.

"Destan."

"Can't say as I recognize that name." Nefu's hand drifted toward his belt, in which Jim had no doubt rested at least one dagger.

"Kaseem," said Jim in a lower voice.

"Better come aboard, then." Nefu's hand moved away from his belt.

Once Jim was aboard, Nefu led him to a companionway in the rear of the boat, one that led down into a middeck. Jim had been on luggers like this and knew this was the crew's quarters, for at least a dozen men if it was a long voyage, fewer if they were hugging the coast and putting in at night. To the rear would be quarters for the captain and one mate, perhaps. There was no galley on a boat this size; all cooking would be done on deck on a brazier, which meant that in foul weather the crew went hungry.

Jim followed Nefu into his quarters, which were barely more than a bed over pull-out drawers, and a single fold-down table for charts and maps. A single lantern hung from a chain above the desk, and a chest nestled in the corner for whatever the captain couldn't cram into the two drawers below his bunk.

Sitting in the only seat, a three-legged stool that was just an inch too short for the table, Nefu said, "Now, what can I do for you?"

Jim thought about what he should say and decided truth was absolutely required, but how much wasn't clear. At last he said, "Kaseem sent me here, with Destan as my guide. We were pursued and he said if he did not return by sunrise I was to make my way here and ask for you."

Nefu was silent for a moment, then said, "Who pursued you?"

"I do not know," Jim answered slowly, looking the old sea captain in the eyes.

After another moment of silence, the captain said, "But you have an idea."

"Yes," said Jim. "I may be mad, but I think they were part of a group not seen for years. Nighthawks."

The captain let out a long sigh. "Where to?"

"I need to get to Sorcerer's Isle."

"Impossible. The Quegans are patrolling between their miserable island and Land's End, and Keshian warships patrol the coast from here to Land's End. The Kingdom Navy is bottled up there, but they send fast raiders out now and again to punish Kesh for her aggression."

"News?" asked Jim.

"Little, but rumors bloom like flowers in the desert after rain." The captain stood up. "If we are to time the run to Sorcerer's Isle, we must leave now."

"I thought you said it was impossible."

Nefu smiled, and suddenly years fell away from him. There was a glint in his eye. "I said it was impossible. I didn't say I couldn't do it. Wait here." He turned and left.

For the first time in weeks, Jim found himself laughing. If Kaseem hadn't already taken this smuggler into his service, he'd recruit him for his own Mockers.

Assuming of course there was still a Guild of Thieves by the time he returned to Krondor.

Assuming there was even a Krondor to return to.

13

DISCOVERY

Child attacked.

The three demons she ambushed turned and presented an impressive array of fangs and claws, and one began to incant a spell. A magic-user! She modified her attack and ripped his throat out before he could continue his magic, and he fell to the rocks, gurgling his cry of pain.

The other two would have overmatched her, but she now had allies and they came swarming over the rocks behind the two remaining demons and, despite being smaller, overwhelmed them quickly.

"Eat," she said to her small band. "But that one is mine," she added, indicating the magic-user, and beckoned for Belog to join her. She desired magic and without a teacher, eating magic-users was her only means of acquiring that ability. Her skills were rudimentary, primitive even. She could channel a push of energy that might topple a small opponent, or cast a small flame, but that was all.

For an unknowable period of time she had been leading this band of demons across a rugged landscape, through volcano-strewn broken lands of basalt and red rock. The sky was dark grey at noon and the sun seemed to be in an odd orbit, never quite sinking below the horizon. Belog said that meant they were reaching a nexus, one of the six poles in their realm: the East Pole. The Darkness seemed to have converged on the Heart Nexus, where the East, West, North, South, Top, and Bottom Poles intersected. Energies cascaded unexpectedly along the surfaces of the clouds above them, and the air stank of ash and bitter minerals as fiery mountains spewed clouds of dark smoke and cinders up into the canopy of grey and black.

Child had begun to gather followers over the last month, allowing those she felt unable to contribute to be devoured by the others. She was even generous in her allocation of who ate first, waiting until the end to claim her portion. She was still struggling to define herself, but at some point she had become aware of the concepts of generosity and gratitude. Being generous could engender thanks, or project weakness, depending on the context. Gratitude could generate true allegiance or feigned loyalty disguising betrayal. She was struggling to find the nuances of these differences.

She was becoming more subtle, and Belog was becoming more fascinated. It was clear to him that she was unique among the People. She was something unpredictable. It was hard to know whether she was his greatest discovery or his most dangerous.

She glanced around as they ate. "I find this place . . . unpleasant. I preferred the last place we rested."

He tilted his head slightly in a gesture she had come to understand meant he was pondering what she had said and was framing a reply. He scratched at his cheek absently with a sharp, gleaming talon and said, "Really? The energy plains are far more dangerous than these volcanic table lands. The vortex rifts and void windows can destroy with a touch or snatch you out of this reality and transport you to another." He made a claws-snapping gesture for emphasis.

She shrugged. "I don't know why, but it pleased me to look at the cascading lights in the night and see the shimmering silver lights during the day. It gave me a similar feeling to when I eat something particularly tasty or look at certain males." As she said this, she cast a glance at one of the young male demons who had been spared because he was on his way to becoming a daunting fighter. Muscular arms hung from a massive upper torso, yet his waist was still small and his legs were slender. Were they still living in the city of Das'taas, he would have long since been killed and consumed or recruited as a soldier in one Demon Lord's faction or another, perhaps even marked to become a city Guardian or palace guard.

Belog observed Child watch the male and sighed silently. She would choose to mate soon, and that could create difficulties. The nature of the People was that procreation was an adjunct to the spawning pits, where life in the realm originated and where demonkind arose. It was from the pits that a demon reemerged after death, with some or all memories intact depending on the circumstances of death. Violent deaths, which were in the majority, often robbed the demon of some memory. But birth was another aspect of creation, and it was relatively infrequent. Demons had mated for pleasure as long as they had been in existence, but the societies in which they lived were never stable enough for young to be successfully produced in any significant number. Rarely did a pregnant female survive, and when a child was born, it was often devoured, often by its own mother in retribution for the pain and inconvenience of childbearing. A few mothers choose to nurture their child, perhaps thinking to create their first vassal, but it rarely ended well. Adolescent demons were always fractious and rarely around for long; those that survived to adulthood tended to the cunning or powerful and picked their conflicts wisely.

The rise of the kings had changed things, in the First Kingdoms and now the Second Kingdoms, and Dahun had been foremost in reforming and remaking his people; the spawning pits still existed—how could they not? But families, a new and alien concept, were mandated and pairs were appointed to breed, Child's mother and father among them.

No one could claim to understand why Lord Dahun had done this, but none would openly question him. It was supposed by the Archivists that at some point he would instruct them on what was to come next in the forced evolution of the People, but the arrival of the Darkness had thrown all into chaos.

When Dahun vanished, society had not just reverted to its former state: it had disintegrated. Those left surviving the anarchy that once was Dahun's Kingdom would be little better than the Mad Ones, let alone the Savages in whose lands they now trespassed. Belog was forced to admit that if it wasn't for the strength of Child's will and personality, this little band would not exist, and he would most certainly already be dead.

He watched as Child finished devouring the brain of the magic-user and applied herself to his torso while keeping her gaze upon the young male. Finally she said, "I like his look."

"Beauty," said Belog. "You have come to appreciate the enjoyment that is derived from perceiving things that are pleasing to look at, irrespective of their usefulness or danger. You feel better just looking at the energy plains or the setting sun, or that young male."

"Yes, I do," she said. "Tell me more about beauty," she instructed, and he did.

They left the volcanic plateau and found themselves entering a realm of thick bramble, black with huge thorns, shot through with meandering pathways that might lead somewhere. "Where are we?" Child asked Belog.

"I am uncertain," he replied. "I believe we are in the region known as the Blasted Plain, a harsh land before we reach the heart of Maarg's kingdom."

"Tell me about Maarg," she instructed. She motioned for her followers to gather around, and Belog realized they now numbered almost two dozen. They tended to be quiet, out of fear, or gratitude, or respect, Belog didn't care to speculate on which. He counted himself lucky that he was critical to Child, and he wished to keep it that way. At worst, that would

ensure he was the last one to be eaten by her. At best, he had
a benefactor and protector who was growing in intelligence,
physical power, and magical knowledge by the day.

He looked around trying to determine which course
through the brambles might suit them best. He knelt for a
minute and felt his jacket bind across his back. It had been
an odd affectation on Dahun's part to dress his Archivists in
black coats and grey trousers. Given the diversity of shapes
among demons, it had made for some particularly odd-looking
Archivists at times. Still, it had made them instantly recogniz-
able as were his Guardians and enabled Belog to move freely
throughout Dahun's realm. However, Child's generosity in
feeding him was causing him to grow, a condition that used
to be prevented by the careful oversight of the King's Chief
Archivist. In Dahun's Kingdom, you could be intelligent or
powerful, but never both.

Finally Belog pointed and said, "I believe that way may be
a wise choice."

She looked at him with an odd expression and then he
heard a sound he had never heard from a young demon: laughter. It was a different sort of laughter than that of the older
demons, who laughed with a maniacal, joyless howl at the
pain and destruction they caused, or at the crushing defeat of
their enemies, or the lamentations and pleas for mercy from
those about to be devoured. But this was something new: this
was a laugh of amusement, not at another's pain.

As he followed Child into the brambles, he thought, *What
are you becoming?*

They hit several dead ends, and on the fourth, Child's
temper erupted, causing her to cast a ball of fire at the brambles that started a conflagration that had them running back
the way they had come. Child collapsed a safe distance away
and began to roar with laughter. The other demons looked
from one to another and tried to mimic her mirth, but failed.

"Can't let my temper get the better of me," she mused as
she stood up.

"You always had that problem—" Belog stopped. Where did that thought come from? Again, he was befuddled by this creature he was following and by his own changes, which he understood no better than he understood hers.

They left the forest of brambles and found themselves on a hillside looking down at an abandoned city, with desolate land surrounding it. "Maarg's city," said Belog.

"Again," she demanded, and he knew what she asked.

"Maarg was the greatest of the Savage kings. He was a glutton and consumed all his enemies, growing massively obese as a sign of his majesty; he savored raw power and his court was formed by combat and by cunning. If a warrior killed his superior, he gained his place and Maarg's favor, for the King felt he was replacing a vassal with a stronger one.

"His court was always a place of terrible balance between loyalty in exchange for protection and the potential for betrayal. It made Maarg especially vengeful and unforgiving."

As Belog spoke he marveled that there was no need for him to explain those concepts, for to understand vengeance you had to understand forgiveness. And forgiveness to any member of the People was an abstract concept. Even Archivists struggled to grasp it.

"Tell me again of the part about him leaving and why?"

"There are only rumors. It is said that somewhere in his city is a hall and in that hall is a gate to the higher realms. Someone from those higher realms opened that gate years past, and Maarg's army poured through, devouring everything in their path.

"It is said Maarg went there and perished, or found another realm to rule; but no one really knows." As they started down a long road to the city, Belog added, "Many kings of the Savage Lands, and even some companies of Mad Ones came here, seeking to take this for themselves. Yet they did not stay."

"Why?" asked Child.

"It is lifeless."

She stopped, and the rest of her entourage did so as well. She said, "Yes, I sense it."

"Sense it?"

She resumed walking. "It's a feeling. What caused this?"

"It is something like the Final Death, I think," he said.

At that the usually silent demons who followed Child halted, some muttering, a few looking at her in abject fear. For a demon there were two deaths: the one that occurred many times in the course of existence, where death returned their essence to the spawning pit. But then there was the Final Death, when all existence ceased, consumed in some fashion by a nameless horror; and that above all else was feared by a demon. From the Time Before Time there was only one way for a demon to die the Final Death, and that was for something to prevent the energies from returning to the spawning pits.

Then came the Darkness and now it was believed that to be touched by it was to die the Final Death. Certainly no being alive from the spawning pits remembered confronting the Darkness and returning. And the Darkness had been growing at the heart of the realm for millennia. Only the oldest, most powerful demons even remembered any of the People who had once lived in the First Kingdoms. And now the Second Kingdoms were being consumed as the Darkness expanded.

Kings and their vassal lords had fled. Some had conquered territory in the Savage Lands, or even in the land of the Mad Ones. Others had found portals to other realms and warred there, conquering all before them, feasting on life that was not enough, never enough. Stories were told, and no one knew what to believe. It was even said that hosts of demons raged across the skies of other realms, warring with mortal races.

Child said to her group, "Follow if you will or return the way we came, but behind lies the Darkness and ahead is merely the unknown."

As if that was reassurance enough, the demons nodded; and when she moved forward, they followed.

They entered the city as the sun was setting. To some demons, day and night were meaningless, since they possessed senses that allowed them to live nocturnally. Others, like Belog, were at risk in darkness, so the band had gotten into the habit of seeking shelter at night. Sleep was unknown to demonkind, except as a means of relaxation, a rare event, or meditation, which was again rare for all but the Archivists.

They entered a building that appeared at one time to have been a barracks or a dormitory, although all the furniture had been destroyed by a series of violent struggles. The walls were darkly stained from blood spattered for countless years.

They had just sat down to rest when the Mad Ones attacked.

Although little more than mindless animals, they were still among the most physically powerful of demonkind. Given equal size, a Mad One would overpower even the most skilled warrior of the Second Kingdom unless he was fully armed and armored or possessed magic.

They came out of the shadows as the sun set in the west, darker shapes against the greying light. They were massive of shoulder and two were four-legged, doglike in their form, with massive heads on powerful necks and slavering fangs. The others were roughly man shaped, but their heads were animal: ram, bull, lion, or bear, with exaggerated tusks and fangs, large horns, feathers, fur, or scales.

Two of the Child's followers were dead before they even knew enemies were upon them, their heads literally plucked from their necks. Child came to her feet and without hesitation put out her hand and a wall of searing flames exploded out in a sweeping wave that caused half a dozen Mad Ones to burst into mystic sparks and vanish.

Another four hesitated and then leaped at her, perhaps thinking her magic exhausted. With a thrust of her hand she shot out a bolt of energy that propelled one of the doglike creatures through the air, slamming it so hard against the wall that its bones cracked.

The other four-legged being launched itself at her and

she simply reached out, swung it around, and threw it hard against the opposite wall, breaking its back. The last two hesitated, and they died for their uncertainty. Child took one step forward and with a slice of her talon slashed open both their throats, causing steaming blood to fountain across the room.

She turned to find the young male she had admired earlier upon the back of the last Mad One, his fangs fastened deep in the bull-headed demon's neck. He howled in pain, but the young male persisted and with a loud grunt of victory finally bit through the thick muscle and the Mad One collapsed.

Instantly all the remaining demons in the Child's party began to feast. Even Belog was overcome with the smell of blood and the release of energies. Child batted away some of her companions as she claimed her victims' heads. She always ate the brains, no matter how primitive the mind: her hunger for knowledge was insatiable.

They devoured every body in the room, including their two fallen comrades. When they were finished, Child studied them. Two were budding flyers, not yet able to sustain long flight but able to hover for a short time and to scout ahead. Five were males who were starting to become warriors. She smiled at the thought of keeping them loyal; she was maturing and the desire to mate was rising daily. There were five worker male demons, two imps, and four immature females. The females would have to be controlled and developed carefully. Unlike the males, who as a rule became warriors or laborers, the females had a variety of potential roles. Perhaps one as a pleasure creature, a succubus, to amuse the males when she needed to have them diverted; and the other three could be many things, including mothers.

She sat back. To Belog she said, "Tell the males to stand guard at the doors, and keep the others quiet. I need to consider things; I need to think."

She retired to a corner, sat down with her knees hiked before her chin, her arms around her knees, and thought. Hours went by.

At dawn she arose and said to Belog, "Walk with me." To the others she said, "Stay here. We will return shortly."

They complied, and Child and the Archivist left the building. "You are growing larger," she said.

He removed his coat and displayed broader shoulders and chest, and arms far more muscled than before. "You are generous with food, Child."

"I no longer wish to be called that," she said.

"What would you wish?"

She paused and said, "Mi . . ." She hesitated.

"Mistress?" he offered.

She hesitated. "No, not Mistress." At last she said, "I do not yet know, but I will tell you when I do. Until then Child will do."

"Yes, Child," he said without mockery. He knew when she was serious, and now she was deadly serious.

"I have lived before," she began.

He nodded.

"Yet my memories of my previous life or lives are not there. Hints, fleeting images, but I can't quite . . ."

She paused, and after a minute, when she didn't continue, he said, "It happens. If your last death was exceptionally violent and prolonged, knowledge fades while you die, so that the energies become fragmented and not all of them return to the spawning pit. You were born of a living mother, so even more energies were consumed in the birth. And if you died at the hands of an energy drinker, there would be very little identity to return to the spawning pits. It would be as if one came close enough to the Final Death to feel its icy chill and somehow pulled back, to be reborn, but greatly reduced."

"No, it's not that," she said dismissively. "The memories are there: I just can't reach them."

He had no idea what to say. Finally, he said, "What is your pleasure, Child?"

"I need to change."

"You have been changing."

"No, I mean, I need to become something other than what I am. There are things in motion, powers roaming out there that demand more than I can give in this form."

After a long, thoughtful moment, Belog said, "There are many powerful beings out there, Child. In the other realms they speak of invisible beings, powerful beings, called gods, who subvert plans and tinker with fate, distort reality, and change time and space by will, providing benefit or harm at whim. In many realms it is said that some lesser beings have risen to become gods."

She was silent for a very long time as she grappled with concerns Belog could only guess at. Finally she said, "Let us return. We must move on. There is somewhere we need to go."

"Where?"

She looked at him and smiled. "I do not know. Let us explore."

The hall was enormous, filling half the massive palace that contained it. Even though it was deserted, there was a presence in it.

At the center of the room a large opening yawned at them. It was a murder pit, where prisoners or others suffering the King's displeasure were thrown to die, either at one another's hands, or by some other means viewed as amusing to the monarch.

Around the murder pit were smaller, shallower feasting pits where prisoners would be bought in chains to be devoured by the King's court. The iron restraining rings in the floor where those chains had been fastened were rusted and mute.

At the rear wall rose a massive dais upon which sat a marble throne. Child walked up to the throne and ran her hand over the surface. Dusty rags, the remnants of soft cushions upon which the monarch had rested, were the last vestiges of this city's once-proud ruler. She stood studying the empty throne, as if she could somehow divine what it had been like when this city was a thriving center of what passed for culture among the Savage Kingdoms. Her head was cocked to one side, as if she was listening to the silence. Then she moved away from it and pointed, "Over there."

Belog looked where she indicated and saw nothing. The wall appeared unadorned except for sconces every ten feet or so where torches or lamps had once rested.

Now Child was touching the walls as she had the throne. Softly she whispered, "Do you feel it?"

He placed his hand upon the wall and felt only cold, lifeless stone. "Feel what, Child?"

"Here there was once a portal, open from the other side, and here Maarg found entry into a higher realm." She turned and looked at her companion. "This is why Dahun warred with Maarg, even though it was in vain. For when Dahun breached this city, he found it led to a lifeless planet, for Maarg had devoured all life there when finding himself trapped there, with no means of returning. In the end he withered to nothing and died without returning to the spawning pits. It happened a long time ago." Her voice dropped almost to a whisper.

Almost afraid to ask, he said, "How do you know, Child?"

She pressed her cheek against the stone. Moisture glistened in her eyes for a moment, then she closed them. "I know," was all she said.

From the city they moved farther east, into the borders of the realms of the Mad Ones. In the month since they had left Child had recruited another score of followers, and these she nurtured as if they were her children. She was a strict mother but gave bounty in a poor land in exchange for loyalty. She now had half a dozen flyers who scouted ahead for the group, and her males were now strong enough to confront all but the most powerful of the Mad Ones in single combat and stand a fair chance of winning. For the most part, small packs of Mad Ones gave them a wide berth. Those few times they had been attacked they had destroyed their foes and feasted, growing ever stronger.

Child began mating with the males. Belog was given the honor of being her first, because he was her first companion, and then one by one she took the others. Within weeks she had them completely bound to her and was learning a new concept: love.

She knew something about it from what she knew of the succubae, but they bound others to them by magic, by charm and glamour. The love she was experiencing was harder to understand. But she knew when she looked at Belog she felt differently from when she beheld the younger males. And although she enjoyed his company, occasionally a feeling of irritation arose in her that she couldn't explain.

Feelings confused her and she needed to understand them, but she was constantly frustrated by her inability to grasp them. Like quicksilver they dribbled between her fingers as she grappled with them.

They felt it before they saw it. Over a rise and out of sight, there was a presence. For more than a week since leaving Maarg's city they had been following a well-worn road into a gently descending valley. It was the only place they had found since leaving the bramble thickets where anything grew.

Tough-looking scrub trees with black bark and magenta leaves were surrounded by bright yellow grasses and tall violet reeds.

Something coursed through Child when she crested the ridge and saw what she had been sensing. The sensation she experienced was one of being drawn, compelled to go closer.

"There is a portal," she said.

"Where does it lead?" asked Belog.

"I do not know, but it is the reason everyone has left Maarg's city. That road was worn by his entire realm having come this way."

"Perhaps it is an escape from the Darkness," whispered one of the males, made bold because Child had favored him with a mating the night before.

She struck back without looking, ripping a gash across his

face. "Speak only when I tell you," she commanded. Of all her companions, Belog was the only one she allowed any discretion when it came to addressing her.

She walked down the path and was accosted by alien scents and odd sounds. A faint vibration, too quiet to make out, emanated from the portal. It was a tall rectangle of grey with a scintillating sheen of colors playing across the surface like an oily rainbow on water.

"It is calling," said Child.

"I sense a desire to enter," agreed Belog. "But we know not what is on the other side."

"Yet it calls."

The tug of desire was mounting by the moment.

"Perhaps safety is on the other side," ventured one of the females, who then cringed in anticipation of Child's wrath.

But Child was unmindful of this second breach and simply said, "No, we do not know what is beyond." When she turned, it was with a grin, but there was no humor in it.

Her features were changing, and Belog was most aware of that since he had seen her in her childhood. She now had high cheekbones and piercing black eyes, a regal nose and a high forehead that swept back to a crest that fanned out behind her head like a crown. Her body was lithe and powerful, but hips and breast were full like those of a succubus. Her teeth were gleaming white instead of yellow or black, with only her eye-teeth pointed, the rest being as flat as those of a lesser being.

She was changing and into what he had no idea, but he said nothing as she finished her thought.

"But we do know what is behind us, and if it takes a lifetime or ten lifetimes, eventually the Darkness will reach this place." She glanced from face to face. "And I will not be here when it comes. Choose as you wish."

She stepped into the portal.

A moment later, Belog followed.

14

FLIGHT

Martin ran up the steps.

Barely dressed as the sun rose, he had been summoned by an urgent call from the sentry atop the highest tower in the castle. When he reached the apex of the tower, the sentry cried, "Sir, the Keshians are moving their trebuchets!"

"Sergeant Ruther!" shouted Martin, and within a minute the old veteran was at his side. "It looks as if the Keshians have grown tired of waiting for us to walk away," Martin told him. Then he added calmly, "Sound the alarm."

With a wave the sergeant ordered a trumpeter to sound the call to battle, and a moment later every soldier and those men of fighting age who had been armed took up their positions.

"I wonder if they're going to ask us to leave again?" asked Sergeant Ruther, his chin jutting as if he was ready for a bar fight.

Suddenly a massive stone came arcing out from the heart of town and smashed into the stonework to the right of the gate. Shards of masonry exploded, and two men fell from the wall nearby, while everyone else ducked for cover. Those townsfolk who were not bearing arms and hadn't yet fled to the rear of the castle were now leaving the front bailey yard at a run. Their screams of terror filled the air, but through it Sergeant Ruther's voice cut: "Steady!" Looking at Martin, he said, "I guess that means not."

The Keshians had been content to sit in the town for five days, sending a message every day, asking for the inhabitants' surrender. They never threatened, but the threat was implicit as more and more soldiers disembarked from the ships now in Crydee Harbor. Already the keep was nearly fully surrounded. Only the heavily forested area a half mile from the rear wall seemed not yet to be closed off.

Martin watched as a second stone crashed nearer to the gate. "They mean to have that gate down before they attack," suggested Martin.

"That's how I see it, sir. Scaling walls is a messy business, and the gate's the easy way in. Usually we wait until we have to pull back into the keep, and then it gets messy for them."

Martin understood. The outer wall was a late addition to the original keep, which had a classic murder room behind the outer portcullis. Although it was easy enough to lift those two gates, they were extremely difficult to breach without a lot of men dying under a hail of arrows from above. "You see any turtles?"

"No, but we can be sure they have them or are building them somewhere in town." The turtles would be covered rams of heavy wooden construction that would be used to smash in the portcullises. The defenders would make the attackers pay a heavy toll to breach the keep, but with enough men and matériel, eventually the Keshians would break through. Martin's sole hope was to hold them at bay until his father and the rest of Crydee's muster returned.

The instructions had been simple. If Lord Henry appeared, the garrison would sally forth in support of his attack on the Keshians besieging the keep. With a strong enough attack, they could roll them up and push them through the town until they found themselves fighting with the bay at their back. Unless they could swim to their ships wearing armor, they would be forced to surrender or be killed to the last man on the docks. Martin chose to worry about the Keshian townspeople after the battle was won. Right now he was focusing on defending this keep.

He looked around and realized that his ancestors had either been geniuses or very lucky. When the original keep had been established by the first Duke of Crydee, this had been a small Keshian garrison, used primarily to keep goblins and the Brotherhood of the Dark Path out of northern Bosania, as this province had been called. The current Free Cities had been their main concern, and the Far Coast had been occupied only as a way to protect their "back doors," as there were two major passes over the mountains. The road east past the Jonril garrison split northeast and southeast and led to the passes, one of which skirted the southern boundary of the Elven Forest, and eventually would clear the Grey Towers at the Northern Pass before descending toward Yabon.

The southern route passed close to the boundaries of the dwarves and the Star Elves, eventually descending toward the Free City of Natal and the Kingdom Port of Ylith. It was infrequently traveled and only utilized if heavy snow blocked off the Northern Pass.

Yet while the Crydee garrison had never been more than a Keshian watch post, it had this bloody marvelous keep: one story, square, and ugly, with a small barbican over the entrance. Martin's ancestor, the first Duke of Crydee, had built a second story above it, extended it on three sides and erected towers at the front two corners, then built a huge wall around it, creating a massive bailey in the front and a less spacious marshaling yard behind. On the north side the stables had been tucked against the wall, while barracks were constructed against the south wall.

The outer wall had two entrances: the main gates and a postern gate in the rear. That was heavily guarded, but the terrain behind the keep made attack from that direction difficult: thick woodlands made marshaling horse and infantry impossible unless they came into the clearing behind and attacked uphill while in range of the bowmen and two ancient ballistas mounted on the towers at the corners. The ancient Keshians knew one thing that every Duke of Crydee had also known: the only way to take the keep was a steep climb uphill and a full-frontal assault.

More boulders came hurtling through the air and more masonry exploded. Shards of stone and choking dust filled the air.

Silently, Martin prayed his father wasn't too long in coming to his aid.

Lord Henry chafed at every moment he was forced to tarry. He paced without let every time they had to stop to rest the horses. Two hundred cavalry had to tend to their mounts while the infantrymen struggled to keep up, lagging perhaps a half-day's march behind.

Brendan watched his father and was hard-pressed to know what to say. He was just as desperate to return as the Duke, but he knew that it was futile to push out too far ahead of the heavy foot. Two hundred mounted soldiers might break a siege, but they would need the support of the twelve hundred men behind them. At last he said, "Father, you taught Martin well. Of the three of us he was always your best student."

Lord Henry turned. He looked as if he was about to lose his temper at his son's words, but just managed to pulled himself back from an outburst. After a moment he said, "You're right. I have always known that you and your brothers might be tested in battle some day. I just thought you'd be older and I'd be there with you." Then his voice lowered. "And your mother is there."

Brendan moved to his father's side. Putting a hand on his shoulder, he repeated, "Martin was your best student. And he has Ruther with him. He may be a boastful drunk on Banapis, but the rest of the year he's a seasoned soldier."

"Against bands of goblins and roving outlaws, yes," said Duke Henry, his dark eyes narrow and his face pinched with worry. "But against Keshian Dog Soldiers?"

"Crydee Keep is battle tested, Father. If the Tsurani couldn't bring it down after months of siege, I doubt Kesh can in a matter of days."

"The Tsurani didn't have Keshian engineers," said Duke Henry. "Even if we arrive the day before the infantry, we may be able to raid from behind and burn their engines, cause confusion, and maybe even scatter them."

Brendan didn't answer, but he knew that was unlikely. They would be coming down from the foothills on the only major road west from Yabon to Crydee. They had been halfway to the Jonril garrison when the fast riders overtook them, warning of the Keshian invasion.

Henry's orders had been to take this command to Yabon, to bolster that garrison should the Keshians sail north or to stand in its stead if the Duke of Yabon was ordered to sail south from Ylith to Krondor. Until the riders came with word of the attack on Crydee, Henry assumed that the likelihood of an attack there was low. He had sent two fresh riders on to Jonril and then to Yabon, ordering the Jonril garrison stripped and force marched to Crydee. He judged they'd arrive no more than three days later than Crydee's own infantry. Yabon would be left to decide what aid they could bring if any. If the Keshians were not moving in the Bitter Sea, Henry was certain Duke Francis would send two or three companies of his own garrisons from LaMut, Zun, and Yabon City to support Crydee. They should arrive within three weeks if Duke Francis moved swiftly.

The Duke gestured to his groomsman to saddle the horses, but Brendan said, "Father, the horses do us no good if we ride them dead before we get there. Ten more minutes?"

The Duke froze in place. He was wearing his armor and the ancient and honored tabard of his ancestors, with a deep brown field upon which flew the golden seagull of Crydee.

His helm rested on the ground near his feet, and he glanced down at it. Then he said softly, "I wish Hal was there with Martin."

Brendan could only nod. Martin may have been their father's best student when it came to strategy and theories of war, but Hal just knew how to do things right and men would follow him anywhere. All he could say was, "Martin will be fine, Father."

Martin walked through the great hall where casualties lay groaning. It had become a makeshift infirmary since the relentless bombardment on the gates had injured more than two dozen men. Most had been workers, attempting to shore up the gate with timbers and stone, delaying the inevitable, when the gate would come crashing down.

He had ordered all the men off the wall two days earlier, having them retreat to the sides of the keep or into the main entrance, ready to man the walls should the need arise, but knowing full well the Keshians would not come within arrow range until the gate was down. He could not help but grudgingly admire the Keshian commander. What his approach lacked in creativity it made up for in effectiveness. His soldiers might be falling asleep in the town out of boredom, but no one inside Crydee had enjoyed a good night's sleep in a week. The best anyone could manage would be to doze off for a few minutes, before being startled awake by the thundering crash of another stone against the wall around the gate.

Martin saw Sergeant Ruther on the other side of the room and signaled for him to join him. The old fighter moved to a corner of the hall where they wouldn't be overheard.

"How are we doing, Sergeant?"

Ruther stroked his chin. "Considering the pounding the gate's taking, better than I expected. No one's dead, just broken bones and cuts from flying stones."

"How long?"

Ruther didn't need to ask what he meant. "Three days at best, two more likely; if they get busy, less than that." He paused, then added, "We need to think about getting the women and children out."

Martin sighed, near exhaustion. "I know. Is the tunnel ready?"

After the Tsurani siege of the castle, Martin's namesake, the first Duke Martin, had ordered an escape tunnel built deep under the keep, far below any that might be dug by incoming sappers. It ran far beyond the clearing to the east, into the heavy forest. The exit was fully disguised by carefully placed boulders surrounding a door-sized rock that had been artfully crafted to look like a solid boulder but was hollow at the back.

"I had the boys down there yesterday ensuring the timbers were still sound and the stone door that hides the entrance can be moved. It will take a couple of stout lads and a long piece of wood to move that door, but it'll be ready when we need it."

"Good," said Martin. "I'm just not certain how we'll get everyone out and when."

"The 'how' is your burden, sir, but the 'when' is soon." He looked at Martin, took in the dark shadows beneath his eyes. "You look all in, lad," he said, though he was in no better shape. "Why don't you try to get some rest, at least an hour?"

"Thank you, Sergeant," said Martin. He knew the old soldier was right. He was exhausted and not thinking clearly. He half staggered to his room and fell across his bed without taking his boots off. In a few minutes he was asleep, unmindful of the dull thud of stones striking the gate outside.

Martin awoke to soft lips pressing against his. His eyes opened wide. "Huh?"

He found Bethany leaning over him.

"You are needed. I thought that was the best way to rouse you."

Flushing, Martin said, "I am roused. What is it?"

"Your mother needs you." She turned toward the door. As she reached it, she glanced over her shoulder and added, "As do I," and left.

Martin sat there half asleep, slightly giddy, and confused. If he lived through the next few days, he would wonder about how he had become the object of affection for the woman he adored.

He had always felt there was something between them, but every time he had dared to imagine what it might be, he had pushed away the thoughts as the idle dreaming of a fool. Now he wondered how things could suddenly change so dramatically. Why did he feel like grinning like a loon when the world was crumbling around him?

He straightened his tunic and hurried to his parents' quarters, which his mother was currently sharing with Bethany, her mother, and half a dozen ladies from the village and their dozen children. The room had always seemed capacious to Martin as a child, being the largest sleeping chamber in the keep with its huge bed, settee, large rugs, and wall hangings, but now it seemed small and cramped.

Duchess Caralin motioned for her son to come to her when he entered the room and took his hands in hers. "How are you, Martin?" Her face was a mask of concern. He knew that look. She worried about him more than his brothers and had ever since childhood. He was not as confident as Hal or as reckless as Brendan, and as the middle child he had often been neglected while his father saw to the eldest and his mother cared for the youngest.

He smiled, though he felt as if he could drop back to sleep just standing there. "I'm fine, Mother. What is it you need?"

"We have people getting sick in the rear yard. It's not bad now, but it will get worse." Collected together tightly as they were, the people of Crydee were ripe to be taken by disease, from something relatively mild like belly flux to something lethal like the red plague or spotted madness. Softly she added, "We must think about getting those who are the most sick away from here."

"Where would we take them, and how would they get there?"

"Elvandar," she suggested. "Your father will surely be coming quickly from Jonril, and the healers will be with him, but many of these people will be dying or dead if we don't get them help soon." Suddenly, she shuddered.

Martin stared at her, alarmed. "Mother, what is it?"

She lowered her voice and whispered, "Ague."

Martin closed his eyes for a second. Several different things could be ague, but those who had it would have the same symptoms: fevers with sweats, then chills, a terrible thirst, and if not treated, hallucinations. If these combined with other problems, death was possible. Usually if someone was struck down, he or she went to bed for seven to ten days and was tended by friends or family in the town. But here ague could leave the garrison incapacitated within days.

"If we're going to get them out, we must do so before they become too weak to travel. I'll instruct Sergeant Ruther to get things organized. We'll have them out at sunset." He paused, then added, "I would like you, Countess Marriann, and Lady Bethany to go as well."

"No," said his mother flatly. "These are my people; this is my home. If you stay, I will stay."

He held up his hand. "Mother, please. Someone needs to take care of the sick, and I can not imagine anyone better suited, and it would ease my mind if you and Earl Robert's family were out of harm's way."

His mother looked at him askance. "Is that so?"

"Yes," he replied, not understanding her question. "More-over, if you won't go, I must send Ruther to lead the escape, and I need him here.

"Very well," she said. "You're enough like your grandfa-ther when it comes to having your mind made up that I'll not argue."

He kissed her on the cheek. "Father's father or your father?"

Frowning slightly she said, "Both."

That made him smile. He kissed her cheek again and departed.

Exhaustion was talking its toll, yet whenever the young commander walked by, people nodded greeting and the soldiers saluted. Martin was uncertain what it was he had done to earn their regard, then as he was leaving the family's wing of the keep and entering the main hall, he realized what it was; they wanted him to succeed. Because if he did so, they would survive. If he failed, they all failed.

Moving through the crowded main hall, with women and children occupying every available space on the floor, took him a few minutes, with several of the town's women smiling or addressing him directly, "Sir" or "Lord Martin"; one even called him "Highness"!

This caused him a momentary pause. He had presumed to name himself prince in the face of Kesh's commander in the field, a self-aggrandizement avoided for generations by his family. His great-great-grandfather for whom he had been named was brother to the King, and he and his son Marcus were both princes of the Kingdom in rank by birth, but Marcus had never chosen to employ the title, nor had his son the first Duke Henry, or Martin's father, the second Duke Henry. Hal would be the third Duke Henry, but the present king was a very distant cousin at best; and the only thing that distinguished Martin, his brothers, and their father from a score of other distant cousins to the King was that they were conDoins. The first Martin had been born a bastard, but he was recognized and named by his father before his death; therefore, he was of royal blood.

Martin shook his head. He must be suffering from fatigue to let his mind wander so.

The day dragged on, and the pounding of the gate continued through the night. As the false dawn approached in the east, Martin hurried out and got as close to the gate as was safe to see how the Keshians were doing. As he stood at the entrance to the keep, a soldier came to stand beside him: a thin, rangy fellow named Means, recently promoted to sergeant from corporal.

"Where's Ruther?" asked Martin.

"Oh, finally got him to get some sleep, sir. I can fetch him if you need."

"No, let him sleep." Another stone crashed into the gate with a resounding thud, and Martin heard a splintering sound and saw the timbers reinforcing the gate shudder. "What do you think?"

"Not my job, sir," said Means.

"A born sergeant," Martin laughed.

"If you mean when do I think the gate will give out, then two days, maybe less. We'd better be ready to fight any time after sunup tomorrow."

Martin nodded. Half the stone surrounding the gates was shattered and cracked, the tops of the walls on both sides sheared to rubble. Men could not stand and fight within half a dozen yards of the gate on either side, for there was no sheltered footing left. Should the Keshians bring a fire ram against the wooden gates, the defenders would be exposed if they tried to douse it and the Keshian archers would have easy targets.

He said to Means, "My mother and the other ladies mean to take the sick from the keep through the escape tunnels. I need Ruther here with me, but I also need an experienced soldier to look after them. I'm putting you in charge of that detail." He glanced around. "We don't have much left for a stand-up fight, do we?"

"Oh, they're a good lot. Your father left a few grizzled veterans mixed in with the boys. And a few of the townsmen are fairly scrappy brawlers—I know that from my drinking days."

"Don't drink anymore?"

"Not to speak of," said Means. "My father couldn't abide a man who couldn't hold his drink. For years I took that to mean I needed to go drink with all the lads and somehow not turn into the horse's ass I usually became. Would have had these stripes years ago if I hadn't been that man. So I learned that to hold their drink, some men just need not to drink that first ale. Haven't had a drink in five years." Then he grinned. "Still doesn't mean I haven't busted a few heads down at the dock taverns in my day." He shook his head. "No, these lads will give the Keshians as good as they get, maybe a bit more. This is their home, sir. This keep will be here when your father reaches us, Commander. I'm certain of that."

"I hope you're right, Sergeant."

Martin went back into the keep and began his routine for the day. He would conduct a personal inventory of stores, ensuring there was ample food for everyone, then he'd walk each post to see how the men were, then take his place on the top of the keep to watch to see if the Keshians were doing anything different. Then he would wait.

"Fire wagon!" came the shout from the top of the keep, and it was relayed down the stairs into the great hall. Martin had just bid his mother and the other ladies farewell before they began their journey to Elvandar. Those too sick to walk were being carried in litters and by best guess it would take a week for the party to reach the River Boundary and the elves. Martin was loath to see them leave in this condition, but he knew a garrison in the grip of even a relatively minor illness would give the Keshians one more advantage he didn't wish to give them.

Sergeant Ruther hurried in. "The Keshians have launched a fire wagon at the gate, sir. They mean to be inside sooner than later, it seems."

Martin nodded and turned to Sergeant Means. "Get them out safely," he said. The escape tunnel led out of the lower basement beneath the kitchen pantry. Those leaving had queued up before dawn and now they were almost through.

Martin ran outside and up to a position on the wall where he could best see through the smoke at the gate. The Keshian fire wagon had been made by filling a wagon with oil-soaked wood and, on top of that, tightly bundled straw. Half a dozen men ran behind it, steering as best they could with a reversed wagon tongue. It was like steering a boat, pulling the tiller in the opposite direction to the one you wished to go in, and the Keshians made a botch of it.

The wagon had crashed into the right side of the gate, opposite where Martin stood. The fire was burning hotly, but mostly against stone. The wood of the gate on that side was smoldering and smoking, but had not yet burst into flames. Crydee soldiers quickly set about throwing buckets of water on the inside of the gate opposite the fire, to help dissipate the heat and keep the wood from burning through. Ruther came to stand beside Martin.

"What do you think?"

"It'll weaken it a bit, but unless they're mad enough to start sending men with oilskins to try and spread the flames to the gate, it'll hold for a while longer."

"Do you think they'll bring a ram after it's weakened?"

"No. They'll not risk getting tangled up in all that mess, especially with flame and embers all around. I'd have the lads dumping oil on them in a moment if they were foolish enough to try that, and they know it.

"No, they'll wait until the flames are out and toss a few more stones to see how much damage they've caused, then they might send another fire wagon, and I'll bet the second time they'll get it right, spot on in the middle."

Martin could only nod in agreement. He let out an exhausted sigh and wondered where his father was at that moment.

Henry, Duke of Crydee, slashed down at the goblin trying to unhorse him. The creature's green-blue face was contorted in a snarl, long fangs bared as it struck upward at the Duke. Brendan came from behind the goblin and struck it across the base of the neck, below the chain where its skin was exposed, and it collapsed.

As bad fortune would have it, they had ridden straight into a goblin raiding party moving through the Green Heart in strength. It was Henry's two hundred riders against thirty goblins on foot.

They made short work of the goblins, most of whom had turned and fled into the deep woods as soon as they realized they hadn't encountered a small garrison patrol out of Jonril. Goblin raiding parties could be very dangerous for caravans and small patrols, but a full company of heavy cavalry was more than they had bargained for.

Henry turned his mount in a half circle. "Report!" he commanded his First Sergeant, Magwin.

"One dead, two wounded, my lord."

"Damn," said the Duke. He was nearly frantic with worry for his wife and son. "I should have had riders on point."

He looked down and saw a spreading red stain on his tabard.

"Father!" cried Brendan. He looked down at the fallen goblin and saw that the creature was holding a blood-covered dirk. He had got close enough to the Duke to wound him.

"It's nothing," said Henry, holding his side. "I'll bind it and we'll be on . . ." His eyes rolled up and he slipped out of the saddle, hitting the ground hard before anyone could catch him.

The Duke struck the ground with the side of his head and shoulder making an ominous cracking sound.

Brendan was at his father's side in seconds. First Sergeant Magwin knelt there and examined the Duke, but Brendan realized his father was dead before the man spoke. "Broke his neck, sir." As if it would be some consolation he said, "He can't have felt a thing."

Brendan's face flushed as tears welled up. "Father?" he said quietly as if expecting an answer.

After a moment, the other soldiers gathered around. The boy wept openly, and at last First Sergeant Magwin put his hand on his shoulder. "Sir, you're in command. We must move on."

Brendan blinked away his tears and took a deep breath. "You're right," he said, his voice nearly breaking.

"What are your orders, sir?" asked the sergeant.

Brendan stood and turned his back on his father for a long moment, remembering every lesson of warcraft taught by the man lying behind him. Softly he said, "Bury the dead, detail two men to accompany the wounded as they follow, and we ride on." His voice rose as he turned. "Mark this spot well, for we will return one day and retrieve our dead and bury them with honor." He looked at the solders watching him expectantly. With a deep breath he pushed aside his pain and said calmly. "We will relieve my brother at Crydee."

To his father, who was now being gently lifted by two soldiers, he said softly, "Farewell, Father." Then he mounted up again thinking, *Hal is Duke now, and he doesn't even know it.* Brendan gestured to his troops. "To Crydee!"

15

ENIGMA

Hal threw a knife across the room.

Ty watched with amusement as the blade struck the wall and fell to the floor. "If you want it to stick, use a meat knife. The bread knives have dull tips."

Hal pushed himself away from the midday meal he had been served. "I'm sorry," he said as he crossed the private dining room upstairs at the River House in Roldem. He picked up the knife and carried it to the table, then wiped it with a serving cloth. "I'm grateful for your father's hospitality and your company. The food is wonderful." He sighed as he sat down. "I can barely fasten my trousers from eating. And the wine! I've never had its like in Crydee. But I'm growing mad with boredom."

The university had all but closed down as students from Kesh, the Kingdom of the Isles, and the Eastern Kingdoms had all hurried home on the first available ships when word of Kesh's fleet sailing north had arrived. Following Swordmaster Phillip's and Lord James's advice, Hal had entrusted himself to the care of Ty Hawkins and his father, Talwin.

Hal pointed his knife at Ty. "You know, I wager I've read

more books here than I would have had I remained at the university. And it's a bit of a relief not to have to listen to every droning lecture, though a few of them were interesting. But I need to get outside. I need to hunt, ride a horse, chase down a stag or bear. Go fishing! Take a walk! Anything!"

"We could practice if you'd like," offered Ty.

Half laughing, Hal shouted, "No! I'm tired of almost beating you."

"You are getting better," grinned Ty. "By the next Masters' Court you will probably be able to beat me. You are a bit faster."

"No," said Hal, falling back into his chair chuckling. "I'm sorry, Ty. I'm just going mad here."

"Until we receive word from Lord James or your ambassador that it's safe for you to travel . . ." He shrugged. "Like it or not, you are related to the King of the Isles. That makes you important."

"Barely related," said Hal, sipping at a light white wine that had been served with the midday meal: a lightly basted roast chicken with steamed vegetables. Before coming to live for the last month at the River House, Hal could not believe such simple fare could be made so delicious by the mere addition of a little savory oil and some herbs. Letting out another exasperated sound, Hal said, "If I ever find a way to steal your cook from you, I will."

"You'd get fat," said Ty with a laugh. He put his feet up on the table and drank his wine. "Francisco is Lucien's best student—Lucien's father's chef in Olasko. I don't think he'd leave Roldem for a rustic destination like Crydee"—he held up his hand as Hal began to protest—"as charming as it may be in its own way. Francisco enjoys the abundance of high living in Roldem, which I believe you will concede is the most civilized city in the world."

Hal nodded. He was not a world traveler by any measure, having never been east of Yabon until his father decided to place him at the university here. He had stopped for a polite visit with Prince Edward in Krondor where they had spent a tedious dinner during which when one spoke the other nodded, because they had nothing in common. The Prince of Krondor had been eager to spread gossip about matters at court in the east, about people of whom Hal had never even heard, and Hal's topics of hunting, warcraft against goblins and trolls, and managing estates all seemed lost on the Prince.

After that it had been an overnight stay in Malac's Cross, then on to Salador where he had endured two nights of being hosted by a very distant cousin, Duke Louis, then a mandatory visit to the King to pay his fealty in Rillanon.

He had been impressed with both Rillanon and the King's court. King Gregory had been welcoming and seemed a bright enough man. It was hard to tell, given the amount of deference shown the man at every turn. Even the Prince of Krondor's court was less formal, and Hal's father's court was casual by comparison. Everyone bowed when the King entered or left the room. One could not sit in his presence unless he sat first, and one could not speak to His Majesty unless spoken to. The sense of impending doom over a social miscue reduced Hal to reticence bordering on constant silence while he was there.

By the time he reached Roldem he had no idea what to expect, but he quickly embraced the rough-and-tumble of student life. The one reception with the King and two of his sons, Constantine and Albér, had proven surprisingly relaxed. The King was a happy, welcoming man, and it was obvious he had been blessed with a family he adored, a family who adored him in return.

Then Hal had been thrown in with the other students, from Roldem, the Isles, Kesh, and a few from the Eastern Kingdoms, to study language, arts, music, history, sciences, and a little about magic. Mainly they learned how to be enlightened rulers, or at least that was the opinion of three of his teachers.

The brothers who ran the university were pious men of the Order of La-Timsa the White, the Pursuer of the One Path. Knowledge was power and with power came duty, they taught.

Hal also discovered that as an abstemious and celibate order they didn't have patience for what passed as fun with the majority of the students. Discipline was harsh and swift, even for minor infractions of the rules, and the favorite instrument of that discipline was the caning wand. Hal had suffered less than most, for he tended to be less fractious than the other boys; a rugged frontier life had made him grow up a little faster than the other lads his age.

He enjoyed the nights out with the other students, but while most were getting drunk and regaling one another with improbable stories designed to impress the jaded tavern girls, he would sit quietly making one ale last half the night. He had never been punished for not returning on time or for being ill from overindulging in drink or drugs the night before.

He rarely gambled and then cautiously, so he never won or lost significant amounts, and he always gave the common girls a wide path. A particularly difficult experience with a town girl one Midsummer's Festival taught him to be cautious, though the other boys seemed to lose all sense when a pretty girl happened by.

"What are you thinking about?" asked Ty. "You've been lost in thought for the last minute."

"Just thinking about the first time I came here." Hal sighed and stood up. "I must get out of here. Even if just for an hour's walk."

Ty was on his feet. With a smile he put his hand on Hal's chest and said, "Wait a minute, my friend—"

Hal grinned, took a step, and then spun around and was past him. With a laughing whoop he half jumped, half ran down the stairs, barely making the complete turn at the landing halfway between floors as he scampered to stay one step ahead of Ty.

It was just after the midday meal, but there had been few patrons, so no one was in the dining room on the main floor to notice when the dark-haired young man raced down the stairs and out of the door with the sandy-haired youth only seconds behind him.

Since Swordmaster Phillip's and Lord James's departure the day after the King's reception rumors of war had erupted into news one day that Kesh had moved against the Isles; as a result, the streets were unusually quiet for this time of day.

Ty caught up with Hal at last. "Wait! If you insist on ignoring your swordmaster and my father and Lord James, at least show the good sense to go armed." He tossed a sword he had grabbed up on the way, and the young Lord of Crydee caught it.

"Thank you." Hal belted on the weapon and took a deep breath. "Sea air! It's different here in Roldem from Crydee. More . . . spices or flowers or . . . something, but it's good. I've lived near the ocean since I was born and can't imagine what it must be like to live in the mountains or the desert."

Ty fell into step beside him. "I've lived in the mountains awhile, but like you lived in a harbor city most of my life."

"Crydee is hardly a city. A large town at best. But it's the capital of the duchy. I suspect every duke before my father considered moving the capital down to Carse—that's the trading center—but . . . ." He shrugged. "I'll probably think about it, too." Then he grinned. "For a few minutes, anyway." He glanced around, drinking in the sounds and noises after being locked away in a bedroom above a restaurant for almost a month.

It was very quiet.

A massive Keshian fleet had sailed up from the south and was striking at Kingdom cities and towns up and down the coast. Although neutral, Roldem was historically close to the Isles, and their navy was a possible threat. While sending reassuring messages to King Carole, the Emperor's chancellor had also dispatched a squadron of ships that had taken up station just outside the harbor mouth in Roldem, to discourage the Roldem fleet from sailing out. It was a strategic move, as the Roldem fleet could easily crush the Keshians, but it would be an act of war, and right now Roldem was working hard to remain neutral. The King wished to serve as an honest broker between the two warring nations, so he ordered his navy to stand down while he sent diplomatic messages to the two capitals.

As a result, people were staying close to home, out of fear of a Keshian assault on the city. Most judged it unlikely that war would come, but fear cared not for likelihood.

Every shop they passed was closed or empty of customers, and every step past a street vendor brought pleas to inspect goods or hungry stares from peddlers too long without sales.

"Is war coming?" asked Ty.

"It's already come," said Hal. "At least to my nation. I don't know if the first arrow has been shot or the first sword blow struck, but if blood hasn't been spilled, it will be soon."

"How can you be certain? Isn't it possible this is some sort of ploy, a means to gain concessions from the King of the Isles?"

Hal said, "One day I will be a duke and while I may not be the brightest student the university has seen, I do know how to listen, read, and try to utilize the lessons of wiser men than me." He was attempting to be light in tone, but Ty could tell he was serious. "Fleets as big as those Kesh has unleashed are not sent into hostile waters as a feint or to spur diplomacy. They are sent out to force concessions or to conquer."

He stopped, looking around. From their vantage point along the river docks, they could see down into the harbor. "You see that clutter of ships?" he said, pointing.

"Yes?"

"Every one of those is owned by a man losing gold. Every hour a ship sits there is an hour that owner is not making profit. Wood rots, rope frays, metal rusts, and men must be paid even if they sit and do nothing; or they must be discharged and leave the owners without crew once business returns, but ships only make money if they are hauling cargo and passengers.

"There are syndicates across the Sea of Kingdoms and in the Bitter Sea where underwriters of cargo are already losing fortunes, because goods contracted and paid for are not being delivered. Men sitting in Barrett's Coffee House in Krondor, Rufino's Tavern in Salador, and Hanson's Inn in Rillanon, men who were wealthy a month ago, now stand on the edge of poverty. Lives are being ruined. Shop owners will run out of goods to sell, and people will go hungry." He turned and looked at Ty. "At least so far Kesh hasn't sent any assassins to kill me."

"That we know of," said Ty. "We've kept you out of sight . . . until now!" He laughed.

"But now we are just two young men spending a pleasant afternoon out and about, walking, taking in the sights, talking about life, and getting out of your father's lovely establishment that is currently my gaol!"

Ty laughed. "Was there ever so fine a gaol?"

"True. But I am getting fat," Hal said, patting his stomach. "I could use a hunt, a few days on the trail, some camp cooking, and I'd be able to get back into these trousers."

"Or you could eat less?"

"Of Francisco's cooking?" asked Hal, looking as if what Ty had said was sheer madness.

"Well, he is very good." Ty looked around and his eyes narrowed.

"What?" Hal's gaze followed Ty's.

"Those men over there. I think they're watching us. Don't stare."

Hal turned his back on them as if he were in conversation about something private with Ty and said, "Tall man, black cloak, short fellow, green vest over dirty grey shirt?"

"Those are the two," said Ty, glancing off in another direction as if listening to something he didn't want to hear.

"Saw them watching us before we came around the corner. I thought they might be following us."

"You didn't think to mention it to me?"

"I didn't want to cause needless alarm." Hal kept his back to them. "What are they doing now."

"Not watching us, and working hard at it."

"Do you know a disreputable ale house not too far from here?"

Ty grinned. "Just the place, around this next corner."

"Back door?"

"On a nice alley. I have had to employ it occasionally."

"Fights?"

"Women."

As they moved down the street, glancing out of the corner of their eyes at the two men, Ty continued, "When we first arrived here, I was new to many things, including the charms of the ladies."

"You don't have ladies in Olasko?"

"I had a mother in Olasko."

Hal laughed. "I understand."

They turned the corner. "My mother thinks I need to settle down. She's . . ." His voice dropped. "My mother went through a great deal . . . well, let us leave it that she would be happier if I found some nice young woman and started a family."

"How does your father feel?" asked Hal as Ty pushed open the door to the tavern. He glanced up at the sign they passed beneath. It showed a painting of a man in fancy livery being chased by a large black dog that was nipping at his heels.

"Father thinks I'll get around to it in my own good time," Ty answered. "He's been through a lot as well, but it's left him with a different perspective." He opened his arms expansively. "Welcome to the Running Footman."

It was just what one would expect of a riverside tavern in a port town: crowded, filled with workers, sailors, river men, and no doubt thieves and cheats. "Not exactly the River House," muttered Hal.

"True, but for me that's the charm, don't you see?" Ty moved to the bar and shouted, "Babette! My love! Miss me?"

The woman behind the bar was at least fifty years of age, possibly more, with sallow skin and a badly applied mask of rouge on her cheeks. She had darkened her eyes with kohl, or kajal as it was sometimes called, and wore the most impossibly red wig Hal had ever seen, including those worn by traveling players and clowns. She smiled. "Ty! You wound me with your absence." Her voice was so gravelly that for a moment Hal wasn't certain she wasn't a man in some horrible mummery; but that might have been the result of the pipe that hung from her lips, or from its smoke, from the very pungent and strong tabac she preferred. "Who's your friend?"

"By name, Henry."

"Hal." He extended his hand, and she took it and gave the fingers a squeeze.

"Pleasure."

"We're thirsty," said Ty, and Hal nodded.

"Two blacks!" she shouted, and a young man behind her grabbed two large porcelain mugs and filled them with a very dark brew. He brought them forward, and Ty slapped a silver coin down. "Let me know when that's used up."

He led Hal to a waist-high shelf against the far wall where they could place their drinks and stand, for there were no empty seats at any table. Hal took his first drink and was greeted by a thick, frothy mouthful unlike anything he had tasted before. It was nutty and slightly bitter, yet it had a lingering sweetness. "This is remarkable," he said. "What is it?"

"Porter," answered Ty. "It's been brewed for years for the porters who work up and down the docks and river. It's unique to Roldem, and what we have here is an example of the best; Black Beauty it's called." Lowering his voice he said, "Just sip it. It's OK to look drunk, just don't get drunk."

Hal nodded. "How long?"

Ty knew what he meant. "If they don't come in after us . . . ? Maybe an hour, then we leave out the back. If they're watching the front and waiting for us, we'll skulk around the corner and see them before they see us."

"What if they're watching the back?"

Ty grinned. "I guess we'll see them at the same time they see us."

"Tell me about Olasko." The two young men had been constant companions for nearly a month since word of the possibility of war had come, and they had gotten to know each other well enough for Hal to count Ty a friend. Yet there was much about him that remained a mystery.

"Not much to tell, really," said Ty. "The original settlers were colonists from Roldem, so the language is much the same, save for an odd word here, or a strange accent there. It's not much of a task to learn the difference quickly. Among the Eastern Kingdoms it was very influential, as the last ruler before the present Duke Varian, a man named Kaspar, was very powerful and held sway. But that was a long time ago." He sighed, and his face became a mask for a moment, and suddenly he looked a great deal older. Then his smile returned and he said, "But the mountains are magnificent and the hunting remarkable."

Hal said, "I should like to see it, and to go hunting."

"Then we shall do so, once this current madness is resolved. What of Crydee? How's the hunting there?"

"Very good. It's mainly forested land from the foothills and up into the Grey Tower Mountains. We have boars that stand man-high at the shoulder."

"Certainly not!"

"We do! The forest boars are big, fast, and mean. You need a boar spear ten feet long with a steel head and bolted cross below it or they'll run right up the shaft and gore you while you wait for them to die! We have brown bears and lions, though they've almost been hunted out, and plenty of wolves and deer, stag, and elk." He shrugged. "And the occasional wyvern."

"Wyvern?" said Ty, looking askance. "I bought the boar, but a wyvern? Dragon kin?"

"So they say, though that's like saying one of those little dogs the ladies at court carry around is wolf kin."

"You've seen one?"

"Ha! My father has the head of one down in the basement. It used to hang in the trophy hall, but Mother made him take it down. Said it disgusted her." He grinned. "It was pretty disgusting, really. All droopy eyes and fangs, and the man who mounted the head for great-grandfather managed to make a botch of the ears, so they sort of went this way"—he made a gesture with two fingers, one pointing up and the other one pointing to the side.

"Ladies?"

It was Hal's turn to laugh. "Nothing like you have here, that's for certain."

"There's nothing like the ladies of Roldem anywhere," said Ty. "Men who hold riches, power, and rank—it's a lodestone for beauties of all ranks, noble and common. Now, the ladies of Crydee?"

"Few," said Hal with a shrug, "if you mean ladies of noble birth."

"Girls, then," said Ty impatiently.

"A few worth spending time with." His expression grew wry. "Remember that problem you have in Olasko?"

"Mother?"

"I have one, too, in Crydee." He sighed theatrically. "And she knows everyone, and I do mean *everyone* in the town. She cares for the ill and makes sure anyone who's fallen on hard times has food, and takes charge of all shopping for the Duke's household . . ."

"So, gossip?"

"Yes. There was one girl, a miller's daughter, who caught my eye and I swear my mother had me in her room, bending my ear about not using my rank to take advantage . . . I was thirteen! It was my first kiss!"

Ty roared with laughter. "So not a lot . . . ?" He shrugged.

"No, not a lot. A few, mostly when mother was away or I traveled, but nothing like here. In Crydee, I'm . . . well, I'm the Duke's son, the next duke, so . . . it's not like here." He took a deep drink.

"Easy," Ty said.

"One won't hurt."

"But it's never just one. Now, what do you mean, it's not like here?"

"Your father, is he noble?"

"In a manner of speaking. He has a patent from the Isles, a knighthood in your part of the Kingdom, from around Ylith or Hawk's Hollow, or somewhere. But we've lived in Olasko so long that it's home."

"Well, there you have it," said Hal. "You can't swing a dead cat in Roldem without hitting a nobleman. So even if you're nobility, you're not *that* noble." Ty fixed him with a mocking gaze. "You know what I mean. I mean if you carouse and end up in some tavern wench's bed or she in yours, it's only something of the moment. If I do it, *I'm the Duke's son.* In a day everyone in the town would be gossiping . . ."

"And your mother would find out."

"Yes," agreed Hal.

"Sympathies, my friend," said Ty, feigning a sip at his drink. With a quick glance he looked to see if anyone was watching, and seeing no eyes upon them, he spilled some of his drink on the straw-covered floor.

"Besides, there's Bethany."

"Who's Bethany?"

"The daughter of Lord Robert, Earl of Carse and vassal to my father. Everyone expects us to wed." He sighed.

"Not pretty?"

"On the contrary. She's . . . quite beautiful. Bright, funny, and can shoot a bow better than anyone in the entire duchy, save perhaps for my brother Brendan. Not counting elves, of course."

"Of course, not counting elves." Ty rolled his eyes. Like most easterners, he found tales of elves, dwarves, goblins, and trolls problematic, bordering on myth and lore.

Hal went on, "She's probably one of the more attractive girls in the duchy, it's just . . ."

"What? You don't like her?"

"I like her well enough, but I'm not in love with her."

"Love?" Ty looked genuinely surprised. "You're a duke's son. You'll marry for political reasons, Hal. Love has nothing to do with it."

"It's different out west," said Hal. "The King hardly cares who we wed, so . . ." He fell silent. Then he said, "Beth is like my sister. I've known her since she was born. She's the same age as my brother Martin. We used to splash around in the same bath, all three of us."

"Well, I'm certain it will be fine. At least it's not like marrying a stranger, like some of these lot do." His gesture indicated the royal part of the island, so Hal knew he was speaking of Roldemish nobility.

"Yes," said Hal. "If I must, I must, and probably I can't do better than Beth, and certainly I could do worse. But . . ."

"What?"

"It's my brother Martin."

"What about him?"

Hal smiled a rueful smile. "He's in love with her."

"He's told you?"

"No, actually, I think he's too stupid to admit it to himself, but there's been something going on between them for the last few years." He shrugged. "Even that would be less of a problem, for Martin's as reliable and loyal as you could want a brother to be, but . . ."

"What?" prodded Ty, now very interested.

"I think Beth loves him back."

"Oh," said Ty, nodding. "A brother who's loyal being in love with your wife is one thing, but your wife being in love with your brother . . ."

Just as Hal was about to reply, his eyes widened.

Ty glanced over his shoulder to see two men entering the tavern. One was a red-bearded fellow in a grey jacket with a sailor's cutlass at his side, and the other was black haired with a dark green waistcoat and two long dirks in his belt. They were not the same men who had been watching them, but Hal noticed they took a good look around the room, their gaze lingering for just the briefest moment on Hal and Ty before they moved toward the bar.

Looking down at his porter, Ty asked, "Did you—?"

"I saw," answered Hal. "They recognized us."

"Follow me."

Ty moved with purpose but not with haste toward the bar and through a door to the right. "They'll think we're going to the jakes to relieve ourselves, but that will be good for less than five minutes."

From the smell of sour beer and human waste emanating from the corridor, Hal had no doubt they were approaching the jakes, but at the end of the hall there were two doors, and Ty pushed open the rear door, then pulled Hal into the one on the side. It was a large closet containing a bucket, dirty mop, two straw brooms, and barely enough additional room to accommodate both of them.

"Be silent," whispered Ty. He kept his hand on the latch and peered through a tiny crack between the door and the jamb.

Five or so minutes passed, then Hal heard the sound of men passing, then running out of the back door. Ty waited for a moment, then said, "Half the wall next to the jakes is down, so it's no task to jump over the stonework and get out into the alley. They are no doubt running around back there looking for us, so we shall go out the front."

They hurried out of the hall, though the main room, and left without anyone taking notice. Outside, they turned back toward the River House and Ty said, "I think that was enough adventure for the day."

Hal was about to reply when the first two men they had seen watching them stepped out of a nearby doorway, weapons drawn.

"Or then again, perhaps not," said Ty, drawing his own sword.

Hal drew his weapon and stepped to the right, giving himself a little room next to his companion. The street had solid shop fronts on one side, and the river on the other, so the two men would be forced to come straight at them. Both young swordsmen relaxed and stood ready. Softly Ty said, "You think these two didn't hear about the Masters' Court?"

As the two men suddenly charged, Hal answered, "I don't think they care." He knew from experience there was a profound difference between formal dueling and combat.

Ty discovered that in the first instant, when he attempted to beat aside his opponent's blade and discovered it was a feint not to gain blade position but so that he could bring up a short knife in his left hand and drive it into Ty's stomach. But Ty was fast enough to recognize the threat. Turning slightly, he let the man go by. "So that's how it's going to be?" He kicked out and left the man sprawling.

Hal knew he faced a brawler from the way the man made one lunge, then retreated into a crouch. Suddenly he realized something. The other two men would be back. "We'd best kill them swiftly and be on our way."

"I know," said Ty. He watched as his man made the fatal mistake of trying to turn while still on the ground and as he stood up, he impaled himself on the tip of Ty's sword.

Ty turned to see Hal's opponent backing away. His eyes widened, and Ty turned around and saw the two men who had run out of the tavern appear, coming from the other direction at a run. Ty crouched as the two men came close.

But rather than attack, the two men slowed and approached with their palms upraised. "Wait!" shouted one, the red-bearded man.

"Why?" demanded Ty, standing over the body of the man he had just killed.

"That," said the second man, pointing behind Ty.

"Hal, what does he mean by 'that'?" asked Ty, not taking his eyes off the two men from the tavern.

"Look," said Hal. From the other end of the street a half-dozen men were coming at a run.

"Come with us," said the red-bearded man.

"How do we know we can trust you?" asked Ty.

"You think you can trust that lot?" replied the man, pointing again.

Ty looked once more and saw the men who were approaching had their weapons drawn.

"Fair enough!" shouted Hal, lashing out with a sudden move that took his close opponent across the ribs. It was not a killing blow but would slow the man down enough to stop him joining in the hunt.

They took off on a mad dash, and the red-bearded man motioned for them to turn a corner and race toward the harbor. Hal glanced over his shoulder and saw the men behind them now numbered a full dozen, all looking ready for blood.

Normally the crowded streets of Roldem's river and harbor district would have been a hindrance, but because business had fallen off, the docks were as empty as if it had been a temple holy day. They charged through one big square, raced down another street, and came to the docks. The red-bearded man turned right, and the other three followed. At the end of the docks a ship was tied up, and before the gangplank stood a dozen armed men.

Ty began to slow, but the dark-haired man shouted, "It's all right. Come on!"

The men in front of the gangway parted, and the four of them ran up to the deck of the ship. They looked back just in time to see the dozen men run up to the men gathered before the ship. They slowed just out of reach and hesitated.

Ty said, "If they attack, do we go back down?"

"They won't attack," said the red-bearded man.

"Why?" asked Hal.

"That's why," said his companion, pointing to the far end of the dock.

Where the dozen pursuers had turned, there now came a squad of men in the uniform of the Roldem city guard. Steel helmets gleamed in the day's sun, and half of them carried pikes.

The leader of the pursuers saw them coming, shouted an order, and they broke into a run and dashed down an alley, away from the docks.

The leader of the watch came to stand before the dock-workers and demanded, "What's all this, then? Got a dead man back around the corner and saw a bunch of men dashing this way."

One of the dock men said, "Jumped one of our lads in the alley and a fight broke out. We came and got them, then they got their friends, then they came here, and tried to fetch our lads."

The watch leader looked dubious then he glanced over and saw which ship he was standing by. "Oh, this is . . . ?"

"Yes," said the dock man. "I think it was a ruse to get aboard."

"Well, we can't have that," the watch commander said. "They're long gone, no doubt, but we'll have a look after them and see if we can find anything." His attitude suggested he wouldn't look very hard and expected to find nothing. With a wave he gestured for his company to follow, and he set off down the alley where the other gang had fled.

"Well, that's done," said the red-bearded man. He turned to Ty and Hal. "Follow me, please."

Seeing no alternative, they did, and he led them through a door to a cabin at the rear of the ship.

In the room they found two people waiting, a young man in naval uniform and a beautiful young woman. She smiled and said, "There you are."

"Ma'am," said Hal, and Ty touched his forelock in salute.

She sighed theatrically. "I am Lady Franciezka Sorboz, a loyal servant to His Majesty the King."

"And I am Albér," said the young officer. "We met at—"

"You're the Prince!" blurted Ty. "Highness..." He bowed. Hal followed suit. "Your Highness."

The young man grinned. "Here I am Captain, not Prince."

"This is your ship, High— Captain?" asked Ty.

"Yes." He motioned for the two men to sit opposite Franciezka on a padded seat in front of the large stern windows. Even though these were the captain's quarters, there wasn't a lot of room.

"We were content merely to watch over you from a distance," said Lady Franciezka, "until you so foolishly decided to go out brawling."

"Actually, my lady," said Ty, "he decided to go out. I went after him to ensure he was safe, and the brawling was not our idea. It just sort of happened."

"It's been a month," said Hal, as if that explained everything. "So were those Keshians? They didn't looked like Keshians."

"Those were common thugs, though I suspect at least one among them may have been a trained assassin," said Lady Franciezka. "You would both have been found dead, or you dead, Prince Henry, and you wounded, young Hawkins, and the story would be that it was a dockside brawl among many men, and the witnesses would have conflicting stories. Create enough confusion and the truth is hidden."

"And while the city watch was sorting things out," added Prince Albér, "my father would have the difficult task of informing King Gregory that a distant cousin of his was killed in a brawl."

Hal realized something. "You didn't answer me? They were Kesh's agents, right?"

"No," said Lady Franciezka. "Despite the fleet looming off the harbor mouth, we're actually on good terms with Kesh these days, at least relative to what the Kingdom of the Isles is dealing with; no, we have sure knowledge those weren't Keshian agents trying to kill you."

"Who then?" asked Ty.

"That's the question, isn't it?" said Albér.

"Yes. It wasn't Kesh and it certainly wasn't Roldem," offered Lady Franciezka. "That means there's another, unknown, player taking a hand."

16

REVELATIONS

Amirantha tensed.

He waited to see if anything went awry as Gulamendis completed his preliminary enchanting. The two had spent most of his visit determining a means of investigating the demon realm without actually exposing themselves to an attack from there.

"I think I'm ready," said the elven Demon Master.

"I'd be calmer if you had not said 'think.'"

Gulamendis glanced at his friend and then gave him what passed for an amused smile; Amirantha had come to appreciate the subtleties of elven expression over the two and a half weeks he had been the Demon Master's guest. He'd also come to appreciate his people more, though the experience was leaving him with mixed feelings.

Amirantha nodded once, and Gulamendis began his final summoning.

The Warlock waited for the telltale bristle of energies that signaled the breach of the barriers between the mortal realm and the demon realm. Gulamendis finished his preparations.

Nothing happened.

"Well, that was disappointing," said the elf.

"What did you feel?"

"Nothing." He looked at his human friend. "Just, nothing. It was as if there was no one on the other side, no demon present."

"Odd," said Amirantha.

Gulamendis and he were standing in the middle of a large empty room, slated to be a storage area in the future, but presently unused. They had been given permission by Tanderae, the Loremaster and highest-ranking member of the Regent's Meet that was not hostile to them to use it, and had taken almost three days in preparing wards against an accidental summoning. The wards were strong enough in Amirantha's judgment to hold anything this side of a demon prince in thrall should one come through, and the intent was not to reach through and bring over a demon but simply control a demon in the other realm long enough to speak to it. Had it gone as designed, they'd have seen the image of the demon standing in the center of the ward and would have been able to communicate with it.

It had been Amirantha's idea for a while that somehow they should be able to see across the barrier into the demon kingdoms, but it had taken a long discussion with Gulamendis and his brother, Laromendis the Conjurer, to come up with a workable plan.

Amirantha had got the idea from two different things told to him, first by those in the Conclave of Jim Dasher's original encounter with the demon cult serving Dahun and the summoning of the image before the mass slaughter overseen by the mad magician Belasco. Then he had taken what Laromendis had told him of portals of scrying, "rift windows" as Amirantha thought of them, rifts you could look through, but not pass through.

Why not combine the two? They had been working on the theory, and more than once Gulamendis had regretted his brother's absence. The conjurer was again in Elvandar, one of those detailed by Tanderae to be an envoy to the Elf Queen's court. Amirantha knew some sort of Star Elf politics was at play, but the details were lost on him. He shook his head. "Well, I remember a story once where a smith forgot to use one last nail on a horse's shoe, and the shoe came off at the worst time and the horse went lame, and the rider of the horse was tossed and killed and failed to deliver a message that kept a king from riding into a trap, and his kingdom fell when he was killed. So a kingdom was lost, all for the want of a nail."

"So what nail did we overlook?"

Amirantha waved his hand at a pile of parchments they had written furiously on over the last few days. "We start again." Then he realized how tired he felt and said, "But perhaps tomorrow? Right now I could use a flagon of what passes for wine here."

The Taredhel did not ferment grapes but had devised a very potent drink from berries. It was called *leorwin*, and Amirantha was developing a taste for it. Or at least for its intoxicating effect.

"Agreed," said Gulamendis. "We'll resume work tomorrow; tonight, wine."

They left the room after extinguishing the lanterns. As they walked away a glowing wisp of vapor formed in the center of the ornate diagram on the floor. It coalesced into a shimmering oval through which a shape could be seen. The shape stopped moving, as if sensing something. It turned as if seeking the source of the sensation, then approached the window and leaned forward, reaching out. Two burning red eyes resolved themselves in a massive face as it grew closer. Then the mist vanished.

Amirantha saw the Lord Regent and most of the members of the Regent's Meet hurrying toward the massive hall used by the Star Elves as their nexus of portals. Gulamendis said,

"From the expression on his face, the Lord Regent is not in a mood to be social. Let's just—keep going—"

Unfortunately, the Lord Regent spotted them and waved them over. "I've been summoned by the Loremaster to the Portals, something to do with demons, he thinks. You two attend me."

Saying nothing, the two Demon Masters fell in behind the group. Amirantha glanced at Gulamendis, clear in his eyes the silent thought, *What now?*

The party mounted the broad stairs leading up to the huge building used to house all portals for the Taredhel. They entered and found several elves scurrying about, or as close to scurrying as Amirantha had seen them. A lithe and graceful race, the Taredhel always seemed to move with elegance and precision even when hurrying.

Tanderae, Loremaster of the Clans of the Seven Stars, was supervising a pair of galasmancers, those magicians responsible for creating portals, or rifts as humans called them.

The Lord Regent stopped a few feet away, his face an unreadable mask. "Yes?" he said in a tone that made it clear he was not pleased to have been summoned. Standing to his right and slightly behind him stood Kumal, Warleader of the Clans of the Seven Stars, and his expression mirrored his master's displeasure. Both were dressed in robes of state, deep purple with sleeves trimmed in yellow orange, every seam finished with silver thread. Gold frogs and loops gathered the robes in front. The Warleader's robe was sleeveless and open at the front, revealing his silver breastplate. He bore gold pauldrons on his shoulders with matching gold bracers on his wrists.

"Why was I summoned?" demanded the Lord Regent.

Tanderae said, "Sire, we have been sending scrying probes though the gates to our old homes, to see if the demons still hunt us. We began to experience difficulties doing so on the world Baladan. Something prevented us from keeping a clear portal long enough to send our scrying probe through, and we have just located the source of that disruption to our explorations."

"For this you practically command me to leave the Regent's Meet and rush here?" Looking pointedly at the Loremaster, he said, "A meeting from which you were not excused, Tanderae." His glance took note of the Loremaster's less formal attire, a simple dark blue robe and woven sandals. The only mark of his office was a silver brooch over his heart.

Tanderae bowed slightly. "This is why I was not at the Meet, Lord Regent, and why I sent for you despite knowing you were occupied with other vital matters. This really cannot wait."

Two senior galasmancers looked caught between regret at the summons and excitement over their find. Both knew the Lord Regent was quick to anger and slow to forgive, and it was often a task to know which mood would be upon him when bringing him news he did not wish to hear.

Tanderae ignored his lord's building displeasure and pointed to the frame that would generate a portal. Glancing to the elf next to him, he nodded.

Nicosia, the Chief Galasmancer, said, "My lord, our problems were not due to any failing on our part. Rather, the difficulties are because someone or something is trying to follow our last flight from Andcardia to . . . here."

Suddenly the Lord Regent's anger vanished and he became attentive, all hint of impatience gone. "You did well to summon me."

He glanced at the portal and saw four Sentinels in full battle array. Despite their ceremonial appearance—spotless purple-trimmed yellow tunics and clean white-lacquered steel breastplates and helmets—these were battle-hardened warriors, and the armor had endured its share of dents, scrapes, and bloodstains before being repaired and donned again. The Lord Regent nodded his respects, knowing that their presence indicated that the galasmancers had never lost sight of the dangers of opening portals to unknown worlds. One never knew what might come through if the portal was not fashioned properly. In theory, they were one-way devices, but brutal experience had taught them that wasn't always the case. The Lord Regent vaguely recalled one report claiming that the human magician Pug knew more about these things, a fact he found difficult to accept.

"Now," said the Lord Regent. "Explain."

Nicosia bowed. "My lord, the demons were able to follow us from the Hub World to Andcardia because we lingered too long in destroying all links between those worlds. It was a flaw in our design that what the humans call our 'rifts' were allowed to be traced from the Hub, allowing the demons to fashion their own portals as we were destroying ours. We are certain we destroyed all links between here and Andcardia in a timely fashion. We have had no hint of demon pursuit since we arrived here."

The Lord Regent was always pleased to hear that. They had returned to Home more than ten years ago and still he worried about the Demon Legion.

"But that doesn't mean they're not out looking for us," said the Warleader, his face set in an expression that could only be called contained rage. He had been first in the battle and had borne the responsibility for the loss of countless warriors of the Clans of the Seven Stars and it weighed heavily on him, even years after the conflict.

"Exactly," said Nicosia. He looked at Gulamendis and said, "Your demon summoner can probably better serve you as to describing their abilities, but we are not aware of any demon possessing sufficient magical abilities to construct a portal, or even exploit an existing one unless it is left open for use."

All eyes turned to Gulamendis who glanced at Amirantha. Seeing no help coming from the mute human, the elf said, "My lord, there is far more we don't know about demons than we do." He found himself bordering on falling into one of his favorite rants as to why that was: because those endeavoring to learn about demons were hunted down and persecuted under this Lord Regent's command, and the Circle of Light, the only body in Taredhel society dedicated to knowledge for the sake of knowledge, had been obliterated. "We know some are magic-users, mostly battle magic."

He glanced at Amirantha again, and this time the Warlock gave him a slight nod of agreement.

Gulamendis continued, "Since meeting Amirantha we've come to understand that the demon realm is a great deal more complex than we presumed."

The Lord Regent looked at the human Warlock and it was clear he expected a comment from him.

"My lord," said Amirantha, bowing his head slightly. It wasn't just that they were all taller by at least a head than he was, it was also that they were such cold, arrogant bastards: even the brothers, Gulamendis and Laromendis, were only less arrogant and more friendly in comparison to the rest. "Since first you arrived—"

"Returned," interrupted the Lord Regent.

" . . . returned," Amirantha amended, "Gulamendis and I have had the opportunity to compare our studies and discover more about the demons than either of us knew before. We believe we have only rudimentary knowledge of the demon realm. As Gulamendis says, it appears it is a far more complex and varied realm than we realized. We think now there may be different societies, some far more like those in our realm than we suspected. So, in short, there may be creatures we call 'demons' who may be intelligent enough and have the magic skills to open rift gates or even create new ones."

The Lord Regent looked as if something inside him had died. For all his faults, he passionately cared for his people. The idea of finally finding their ancestral home world, only to have to contend with the fear that once again the Clans of the Seven Stars might have to flee the Demon Legion, was devastating.

Sensing an opportunity, Amirantha continued, "My lord, it would be of immense benefit to all if we could uncover more about this terrible threat. Knowledge is the key."

The Lord Regent's eyes narrowed. "What do you propose, human?"

"Only that you allow Gulamendis to return with me for a time to my home island. There are other magicians, with different skills, who might be able to aid us in gaining more information on these demons." Seeing the Lord Regent begin to frown, he added quickly, "More useful information, I should have said."

The Lord Regent glanced at the Warleader, who barely moved, but Amirantha was beginning to learn to read the subtle expressions of the elves and suspected that the old warrior had just given his leader a shrug of uncertainty. Then the Lord Regent looked at his Loremaster.

Tanderae said, "It cannot do any harm, my lord. While none live who are more gifted in constructing portals" (which was probably not true, Amirantha thought, but now was not the time to digress on the topic of Pug's knowledge of rifts compared to that of the Star Elves), "the human magic-users are familiar with a great body of magical knowledge that has been for a time outside our areas of interest."

Both Gulamendis and Amirantha knew that for an elf, that was a dangerous statement, for implicit in it was that the reason the areas of magic study among the Taredhel were narrow was the Meet's obliteration of the Circle of Light. Magicians who were not in direct service to the Regent's Meet were seen as a threat.

If the Lord Regent sensed the reference and the implied criticism, he ignored it. "Very well. Leave at once."

Dismissed, Amirantha and Gulamendis turned and left the great hall. Moving down the stairs, Amirantha said, "What just happened?"

"Taredhel politics," said Gulamendis. "All of which is not of the moment. Now I get to study that damn odd book and talk to some people who might know a little more than I do." He actually smiled. "This is good."

This was as enthusiastic as Amirantha had ever seen him get.

Once the two Demon Masters had departed, the Lord Regent turned to Tanderae. "Now, what have you discovered about our exploration and why it was obstructed?"

The Loremaster indicated that the Chief Galasmancer should answer.

"The problems we have had were intermittent," said Nicosia, "and there seemed little consistency in how they were impacting our—"

Holding up his hand, the Lord Regent said, "I do not need to know the . . . specifics. I need to know *who* interferes with our work. Is it demons?"

"I think not," said Nicosia. "The magic used to reach out to find us is . . . alien. It is nothing like the magic the demons use."

"Some of our lost brethren?" asked the Warleader with the slightest hint of hope in his voice.

Tanderae said, "Probably not."

"We would recognize our own magic," said Nicosia. This is nothing we've encountered before. We know our own and demon portal-magic well, and I've studied some human craft, and would recognize that. This is . . . different."

"Then what do you propose?" asked the Lord Regent.

"It was the human who just left who gave me the idea, Lord: we can open a scrying portal, one that cannot be passed through but one that would allow us a glimpse of what was on the other side, a 'window' to use a metaphor."

The Lord Regent nodded. "I'm familiar with such. Laromendis the Conjurer used such to show me this world when he came back to Andcardia with word that he had found Home."

"Just so," said Nicosia. "But the difference here is that it is more difficult to do with a portal we didn't create. We are attempting to reach out and view the source of the interference, to see who reaches out to us." There was a hint of pride in their achievement in his voice.

"Then begin," said the Lord Regent, obviously unimpressed. "I want to know who is seeking us so that we may plan how to deal with them."

The two galasmancers turned and quickly set about placing crystals in receptacles at the base of the portal device. As they did so, the four Sentinels moved as if to make ready to intercept any intruder. They had heard Nicosia say that nothing could come through, but old training overrode logic.

The spell was quickly begun, and a humming filled the air. Suddenly a grey void appeared within the confines of the two massive wooden poles that rose up from the portal device's base, and then suddenly between them there was an oval of darkness.

But there was nothing there.

"What is that?" asked the Lord Regent. "Is it night there?"

"In a cavern, perhaps? Or an underground vault? We have used such in the past," suggested the Warleader.

Takesh, the younger of the two galasmancers, moved toward the device and peered closely into the darkness. "I can see tiny hints of movement. Wherever this place is, there is almost no light—"

Suddenly a shape loomed in the portal, and two things were instantly evident. First, that it was nothing previously perceived by any elf in the portal room; and second, that it was a thing of baleful aspect.

Size was impossible to judge as there was nothing else in the frame to lend it perspective, yet the Lord Regent and everyone else observing the creature sensed that it was large, even immense. It was a thing of black smoke and shadows, with a silhouette of roughly elflike proportions, but massive of shoulder and arm.

Everyone but Tanderae found themselves blinking as if somehow their vision was betraying them, as if the image was a trick of the light. As it neared, two malevolent red glowing eyes were revealed, and it peered into the room. The creature was a thing of pain and hopelessness, and it seemed, terrifyingly, to look deep into their souls. Then it leaned forward, revealing a crown of flames circling its head, shimmering crimson and orange, alight yet seeming to cast no illumination on the being's features.

"Can it see us?" asked the Lord Regent in almost a whisper.

Tanderae acted, and his sudden movement caused the Sentinels to draw their silver blades and raise their golden triangular shields as if the thing might somehow step through the portal. The Loremaster pushed aside the two transfixed galasmancers and pulled a crystal from the base of the device, causing the image instantly to collapse in on itself.

"What was that?" asked the Lord Regent.

Tanderae was visibly shaken. "My lord, if . . . I must speak with you alone."

"Why?" asked the Lord Regent.

The Loremaster leaned forward so that his face was next to his master's and whispered, "It is Forbidden."

"Leave us," commanded the Lord Regent, and the galasmancers and the Sentinels departed at once. He looked at the other ministers from the Meet and said, "You may go, too." All left but Kumal, whom the Lord Regent permitted to remain with another subtle nod.

Tanderae repeated, "What I know is from the Forbidden."

The Forbidden was the ancient lore, stemming from the time of indenture to the Dragon Lords, the Valheru, and it was denied to any but the Loremaster. Even as heir to the office and senior assistant, Tanderae was not allowed to see it. Upon achieving his office, prime among those charged with conserving the history and culture of the Taredhel, he had delved into the documents and tomes. He understood why much of what was contained within was denied the Taredhel, because it spoke of centuries of crushing slavery, with the Edhel being chattels, with all that entailed: death, rape, endless labor and brutality. The Valheru were cruel and capricious, and any reminder of that history had been subsumed into a vague "before" in the history taught to the citizenry, which focused on the rise of the Clans of the Seven Stars since they departed Midkemia for other worlds.

"I remember what I read in the Forbidden as if I had studied it all my life. What I fear is that which is seeking us is far worse than the Demon Legion. What you beheld was a child of the void, a member of a race known as the Dread."

"The Dread?" asked Kumal.

"A Dreadlord is a thing to make a Demon King tremble," said Tanderae. "Even the Valheru feared them."

"Truly?" said the Lord Regent.

"My lord, what I have learned from those humans, such as Amirantha, that I have come into contact with, who know anything about the Time Before, is that that which is recorded in the Forbidden is true.

"A single Dread is the equal of all but the most powerful demons we have encountered. A Master of the Dread would challenge a dozen of our best spellcasters and a score of Sentinels. A Dreadlord is a being who might challenge a great dragon or even the Valheru themselves . . ."

"What else?" asked the Lord Regent, visibly shaken.

"As little as we know of demons after our years of struggle, we know a wealth about them compared to what we know of the Dread. Almost no one who has confronted one has survived, and their realm is outside the normal concepts we have of all the various realms, but we do suspect that out there"—he waved vaguely at the now lifeless portal—"there exist even more powerful creatures, perhaps even a Dread king."

The Lord Regent was speechless. He stood silently for more than a minute forming his thoughts. "Do you think he sensed or saw us?"

"It is impossible to know. Something drew the creature to the other side of the portal. It may be that it emitted a sound or some energy that the creature sensed, but that it saw us, knew who we were, or where we were, I think not."

Again the Lord Regent was silent; then he said, "We will stop all work on the portals now."

The Warleader nodded in agreement.

To Tanderae, the Lord Regent said, "Do what you must, but your task now is to seek out lore and knowledge about these creatures from whatever source you can."

The Loremaster was thoughtful for a moment, then he said, "Then I must begin with Lord Tomas."

An expression of pure displeasure greeted that remark. The Lord Regent was still unhappy with his people's reaction to Lord Tomas's visit to E'bar when first the Taredhel had returned to Home, as they called Midkemia. It was a foundation of his beliefs that the Taredhel reject anything remotely related to their subservience to the Valheru, all that was recorded in the Forbidden. Yet ancient ties of blood were still strong. It had taken steel-willed self-control not to drop to his knees in Tomas's presence. It was clear to anyone who had any insight into that first meeting or perspective on the two leaders that a conflict would be inevitable.

Tanderae didn't fear that; he had no love for this Lord Regent and despised his Meet for their jealousy and obliteration of the Circle of Light. As a historian, he revered knowledge and learning. No, he feared what that confrontation would do to the Taredhel.

Finally, the Lord Regent said, "If you must, then go speak to him. But only you. I have concerns about this so-called Queen and her consort and their designs on us."

Saying nothing, the Loremaster of the Clans of the Seven Stars bowed slightly and withdrew, then turned and hurried away. He needed to catch up with Gulamendis and the human, for he knew now that certain things needed to be accomplished and that these things needed to be put in motion now.

Then he realized that even now it might be too late.

He fled through the night with the image of a black shape with burning red eyes haunting him.

17

SURRENDER

Sandreena groaned in pain.

She had been beaten, questioned, beaten again, drugged, and transported, to where she had no idea. She knew she was aboard a ship somewhere, deep in a dark, dirty, wet hold, chained to a wall. Something in the drugs she had been given had not only dulled her senses but seemed to deaden her ability to use some of the spiritual gifts her order had given her.

Unlike the priesthood of Dala, who used magic on a daily basis, the Sisters and Brothers of the Martial Order of the Shield of the Weak had rare access to the prayer power given by the Goddess. Most of that magic was dependent on rites practiced in the temples, or on artifacts given by the order, as well as some magic that was inherent in the training for combat. In fact, most of her training was in combat magic, useful when avoiding a crazed magician's energy blast or in banishing a demon back to the demon realm, but fairly useless when it came to escaping from the hold of a ship.

During her questioning, the topics had ranged from the obvious to the bizarre, and throughout she had endured the punishment and stuck to her original story: she was an itinerant Knight-Adamant of her order, which was true, who happened into a situation in which she had perceived something of interest, again true, and had chosen to investigate, again true; but she neglected certain details and volunteered no additional information.

Her captors seemed to know a fair bit about her, though, which corresponded with what the hired archer Ned had said when he mentioned they knew her name. She hadn't been interrogated by the man in the robe who had ordered Ned's killing, but by others who seemed content to ask her a series of questions that appeared unrelated and to beat her from time to time, seemingly irrespective of the answers she gave.

One in particular, a reed-thin man with a hooked nose and a heavily pockmarked face that he tried to hide with a thick beard, seemed to take pleasure from causing her pain. She had known his type when she had been a whore in a brothel in Krondor, and fortunately her beauty had prevented her from their predations, because the owner of the brothel had wanted her undamaged. But she remembered the other girls who had returned from time with those men bleeding, bruised, and sometimes cut and scarred. Many of them escaped into drugs, and a few took their own lives.

She thanked Dala every day for Brother Mathias, the Knight-Adamant who had saved her and brought her to the path of the Goddess. Though on days such as today where she awoke chained to the stinking hull of a ship, with dirty bilgewater splashing up on her every time the ship struck a comber bow-on, in a hold that contained enough rats to populate a sewer in Krondor, she wasn't sure how much thanks was appropriate.

She had no sense of time. Even the passing of night and day was impossible to judge, since she was so far below in the ship that night and day were not distinguishable. She did know her own body well enough to realize she had been there for at least a week. She was trained to go without food for a long time, and had to endure hunger before, and the way she felt now told her it had been at least three days since her last meal, a bowl of half-boiled millet and some salt pork.

She was thirsty, as well, and knew she had been given a cup of water some time the day before, but now she had to fight the urge to splash bilgewater up to her face and drink. There were spells used by the more gifted in her order to purify water, even, it was said, a few for the creation of food, though she had never met a Knight-Adamant who could achieve that. She wryly thought it would save so much time and coin if you could just whistle up a side of beef, some steaming potatoes, and a flagon of ale.

She sighed and felt her head clear. She had been left unattended for a long period of time as far as she could tell, but at least she was more lucid than she had been when taken captive. She had ridden to the shore with her captives and then someone had struck her hard across the back of the head, and she had awoken in this hold, stripped of her arms and armor and chained to this wall. But at least this time she had not been raped and thrown off a cliff.

She stretched and realized that her body didn't hurt as much as it had the day before. She still had aches and sore spots all over her body, as well as raw wrists and ankles from the chafing of the chains. She sat back, extending her legs as far as the chains would allow, not too far. At least she could sit with knees bent and her back against the hull. She closed her eyes and turned her mind to a healing focus she had learned early in her training.

Soon her body tingled, and she felt energy coursing through her. She hadn't felt like this since her last encounter with a healing sister of the Temple of Dala. She kept her eyes closed despite an urge to open them from surprise, and returned to her prayer, sinking into the feeling of wellness as she had been taught. It was a healing bath of the Goddess's powers, and she let it wash over her and consume her. She felt pain slip away, felt the fear slip away, and finally felt contentment seep into every fiber of her being.

At last even this feeling slipped away, and she regarded her wrists. The chafing had vanished, and her skin was intact. What bruises she had been able to see in the faint light allowed into this room by the single lantern hanging at the rear of the hold seemed to have vanished as well.

That was surprising.

She was, though, a worshipful devotee of the Goddess; and even if Dala had taken pity on her faithful servant and healed her, there were far more impressive miracles recorded by the temple. Sandreena had just never expected to be on the receiving end of even a little miracle. In fact, she often thought the Goddess's main means of instructing her daughter were by pain, obstacles, and frustration.

She sighed, feeling better than she had since her captivity, though she was still hungry enough to eat a hanging side of beef, raw. She stretched a little and found she was still weak and sore despite her healing magic. She sat back and thought about it. She knew she'd healed fast before, and she had survived a nearly lethal encounter with the Black Caps, thrown off a cliff onto rocks below in the surf. Up till now she had considered her survival a matter of luck. But perhaps it was more than luck. Perhaps it was the Goddess's gift.

She let out a long sigh. If only there was a spell to make shackles fall away. She was sure there was, but it was probably the province of the worshippers of Ban-ath (also called Kalkin), the God of Thieves.

The hatchway above opened and a rope ladder was lowered. From the shaft of light she deduced it was somewhere near midday. The skinny, pockmarked man came down the rope ladder again, and Sandreena began a mild meditation in anticipation of another beating.

Another man followed the first, the robed man she had encountered on the road where Ned was murdered, and behind him a third. Something different was about to happen, and Sandreena readied herself for death, if that was the Goddess's will. For one second she had an irrational urge to hit Amirantha one more time, and she let that go and the Warlock's image was replaced by an image of Grand Master Creegan. For a moment she was overwhelmed by a sudden sense of loss at the idea of never seeing him again. She forced herself to breathe slowly.

The three men came to stand before her, and the third man, the one she'd never seen before, said, "Release her."

The pocked man produced a key and unlocked her shackles. The third man was portly, though she suspected there was muscle underneath the fat given how nimbly he had come down that ladder. He had a gravelly voice and a nondescript face, round with brown eyes, a small nose, and a small mouth. He said to her, "Can you climb that ladder?"

She stood up slowly and found that her healing magic had given her enough strength not to stagger. "I can," she said, her voice sounding hoarse in her own ears.

"Come," is all the man said. He turned toward the ladder. The other two men, the one who had questioned her and the one she had met on the road, stood one on each side, ready to respond if she tried anything. Realizing she was still too weak to fight effectively, she judged it best to come peacefully. Besides, she knew they had weapons secreted upon them, and if she was to try for an escape, up on deck was better than here.

She walked slowly to the rope ladder and climbed up. As she reached the hatch above, two rough-looking sailors hauled her out onto the deck. She blinked at the bright afternoon sun after all the time she had spent in the hold. She appeared to be on a ship anchored offshore, amid a fleet of other ships, all in the process of being unloaded. There was a seemingly endless traffic of boats rowing to and from the shore, where a throng waited to haul the cargo up onto the beach. There, a camel caravan waited. As her eyes adjusted to the light she decided she was somewhere in the Bitter Sea between Ranom and Durbin. There was no other sea coast on Triagia that she knew of with blowing dunes and she seriously doubted she had been at sea long enough to be anchored off the coast of Novindus or Wiñet.

Twenty armed men were arrayed in a circle around her, and another dozen sailors were scattered through the rigging watching. The majority of them wore some sort of black headgear: hats, kepis, berets, or flop hats. She was certain she was in the hands of the Black Caps.

The third man said, "Come," and moved toward the stern of the ship. He entered a cabin in the stern-castle with two armed guards posted outside the door. Inside there was a table with food and wine on it. "Eat," he told her.

She hesitated only for a moment, then sat down and began to tear at the roast duck. She sipped the wine and pushed it away. In her weakened condition she knew wine would quickly go to her head. She asked, "Can I have water?"

He clapped his hands and one of the guards looked in, sword drawn and ready for trouble. "Bring water," her host said, and the guard disappeared. He was a hard-looking man, despite his ample girth, perhaps forty or fifty years of age, but there was nothing about him that wasn't dangerous. She'd seen his kind before, a stout man of jovial humor who could turn murderous in a moment and never lose his smile. He moved easily as a trained warrior might move. She saw scars, many of them, tiny ones on his hands that told of brawling and one on his neck where someone had almost taken his life. His eyes were dark as he studied her. His features were classic Keshian, but not Trueblood. He could pass for a man of the desert or any of the smaller cities around the Overn Deep. His accent was slight, as if he had traveled and spoke many languages.

They sat in silence waiting until a minute later the guard appeared with a large pitcher of water and a mug. Sandreena ignored the mug and drank straight from the pitcher. She hadn't realized how thirsty she had become chained in that hold.

"The wine not to your liking?" asked her host.

"I'm weak enough that two mouthfuls and I'll be drunk," said Sandreena.

He chuckled. "I've always admired one thing about all the martial orders, no matter which god or goddess they serve: no matter the circumstance, you're always ready to give up your life for a higher cause, and to ensure you're able to do that, you remain sober."

"I've had my drunken nights," said Sandreena. She could feel strength returning to her as she wolfed down the food.

"No doubt," said the man. He waited until she slowed her eating, then said, "To business. I have a proposition."

She put down the bowl of potatoes she had been devouring. "Yes?"

He sat back and looked at her. "I believe we have some common interests."

Her eyes widened. "Go on."

"Do you know who we are?"

She paused, then said, "I believe you to be part of an organization called the Black Caps by the people who live near the Peaks of the Quor."

"As good a name as any." He gazed out of the window, then said, "We are what is left of a very large organization that has been reduced to what you see here, a small band of desperate men and women. Let me indulge myself in a short history, if I may.

"Three hundred years ago, a baker by the name of Shamo Kabek resided in a small town a day's wagon ride from the city of Great Kesh. He and his two sons were plagued by a tax collector who had designs upon Shamo's young wife. Despite appeals to all and sundry, the tax collector continued to make unwelcome advances. One day returning from the mill with his week's flour, Shamo found the tax collector had assaulted his woman, in front of two very small and frightened boys."

Sandreena frowned; this story was designed to appeal to a member of her order, she knew, but what did it have to do with her current situation?

"Shamo confronted the tax collector. He was Keshian Trueblood, Shamo was not. Shamo assaulted the man and was sentenced to carry out hard labor for twenty years.

"As is common in such circumstances, he never lived long

enough to regain his freedom, dying in a mining accident six years later. But he left behind two very angry little boys." The man paused and poured himself a flagon of wine. "When they were little more than boys, the two slipped into the tax collector's house and cut his throat while he slept. Apparently someone else in the household awoke, for the next morning a city watchman found everyone in the house dead. The boys had been fast, efficient, and merciless. The tax collector's wife, daughter, small son, and three servants all paid the ultimate price for the tax collector's uncontrollable lust.

"Thus were the Nighthawks born."

"True?" asked Sandreena.

"True enough. There may be an embellishment or two. The boys may have ambushed the tax collector on the road and hit him over the head with a rock for all I know. But that is what we are taught when we pledge to the Brotherhood of Assassins."

"You're Nighthawks?"

"Nighthawks, yes. Black Caps as well. And we have several other names as well when it suits us. I am Nazir, and my title is Grand Master, much as your Creegan is in your order."

"Rumor is you were wiped out some years back in northern Kesh."

"A rumor that suited our purposes." He sighed. "We were for nearly two hundred years a very small organization. While it may seem a great many people in the world need killing, in fact there are far fewer than you might think; and even more to the point, there are even fewer who are willing to pay for the service. But there are always enough that a handful of trained killers can make a decent living. For years we traded on our reputation and made a good living. When we were not out plying our trade, we lived in a small town in the north of Kesh, the name I will not share in case this discussion does not bear fruit. We had families; we trained our sons, and our daughters were permitted only to marry those young men we brought into the Brotherhood.

"A hundred years ago that changed." He sighed again, as if it were a personal memory he was recounting, instead of lore. "What do you know of the Pantathians?"

Sandreena paused. She had eaten too fast, and her stomach was starting to object. She sat back. "Little. A race of serpent men, had something to do with the Great Uprising of the Dark Brotherhood, something like that?"

"Something like that," he said dryly. Sandreena could sense that something in this man was profoundly tired, almost defeated. He continued to look out of the window as he said, "They are an interesting people."

"Are? I was told they had been obliterated."

"Yes, you would hear that." He turned to face her. "The Pantathians were a created race, raised up from snakes by a being named Alma-Lodaka, of a race called in their tongue the Valheru. Our lore speaks of them as the Dragon Lords."

Now he had her full attention, her meal forgotten. "Few know about these things."

"In the common population, yes," agreed Nazir. "But as in all such organizations, the Brotherhood of Assassins has a strong dedication to tradition." He sighed. "But that tradition was subverted, distorted, and eventually used to enslave us, as we became a cult of demon worshippers."

"Dahun," said Sandreena.

"Yes," said Nazir with a smile. "You were there, when the gate was destroyed by the magician Pug and his . . . what do they call themselves? The Conclave? It is no matter. Many of us died, but there were others there as well."

"What does this have to do with the Pantathians?"

"I'll return to that in a moment. Those you call the Black Caps are those in the Brotherhood who eventually rejected the demon worship and tried to return to our old traditions."

"Tried?"

"Demons and their servants do not brook betrayal with grace. We were not permitted to withdraw quietly from their company, and many of our brotherhood were true believers. In short, we became less trusted, less privy to the inner workings of Dahun's servants' plans, and we were watched. Moreover, we were forced to take into our ranks mercenaries with no bond to us whatever. In short, it was an unhappy circumstance."

"Not to sound indifferent to all this, but why is it of any import to me?"

"Despite your belief in your goddess and her plan for you, I assume you would prefer to live, rather than the alternative?"

"A fair assumption," said Sandreena. Between her unexpected healing magic and this meal, she felt ready to fight again if the need arose.

"Then imagine how it was for those of us in the family to realize when we were children that our parents had bound us to serve a demon with our lives if need be. We were promised chieftaincies, eternal life, and . . ." He waved his hand. "The usual demented nonsense."

She said nothing.

"Over the years, there were those of us who recognized in each other that same sense that we were trapped in madness. A group of us managed over time to create a separate brotherhood within the larger one, a brotherhood dedicated to one thing: survival."

"Why not just leave?"

"Leave? Just walk away from our families and heritage?" He chuckled. "A few did, those whose temperament was ill suited to our trade and practices. Most were relegated to support roles, as cooks, menial labor, and tradesmen: useful in many ways, especially as eyes and ears throughout the Empire and Kingdoms.

"But at our heart we are family; even after the influx of those not related by blood, we still felt a kinship, because despite our differing reasons for being in the Brotherhood, by birth or recruitment, we swore an oath."

"To Dahun?"

He shook his head. "Before Dahun. We swore an oath to one another."

"And those who tried to leave?"

"Hunted down and executed."

"Hardly a familial act."

"Betrayal is the ultimate insult. And while you of the Shield of the Weak may be more kindly disposed toward those who elect to leave your ranks, not all templars are: the Hunters, the Arm of Vengeance? Those were the martial orders of the temples of Guis-wa, the Red-Jawed Hunter, and Kahooli, the God of Vengeance."

She shrugged. Martial orders of the temples often had their differences, sometimes ending in bloodshed. In ages past her own order had been involved in a years-long armed struggle with the Brotherhood of the Hammer, servants of the God of War, Tith-Onanka. "What am I to do with all of this? Why haven't you just hit me over the head and dropped me over the side?"

"There's use for you yet, Sister Sandreena." He put his hands on the desk and stood up. "We have no wish to bring the temples down on us. Sparing you may gain us a slight advantage in the future. Chaos runs amok across the lands, and armies are on the march. We of the Brotherhood of Assassins not caught up in that madness seek less strife, not more. Moreover, even were we to find a tiny corner of the world in which to hide, a jot of land no one else wanted where we could reside in relative peace and comfort, it would be small consolation to us that we were the most peaceful, comfortable inhabitants of a world when it came to an end."

"End?"

He sighed, sat back, and held up a finger, "And that brings me back to the Pantathians and to why we need you alive, and to the ultimate point of all this: I know why Dahun was trying to come to this world." He sighed. "And I need you, because there is something out there that terrified a Demon King, and we must eventually face it together."

18

EVACUATION

Martin shouted his command.

Every bowman on the walls fired down into the surging mass of Keshian soldiers storming the gate. For two days the gates had smoldered, as townsmen doused the back of them with water, slowing the burn, risking injury or death as the Keshians continued to hurl rocks at their target.

The second night Sergeant Ruther had quipped there probably wasn't a rock left on the beach a man could carry.

When the gate gave way, it collapsed suddenly. Martin barely had time to order the retreat into the keep. The last three days had been unnerving. Martin had read histories of sieges, specifically the previous siege of Crydee by the Tsurani, but they had lacked the great siege engines Kesh employed.

He had also read about sieges of other cities and what their population endured. Crydee was not built for such a thing. The legendary siege of Deep Taunton until relieved by Guy du Bas-Tyra had lasted months. That population had been near starvation when the Keshians had fled.

This siege would last perhaps two days longer, no more and possibly less. If the Keshians' rams were big enough and durable enough, they could be inside the keep before dawn tomorrow. If the defenders could fire a ram at each portcullis, the Keshians would be forced to withdraw, then clear away the debris and start again.

But Martin knew he was only buying time. Time in which he hoped his father and the relief column would arrive.

The Keshians were returning bow fire as best they could, and Martin knew that once they climbed the stairs up the inside of the wall, most of the defenders' height advantage would be lost. With no stonework to protect them from archers atop the keep, the Keshians would bring large shields and two well-trained men could crouch behind them, with their archer risking only a moment's exposure to shoot at the defenders. The Keshians wouldn't care how many defenders they killed; their purpose was to keep the bowmen from Crydee crouched behind their walls, heads down so the massive rams they brought were allowed to reach the outer portcullis of the barbican without those moving them taking too many casualties.

The last remnants of the outer wall's huge gates collapsed in a shower of char and sparks, and the Keshians now flooded into the bailey. Sergeant Ruther said, "We're going to run out of arrows before they run out of soldiers, sir."

"I know," said Martin, exhausted from a week of little sleep, scant food, and worry. He had ordered the last of those in the outer bailey into the castle an hour ago, and now they were locked in.

The keep's entrance was essentially an open box with double portcullises. Entering that box, attackers would be staring at a stone wall, and beyond the second iron portcullis were two doors, on the right and left.

Between the two portcullises was the "murder room." It was there attackers would be caught between the two heavy metal gates while bowmen from above could fire down through archer's slits. It would be in that thirty-five feet where the Keshians would lose the most men in the shortest amount of time if they tried to cross the space exposed to the archers and hot oil from above.

Martin knew they wouldn't. Their rams would have broad-tented roofs of wood and treated leather, slow to catch fire unless doused with the hottest flaming oil.

Once the second portcullis was down, the Keshians would have to choose which of the two reinforced wooden doors to assault. Either or both could be blocked or defended depending on what the occupants decided was the best choice, and the attackers would be forced to pick one and hope they could get through it without massive losses in the murder room. It was the genius of the design that the defenders had half a chance that attackers would waste valuable minutes and lives assaulting the wrong door.

Martin worried whether it would be long enough for his plan to work.

Sensing the young man's mood, the sergeant leaned forward and spoke so as not to be overheard despite the clamor all around. "You've done well, Martin. Given what you had to work with, your father couldn't have done better. No man could."

Martin was silent for a moment, knowing that Ruther wasn't just being kind. This was his first conflict against an organized force, but he had been a student of the Kingdom's military history as well as much of Kesh's, and he had known from the outset the best he could do was hold out for relief.

And that relief would not arrive in time. Should his father come riding up at this moment, the best result the defenders could hope for would be a momentary withdrawal by the attackers, before a resumed offensive would once again jeopardize the keep. The simple truth was the battle was lost.

He took another deep breath and said, "Sergeant, we cannot hold this position, as you well know. Father told me if victory eludes you, the next best choice is determining how you endure defeat."

"Sir?"

"Let's get organized. We're taking this garrison out from under their noses tonight."

The old sergeant smiled. "We go into the forests, hit them from there?"

"No, this coast is lost," said Martin. "We have no reason to think that Robert has held Carse or Morris has held Tulan. Even if they still hold them now, they'll be starved out within two months. They were no more prepared for this than we were." He let out a long breath. "I'm sure Prince Edward will have more to worry about than relieving the Far Coast any time soon."

"Where to then, sir?"

He put his hand on Ruther's shoulder. "I want the wounded and escorts out tonight, first, and send them east, up into the mountains, toward the southeast fork road to the Free Cities." The main road, a continuation of the King's Highway, ran due east to Ylith, but there was a traders' road that ran down to the nearest outpost of the Free Cities. "They'll shelter the wounded. And the rest of us will hold for a while longer, then we'll follow. Once away from here, we'll take the straight road to Ylith."

"A desperate plan, sir," said Ruther.

"Is there any other kind in these circumstances?" asked Martin with a faint smile. Then he asked, "Lady Bethany?"

"With the wounded, as always."

Martin shook his head at her stubborn defiance of his order to leave. He had only discovered she was still in the keep half a day after all the other women and children and the gravely wounded had departed.

Down below, the battle was going exactly as he had expected, with the Keshians setting up firing positions, their shields forming turtles, turned up toward the archers in the keep, preventing arrows from penetrating, though occasionally a shaft would find an exposed leg or foot and a man would go down, but for the most part the positions remained impervious to Crydee's archers. Soon they'd have teams of two and four men working their way up the steps leading to the walls where more archers would start clearing the keep's windows as best they could in anticipation of the assault on the entrance.

"Stay here and maintain discipline," said Martin. "I know the men are tired. If they move on the portcullis, send someone to get me."

"Sir," said Ruther with a slight smile. The Duke's second son had initially been overwhelmed by the responsibility of commanding the scant garrison, but he had grown into the role by the day.

He hurried downstairs and found Bethany boiling bandages in the kitchen. It was a time-honored tradition that if bandages were boiled and left to air dry, wounds bound with them were less likely to fester and require a healing priest. The keep at Crydee had a chapel in which any member of the household could pray to any deity, but there was no resident prelate. Old Father Taylor had died two years before, and Martin's father had been remiss in petitioning the Temple of Astalon in Krondor to send out another priest. There were shrines in the town, and traveling priests of several orders visited, but healing by magic means was no closer than Carse under normal circumstances.

Martin paused for a moment and watched Bethany. He had lost all anger at her defying his order to leave with their mothers and instead savored both her beauty and her industry.

Finally he took a breath and came over behind her. She sensed him and turned. "Could you grab that bundle of rags over there for me, please?"

He complied and when they were dumped into the pot, he said, "How many of the wounded can travel without help?"

"Not many. Those who can stand are still on the walls, some doing nothing more than showing the Keshians a face so they'll think there are more defenders than there are."

"We'll be evacuating the entire garrison after sundown. If a man is wounded but can help, I'll send him to you." His voice fell. "How many cannot be moved?"

Grimly she said, "None. Those have already died. Some will have to be carried, but all can move."

Martin sighed. "I want you to leave with the wounded. The first group."

"Where are we bound?"

"The Free Cities. The rest of us will go on to Yabon."

"You sent our mothers north to the elves."

"It is a safer destination . . . The elves would welcome our wounded and the woman and children, but as well as we've got on with them over the years, I have my doubts about them welcoming an army. Besides, I've got what's left of Crydee's garrison here, and most of us can still fight." His voice lowered. "We just can't fight here."

"You did the best you could," she said and put her hand on his arm. Then she kissed him lightly. "You really did, Martin."

He tried to smile. "Still, it's a bitter thing to lose your first battle."

She tried to look brave, but her eyes welled up with tears for his obvious pain. She grabbed him and hugged him. "You did do everything any man could do." Then she kissed him hard on the neck, then added, "And I do love you so very much even if you are a humorless fool at times."

Despite his fatigue and black mood, he was forced to chuckle. "Humorless fool? Faith, lady, I am injured."

"Just your vanity." She grinned. "I'll start making the wounded ready."

"Good. If I can't be back before the sergeant orders you out of the keep, stay well. I will find you when we are on the trail."

She nodded and went back to the boiling bandages. Using a large wooden spoon, she began picking up the dripping linen and hanging it in front of the fire to dry.

Martin did a quick inspection of the wounded himself, then hurried down to the basement and inspected the tunnel entrance. Two guards had been stationed in the subbasement against the possibility of the Keshians finding the exit in the forest beyond and coming up through the tunnel. It was a faint chance if the entrance had been covered properly when the first group had left days earlier, but it was still a possibility.

To one of the guards he said, "Go to the old tack room. You'll find a dozen bales of straw. Get some men to carry them down here. And then find a pot in the kitchen. So big." He made a circle with his hands showing something that would hold five or six quarts. "Fill it with lamp oil and bring it here."

"Sir," said the guard and hurried off.

Martin looked to the other guard and said, "How long have you been at this post?"

"Can't rightly say, sir." The guard was barely a boy, younger than Brendan from his appearance, and his uniform was ill-fitting.

Martin smiled. "I know every man in the garrison by sight. You're not from the garrison."

"No, sir. Name's Wilk. I'm the cobbler's son. The sergeant said it would look better should the Keshians come if those of us bearing arms had uniforms on. Something about rules of war and the like."

Martin nodded. It was a nice-sounding story, but not true. Civilian or soldier alike, he had no doubt what end would greet anyone found bearing arms when the Keshians finally broke into the castle. Though, given the reputation of Kesh's Dog Soldiers, he doubted that bearing arms would make much difference. Those found within would either be put to the sword or sold into slavery.

Martin said, "I'll see if I can get someone down to release you, Wilk. You should get a little rest. It's going to be a long night."

He hurried back to the topmost vantage point and found the Keshians had established two firing positions opposite the barbican and were trying to drive defenders off the roof. Sergeant Ruther was crouched down behind a merlon, and Martin waved for him to approach. The sergeant ran in a crouch, and when he was safely inside, Martin said, "We can't wait. Start the wounded on their way and then organize the men. When the time comes, I want everyone but your ten best archers to leave on my command and run to the tunnel."

"When will that be, sir?"

"When the Keshians get a ram through the outer portcullis, or I give the order, whichever is first."

"Sir."

"One more thing," said Martin.

"Sir?"

"If I don't make it out, make sure you keep everyone together. Head east, and with fortune, you'll encounter Father somewhere along the way. Report what was done here. If you don't encounter him, send the wounded to the Free Cities with Lady Bethany, and take the garrison to Yabon."

"We'll find your father, sir. You'll tell him yourself."

"If, Sergeant."

"Yes, sir."

"Now, form a flying company to gather in the great hall, twenty of your best men with short swords and knives, for close-in fighting."

Yes, sir," said Ruther. "I'll get twenty of my best brawlers and have them here straightaway."

Martin glanced around as if looking for something to do and realized that for the moment his only choice was to get back on the roof of the barbican and possibly take an arrow for no good reason, or sit and wait until he got word that the Keshian ram was in place at the outer portcullis.

He found an empty bench in a hall between the great hall and some guest quarters and sat down. He leaned against the wall and felt fatigue in his bones and wondered how he could be so wrung out when he'd barely lifted his sword save to command bow fire down on the Keshians. He supposed he could have taken a bow and stood in the crenels shooting down, exposing himself to enemy arrows, but given how bad he was as an archer, it would probably have been a waste of arrows. That they could not afford.

He wished desperately his father or Hal or both were here. Even the sight of Brendan would have cheered him. He was not the man to be in command. He barely considered himself a man, despite having passed six summers since his "manhood" day on his fourteenth Banapis Festival. Yes, he had drawn enemy blood before, but those were rabble: goblins and outlaws. This? This was war, and opposing him was a seasoned Keshian commander with battle-hardened soldiers at his disposal.

When he thought of war, he thought of the great battles told of in the archives. When Borric I had charged across the plains northwest of Salador, he was outnumbered by half again as many soldiers under Jon the Pretender. Martin had wondered more than once if he had been a member of the Congress of Lords, which side he would have chosen. Borric had the claim, as eldest son of the King's younger brother, but Jon had been Borric's bastard cousin and was immensely popular. History was written by the victors, his old teachers had told Martin, so the chronicles were canted in Borric's favor, but there was enough to tell a careful reader that Jon's claim was no less a claim.

When he thought of warfare, Martin remembered reading the various accounts of the siege of Crydee, during what was commonly known as the Riftwar, the Tsurani invasion. It was all the more vivid because he could walk the walls and visit each location recounted in the narrations. As a youngster he used to take the text and stand where Arutha was when Fannon was felled by an arrow and walk to where the Prince had stood rallying his soldiers to repulse wave after wave of attackers.

Martin had always been Arutha in his imagination, despite his own many-great-grandfather and namesake, later Duke Martin, being a significant figure of the battle.

He couldn't imagine how Arutha would have dealt with this situation, being forced to withdraw in the face of overwhelming odds. He closed his eyes for a moment.

In what seemed to be a second later, Bethany was shaking him awake. "It's sundown and the Keshians haven't come yet," she said, softly. "The wounded are ready to leave."

He blinked and shook his head, not entirely awake.

She repeated herself and he stood. "Sorry, I fell asleep."

"Obviously." She slipped her arm through his. "You drive yourself too hard."

"Just before I fell asleep, I was wondering what Prince Arutha would have done in my place."

"Exactly what you're doing: trying to make the best of a terrible situation."

He smiled tiredly. "Let's get started." He disentangled his arm from hers and led her down to the subbasement, where six litters were being carried by a dozen men.

Sergeant Ruther said, "Ready, sir."

"Begin," said Martin.

The tunnel was low, so the litter bearers had to bend forward a little, but they managed to get the six men too wounded to walk through. Then those who could walk began to enter the dark maw of the tunnel.

After the last of them had gone through, Martin turned to Bethany. "Now, I want you to round up the few remaining women, and I want you out that tunnel within the half hour." When she seemed ready to object, he said, "It appears the Keshians may wait until first light to begin the assault on the keep itself, so we shall all be far from here when they do."

"You're coming after us?"

He nodded. "I will be the last to leave, but I will leave, that is a promise."

She didn't appear convinced, but nodded. "Just don't do anything heroic and foolish so that someone writes some damned chronicle about you one day."

"That's unlikely," said Martin with a fatigued smile. "Now, go."

She ran up the stairs, and the sergeant said, "Sir, if I may?"

"Sergeant?"

"Let me be the last to leave, sir."

"Why?"

"Three reasons, sir, if you don't mind the truth."

"I'll probably mind, but say on anyway, Ruther."

"Thank you, sir. First of all, you're tired beyond thinking, and men that tired do not have the wits the gods gave a turnip. You might make mistakes that will get men killed.

"Second, you're young and just might do what Lady Bethany said, try something heroic and get yourself killed, and I do not want to explain to your father how I managed to let that happen.

"Third, if you're going to marry that girl, you should make sure you both stay alive."

"Marry—?"

"Do you think no one else noticed how you are when she's around all these years, Martin?" Ruther gripped the young man's shoulder. "Maybe your father was too busy being Duke to pay attention to his sons as close as he could—heaven knows I think of him as a good man and wise ruler, but fathers sometimes miss things about their sons. But no one who's seen you around Bethany since you were fifteen could mistake how you felt about her, and it seems she feels the same way about you."

"Well, her father and mine may have different plans," said Martin.

"That may well be, but you will have no chance to discuss the matter with your father if you're lying facedown on the stones of this keep in a pool of your own blood, now will you?"

Martin couldn't think. "Very well, how will you proceed if I allow you to be last out?"

"That flying squad you asked for, of brawlers and hooligans. Brilliant. We will hit hard any company that comes through this side of the barbican's rear door; we'll barricade the other side door so they will choose this one. We'll fight as we retreat, and we'll dump a few traps along the way so we can get to the basement. We'll fire the hay along the way, and if we're lucky, the tunnel will collapse on a host of them when we're out the other end."

"Sounds like a wonderful plan, Sergeant," said Martin. "That's exactly what I plan on doing. Now go get those twenty brawlers to rest a bit, organize some traps for me, and when you have finished, I want you personally to see that Bethany, the other women, and half the garrison leave. It's your charge to see them safely to my father or Yabon. Understood?"

"You're not going to let me talk you out of this, are you?"

"Understood?" repeated Martin, his eyes narrowing.

"Understood, sir."

The sergeant led the way out of the subbasement, and Martin asked as they climbed the stairs, "How do you do it, Ruther?"

"Do what, sir?"

"Stay awake for four days."

"I don't. You learn to grab sleep when you can, a few minutes here, a half hour there, sitting in the corner, lying under a table, whenever you can."

"I have yet to learn the knack."

"Go to your room," said Ruther softly. "Take at least an hour. I'll bid the Lady Bethany farewell for you; she'll know better than anyone you need sleep more than a bittersweet good-bye. I'll wake you before dawn. If you're going to survive your delay, young prince, you'll need your wits about you."

Martin said nothing, then nodded once and turned toward his room when they reached the top of the stairs. He half staggered to his quarters, pushed open the door, and fell face-first across the bed.

He was deep in sleep when Bethany came in, saw him there, removed his boots for him without waking him, and covered him with a blanket. She bestowed a light kiss on his face, whispered good-bye, then closed the door behind her.

19

RETREAT

The portcullis crashed loudly to the stone floor.

Martin was ready, his men arrayed outside the unblocked side door. He signaled for them to wait.

The Keshians had brought up the first of two rams at dawn, and it had been a very well-built one. An enormous log suspended from heavy ropes and chains and a massive iron boot covered the front end of the log. A wooden "tent" roof protected the men pushing it, a dozen crouched over long wooden poles that ran through the frame of the massive war engine.

Horses had been used to pull it up the hill from the town below, but when they came into the courtyard, they released the ropes used to pull the device and their riders had peeled off to the right and left, leaving it for the two dozen men under the protective roof to keep it moving forward until it slammed into the outer iron portcullis.

Then the pounding began.

A portcullis's first grace is that it is heavy. The thick iron bars require a hoist and a winch inside the barbican, tantalizingly close but just out of reach. So the portcullis must be knocked down, literally pounded until it folds in on itself and shatters, releasing the attackers into the murder room.

Then the second portcullis must be destroyed, while the defenders above are free to fire arrows or pour boiling oil on the attackers.

The first ram had burned, and it had taken most of a day for the Keshians to clear it away and bring up their second. But the first had done enough damage to the inner portcullis that Martin knew it would not endure until night.

Some time late in the day, Kesh's Dog Soldiers would be within Crydee Keep.

Martin had expended most of his arrows and a lot of energy convincing the Keshians that the defenders were still inside in numbers. Men had run from position to position firing off the roofs of the keep and barbican at enemy archers on the wall, shouting from various locations, trying to give the impression of being in two places at once. At one point Martin had shouted orders for a sally, and a squad of Keshians had actually retreated behind their barricade and waited for nearly half an hour for a counterattack that never came.

Once the outer portcullis had come down, he had ordered the men off the roof. Two had occasionally shot arrows down into the murder room, and then the fiery oil had been poured down on the first ram.

Once that was ablaze, he had ordered them to stand down and rest. The first portcullis had endured until midday, but he knew the Keshians would breach the second before midafternoon.

Inside the keep Martin shouted random, meaningless orders while his men rested. Occasionally one of the men would shout a faux reply, trying to make it seem as if men inside the keep were waiting.

Martin made ready, knowing that the second iron portcullis was about to fail. Once it was down, the Keshians would tie ropes to it and drag away the impediment to their attack. Then they would be faced with a massive stone wall with two entrances into the building. The one on their right had been blocked with every piece of furniture, fallen stones, and debris that had come to hand to stop that door from opening.

The left door, the one behind which Martin and his twenty men waited, had been blocked just enough for Martin to make it appear the garrison was putting up a last, desperate fight.

The crash of the last gate was accompanied by the shout of Keshian Dog Soldiers outside. They apparently felt as if the day was already theirs, perhaps were even thinking the remaining garrison was holed up inside behind makeshift barricades, waiting for the final slaughter.

Suddenly there was pounding on the door before them and Martin turned. "Get ready."

His twenty men were arrayed in two lines, with their backs to the corridor leading to the kitchen and the subbasement below. The first ten bore shields, and the second bows and arrows, despite few of them being skilled archers.

A rhythmic pounding began on the doors. It would be only a matter of minutes before the one on the attackers' left, behind which the defenders waited, would begin to buckle.

Martin's mad plan was about to begin and he prayed for a brief moment to Ruthia, Goddess of Luck, to take pity on him and his men.

The timbers on the heavy wooden doors shook and splintered around the hinges, and the large wooden bar cracked. Mortar fragments rained down from the stonework above the supports, filling the air before the door with a fine haze of dust.

"Easy," said Martin. "Wait."

Another thud and the bar cracked more, torquing itself apart. "Wait," he repeated.

With a loud thud and the protest of iron fittings being ripped out of masonry, the hinges were pulled loose. For a pregnant moment the door hung slightly ajar, the splintering bar holding it against the door on one side.

"Now!"

Crydee bowmen fired into the narrow opening, and the Keshian attackers screamed in pain and anger. The bowmen ran to the second position, while the ten men with shields crashed against those Keshians trying to enter the keep.

Martin was behind them, his sword held high as he struck downward over his men's shields, his only objective to slow the Keshians down for one more minute.

It was mad chaos at the door, with men grunting, cursing, shouting, and bleeding. The brawlers selected by Ruther were skilled at close fighting, and from behind their shields they were content to wait for any sign of exposed Keshian flesh and slice at it with daggers and dirks, not trying to kill, only to make the enemy bleed, and to slow them down.

The Keshian Dog Soldiers all wore iron cuirasses, leaving their arms and shoulders exposed, while the Crydee defenders wore mail coifs over mail shirts with sleeves down to their wrists. No fatal blows resulted from the first two minutes of fighting, but a lot of Keshians would be sporting scars on their arms, shoulders, and faces if they survived the day.

There was a moment when the fight seemed to take a breath, as the Keshians collectively pulled back to adjust the crowding at the doorway.

"Back!" shouted Martin, and the ten men and he turned, then sped down the hallway toward the kitchen. Martin waited for a moment, allowing the others to pass him. Then the door finally fell to the stones, and the Keshians came boiling through the entrance.

"Down!" Martin yelled, and the men before him all knelt while a flight of ten arrows sped overhead, striking the first two Dog Soldiers. The others ducked back inside the shelter of the barbican or crouched low, but it gave Martin and his men another moment. "Now!"

Hanging above Martin in a net were three bales of straw soaked in oil. A pair of fire arrows were shot into them, setting the bundles ablaze. The rope holding the bales was cut and the pile came down. When it struck the floor, it exploded into a massive ball of fire, forming a curtain of flames across the hall that would halt the Keshians for another two or three minutes.

Martin crawled furiously forward, having been missed by the falling bales by less than a yard. He felt the heat wash over him as he gained his feet and started to run into the kitchen. The straw would burn out quickly, and soon the Keshians would be kicking the smoldering remnants out of their way.

Martin hurled himself down the stairs to the first basement. The entire room had been filled with more oil-soaked straw with every loose piece of timber, furniture from the rooms above, and kindling they could find stacked on top. A soldier waited for him, torch in hand.

As he reached the man, he said, "Now!" and the soldier threw the torch as far across the basement as he could, and then both of them dived through the portal while two others pulled the heavy wooden door shut behind them.

As they secured the door with a large brace jammed into place they heard the whooshing sound of the flames igniting. "We don't have much time," said Martin.

They ran down the steps to the smaller subbasement where men were already entering the escape tunnel. He motioned for the man before him to enter and waited until he vanished from sight. Shouting after him he cried, "Clear the tunnel as fast as you can."

He could hear the crackle of flames above and knew that it would be close to a half hour before the Keshians could brave the fire in the basement below the kitchen. Martin wasn't going to give them a half hour.

He waited until he was certain that his men were more than halfway through the tunnel, then went to a large chain in the corner of the room. It led up through a series of pulleys in the wall to the roof of the tower known as the "Magician's Tower" because it was where Pug and his mentor, the magician Kulgan, had resided decades before. He hauled down hard on it and, as he had suspected, was met with resistance because the old mechanism hadn't been used in almost a century. His grandfather had tested it once, but since then the old valvework at the top of the tower had remained untested. Martin hoped it still worked and that the trap his ancestor had devised would still be effective.

At the very top of the Magician's Tower a mechanism released a canister of twenty gallons of what was called "Quegan Fire": a mix of naphthaline, sulfur, limestone, and fine coal dust. This would create a massive fireball when dropped into the flames in the keep entrance, two floors above Martin's head. It had been constructed as a last resort, a means of denying the castle to an invader.

As soon as Martin felt the click of the mechanism engage, he yanked hard, then sprinted for the entrance. He was forced to make his way bent forward, for the tunnel was too low for him to run upright. He reached the first marker and grabbed the two ropes attached to the supports for the overhead shoring. He hauled on them and felt earth fall on him and heard timbers creaking. A short moment later he felt a compression of the air as the tunnel collapsed behind him. Then there was a dull thud and he knew the Quegan Fire canister had exploded.

It would burn hotter than a blacksmith's forge. Any man in the keep not able to reach a door would be incinerated or die as the air was sucked from his lungs by the voracious fireball. If, as Martin suspected, the Keshians had pressed hard expecting desperate resistance in the keep, the Keshian commander would just have lost at least two hundred Dog Soldiers in the conflagration.

Martin reached a second set of ropes and pulled them, even though he knew the first fall had worked. More earth fell as he hurried along.

It seemed to take forever to get out of the tunnel and then suddenly he was outside. Instantly a pair of arms wrapped around him, and Bethany was hugging the breath out of him.

He hugged her back then held her at arm's length. "I thought I told you to leave with the wounded, again?"

"You did, again." She was dressed in the same hunting clothes she had worn when last she had come to Crydee, when her arrow had taken down the wyvern that he and Brendan had faced.

"Why are you still here?"

"Waiting for you," she said, as if that was all the explanation needed.

He glanced around and saw that Sergeant Ruther was there as well, with an additional ten men along with the twenty who had preceded Martin through the tunnel. "Report," said Martin.

"Everyone safely out, sir." Ruther smiled. "Everyone," he repeated.

Martin looked back, but his view of the keep was blocked by the large rise from which the tunnel exited. He climbed up on top of it, over the reinforced door. He could not quite make out the keep through the trees between himself and the castle, but he could see a massive pillar of dark smoke rising overhead.

Bethany came to stand beside him and said, "Now?"

"Now we head east. The Keshian commander needs to regroup and reorganize. We may steal a day on him, no more."

He took her by the hand and led her down from the rise.

Sergeant Ruther said, "That's a nasty business old Duke Martin built into the keep, isn't it?"

"According to the histories, he had some experience with Quegan Fire used to destroy a position so that the enemy couldn't occupy it," said Martin. "The retreat from Armengar; I read his notes on why he installed it, how to maintain it, and when to use it."

With a grin the sergeant said, "It's a lovely thing you're such a fine student, sir."

Martin shook his head in self-disgust. "Fine student? I lost the keep in less than a week. Even the Tsurani couldn't take it in months."

Sergeant Ruther's expression turned stern. "You're tired, young sir, but that's no excuse for losing your perspective.

You held out for a week with less than a hundred trained soldiers and a handful of boys and old men.

"Prince Arutha had Swordmaster Fannon and Sergeant Gardan, Martin Longbow himself, and over three hundred trained soldiers, and another three hundred men of the town. You're not the only one who's read some history." He put his hand on Martin's shoulder. "You got everyone out, sir. From the start of the siege until today you've lost two men, both on the wall before the retreat, and three unfortunate town lads who were by them, and suffered less than two dozen wounded. Even some I thought wouldn't make it did, thanks in great part to Lady Bethany's tender care." His voice became hoarse. "Think about it. Two soldiers, no more. Now, put on a stern face and lead this lot. We still have a long way to go to reach safety."

Martin took a deep breath. "Who do we have?"

"Your twenty, my ten, and the lady."

Martin glanced at Bethany and grinned. "Well, at least we have one decent archer with us."

"That we do."

"East now, and let's put as much distance between us and Crydee as possible. That Keshian commander will have to wait a fair bit before that fire cools off enough to inspect the wreckage of the keep."

"True enough," said Ruther. "Never seen anything burn hotter than Quegan Fire."

"But once he does he's going to notice there are only Keshian bodies in the rubble and if he bothers to dig, he'll find the subbasement, or even if he doesn't, he'll assume there was such a way out and come looking for us. We'll go east and if we don't encounter Father and his column before we get to the Jonril cutoff, we'll head to the garrison there and hunker down until he does show up. We'll send a lookout up to the cutoff, and when he arrives, we'll join him. If he doesn't . . . That will mean either the fast riders didn't overtake Father before Ylith or were killed before they reached him. If we don't hear from Father within ten days, we move on to Ylith."

The sergeant nodded. "Wise plan."

They moved out along a game trail that would lead them to the eastern road two miles away. Once there it would be easier to move, but they would be in the open, exposed. Much of the heavy forest to the north and south of the road had been cleared for farmsteads, cattle pasture, and sheep meadows.

As they moved along the trail, Martin asked Sergeant Ruther, "How are we for provisions?"

"Well enough. Each man carries a bag of food and a skin of water, enough so that we won't have to worry about starving until we reach safety."

"Any sign of Keshians while you waited?"

"None to speak of. One bunch came looping around behind us an hour before you set the trap. Small patrol, about six men. We let them go by, and they had no idea we were near. I don't think this particular lot has any forest skills. Made enough noise that we heard them coming and were safely hidden. Don't speak their language but they were jabbering about something like a bunch of fishwives." He glanced around. "Nothing since then."

They continued to move, strung out in loose formation, moving purposefully and as quietly as possible. The sounds of chaos from Crydee quickly fell behind them, and they reached the road without incident.

"We've a full six hours of good light," said Martin. "Let's rest for a few minutes, then get moving." He glanced at Ruther. "I want a man ahead and a man behind. Your fastest runner behind, for if we're overtaken, he'll need to scurry along."

"Jackson Currie!" shouted the sergeant.

A slender soldier ran up, "Sir!"

"Run down the road, see what's behind us, and linger a bit. Don't catch us up until sundown, there's a good lad."

The soldier nodded, saluted, and ran off down the road. Sergeant Ruther detailed another soldier to go ahead and act as point, while the remainder of the company rested a little. At last Martin said, "Let's go."

They began their long march from their lost home to what they hoped would be safety.

The rear guard came racing up the road, shouting, "Riders!"

Martin hesitated only for a second, then he motioned for everyone to sprint into the trees and brush, a dozen yards off the road down a slope. They half ran, half tumbled into the thicket and lay motionless.

Peering through the undergrowth, Martin saw a dozen riders coming up the road from Crydee. They were loping along and glancing from side to side occasionally, but not showing any particular urgency or alertness. They were dressed in a similar fashion to the Dog Soldiers who had stormed the keep, except that instead of a steel spike atop their helms, they had a sharp blade running fore and aft. Their helmets had nose guards and their cloaks were very dark blue, almost black, thrown back to reveal the usual cuirass and flannel shirt beneath, and heavy trousers tucked into their boots.

The one unusual mark was a belt of leopardskin that was worn around the lower edge of the helmet where the neckguard chain was attached.

After they rode past, Ruther said, "I've heard of them. They're called the Leopards." He rolled over onto one side and continued to whisper. "I didn't see horses unloaded, and the Keshians didn't appear to have any. We certainly didn't leave any ridable mounts behind: your father took them all."

"They must have off-loaded them yesterday, before the final assault."

"But what is an outfit like that doing riding down the road out here?"

"Looking for us," said Bethany from behind Martin.

"No," said Sergeant Ruther. "I mean of all the places Kesh could have chosen to send a top-of-the-line command of cavalry like the Leopards, why the Far Coast? You'd think they'd send them to Krondor or maybe into the Vale where the fighting is bound to be heaviest."

Martin said, "Unless you want them where they didn't expect much resistance." He looked thoughtful. Eventually he said, "Sergeant, I want you to take to the forest and move parallel to the road. Those Keshians aren't going to be patrolling for more than another hour so you should catch them coming back, then take to the road and keep going. I'll catch up with you as soon as I can."

Bethany grabbed his arm from behind. "Where do you think you're going?"

"Back to Crydee." He gently pulled away from her and stood up. Kneeling before she could rise, he gave her a quick kiss and said, "I have an idea and I need to see what is going on in the town. Now, go with Sergeant Ruther and try not to cause too much trouble." Then he was off, darting through the trees.

With a sigh, Ruther stood and extended his hand down to Bethany. When she slapped it aside, he chuckled and turned to the line of men in the woods. He covered his mouth in the sign for "no talking," pointed into the woods, then pointed toward them, then back to himself, telling them to fall in behind and follow him.

"Do you—" began Bethany.

The sergeant quickly but gently covered her mouth. "No talking, Lady Bethany. Now, let's go."

Before she could say another word, he moved into the trees and the other men began to follow.

Martin ran down the road and then slowed to a trot. He'd have to pace himself or he'd collapse before he even knew exhaustion had hit him. He was young and fit, but he had been without sleep for the better part of three days, had hardly eaten, and had endured his first battle. He stopped, put his hands on his knees, and took a deep breath. He was feeling dizzy. Certainly not a good sign.

He slowed his breathing for a moment, then heard voices coming from the west. His fatigue forgotten, he hurried down the side of the road to a stand of trees and moved parallel to the road as best he could.

He could smell char and smoke and knew the breeze from the harbor was blowing it toward him. At least the Keshians wouldn't smell him coming.

He saw a small copse of wild apple trees and grabbed one of the fruits. It was slightly sour, but he needed the nourishment. He chewed slowly, not wanting to give himself a stomachache.

It took him nearly an hour to work his way carefully northward, first crossing the main road, then moving along a series of game trails through thinning woodlands. He and his brothers had played here as children, then later had hunted in this vicinity.

Crydee Harbor was marked at the southern end by a pinnacle of rock and a rising bluff known as Sailors' Grief. To the north the circle was suddenly cut off by a massive bluff with a fifty-foot drop to the beach below. From the junction of that bluff and beach a series of stones that jutted above the water even at high tide ran out to a small island. That rocky path and island had been filled in with quarried stones until a man-made jetty with dock had been fashioned, named Longpoint. At the end of it rose up the Longpoint Lighthouse.

The bluffs to the north of Longpoint had served the first Duke and his son as a makeshift lighthouse and lookout station until a proper lighthouse had been constructed. On top of the bluffs the stones of that old watch post still rested.

Martin reached that point after an hour of climbing and looked down onto Crydee Harbor. "Gods!" he said aloud.

What looked to be at least two hundred Keshian ships were at anchor. He could see two more sailing out to sea, and another two sailing in while about thirty ships in the harbor were being serviced by a dozen or more ferries, carrying cargo to the docks. The activity was frenzied and so widespread that the Keshians were off-loading cargo onto the rocky shore to the south of the town's docks, and thence to the rickety smaller quay before the fishing community directly below where Martin stood.

But what astonished him the most was that more and more people were coming ashore. A second wave of men, women, and children were entering Crydee Town, and from their varied skin color and garb they were obviously from many different places in Kesh. Many of them had animals, oxen pulling wagons, horses on leads—not warhorses but dray animals—donkeys, mules, and cages of chickens and geese. Even a brace of spitting angry camels were being led into the town.

Martin stood in stunned amazement.

He sat down and took a deep breath, collecting his thoughts. Nothing he saw below him made sense. Out of the three brothers, he was the student of history. More than just studying battles and the lines of nobles, he had delved into the causes of war and the results.

Kesh had expanded rapidly over the three preceding centuries, its people moving across the Straits of Darkness from Elarial up to what was now Tulan. They had built their first garrison there, then an expedition north from there had found the wonderful harbor at Carse and the smaller harbor below. A fourth harborage far to the north also was found, and at one point Kesh tried to build there, calling it Birka. But that settlement had been the first obliterated by the dark elves, the Brotherhood of the Dark Path as humans came to call them.

History showed that Kesh had expanded too far and too fast, and it could not support the ancient province of Bosania, as Crydee and the Free Cities were called. The coast of the Bitter Sea colonies prospered, so that when Kesh withdrew, its people had been strong enough to resist the expansion westward of the Kingdom of the Isles. But it had been Martin's ancestor who had ridden over the very trail from Ylith that his men were now fleeing down, to arrive here at Crydee.

The only reason Crydee had become the capital of the duchy was that his ancestor had taken the old Keshian fortification and built upon it, waging a ten-year campaign to conquer Carse and then Tulan. When it was over, Queg was an independent kingdom, the colonies in Natal had become the

Free Cities, Ylith had become the southernmost city of Yabon Province, and that had remained the status quo for more than two hundred years.

Now Kesh was back, and it was clear the Keshians were reclaiming all of ancient Bosania. They were not only bringing their armies, they were bringing in colonists hard on their heels. They were obviously going to be bringing in their own logistical support, occupying farms and pastures, logging camps and cutting mills, mines, and fisheries with Keshians.

Martin was no expert on such subjects, but it looked to him as if they had brought enough of Kesh with them that they could occupy the entire Duchy of Crydee ... He stopped.

Suddenly he knew exactly what Kesh was doing. If Martin desired one thing in life as much as Bethany's kiss, it would be word from her father as to what was occurring in Carse. Because if he was to wager everything he had, he would bet that the entire Keshian invasion force had sailed right past Carse and Tulan, perhaps leaving a screen of ships to keep the Kingdom warships bottled up in those two harbors, and then landed here. They weren't going to occupy all of Crydee, just the north!

And he knew why.

Wishing he could just lie down here on the rocks and sleep for a week, Martin pushed aside his exhaustion and started back down the hill. Glancing at the midday sun, he considered that with luck he might be able to overtake his men and Bethany after sunset.

He ran down the slopes from the bluffs into the woods below.

As he reached a drop in the road, in darkness, Martin could make out fires ahead and hear the sound of horses. He wondered if it might be those Keshians Ruther called "the Leopards," and if so, where were Bethany, Ruther, and the men?

He crept up to the edge of the clearing and saw men there in the brown tabards of Crydee. Feeling relief flood through him, he shouted, "Hello, the camp! Coming in!"

One step later he was surrounded by guards, who took a moment to recognize him. "Martin!" they greeted him.

Bethany was sitting near the fire next to Brendan. Martin smiled and walked over as quickly as he could. He smelled food cooking and was suddenly ravenous.

His brother rose and came around the campfire to embrace him. "Martin, I was worried."

"We all were," said Bethany, and Martin saw an expression on her face that made his heart sink.

He looked around and realized something momentous. "Where's Father?" he asked quietly, knowing the answer before it came.

Brendan looked to the east along the road. "Goblin raiders. They jumped us before they realized how many we were. One wounded Father and he fainted, but when he fell . . . he broke his neck."

Sergeant Magwin joined them. "We buried him near the road, Martin, and marked it well. When this is over, we'll fetch him home."

Martin felt empty inside. Of all the things he had imagined, his father not being at the head of this column had never been one of them. He sat down next to Bethany, and a plate of food and skin of water was presented to him. "Eat, drink," she said. "I know you've no stomach after such news, but you must revive yourself."

Martin was numb. Exhaustion, fear, and the stress of battle had worn him to a nub inside. He knew he should be weeping or shouting in rage or something at the news of his father's death, yet he felt almost nothing, as if the sense of loss was a distant thing. He was silent for a long moment, then just said, "Father?" He let out a long sigh and took the food.

"What of Crydee?" asked Brendan.

"They're not simply landing an invasion force. They're moving a colony in."

"Colony?" asked Ruther.

"Those men, women, and children that landed with the first wave were just the beginning. Hundreds, maybe thousands more are sitting in ships off the coast waiting to be off-loaded."

"But why? Of all the places in the Kingdom, why the Far Coast?" asked Brendan.

"Not the Far Coast," answered Martin. He forced himself to chew and swallow a spoonful of tough meat in a thick stew, despite having no stomach for it. "Crydee."

"Why?" asked Brendan.

Martin took a dagger from his belt and quickly drew a rough map in the earth. "The Bitter Sea," he said after he'd drawn a diamond shape. Then he drew another line to the left of the diamond. "The Far Coast, and we are about here . . ." He dug the point of his dagger in. "I believe Bethany's father and Morris down at Tulan are not being attacked, but rather are being bottled up and prevented from moving north to aid us.

"I think there's a squadron or more of Keshian ships sailing up and down the Far Coast ensuring that no one gets out of either harbor or any of the fishing villages between the Straits and Crydee. I also believe that once they've established themselves in Crydee, they'll keep coming east, along this highway to seize Ylith. If they do, they'll have removed the King's Fleet from the Far Coast and prevented Yabon from sending anyone south. Duke Gasson will be bottled up, unable to come any farther south than Zun, and with that move Kesh will have trisected the Western Realm.

"They can then move in strength against Krondor from the south, leaving the Kingdom in tatters. I cannot let Krondor be surrounded without support from the north. The only relief from the east is in Salador, and that would take weeks, and who can guess what Kesh is doing in the Sea of Kingdoms? The King may be very ill-disposed to stripping any of his eastern garrisons to come to Krondor's aid."

"But how?" asked Brendan. "How could they put so many men in the field at once?"

"That, my brother, is the question," Martin said. "For the moment, we need rest."

"You and the others from Crydee sleep," said Brendan. "We'll keep watch."

"What happened to that band of Leopards?" Martin asked.

"Brendan happened," said Bethany, patting him on the arm.

"They rode right into us not knowing we had them by five to one," said Martin's younger brother. "They are good, but it was over quickly." Then he smiled. "But we have their horses, so you don't have to walk to Ylith."

Sighing, Martin lay down, putting his head on a pack someone had set down behind him. "Ylith." After a moment as his eyes grew heavy, he said, "If Robert is bottled up in Carse, and Gasson cut off up in Yabon . . ."

Bethany came and lay down behind him, snuggling in close as if to keep him warm for the night. Bethany closed her eyes and was quickly asleep as well.

Brendan saw his brother slip into deep slumber and turned to look at the two sergeants. "With Father dead and Hal in Roldem, that puts Martin in command."

Ruther looked at Magwin. The two sergeants were the oldest members of the garrison, save for Swordmaster Phillip who was with young Henry in Roldem for the Champions Tournament at the Masters' Court. Finally Magwin said "Title or not, that makes him the King's Warden of the West."

Ruther looked at the sleeping youth and said, "Now all he needs is an army."

20

CONFLUENCE

Jim groaned.

His arms felt as if they were about to fall off, yet he knew he had another half hour or more of pulling hard on the oars of this boat. He glanced over his shoulder and at once regretted it. Sorcerer's Isle didn't look a foot closer than it had the last time he had looked.

His Keshian guide Nefu had proved as wily a smuggler as he had hoped, and if he had the chance he'd use him himself, if Kaseem would let him. They had run up the coast on a downwind tack, then turned and run before the wind northward. Twice they had seen sails on the horizon, and Nefu had deftly sailed away before they were noticed.

They had reached an imaginary line between the southwest tip of the island nation of Queg and the distant point of Land's End over the horizon and found that it was just as Nefu had feared: heavily patrolled by Keshian warships. He had quickly produced both a Keshian flag and a courier's pennant and affixed them to the mast. As long as he kept sailing, and didn't get stopped and have to answer questions, it would be fine. Though Jim judged it likely that Kaseem abu Hazara-

Khan had provided Nefu with a fairly comprehensive set of false papers. There was a likelihood that because Kaseem had been betrayed and his network compromised, many of those patents and passes were no longer valid, but unless those who stopped the smuggler were privy to the most recent changes in the top echelons of government, they might get them through. Jim also knew that had he been in charge, Nefu would have a packet with a lot of impressive-looking seals that were to be opened only by a specific noble, one who wasn't on whatever boat was stopping them.

He was relieved they had not had to test those ploys. For Nefu was even more resourceful than Jim had imagined. They sailed along the line of ships, staying to the east and looking as if they were bound on Imperial business for some destination behind the lines, until sundown, at which point Nefu sailed around in a lazy circle until he was where he wished to be. He had lowered the sails and sculled the ship silently through the darkness. Sculling was a primitive means of propelling a boat, probably used centuries before sail or oar. Jim was amazed to see the long oar come out of the hold; it was in sections that were quickly fitted together and put over the stern as the rudder was hoisted out of the water by means of a clever winch-and-cable mechanism. Then Nefu and two of his men fixed the twenty-five-foot-long oar in an iron cradle bolted to the stern of the boat, slipping it through a cut-out that Jim had assumed was a common feature to allow water splashing up on the deck to run off.

Sculling took a lot of power, and this oar was massive, so two men worked it. It was a slow and tedious way to move a boat, but move the boat it did, and silently they crept between two sentry ships anchored along the line Jim had drawn on the imaginary map in his mind.

By dawn an exhausted crew raised the sails and they set a course for Sorcerer's Isle. They took down the Keshian pennants and kept a sharp watch for Kingdom warships.

A day later they came within view of two things simultaneously: a smudge on the northeastern horizon that Nefu claimed was Sorcerer's Isle, and a dot of white to the southeast that the lookout claimed was a squadron of Kingdom warships.

Despite Jim's assurances that he could convince the commander of any Kingdom squadron they were there on official business, Nefu declined to see whether Jim could effectively keep him and his crew out of a Kingdom prison and his boat from being confiscated. The fact that Jim was without identification of any kind, that the Kingdom was in a state of war, and that there was no guarantee that this particular squadron commander had ever met Baron James Jamison all weighed heavily in the smuggler's decision.

Hence Jim found himself rowing furiously against the current trying desperately to take him away from his destination. Not for the first time that morning did Jim curse Destan for disabling his Tsurani transport orb.

Jim's shoulders ached and his back hurt, and he knew that this was the first time in his life he was seriously beginning to feel his age. At forty a man's body begins to betray him, and it's only male vanity that makes him not believe it.

Jim was well past forty.

He worked hard at staying fit, drinking little and eating well, but the rigors of his trade, both as leader of the Mockers and supervisor of the King's Intelligence Service, conspired to keep him from taking care of himself as much as he should.

Never in his life had he regretted that fact more than now.

As he pulled hard on the oars, he wondered if it might really be time to settle down and start that family—assuming there was still a Kingdom in which to raise them after this war was over.

Of course, if Kesh was victorious, he could probably find employment in Roldem.

Then he wondered if Franciezka was honest about her feelings for him. He had been thinking of her a great deal lately, a fact that both did and didn't surprise him. It did because he had walled off his feelings toward women early in life, a necessity given his career; it didn't because Lady Franciezka Sorboz was far and away the most interesting and devious woman he had ever encountered. Life with her would never be dull. And it didn't hurt his little daydream that she was still the most arrestingly beautiful woman he knew. But most of all, she was the most intelligent woman he had ever met, and he had met a lot of intelligent women. They had to be intelligent to put up with the idiots they married. That then raised the question of how they could marry idiots and still be called intelligent, at which point Jim decided to put aside the question and concentrate on something simple, like who had started this war, why, and how he could convince Pug to save the Kingdom.

Jim kept rowing.

The boat rose and fell and in the distance Jim could hear the sound of surf, but he refused to look behind, knowing this to be a cruel joke being played by Kalkin, God of Thieves. He knew if he looked, the island would be back where it was when Nefu had first put him over the side into this boat.

Twice more the boat lifted, and then Jim remembered there were rocks along the western shore of the island and then he looked.

White surf crashed against a massive rock face and Jim started frantically pulling with his right oar, while backing with his left, pulling his little boat around onto a southerly course.

He had rowed until he felt his arms would fall out of his shoulder sockets, and now he let the boat drift. He just shipped the oars, sat back, and watched. Currents took the boat around the island, slowly moving past the rocks to an open, sandy area. Jim had been to Sorcerer's Island more than once, but he hardly considered himself an expert on geography. His usual landing site when he came by ship was on the southeast corner of the island, and he was now at the southwest.

Given the belligerency of almost everyone currently sailing on the Bitter Sea, Jim expected Pug to have lookouts posted around the island. Then he realized that Pug probably had some magic device or spell that let him know when trouble was on its way.

Jim took a long breath and let it out. At this point he decided he would rather walk for a day than row, so he grabbed the oars and turned the boat toward shore.

He started rowing again.

Magnus watched as the boat came ashore. He used his distant sight to see who had come across the Bitter Sea in a rowing boat designed to cross a harbor at most.

At first he wasn't sure who the scruffy-looking sailor was, but when the boat rode in on a breaker and the man jumped out, Magnus smiled. Of course.

He willed himself to the beach and Jim nearly leaped from surprise. "Damn, I wish you wouldn't do that! Couldn't you appear a few yards away, yell 'hello,' and then walk up in a civilized manner?"

Magnus leaned on the staff he always carried and smiled, genuinely amused. "Hello," he said. "Tell me, how did you get to here in a rowing boat? Tell me you didn't start in Vykor or Durbin."

"I didn't. Got dropped off by a smuggler about half a day's sail out, which is why I've been rowing for the entire day." He glanced around at the light. "At least I think so. It is close to sundown, right?"

Magnus pointed. "That's west. That bright round yellow thing hanging above the horizon is the sun. Yes, it is close to sundown."

Exhausted, Jim said, "Just take me to your father."

Magnus reached out and put his hand on Jim's shoulder, and abruptly they were in Pug's presence.

Jim looked around, confused, as he had expected to be

taken to the castle. He smiled at Pug as the magician turned to greet him. Pug still wore the black robe he had always worn since his time in the Assembly of Magicians on Kelewan, where he had learned his craft in Greater Path Magic.

"Jim," he said, extending his hand.

"Pug," said Jim, looking around. "Rebuilding, I see."

The villa was nearing completion. With the aid of talented magicians as well as skilled craftsmen, a year's worth of work had been finished in a month. Pug said, "Making changes, but it's much the same as before."

Left unsaid were the people who would be missing.

Jim said, "I'm exhausted. Have you a cup of wine and somewhere we can speak?"

Magnus said, "I'll get the wine, Father."

Pug motioned for Jim to follow him and led him through the entrance to the main building. It was just as it used to be, a massive square with a huge garden in the middle. Currently the fountain was restored to its formal beauty, comprising three dolphins that would spew water in graceful arcs into the pool around them. It was currently empty, waiting for water. And the soil in the garden was bare, having recently been denuded of weeds.

Jim followed Pug to his office within his personal quarters. The room looked very different. Instead of the large sprawling desk Pug had used for years, there was a small work table and a single chair. "I thought it time for some changes," said Pug. He motioned with his hand. "I'm leaving the walls as white plaster. It was Miranda's idea to paint the quarters that light blue she loved so much." At the mention of his wife, Pug's voice echoed a distant sadness.

The magician motioned for Jim to pull up a chair. "So how is it you come to us in a boat, Jim? Magnus was alerted that someone approached and went to investigate. I will confess I was surprised to see you. Why didn't you use the orb I gave you?"

"Broken," said Jim, deciding to leave the details until later.

"Ah," said Pug. "Tell me what you can about the madness I see going on across the whole of the Bitter Sea."

"Across the whole of Triagia," said Jim. "Kesh has marched against the Kingdom, on all fronts, apparently."

Magnus appeared with a pitcher of wine and three mugs on a tray. He poured one for Jim and his father, then one for himself.

"I will confess I've been completely caught off guard," said Pug. "When we saw the Keshian fleet sailing to the south of us, we began our inquiries, contacting our agents. Without success."

"My agents south of the Girdle of Kesh have been eliminated."

"All of them?" asked Magnus.

"They've all dropped out of sight. Probably murdered." Jim sipped his wine. "In my craft, it's best to assume the simplest explanation." Then he considered Amed Dabu Asam. "But I could be wrong. My most trusted agent in the Jal-Pur was turned and tried to kill me."

"Turned?" asked Magnus. "You mean he was secretly working for Kesh?"

Jim shook his head. "No. That's the maddening thing." He glanced from Magnus to Pug, then took another drink. "My arms are going to fall off from all that rowing," he said with a sigh. He put down the mug. "There's another player in the game."

"Who?" asked Pug.

"I don't know. I know it's not Roldem's agents, because I have a good relationship with them now, and there is no gain for Roldem and much to lose. Kesh's intelligence leader is well known to me, and he was caught by surprise: key members of his staff were being murdered when I last saw him. And now you tell me your agents were kept ignorant of the coming war." Jim looked as if he was ready to weep in frustration. "Some of this is possible, but all of it?"

Magnus said, "There's one possibility, one that even we didn't think of."

"What?" asked Pug.

"Magic," said Magnus. "Whoever has balked all our information gathering—neutralized it, compromised it, fed us lies—it could all be done with magic."

Pug was silent for a while, then said, "My best contact for years in Kesh, Turgan Bey, Lord of the Keep and personal adviser to the Emperor, has retired. My next highest contact, Januk Hadri, Privy Counselor to the Emperor, has been silent."

"I always thought it odd that Bey would 'retire,'" said Jim. "Some of those Truebloods love the life of leisure, but not Bey. Some other man might see a political sea change coming and retire to a villa on the shore of the Overn with a dozen beautiful women, or go hunting for lions or whatever else it is retired Keshian nobles do, but he loved the infighting of politics. I expected him to die on the job." Jim leaned forward. "He was your agent?"

"I told you the Conclave had many friends."

Jim sat back, his hands in his lap. "I thought I had a good conduit to Kesh's court intrigue, but Turgan Bey?"

Magnus smiled.

Jim shook his head. "I'm impressed." Then he looked at Magnus and said, "It must be magic."

"A lot of it," said Magnus. "A spell of influence to get a noble to decide it was time to retire, for instance. It is much more subtle than any overt enchantment or spell of control. Just make a man slightly tired, slightly less interested in the day in and day out, and you might not even have to suggest it's time to step down. He may even do it on his own."

Pug said, "Yes, magic playing on your man in the Jal-Pur's divided loyalties, or his greed, or . . ."

Jim closed his eyes. "Of course. Amed was of the desert tribes and blamed the Truebloods for his father's murder, which is why I could turn him against the Empire, but . . . he was Keshian."

"A call to slumbering patriotism," said Magnus.

"It's still a lot of magic, Pug," said Jim. "And it would take years. Agents would have to be identified, influenced, plans made . . ."

"But it could be done?" asked Pug.

Jim was silent for a while, thinking. After a few moments, he said, "Yes. If they can identify that first agent, if he or she is highly placed enough." He sat tapping his cheek with his finger. "I use blinds—that is, agents who do not know who they are working for. But if you get to someone high enough, they may be able to give you the identity of others, and if you can get to them . . ." He outlined quickly how the three intelligence services of Isles, Kesh, and Roldem were structured and utilized, glossing over a lot of detail, but ending on the point that many agents knew who was working for the other agencies. He finished by saying, "So one of mine gives up one of Franciezka's, and in turn her agent gives up one of Kaseem's."

"And at some point, one of them turns out to be working for the Conclave," said Magnus.

"So this has been going on for years, now," said Pug.

"Who?" asked Jim. "Who besides you has . . . this ability, this power?"

Magnus said, "There are only two possibilities. If the temples were to work together, even only two or three of the most powerful, they could do it. They have magic, though it is of a very different nature to what we are used to—"

"Which might be of benefit," interrupted Pug. "It might be harder for us to detect the influence."

Magnus added, "Or it could be the Academy."

Jim looked shocked. "The Academy? Why? I mean, who? Don't you still play a role there?"

Pug said, "A little, and we have agents there as well." He looked troubled as he gazed out the window. "I don't know how such an undertaking could . . ." His voice trailed off, and he was silent.

Jim asked, "Do the Pantathians have that much magic?"

Magnus said, "Why do you ask? They were obliterated."

"I was there when their birthing crèches were destroyed in the Ratn'gari Mountains."

Without humor, Jim said, "You missed some."

Pug stood up. "What?"

"On a boat in the south of Kesh I saw a scaled green hand with black talons sticking out of a robe, and if that's not a Pantathian, then I've not read every report on them in the archives in Krondor."

"Where was this?" asked Pug.

"Off the big island called the Island of the Snakes. Wondered what he had to do with things; maybe that's your answer."

Pug sat down again. "It's possible. The Great Uprising was about the Pantathians getting the Moredhel to invade the Kingdom. With that relatively small force, they manipulated the Brotherhood of the Dark Path and that ended with the destruction of two cities, first Armengar and then Sethanon. With Kesh's might at their disposal . . ." He shrugged. "They have the ability to appear as other races, elf, human . . . yes, if they are back and in numbers, it's possible."

"Kesh and the Kingdom at war? To what ends? How does that benefit the Pantathians, if it is them?"

Pug looked uncertain. "What I do know is that when they first took a hand, at the end of the Riftwar, they were bent upon securing the Lifestone—" He looked at Jim.

"I know about it. My great-great-grandfather was detailed in his remembrances. He was at the Battle of Sethanon, remember, with Prince Arutha?"

Pug was forced to smile. "Not many of us within that chamber knew the Lifestone existed then, and none of us ever understood its true nature; even later when Calis 'untangled' it, for lack of a better way to put it, we hardly understood it better. The Pantathians wanted it, as did the Demon Lord Jakan later, because it was an artifact of great power.

"But neither the Pantathians nor the demon knew its true nature, or that it would ultimately be useless to them.

Whatever the Dragon Lords planned to do with it was never apparent. I know they were desperate to regain it during that battle."

Jim said, "I know its nature was unknown to James . . ." He interrupted himself. "This is one of those moments when I have to remind myself that you knew him."

"My daughter was married to him," Pug reminded him.

"You knew all of them, Prince Arutha, King Lyam, Guy du Bas-Tyra, all the great figures of history."

Pug's smile was rueful. "Hardly all of them. And not all were mentioned in the histories." For a moment a fleeting kaleidoscope of images played through Pug's mind, faces of those he had known and loved: Squire Roland, his rival for the affections of Princess Carline, then Katala, his first wife, and Laurie of Tyr-Sog, who wed Carline. Then came others, Lord Borric, Swordmaster Fannon, Father Tully, Kulgan, and Meecham, those the years had left behind.

Pug pushed aside the flood of memories and said, "Jim, your great-great-grandfather, like those not within that chamber, was told what we believe he needed to know."

"We?"

"What would later become the core of the Conclave, along with Tomas." Pug looked off into the distance as if remembering, then added, "Lord James, the legendary Jimmy the Hand, had just died when Calis unlocked the mystery of the stone. It was . . . life. Somehow when the Valheru contrived to overthrow the gods during the Chaos Wars, they created it. Apparently they placed some of their own life energies within it, creating a tool only they truly knew how to utilize. We surmise it was a weapon or source of great power to them, for it was they who manipulated the Pantathians to attempt to seize it. Over all these years, especially since the Lifestone was destroyed, we've never attempted to assess what the real nature of the device was."

Magnus said, "You have been otherwise busy."

Pug and Jim both looked over to see if he was joking.

Pug said, "Yes, but still, it was a watershed creation in the history of this world." He let out a long sigh. "What we know is this: the Pantathians are artificial creatures, not natural beings, but rather snakes raised up to human form, given existence by their Dragon Lord Mistress, Alma-Lodaka."

"Could they really do that?" asked Jim. "I mean, create life?"

"No, not exactly," said Magnus. He glanced at his father, who nodded for him to continue. "They could manipulate it, not create it. The Valheru were beings of enormous power, godlike even, but they were not gods. And the Pantathians were not the only product of Valheru tinkering."

"Really?" said Jim, his fatigue wearing off as he became more interested. Here was a discussion about important things that didn't involve people trying to kill him or destroy the Kingdom.

"There's a race of tiger-men near the Necropolis, called the City of the Dead Gods, in Novindus. And once a race of giant eagles, big enough to carry a man, flew the skies."

Jim frowned. "Perhaps we should go back to things I might comprehend.

"If this Lifestone no longer exists, then, assuming for a moment the Pantathians are behind every mad thing that is under way right now, what could they be after that would possibly benefit them by having the Kingdom and Kesh plunged into total war?"

"I have no idea," said Pug.

"And, while we're on the topic of madness, can you even begin to suggest the part the demons have in this?"

"No," said Pug.

"Except," said Magnus, "they did manage one thing."

"What?"

"It just occurred to me that they did force the Star Elves to return to the world of their birth."

"You think that was by design?" asked Pug.

"I have no knowledge of design, Father, merely results."

Pug was silent again for a long time, then said, "These are the moments I wish Nakor was here." He paused. "And your mother. We could use their wisdom."

Magnus's expression turned dark. "We could."

Jim did not know what just passed between father and son and decided against inquiring. He said, "I have never officially been one of you, but you have always treated me with courtesy. Certainly you have no desire to see this bloodshed continue."

"No, in this we are as one," said Pug.

Magnus said, "But we still lack information and we need to gain more intelligence before we know how to act. Father and I can no doubt tip the balance in a battle, say to defend the walls of Krondor or turn a fleet to a new course; but to end a war takes a willingness on the part of the combatants that is not in evidence now."

"Kesh has aggrieved the Kingdom, certainly, and the Kingdom will seek retribution and to take its land back, of that I have no doubt," said Jim. He got up from his chair. "Can I rest here for the night, then perhaps you could aid me reaching Rillanon?"

"Not Krondor?" said Pug.

"Krondor is either safe or not, as it will be, but I must know the King's mind and gauge the temper of the Congress of Lords. War madness will no doubt be upon many, but some see the west as no significant loss. For all I know some Keshian general is even now playing with the animals in the King's zoo."

"The King has a zoo?" asked Magnus.

"A small one," said Jim. "Near the garden behind the palace, overlooking the river. It's quite nice, actually." He stopped, overcome by fatigue. "Moreover, I must begin to find out who has betrayed me, and in so doing, betrayed their nation."

"If indeed, it's betrayal," Magnus reminded him, "if magic was employed."

Jim's eyes closed for a moment. "Apologies. I'm tired and it's easy to forget. No offense intended, but there are days when I wish I had never heard the word 'magic' and had to deal with its confusions and complexities."

Pug chuckled. "I can appreciate that."

Jim said, "What do you think you'll do next?"

"If the Pantathians are in fact back in numbers, then they must be sought out."

"I will go, Father," said Magnus.

"You?"

"You're needed here, and if things are coming quickly to crisis, you can't be away. I can travel faster than you," Magnus said without boasting, "and you have a more critical task."

Pug looked pained. "Yes, I think I didn't want to see that."

"What is that task?" asked Jim.

"Like you, I must begin to find out who betrayed us."

21

TREACHERY

There came a pounding on the door.

It was the dead of night, but Hal and Ty were both out of their beds with swords drawn before they were fully awake.

Ty pulled open the door to find a servant with a lantern standing there. The man said, "Quickly. My mistress says to dress and come at once."

Both young men hurried to do as they were told and were dressed, with weapons buckled on, and moving down the corridor following the servant within moments.

Lady Franciezka was dressed in leather breeches, a heavy woolen shirt, a cloak, and a pair of heavy leather boots. "Come," she said and led them down the stairs.

As they reached the front of the large estate house in which they had been guests for a week, both boys heard pounding at the front door and a man's voice cry, "Open in the name of the King!"

They scurried to the back of the house, and she showed them to stairs leading down into the basement. The pounding on the front door became more insistent as they reached the bottom. She pointed to a storage shelf and said, "That is a false shelf. Move it to the right and it will swing out. Behind is a safe room. Wait there until I come back."

"What if you don't come back?" said Ty.

"Then things are in far worse shape than I think. If I don't return by tomorrow, go to your father's restaurant any way you can. He'll know what to do."

She hurried back up the stairs as the young men heard angry male voices.

"By whose authority—" The voice of Lady Franciezka faded out of hearing range.

Ty and Hal found it easy to move the shelf and it did swing away to reveal a hidden room. They entered and lit a single candle, then closed the shelf behind them. Inside, there was only a bed, a stool, and a table. Hal took the stool, leaving the bed for Ty.

They sat and said nothing. After a few minutes, they could hear the muffled sound of boots on the stairs to the basement, and some indistinguishable voices coming from the other side of the false wall.

The search of the basement took about ten minutes, then they heard more steps up the wooden stairs, and finally silence.

Hal held up his hand and mouthed, "Wait."

A minute of silence went by, then they heard faint sounds of movement, then fainter creaking on the stairs.

Whispering, Hal said, "Leaving someone behind to see if anyone was hiding is what I would do."

Ty smiled. "Sneaky bastard."

"What do you think is going on?" asked Hal.

Ty shrugged. "Your guess is no worse than mine."

The night passed slowly and they played "odds and evens" to see who got the bed. Ty won. Hal made do with sleeping on the chair with his feet up on the tiny table and was rewarded with a night spent dozing while trying not to fall off the chair.

They were both awake when the false wall suddenly swung aside and Lady Franciezka stood there, one of the servants beside her holding a lantern. "You may come out now."

Ty said, "Lady, what was that about?"

"I was summoned to the castle." She led them upstairs and back to the kitchen at the rear of the house. "I expect you're hungry."

"Always," said Hal with a laugh. "Father says I'll be as fat as a prize hog if I don't keep busy."

"Yes, thank you," said Ty.

Food was served with a hot pot of Keshian coffee. "Enjoy that," she said, indicating the steaming black liquid as she poured herself a cup. "The way things are, it may be hard to get in a few weeks."

"What news?"

"I was summoned by Lord Worthington."

"Worthington?" said Hal. "Sounds like a man of the Isles."

"Our two nations are closely linked. His forbears were from the Isles, but he is minor nobility of Roldem, very minor." She let out an irritated sigh. "He's a jumped-up, but very ambitious, fellow distantly related to some important nobles, but that's true of almost anyone with a title on this tiny little island we call home.

"But in the last five years he has risen fast and has grown very influential. He is said to control many voices in the most important circles of society and, more, has many friends in the House of Nobles. It's also rumored he has a strong desire to see Princess Stephané married off to his son."

"Can't spite a man for ambition," said Ty, "but for all of that, how does he get off summoning you? I mean, from what I know, you're very close to the King yourself."

She looked at Ty with a narrow gaze. "Few people know that, and I would advise you to consider keeping it that way. I am officially a minor court lady, occasionally a lady-in-waiting to the Princess, living on an inheritance from a rich father. I know I am considered desirable—" She held up her hand. "None of your childish flattery; I'm not in the mood, don't have time, and you're not very good at it, Ty. Now, your father, he could charm the ladies from what I hear, but that's for another time.

"Anyway, Lord Worthington has no idea who I really am, a situation I'd like to continue. I have seen many ambitious lords come and go, especially when the two princes were in their young 'I love everyone when I'm drinking' phase of life. The list of suitors for the Princess is breathtaking, so normally I would expect to see Lord Worthington spend his brief days, a few months perhaps, in the glory of the King's sun, then fade back into gloomy obscurity, but there is nothing normal about these times." She took a deep breath. "For the duration of this emergency, by the King's order, Lord Worthington has been named Chancellor of Roldem, with extraordinary powers."

"But what of the old Chancellor?" asked Ty.

"Suddenly retired, apparently, and he never had the powers granted to Worthington."

"You suspect him of—"

"I suspect everyone right now, except for you two, and only because you"—she pointed at Hal—"are vouched for by someone I trust implicitly, and you"—she pointed at Ty—"because I've known your father since I was a child. Everyone else right now is suspect."

Ty detected something in her voice. "What is it?"

"Worthington has declared martial law."

The two young men exchanged glances, and Hal said, "With the Keshian fleet anchored off the harbor mouth that's not entirely unreasonable."

"With Kesh sending love poems to Roldem, indicating that their business is with the Isles, yes it is. It creates strife and engenders fear and panic where none need exist. Moreover, he's secured the palace. No one enters or leaves without the Lord Chancellor's writ."

Ty said, "Does that mean the King and his family . . ."

"Are virtual prisoners within their own villas in the heart of the palace. No one can get near them without the Lord Chancellor's permission."

"The King approves of this?"

Lady Franciezka's blue eyes flashed. "How would I know? No one can get near the King to ask him, save with Worthington's seal on a pass."

"What of Constantine and Albér?"

"On their ships, at anchor in the harbor, under 'protection' by the King's Own Royal Marines."

"Grandy?" asked Ty.

"The young general has gone missing," she said with a smile.

"You know where he is!" Ty looked delighted.

"No, but I think I do, and I will know if I'm right in a few days."

"And the Princess?" asked Hal, and Ty threw a glance at him.

"With her mother and father," said Lady Franciezka. "You let me worry about her. I saw the way you two young peacocks strutted when presented to the royal family. She is the prize young hen in Roldem, in the entire Sea of Kingdoms, and I'm not about to let either one of you romantic fools get any closer to her than I am allowing Worthington's son. She will marry the next King of Isles or highest-ranking duke's son I can find.

"This war has shown that Kesh is flexing its muscle again, and if the Isles survive, they must be made whole, and quickly. For Kesh without Isles means Roldem's end eventually. It's that simple."

She stood up. "Finish what you will, then rest. Ty, I want you to leave after breakfast and find your father. Ensure that all is well and ask what he has heard from Jommy, Servan, or whoever else might have news of Prince Grandy, but be discreet. Make sure no one, and I mean no one—not friends, not trusted household staff, no matter how long they've been with you—no one overhears you. Hal, you'll stay here one more night. It should be safe."

"Then what?"

"We move you. Someone wants you dead or captured, that's certain, and my men have no idea who. Those men who attacked you are not known to us; they are not agents of Kesh, Isles, or anywhere else we know of. Nor are they local thugs for hire. After asking everyone we can think of, we found they came into the city by ship just before war broke out."

Hal didn't know what to say so he just sat back in his chair. "Very well." After a second he asked, "Have you anything here I might read? It's tiresome being alone in a room."

"I have books." She looked at him. "I may have to reappraise you, young lord from the wild frontiers. There may be more to you than meets the eye."

She rose, and the young men stood up and bowed. When she left, they sat down again and returned to finishing their meal.

"She's quite something," Hal said at last.

"My father once told me she was dangerous. I guess he knew of what he spoke."

Hal scratched at his cheek. "Did we really act like peacocks?"

Ty grinned widely. "You did. I was a perfect gentleman."

Hal took a linen napkin and threw it at him.

Sandreena rode with three other knights along the trade road from Durbin to Land's End. As expected she had been halted by Keshian forces moving against the Kingdom three times since they had left Durbin. Her position as a Knight-Adamant of the Temple gave her a certain carte blanche when it came to traveling through such conflicts, for neither nation wished to earn the enmity of any temple, especially one with as powerful and influential a martial order as the Temple of Dala. If need arose, Grand Master Creegan could field more than four hundred veteran knights, a force that could tip many battles, if he felt one side was dominating, and at the moment the Keshians certainly appeared to have the upper hand.

All Sandreena did was to acquaint any Keshian officers who sought to impede her travel with the fact that the High Priest of Dala in Kesh was personally interceding with the Emperor to cease hostilities and allow the temple to take a role in resolving further conflict.

This time she faced a different impediment—a full legion of Keshian soldiers, not the traditional Dog Soldiers of the northern command, but an Imperial Legion with all the trappings: camels as well as horse cavalry, siege engines, a luggage train stretching back two days' march, camp followers and merchants numbering nearly as many as the fighting men. All were athwart the caravan trail, and the commander was disinclined to allow anyone, for any reason, to cross the frontier.

Looking annoyed at having to deal with this, the commander had come out of his tent to regard the four Knights-Adamant as they sat astride their mounts. He was an ideal model of a Keshian Legion Commander. His armor was of polished black lacquer, his helmet crowned by a dyed red horsehair plume; he wore a black cuirass, with black leather pauldrons, a black skirt, and shining knee-high boots. His breast was emblazoned with a relief of a snarling lion's head, signifying that this was one of the Inner Legions, rarely seen outside the immediate vicinity of the Overn Deep. With barely contained irritation, he said, "I have nothing but respect for your order—"

Sandreena pushed up her faceplate. All four had been wearing full helms, not her personal preference, but necessary for this journey.

"Sister—"

"Sergeant, Commander," Sandreena interrupted. "I'm a Sergeant Knight-Adamant."

"Sergeant, then," he amended, looking frustrated. "As you can see I have a war to conduct, and as I was about to say, I have nothing but respect for your order, but I cannot permit potential combatants for the other side to cross the field uncontested. I know enough about your practices to believe you will be behind the barricades at Land's End when we move on it."

"Commander, normally that would be the case, but in this instance I am under orders to take ship from Land's End to another destination with utmost urgency. I will not be lingering to oppose your assault on a weaker position, no matter how much it might be in my nature to do so. You have my oath, by the Goddess, that I will not be stopping in Land's End for any longer than it takes to eat a meal and secure transportation."

He calculated. For her to be seeking a boat from Land's End meant a destination somewhere up the coast between Port Vykor and Ylith. If that was true, it made no difference to his efforts. "If you will swear you will give no information on our disposition, nor advice to the enemy, then you may ride on."

"Commander, the only advice I might give to any Kingdom officer I meet would be to quit his position and make haste to Port Vykor and hide behind the Kingdom Navy there. For in all my travels I have never seen such an army as you command here today."

He nodded. He wasn't entirely sure if that was a compliment or not. He waved over one of his guardsmen and said, "Escort them through the line and permit them to pass over to the Kingdom side."

They walked their horses behind the guardsman who took them through the camp. The sheer number of soldiers was impressive, and Sandreena knew that only the Prince's army in Krondor could withstand the siege this commander would bring. Everything between here and Krondor would eventually be swept away. And for the Kingdom to drive out the invaders, another army in support of Krondor would have to arrive from the east. The last time the Armies of the East had appeared in the Western Realm had been over a century before to meet the Tsurani invasion. And before that war was over, a king died.

Sandreena and her companions reached the barricades, and she noted they were nothing more than straw bales upon which dozens of pikes and spears had been lain. She took this as an indication that the Keshians expected no counterattack. A sudden appearance of even a small company of horse archers with flaming arrows and the front line of this army would be beating a hasty retreat. It wouldn't help the war, thought Sandreena, but it would be amusing to watch.

The no-man's-land between the Keshian army and the outer defenses at Land's End was over two miles, which was, from Sandreena's point of view, a good indicator that the Keshians were not in any hurry to advance. If you wish to sack a town, you move on it. Any student of warcraft knew that. If it was a walled city or other fortification, you surrounded it. You did not permit reinforcements easy access, or those in the town easy escape.

There was something decidedly odd about this war, but Sandreena had yet to put her finger on what it was.

Right now her mind was on her current plight, and her annoyance with her companions wearing the garb of her order was constant. The three other men were Black Caps. Nazir, their leader, had promised to reveal what he knew about the demon presence on Midkemia and why Dahun had provoked a massive war in the demon realm for the sole purpose of sneaking into Midkemia in human guise, but he refused to tell Sandreena.

He would only speak directly to Pug and the Conclave.

Sandreena had taken the better part of a day deciding, but he had been intractable. His small loyal band of Black Caps, the last "true" Nighthawks, were quite capable of vanishing into the night, never to be found again unless they chose to be found. Better to deal with him now when he was in a mood than later when he was not, she decided.

But getting him through the lines into the Kingdom was risky. Smugglers who could do it by boat were few and far between, and after consultation, this charade seemed the most straightforward method.

They walked their horses to within sight of the Kingdom pickets who had alerted their command by the time Sandreena and her companions reached their lines. A young militia lieutenant said, "Your business?"

Sandreena pushed up her helm. "I am Sandreena, Sergeant Knight-Adamant of the Order of the Shield of the Weak. I have been given orders to come to Land's End and take a boat north."

"Orders by whom?"

She smiled indulgently. "By the Grand Master of the Shield."

He clearly did not know what to do. After a moment, he said, "Wait here."

He ran off, and Sandreena looked around. Wherever the small army of Land's End might be, it wasn't here. The barony of Land's End was one of the poorest and least important in the Kingdom, save for the fact that it was the last town of size before leaving the Kingdom and entering Kesh. But it was part of the Principality of Krondor, specifically under the care of the Duke of the Southern Marches, Lord Sutherland, who was headquartered in Port Vykor. His mandate precluded giving up this town and pulling back to a stronger position, which was the expedient thing to do. Instead he had to make a show of defending it, which meant leaving a lot of ill-trained local boys and old men to fight against a trained army.

A few minutes later, the young officer returned. When he grew near, Sandreena asked, "What did your father say?"

The boy said, "My fath—" His eyes narrowed. "The Baron said for you to come to the command center."

"And where is that?" asked Sandreena.

"The big house up on the hill," he answered quietly, obviously feeling self-conscious.

"Thank you," said Sandreena.

As they rode away she heard Nazir ask, "The Baron's son?"

"A lucky guess," said Sandreena. "He looked the eager type who'd convinced his father to let him man the barricades. Not a lot of locals with military experience serving in the militia. The real soldiers are up with Sutherland in Port Vykor."

Nazir said, "These poor fools won't even slow the Keshians."

"This is their home," was all Sandreena said in response.

The Baron's estate was easy enough to find, being the only large estate house overlooking the town from a vantage that was clearly visible from the road, and they took the ride up to the house. Sandreena was struck by its construction. It was close to a villa in style, but two stories tall. A low stone wall surrounded the estate, to keep sheep and cattle from wandering around rather than to repel any invading army.

This was a community that had known a relative peace despite being on the frontier. It was clear it was a place no one else wanted.

Servants came out, looking oddly comic in ill-fitting tabards bearing the crest of Land's End: a stylized stone keep on an up-thrust rock, white tower, black rock, and deep olive green background.

Sandreena said, "Wait here," and if Nazir didn't care to be left out, he kept his own counsel. On this journey he was at her mercy and he knew it.

Sandreena entered the estate building and was appalled at what a musty, dreary old shambles of a place it was. She knew Land's End to be a backwater, but surely they could afford better than this.

The Baron was standing in front of a fire in his office, and from the look of the massive roaring flame and the pile of parchments and papers he was feeding into it, it appeared he didn't plan on staying long. He glanced up and said, "You're the woman who was rude to my officer?"

"I'm the woman who told your son to mind his manners," she returned, then almost as an afterthought, added, "my lord."

"You came through the Keshian lines?"

"Yes, my lord."

There was a resemblance between the Baron and his son: both were round faced, but whereas the boy simply looked callow, this man looked already in ruin from excessive drink and food. And the way he kept staring at Sandreena, despite her armor, road dirt, and less than charming behavior, told her he was a lecher as well. Despite being less than fifty, he looked to be a man of sixty years or more. His armor would have appeared comic if it wasn't so worthy of pity.

She put aside her personal, instantaneous dislike of the man and said, "I have seen the entire Keshian army arrayed against you, my lord, on my travel to Land's End."

The Baron didn't even flinch; he kept on throwing documents into the fire. "They mustn't have any of these," he said. "These are vital to Kingdom security."

More than likely a record of bribes paid and taken, accounts of taxes withheld from the Crown and other felonious activities. Sandreena merely said, "They don't seem to be in a hurry. I think you have ample time to destroy all your . . . sensitive papers, my lord."

"Are you sure?"

"They are dug in, my lord."

"Ah, afraid to advance," he said, suddenly infused with false bravado. Then he returned to the edge of panic. "Are they waiting for reinforcements?"

Sandreena said, "My lord, they appeared content to wait upon orders, perhaps from the Emperor himself, to advance. But they have ample forces in the field deployed against your position and can advance with little difficulty. If I may suggest, you might do well, once you've finished denying them this critical intelligence, to remove yourself and your forces to Port Vykor. Lord Sutherland's commanders could certainly use the help."

"Are you certain?"

"Most assuredly," she said. She knew that he would use this as his sole reason to abandon his home and run like a scalded rabbit up to Vykor. At least it saved him the pain of leaving his son to die on the barricade while he ran, assuming he was capable of feeling parental love. She knew many fathers who did not.

She saw his calculating expression and realized that when he reported to whoever was in charge at Vykor, he would claim he had been ordered to withdraw, by someone whose name he could not recall, but a knight of some sort, bearing heraldic badges (he would neglect to recall they were temple badges without any rank or standing within the King's Army of the West).

"Now, to the business of your being here," he said.

"I need a boat."

"Well, I won't stand in your way. Go to the docks and see what's there. I suspect everything that floats is already heading north, but if you can find one, you're free to buy or hire it."

Sandreena thought of several things to say, none of them respectful, thought better of it, and said, "If your dock warden is doing his job, my lord, he'll need authorization from you to permit a boat to leave."

The pasty-faced man blinked for a moment, then said, "Oh, yes, that."

He stopped tossing documents into the fire, reached out and took a blank sheet of parchment from a stack and scrawled a hasty note. When the ink was dry, he picked up a candle and melted a dollop of wax on it, into which he pressed his baronial signet ring. "There, that should suffice, I think," he said as he handed the document to Sandreena.

"Thank you, my lord," she said and withdrew.

As she left the building she realized they could have ridden past straight on to the harbor and no one would have noticed or even cared. And she could probably have bullied the dock warden. Assuming he was still at his post and not sailing north as any wise man should.

As expected, the dock warden was absent, and there were few boats left, but one enterprising owner smelled a panic coming soon and was determined to get the most out of the situation as possible. Sandreena knew if the world caught flame, people like this would be trying to sell water.

She quickly convinced him to take her where she wanted to go in exchange for a fair price: the four horses, three sets of arms and armor, and staying on her good side. It was a single-masted, lanteen-rigged coaster easily crewed by two men, de-signed to ferry cargo and people to and from larger ships at anchor, but it would serve.

The trip was straightforward. They beat a tack up the coast as the Keshian fleet was lying off to the northwest, in a line that ran to the south of Queg, and then when they were far enough away and the Quegan sails could not be seen, they turned their course for Sorcerer's Isle. As they were sailing on the Kingdom side of the line with an almost-illegible scrawled note from the Baron of Land's End, Sandreena thought it un-likely that any Kingdom captain would prevent them from reaching their destination.

Sandreena ordered Nazir and his two bodyguards to divest themselves of their false gear, and they were now dressed like the thugs she thought them to be.

The wind was favorable, and they made the journey in less than three days, a half day earlier than expected. Nazir and his companions slept on the deck with the captain and his one deckhand, while Sandreena occupied the solitary berth below; given the stench in the cabin, she considered the others had got the better part of the bargain.

The captain deposited them in the waist-deep surf, as close as he was willing to get without the risk of the boat getting beached.

By the time they got out of the water, three men waited to greet them. "Pug, Jim, Magnus," said Sandreena.

"Greetings," said Pug. "Who are your friends?"

She laughed. "Hardly that, but they are under my protec-tion and you should listen to them." She turned to her com-panions and indicated the first of them. "This is Nazir. He is the leader of the group I ran afoul of down in Kesh: the Black Caps.

Jim said, "The ones that beat you, raped you, and threw you over a cliff?"

She nodded.

"You're more forgiving than I am," said Jim.

"Hardly that, but we have a truce and I'll honor it, and I expect you to as well."

He put up his hands, indicating he was willing to abide by her decision.

"The Black Caps are also a splinter of another group you know very well, Pug: the Nighthawks."

Pug's brow furrowed, and he looked from face to face. Finally Nazir, the man in the middle said, "What she says is true. I have an offer for you."

"You know who I am?"

"Of course. Pug, the Black Sorcerer. We are trained to know our enemies."

"What do you offer, and what do you expect?"

"I offer truth, and I expect only this: that when you hear me out, you arrange for transportation for myself and my men to a tiny little corner of the Empire that is relatively calm, where I will be content to hide until this insanity is over. After that, feel free to come looking for me and my brethren. You will not find us."

"No more than that?"

"No amnesty, no pardon, no forgiveness. Just a head start."

"Very well," said Pug. "If we hear truth from you."

"Oh, that you will. As I told Sandreena, this is something you need to know, you more than anyone else, for while others will want to know what I am about to tell you, you alone can prevent utter destruction.

"I know why Dahun was trying to enter Midkemia in disguise and what he was fleeing from."

22

AWAKENING

Child screamed in defiance.

Her small force arrayed behind her, every weapon they possessed presented. Those who were magically enabled began either defensive or offensive spells as they had been instructed, and the flyers sprang into the sky of this alien world.

Another band of demons, this one ragged and dispirited, backed into a defensible position, ready for combat. They were thin and weak, but they would fight with whatever ferocity was left to them and Child wished no injuries to her followers.

She signaled and her band attacked. It was over almost as soon as it began, as her bull-headed males charged. They could withstand the feeble claws and fangs of those in the enemy's vanguard, while the magic-casters were struck by her flyers, interrupting their conjurations. It was a quick battle and scant feast afterward, but any food was better than starvation.

She had come into this world through the portal, and as soon as she had entered she had known she was in a different plane of reality. This place reminded her of the Savage Lands in her own world, but only superficially. It was rocky, barren, and strewn with volcanoes that spewed pillars of dark smoke and ash into the air, coloring the sky red and orange during the day and providing a canopy that hid stars at night.

There were demons everywhere, small pockets of them who fought over every scrap on this world. Newly come to this realm, Child and her retinue were more powerful than any they faced. The problem was that those they consumed provided the barest sustenance. She and Belog had thought that this world was in the mortal realm, a place demons had visited repeatedly, but one that was reputed to be abundant with life energy, providing endless feasting. But this planet was hardly that.

The week before, they had found a valley, and across it were strewn banners and other remnants of a mighty battle. Certain corners of it were blasted as if mighty magical spells had been used, and weapons of all sorts littered the landscape.

Upon a rise overlooking the valley was a faded, tattered banner that Belog claimed to have borne the mark of Maarg. Yet as long as Maarg was reputed to have vanished, this battle could only have occurred much more recently. Leather harnesses still retained their form, cloth tatters still waved as banner poles swayed in the acrid breezes. The acids in the air would have destroyed them long ago had this army been present when Maarg vanished. This was proof of a far more recent struggle.

Belog had said, "Perhaps this is where he came. Perhaps his army raged across this world for years, decades. Now he is finally gone, having consumed all in his gluttony."

"But that is not the case," said Child. "Not all is gone. Most, but not all."

"Perceptive," said Belog.

"We are at a place between," she said.

"Between?"

"I can smell the lingering aroma of blood that is not demon, the blood of lesser beings, yet still so savory!"

"Savory perhaps," agreed Belog, "but hardly satisfying unless we have more. We are weakening: every day we are growing weaker."

"How do we stay strong?"

"Magic, eating," he said.

She closed her eyes and said nothing, extending senses she hardly understood, then her eyes snapped open and she pointed, "That way!"

She led them though a long valley to an abandoned, ancient castle. She closed her eyes again. "Many lesser beings once resided here."

"What is this place?" asked one of the male demons.

Child snarled, and the other fell silent. "Do not speak!" she commanded, and the other demon realized he had barely survived. He quickly lowered his eyes in the sign of submission.

Despite the young male's apparent subservience, Belog realized he was now physically strong enough to contest Child for the leadership. He had presumed himself above the others because he was the male with whom she mated most frequently, which in itself seemed strange, because mating required energy that could be harbored. It was as if she was seeking something in the act itself.

"Come," said Child. "We have a distance to travel."

How did she know? Belog wondered.

They came to a large complex of buildings, and from the skeletons scattered everywhere, the abandoned arms and armor, it had clearly been the scene of a vicious struggle.

"They fought to protect this place," said Child.

"Who?" asked Belog.

"The Taredhel," said Child. "Those elves who called themselves the Clans of the Seven Stars. This was the nexus of their transportation from world to world. This place is called Hub."

"How do you know this?" asked Belog.

"I do not know."

They moved along a broad street to a building at the end. Child climbed the broad steps and entered a huge room containing a circle of devices, each set upon a large round base. Two gracefully curving arms of wood and metal rose from the base inscribing a massive circle. One at the back of the room dwarfed the others.

"That one," she said, "was the first, from a world called 'Andcardia.' We troubled them there first, and last. It was their final refuge before they fled to another world."

Belog looked around the dark room and said, "But we cannot follow."

Child said, "We can. Just not through here." She looked slowly around the room. "We would not wish to. The elves would have death awaiting any who came through." The last was said with a tone conveying she expected him to know that already.

Belog sighed quietly. She had now moved beyond his ability to comprehend. She knew things she could not know. She recounted things she had not been witness to, and she grasped things that should be beyond her capacity. She was unique. Yet there was something also familiar about her, as if he had known her for a very long time. He found that puzzling, as well.

She turned and left, bidding the others to follow or not as they wished. Here only death remained.

They wandered through broken lands and burning lands without a hint of life. Armies of demons had ravaged one another in battles of titanic proportions, leaving only a few bones and scattered weapons covered by windblown dust. Banners long shredded by those acrid winds had tatters snapping angrily in a bitter breeze as a glowering orange sun rose to greet another lifeless day.

Mounting the summit of a range of small hills, Child looked down into the shallowed valley below and said, "There. It awaits."

"What is it?" asked Belog.

"Can't you see it?" She looked at him with genuine confusion.

"See what, Child?"

"Come. I'll show you."

She marched down the slope with the remaining members of her band. There were fewer of them than when they had arrived. One flyer had misjudged how close he could come to a seemingly benign hillock only to be consumed in flame when the crest exploded with volcanic violence.

Another stumbled on a narrow trail, injuring himself in the fall, and was devoured by the rest. Child had torn the throat out of the presumptuous male after their last mating, when he had dared to question her leadership. She had devoured him alone, provoking sullen envy in the others, but they failed to realize that act prolonged their lives. Two others had had a falling-out and fought, sustaining wounds, and the smell of blood and the unleashed rage swept aside all inhibitions and the others fell on them and feasted.

Now there were six besides Child and Belog. One flyer, one male, and four magic-users.

They trudged down the hillside, fatigue visiting again like an unwelcome companion. Hunger was rising up inside as well.

They came to the center of the little valley and Child said, "Behold."

Belog said, "Child, we see nothing."

"You do not see a portal, hanging in the air as if beckoning?" Her tone was impatient, as if she expected more of them.

"No," said one of the magic-users, risking his leader's wrath. "Not by eyes or arts can I see."

She looked at Belog. "You?'

He strained as if trying to see. "No, nothing, Child."

With an odd, exasperated tone she said, "I see it as clearly as I see that rock over there." She pointed to a boulder.

"What is it you see?" asked Belog

"As I said, a portal. An energy vortex that will lead us from this place to another."

"Which place, Child?" asked her first teacher.

"I expected more of you," she chided. "There is nothing for us here. Here I will eventually devour all of you, then myself perish from hunger. There is perhaps a better place on the other side of that portal, but it can be no worse than here. Even a quick death is better than a long, lingering, painful one."

With that, she turned and unleashed a shimmering bolt of silver-blue force that struck the flyer and the male, sending them senseless to the ground and shocking the magic-users to immobility. She leaped upon the powerful male, who was just regaining his feet. He had scant time to defend himself before she had her fangs in his neck.

The flyer scrambled backward, still dazed, and as Child overpowered the male, the flyer leaped to the skies, speeding away as quickly as his wings would enable him.

Child tore out the male's throat, then turned to Belog. "Feast, but harbor your energies well. Master your hunger and feed your mind. Leave your body as it is."

He fell to and began to devour the huge dead demon. Her instructions were clear, but it took all his conscious effort not to let his body grow, not to build more muscle and sinew, but rather to feed only his intellect. Only his training as an Archivist kept his feeding frenzy under control.

Now Child devoured the magic-users, eating their brains first while their knowledge of magic still lingered. When she finished, she lingered over their bodies.

When the orgy of feeding was over, Child stood and looked around. She observed, "What a wretched place, indeed." Turning to the portal only she had been able to see, she said, "Do you perceive it now?"

Belog stood and she noticed his posture had changed, as if somehow his mind had made a shift to a new set of memories, habits, and inclinations, so that even the act of walking had become different.

He grinned. "Ah, now I do."

She reached out to him. "Take my hand."

She led him into what looked like a step from one place to another.

And suddenly they were somewhere else. It was a long road, wide enough for a decent-sized caravan to travel, but on all sides a grey nothingness spread out. Every so often on either side, portals were present.

"Where is this place?" asked Belog.

She did not answer his question but merely pointed and said, "That way."

She led him down the Hall of Worlds.

Pug regarded Nazir with a cold stare. "You live only because of Sandreena's guarantee of safe conduct, and as we agreed on the beach, if I hear truth from you, I will grant you safe conduct away from this island. After that you'll be hunted."

"Fair enough," said the leader of the Nighthawks. "I've spoken to your friend about the history of my brotherhood; should you care to know it, she will convey it to you." He nodded to Sandreena, who stood quietly in the corner, just behind Pug's seat. In another corner, Amirantha observed without comment.

"Let me begin here by saying that more than a century ago, there arose within the Nighthawks a faction that became embroiled with a cult of demon worshippers. Promises were made and in the main they were delivered, so more and more of the Brotherhood of Assassins fell under their sway. Those of us who did not . . . let us say that we saw how the wind blew and kept our concerns to ourselves.

"Given your legendary reputation, Pug of Sorcerer's Isle, I have no doubt you're well aware of the events that took place over a hundred years ago in that very fortress where you destroyed the Demon Gate recently. That was the first attempt at a summoning of a Demon Lord." He stopped. "There is much to say. Might I have some wine?"

Pug said, "Bring water," and sat back.

Nazir shrugged as if it were of no importance. "What none of my brethren knew was that those in league with the demons were using them, giving them small gifts in exchange for blindly following orders. That fellow you called Jimmy the Hand, who later became Lord James, he nearly single-handedly destroyed us with his meddling in our first summoning, but while he set back that faction and harmed the Nighthawks severely, he also served the demons."

"How?" asked Pug, now genuinely curious.

"He gave the demon faction an excuse. There were things those in the Nighthawks not already serving the demons wanted: powerful magic, devices of great art, things to raise up the Brotherhood until empires trembled at our name, but now we had an enemy, a talented, insidious enemy, Lord James and his agents. It gave us a unifying motive: a common enemy.

"For decades James and his intelligence service were our excuse when we failed. And most of the Brotherhood accepted this: all our success was ascribed to our demonic benefactor; all failure to Kingdom spies, Keshian spies as well, and later spies from Roldem. But there were enough victories—gold, blood, women—to keep the Brotherhood from turning their backs completely on the demon cult. But slowly the demon servants again rose to dominate the Brotherhood. And they provided us with much."

"Such as?"

"The usual. Wealth, power, influence." Nazir shrugged.

A tray was brought in and he was given a mug of cold water. He drank deeply, obviously thirsty, then nodded and Magnus refilled his mug.

"Where was I? Oh, yes, the demon cult came again into the ascendancy, and those of us who treasured our family traditions went deeper underground. But there came a moment when several of us, myself especially, had to be convinced by the demon worshippers to lend our support to that monstrous undertaking you so wonderfully ruined down in Kesh. It took all our considerable wealth and calling in most of the favors owed us by others."

"Favors?" asked Magnus.

"An official who marked down a shipment of tools heading to our camp as farm implements; workers gathered by slavers—though you freed most of them. We also needed safe passage through the desert to the Valley of Lost Men, which meant knowing when patrols were due out of the local garrisons, that sort of thing.

"I agreed to the demon cult's request, but only if I were to know the real reason behind all this insanity." He took another drink of water.

"Continue," prodded Pug.

"I loved many of my brethren among the demon cult, seeing them as no more or less misguided as that lovely woman who escorted us here"—he indicated Sandreena who gave him a sour look. "To give over your entire life to one thing is to deny yourself so many other pleasures." He shrugged. "But people do as they do. That is when I was told a story, and it is for that story I will expect my freedom."

"You have been promised your safe passage anywhere we can take you."

Suddenly Nazir smiled. "I think I need more than that."

Pug came out of his chair. "What?"

"It occurs to me that your Conclave of Shadows has cost me and my brotherhood dearly, Pug. It is not enough we just be deposited somewhere quiet. We need a few things to make our life bearable."

"Such as?"

"Gold, enough to buy comfort and security."

"How much?"

"A hundred thousand Kingdom sovereigns would be sufficient, I imagine."

Pug sat back down. "I'm sure. Where would you expect us to get a sum like that? That's taxes in the Western Realm for ten years."

"You have the largest group of magic-users in the world, Pug. Someone must be able to find gold with a spell or turn base metal into gold, or just create something to sell for gold."

Pug looked as if he had tasted something bitter. "And if we don't comply?"

"You can kill me now if that is your pleasure. It is not important, because you and I need each other." Nazir smiled like a gambling man whose winning card has been dealt. "I'll amend my demands, then. If we survive, then you'll pay me."

"Survive?" asked Magnus.

Nazir looked at Pug's son. "My friend, what I know is simple. There is something out there that makes the Demon Kings tremble. It puts fear into the very gods themselves, and if you do not defeat its purposes, then all here is lost anyway, and dead with gold is no better than dead without gold. Dead is dead."

"What is this thing they fear?" asked Pug.

"They call it the Darkness."

Pug sat back, and the blood drained from his face. He remembered a time when he had heard that phrase, but in the Tsurani tongue, and he knew what it had meant at that time. The mad Pantathian Serpent Priests had sought to bring into this sphere of reality their lost "goddess," the Dragon Lord Alma-Lodaka, she who had created them. What they actually brought in was the disembodied essence of another, by the name of Draken-Korin, the Lord of Tigers, who was defeated by Tomas at the battle beneath the city of Sethanon. But even more unexpected had been the appearance of a Dreadlord, who had battled with the great dragon who had become the Oracle of Aal.

Calmly Pug said, "If we survive, I'll pay your price. You have my word."

Magnus looked at his father with surprise, but said nothing.

Nazir said, "Then know this. The father of all irony is that Dahun sought to sneak into this world in the guise of the mad magician Belasco. You and his brother"—he indicated Amirantha—"saw through the ruse and destroyed both of them. But Dahun did not come here as a conqueror. He came as a supplicant, to seek out the most powerful magic-users in this realm." He waved his hand around the room. "He was going to ask them for help." He laughed. "He wanted to beg you for protection, Pug. For the Darkness was day by day destroying his world."

Pug cried, "Amirantha! Get that book."

The Warlock didn't need to be asked which book it was Pug wanted. He hurried to his quarters where he found Gulamendis poring over the very tome. Unceremoniously he pulled the massive volume off the table and said, "Come along. You'll want to hear this."

They both returned in haste to Pug's quarters, and Amirantha laid the book down. It was the *Libri Demonicus Amplus Tantus*, literally the *Really Big Demon Book*. It was both large in size and vast in scope. As bad as some of the scholarship in it was, some parts were brilliant and accurate. The trick had been puzzling out which was which.

"The map," Pug said, and Amirantha set about unfolding the huge map that was attached to the book, glued inside the front cover. Amirantha laid it out and everyone in the room looked down on it.

The map was laid out as if the demon realm were a massive disc, with a large circle in the middle. In the ancient Quegan dialect employed to write this tome were the words *Ater Irritius*.

"There," pointed Nazir, his finger stabbing the center of the map. "That is what they fear."

Amirantha said, "We translated that to mean 'void.'"

"It may," said Nazir. "I speak no Quegan, modern or ancient, but they call it 'Darkness.'"

It was Pug who said, "It means both. And now I understand fully . . ."

Before he could speak again, Nazir said, "What is this?" His finger circled the edge of the void.

Amirantha said, "The Demon Kingdoms, from what we can translate. There seem to be a group in a ring about this void, called the First Kingdoms, then around that a second ring, called the Second Kingdoms. Then come the Savage Kingdoms, and around the edge what is called the Mad Lands."

"Well, it's an old map," said Nazir. "Because Dahun's kingdom is being devoured by the Darkness." He looked at Pug. "There aren't any First Kingdoms. They are all gone."

Pug closed his eyes for a moment. Then he nodded. To Sandreena he said, "If you don't mind, escort Nazir back to his room and have someone keep an eye on him. Then please return. I'm going to need to send messages to your temple and the others."

After Nazir was gone, Magnus said, "What is it, Father?"

Pug sighed. "All the signs were there. All the way back to the Riftwar when Tomas and I were looking for your grandfather. Right up to the struggle with the Dasati, the capture and imprisonment of their gods, the false Death God and . . . It's the Dread. They're destroying the demon realm and seeking a way back here."

A silence fell over the room.

23

ARRIVAL

The horse stumbled.

Martin almost lost his balance and forced himself awake.

"We're almost there," he heard Bethany say. At her side rode Brendan.

Martin glanced at both of them and said, "Sorry."

Bethany said, "You've been without rest for most of a week, Martin. It's no wonder you're falling asleep in the saddle."

They were coming down out of the foothills on the road to Ylith. They had passed one outpost already manned by local militia who looked barely able to hold their pikes, let alone use them effectively. When challenged, he had merely answered they were "the muster from Crydee," and they had ridden past without pause, the sentries showing no inclination to challenge them any further.

Riding slowly by the makeshift barricades—two long lines of overturned wagons, covered with sandbags and hay bales lashed down with tarps—Martin could barely repress a shudder. The design was basic, two lines from opposite sides of the road, forming an "S" in the road that a rider could walk his mount through while a galloping rider would be unable to navigate it. Some would-be military genius in this lot had decided not to block the entire road, in case someone needed to pass by. Sound logic, until one realized that the Keshians would merely pull up, start shooting arrows until the defenders fled, then quietly ride past at a slow posting trot.

The three days since encountering Brendan and the men had been somber ones. Both brothers were mourning the loss of their father and fearful for the fate of their mother. They prayed the women had reached Elvandar and were under the protection of the Elf Queen and Lord Tomas.

As they reached the heights above the city, they could see the situation. Kingdom ships were mostly absent, save for a few luggers, fishing boats, and some small ferries, all nestled against the docks or anchored close in. Out to the south some sails could be seen on the horizon, but Martin didn't know if they were Kingdom, Keshian, or Quegan.

When they arrived at the North Gate, they found it closed and barred. From above, a sentry called down, "Who are you?"

"Martin of Crydee," he shouted back, "with the Crydee Muster. Open the bloody gates!"

The gates opened a moment later, and Martin signaled for his column to ride in. When he had cleared the gate, he turned to the nearest guardsman, a boy barely in his teens, and asked, "Where's the officer in charge?"

"Of the gate? There isn't one, sir."

"Of the city, then?"

"Oh, that would be the captain. He's up at the mayor's house, having tea, or else he's up at the Baron's castle on the hill over there." He pointed in a vaguely northwesterly direction. Glancing around, the soldier lowered his voice. "It's almost certain he's at the mayor's, sir; the mayor, he's got a lovely daughter."

Martin looked as if he had found himself in a bad dream. "Just tell me how to get there."

Directions were given. Then Martin asked, "What is this captain's name?"

"Bolton, sir."

"See that the men are directed to the stables. I want the horses cared for and food for them."

"Sir?" He looked confused.

"I said I want my men and horses cared for. Is that too hard to understand?"

"No, I mean it's not, sir, but it's just that—"

"What?"

"Well, I don't know who's supposed to care for that sort of thing, the horses and men, sir."

Martin looked ready to explode. Brendan interrupted. "Where's the quartermaster?"

"There isn't one, sir," said the boy. "I mean, there is, but he's not here."

"Where is he?"

"Gone, sir, with the Duke."

"The Duke of Yabon?"

"Yes, sir. He, the Baron of Ylith, Baron of Zūn, Earl of LaMut, with the entire army of Yabon; they were all here and then they traveled on."

"Where?"

"To Krondor, sir. They've all gone to meet with the Prince in Krondor."

Suddenly all Martin's fatigue evaporated. "What's your name?"

"Tommy, sir."

"You're now Corporal Tommy."

The boy blinked in surprise.

"There's no enemy coming down that road for at least two or three days. I want you to get these boys off the wall and help my men find shelter for our mounts. If there's no garrison stable in town, find what you can, then lead the rest up to the Baron's castle. Tell whoever is up there to take care of my men. If the Baron's gone south, the barracks are empty. I want my men fed and if there's a healer left in this city, find him and send him along."

The newly minted corporal hesitated, then ran to the wall and shouted for the others to come down. The column from Crydee continued to enter through the city gates. It was clearly going to get crowded in a hurry if those entering weren't given somewhere else to go.

Corporal Tommy ran to the first boys coming down the stairs, shouted instructions, and pointed, and they came over to lead away a squad of riders.

The two sergeants moved to either side of the entering column, and quickly order was restored as more men of the city came to direct those entering.

Martin shook his head. How was he going to defend this? He looked at Brendan and Bethany and said, "Let's go find this captain." He turned without seeing if he was being followed and rode into the city. Shouting "Make way!," he forced his exhausted mount into one last run toward the building described by the boy.

Reaching it, he encountered a closed gate in the middle of a low wall, beyond which he could see a very elegant building, the mayor's home. Using the pommel of his sword he banged on a closed gate. When it opened, Martin pushed past an astonished-looking porter, who leaped aside. Brendan and Bethany followed. Martin tossed the reins of his mount to a lackey and told him, "Water him but not too much too quickly. Then if you have grain, feed him a handful, no more." He crossed the small courtyard and ran up a wide set of steps to the house.

As he had expected, there were no guards, just servants. The porter who had answered the gate ran after him shouting, "Who should I say is calling, sir?"

Martin ignored the man and pushed open the main door. A maid shrieked at seeing a man in fighting togs covered in road dirt enter unannounced. "Keshians!" she screamed and ran.

This had the desired result of calling the attention of the entire household to the fact that Martin was on the premises. From a door at the end of the hall two men appeared, one in fine clothing and the other in the uniform of Zūn, a wolf's head on a blue tabard. As they approached, the man in the uniform began to draw his sword, but before he could get it free of the scabbard, Martin stepped forward, grabbed his wrist, and forced the blade back. "Don't!" he snapped as Brendan and Bethany caught up.

"Who are you, sir?" demanded the man who could only be the mayor of the city.

"I'm in command of the muster from Crydee."

"Well, it's about bloody time you got here—" began the captain, a pinched-faced blond youth about Martin's age.

"Don't!" said Martin again, fixing him with a murderous eye.

All the remaining color drained from the face of the already pale captain.

Brendan walked over and said, "We were delayed by an army of Keshians."

"Keshians?" said the mayor, almost spluttering with confusion. "This far north?" He was a portly man given to fancy brocade shirts even in daytime and a heavy rich woolen surcoat, even though the day was hot. His grey hair was receding, so he wore it long at the back.

"Do you have a map?" asked Martin. "Of this region?"

"In the Baron's castle," said the captain.

"I have one in my study," said the mayor.

"Bring it," ordered Martin. "And some food and wine for Lady Bethany."

Seeing the young woman and hearing a noble title, the mayor turned and called, "Lily!"

A few minutes later a fair, willowy girl appeared at the door from which the two men had exited. She approached and said, "Yes, Father?"

"Could you see to this young lady. She has traveled some distance."

"From Carse," said Brendan. "She's the Earl's daughter."

"Oh!" said the mayor, suddenly respectful. "Please, then, come into the study. I'll send for some food and wine."

"Thank you," said Martin.

The study was a large office where a long table with half a dozen chairs were arrayed. "Our City Council of Burghers meets here," said the mayor. He fetched down the map and unrolled it.

To the captain Martin said, "Your name Bolton?"

"Yes," said the captain. "My uncle is the commander of the Earl of LaMut's guard. They left me in charge."

Martin glanced at Brendan, who nodded once. They both decided they didn't like this puppy.

"How long ago did the Duke of Yabon leave?" asked Martin.

"Four days ago. The infantry began marching south the day before that, while the Duke and the other nobles left by ship the following day with the cavalry. They'll put in at Sarth—sooner if they see a Keshian blockage—then ride for Krondor to come to the Prince's aid."

"Krondor is under siege?"

"Not yet," said Bolton. "But the Prince anticipates a full attack by Kesh at any moment."

Brendan rolled his eyes as Martin said, "The idiot."

The mayor was taken aback, and Captain Bolton said, "See here, now—"

"You see here, now, *Captain*," said Martin with some contempt in his voice. "Prince Edward is falling into the exact trap the Keshians want him to. They are not attacking Krondor."

"Where are they attacking?" asked the mayor.

"Here!" said Martin, stabbing the map with his finger. "Crydee has fallen and within a week, ten days at most, three thousand or more Keshian Dog Soldiers and a thousand or so cavalry, with siege engines, will clear the border of Crydee. That will put them outside your city gate in less than a month." Martin drew in the air with his finger. "They will sweep down and besiege Ylith: it doesn't matter if they take it, they just want it bottled up. The Duke and almost all the Army of Yabon is down in Krondor, and the rest of the Army of Crydee is still in Carse and Tulan. My two-hundred-odd men plus what you have here is all we have."

"We must send word to the Duke of Yabon!" cried the mayor.

"Where is the Duke of Crydee?" asked Captain Bolton.

"Dead on the road," answered Brendan. "Five days ago. Goblin raiders."

Bolton said, "Well, we must do something."

Martin shook his head. "Here's what you'll do. Send a runner, your fastest rider on the best horse you have, and get the infantry turned around. I doubt any ship can overtake the Duke before he reaches Sarth, but you'll try. If any smugglers haven't already fled town, find one, offer him as much gold as it takes to sail their fastest sloop down the coast. Those luggers and fishing boats I saw in the harbor won't do.

"Send messages north to Zūn, LaMut, and Yabon. Every man able to bear arms is to grab whatever weapon he can and march south as quickly as possible."

"Is that wise?" asked the mayor. "Shouldn't we perhaps evacuate and go north, instead?"

Martin took a breath, and a servant appeared with wine. He took a flagon without waiting and drank deeply. "No, we will defend Ylith until we are relieved. If the Keshians take this city or even surround it, Yabon and Crydee are both lost. The kingdom will never recover control of them. If the infantry can reach us in time, and we can break the siege, we will retake Crydee."

Captain Bolton said, "I don't know if this is a wise plan."

Losing his temper at last, Martin barked, "Did I ask what you thought of the plan, Captain?"

"No, I mean . . ." Then with color rising in his cheeks, the captain said, "Now, just a quick minute here. I was left in charge of the city and the rest of the duchy. Who are you to come riding in here and take charge?"

Martin glanced at Brendan, who nodded once.

"I am Martin conDoin, son to the late Duke Henry, brother to Henry, now Duke of Crydee. I am a prince of the blood royal and I am now assuming command of the defenses of whatever is left of the King's Army of the West in Yabon."

Brendan smiled at his brother and there was a sheen in his eyes.

TRANSFORMATION

C hild stood before a door.

Several times along the way they had encountered others traveling the Hall of Worlds. All but one time the encounters had been peaceful; the one exception was a band of roving slavers who had sought to subjugate Child and Belog. She killed them all and they feasted on them.

"We're here," she said softly, looking at the glyph above a door.

"Ah," said Belog. "I remember." He suddenly looked sad. "Kalkin," he whispered.

"Yes," said Child. "That bastard. He just won't stop meddling."

"Where does this one exit?"

"LaMut, in a tavern."

"I know that place. It's rough-and-tumble, but as we are we'll alarm them."

"We'll change our appearance. We know how."

Again he paused, thinking. Then he said, "Yes, now I remember." He closed his eyes and suddenly his form shifted. Where the squat, broad-shouldered demon had stood now there was a small, bandy-legged man, with a balding head surrounded by a fringe of wispy white hair. He wore a slightly tattered and faded orange robe, as well as a long faded blue cloak. He grinned. "Going to have to learn to eat like I used to. That should be a very interesting trick. I've forgotten what it's like to eat something that wasn't alive just a moment before."

She nodded. "We have many things to relearn." Then she let out a long sigh. "What was the last thing you remember?"

He didn't need to ask what she referred to. "Something wondrous. A god returning and a horror defeated. When we get something to eat, I'll tell you about it."

Just before she stepped through the doorway to Midkemia, Child's shape began to change. Her features flowed and re-formed, and she shrank until she was a third of her previous size. Now she was a human woman with dark, grey-shot hair, vivid dark eyes, high cheekbones, and a slender body wearing a blue ankle-length dress. "That made me hungry," she said. "Do you have any oranges?"

Reflexively, he reached for a satchel on his hip that wasn't there. Sadly he said, "No, I don't."

"You always used to, you annoying little man." She spoke with affection more than scolding, and her now-human features struggled to process memories she knew were not her own. She took a breath, as if steeling herself to something ahead that was going to be very difficult; then she turned and stepped through the door.

Belog had never seen that expression before; but the memories of the man he now was had seen it many times before. The woman he knew as Miranda was deeply worried.

The demon body that housed the memories of Nakor the Isalani now followed her through the portal.

Men shouted and screamed as the attackers roared. The assault was loud and unexpected and threw the smugglers' caravan into confusion. Hardened mercenaries turned in panic to confront enemies on all sides. The forest was thick, with a triple canopy of branches blocking out most of the sun, threatening to envelop them on all sides. It was late summer in the southern half of Midkemia, but this part of Novindus was already chilly at night and temperate during the day. It had been the perfect time to risk the deep forests west of the Ratn'gari Mountains.

Braden of Shamata didn't hesitate, a decade of battle-honed skills coming into play. Neither overly cautious nor impulsive, he trusted his instincts to keep him alive more than the commands from officers whose only right to give orders came from a purse of gold or a marque handed down by an official in some faraway government. He glanced to his right and saw his old companion Chibota nodding as he gripped his sword and readied himself for the attack. Others were turning to look where the screams originated, but these two practiced fighters knew better. The attack would come from the nearby brush. They flexed their knees and hoisted their shields, turning slightly outward from the line of march so as to almost be back-to-back. Each man trusted the other not to make a mistake that would get them killed.

Time seemed to slow as the attack unfolded. The rear was hit first, causing most of the men to turn to see what was behind, thus drawing their attention from the closer threat. They were on a narrow trail, barely enough room for three men to stand shoulder to shoulder, with enough deep brush under the trees to hide attackers. Those attacking the fighters were familiar with the terrain; the mercenaries were not.

As both Braden and Chibota had anticipated, the attack came from their right and left, respectively, but the form of the attackers shocked both seasoned warriors, causing hesitation that almost cost them both their lives. For the attackers were not human, but creatures unlike any either man had encountered before.

Men and tigers had been blended in a horrific fashion, giving them huge upper torsos and broad shoulders. Their powerful arms ended in outstretched claws, and their ability to leap over the men they attacked had them instantly in the midst of the melee. These tiger-men were dressed in short-sleeved tunics of black, trimmed with orange, and short trousers cut above the knees, but otherwise were unarmed. With the fangs they bared and the claws that slashed at the mercenaries, it was clear they did not need weapons.

Braden glanced at his longtime companion, who nodded once, and then they attempted to battle forward. The tiger-men's attack was without art: the stealth before the ambush had been almost perfect and there had been only seconds for the most practiced mercenary in the company to anticipate the assault. But the closing circle had gaps in it, and one of the attackers stood before the two fighters from the north. Like all big cats, these creatures could cautiously stalk prey, but once the assault began, it was all sound and fury. They fought like tigers. Unlike lions—or even packs of coyotes—tigers were solitary ambush predators, and now it was an uncoordinated brawl.

Braden shouted, "Move forward!" Chibota grunted an answer as he slashed downward with his sword against a creature trying to rake his shield with its claws. The sword dug deep into the monster's shoulder just below the neck, and as the dark-skinned warrior yanked the blade free he was rewarded with a catlike scream and a fountain of blood. He turned a half step and rammed the point of his sword into the exposed side of the creature attacking Braden, causing that tiger-man to howl in shock. Braden quickly ended its life.

Both turned as one and saw they were alone in withstanding the assault. Behind them their comrades were going down under a swarm of the creatures and even farther behind them the animal-men were on top of the baggage carts, having killed the drivers and handlers.

"Run!" shouted Braden, but as he turned back he saw that Chibota had already apprehended the situation unfolding around them and had come to the same conclusion.

Racing down the narrow trail, they came to a slight clearing out of sight of the fight, pausing for just a scant second to sheath their swords and swing their shields over their backs, then they were off again, running as fast as their feet could carry them. Over hard ground and through heavy undergrowth they lengthened their strides to a dangerous pace. The forest provided scarcely enough visibility for them to move forward at any speed. Braden had no doubt the tiger-creatures knew their way around without hesitation and would be on their trail in minutes.

Crashing through low-hanging branches, they heard the sound of their footfalls change. Braden glanced down and saw a patch of stone beneath the trail. "Hey!" he said, panting from exertion. He pointed down and Chibota nodded. This trail was crossing an ancient road of some sort. Perhaps it might lead to a defensible shelter.

"Which way?" asked Chibota, as the sounds of pursuit became audible.

Making an arbitrary choice, Braden picked the right-hand side of the road. "That way!"

Sounds from behind them announced that the chase was on, and Braden hurled himself forward, unmindful of tearing brambles and undergrowth. He knew their only chance lay in finding a good strategic position, somewhere they might defend until the tiger-men grew weary and left. In an open fight, they were doomed.

The ancient stone path led slightly uphill, then leveled off, and suddenly the two fleeing mercenaries bolted into a clearing. A stone building almost invisible until they were nearly upon it rose up suddenly before them. It was covered in ages of dirt and detritus, with plants gripping it as if fearful of losing their hold.

They had little time to examine the structure, any curiosity they might have otherwise felt obliterated by the surge of panic within as they realized this was where the ancient stone pathway ended and there was no way around. Behind the stone building rose a hillside thick with trees and brush; if there was a way up that hill, it was not obvious and the exhausted fighters had no time to scout around.

As one, they turned and backed toward the ancient building's open doorway, a black maw behind them that was inviting only relative to the terror that was coming rapidly toward them. "Into the doorway," said Braden. "That will keep them from—"

A growl of rage accompanied an orange-and-black-striped form as it hurled itself into the clearing and in one leap was upon them. Chibota lashed out with his sword. But he was a moment too late. The blade cut through air instead of his attacker, and the shield didn't keep claws away from his throat.

A crimson fountain sprayed for a moment, and Braden barely had time to lunge with his sword as the creature turned with a cat's fluidity. The point of the sword scraped across bone and hard muscle, causing enough pain that the tiger-man recoiled with an angry yowl of pain. But the lunge pulled Braden off balance, and he stood exposed for a moment with his shield held away from his body. Before Braden could recover, the tiger-man lashed out with talons that sliced right through Braden's chest armor. He wore simple jack: heavy padding covered over with quilted fabric, double stitched for reinforcement. Surprisingly durable against sword points and daggers, it was all he could afford to purchase on his meager earnings as a caravan guard. His willingness to go along with this smuggling attempt had been fueled by his hope of buying better arms and armor when they reached their destination. The pain that shot across Braden's chest as the claws sliced through his muscles made him gasp. He was slow in bringing up his shield to protect himself, and the tiger-man struck again, giving Braden a deep cut on his shield arm just below the shoulder. Instinctively Braden stepped back, deep into the doorway, feeling his left arm go completely numb. He knew he was moments away from being gutted by this creature if he couldn't somehow fend him off, and even if he did, other tiger-men would soon arrive. Braden struck out again with his sword, and the creature retreated.

His left shoulder was in agony, and he could not move his left arm at all. He felt the dangling weight of his shield, hanging useless at his side. His sword came up feebly to receive the creature's next assault.

But the tiger-man hesitated and crouched, his ears flattened back against his skull as his face contorted into a snarl and then a hiss as if his rage had turned to fear. Braden could feel blood running beneath his armor and knew that he had two wounds to stanch if he was to live through the next hour. He crouched, breathing slowly to keep from fainting.

But the creature didn't attack. Snarling, it kept its yellow cat eyes fixed on Braden, but it would not cross the threshold. Suddenly two other tiger-men appeared bounding into the clearing, but like the first, they paused at the threshold of the stone building and withdrew a step.

Braden had no idea why they refused to come into this darkened hall, but he counted it a gift from the gods. He backed deeper into the tunnel, which he realized now was heading downward, into the heart of this hillside.

The three tiger-men paced outside the entrance, yowling and snarling. Braden backed slowly until he was sure they would not follow, then turned and moved into darkness. The light from the entrance fell away quickly and he had to feel his way along. He put away his sword, as his left arm was useless and he needed his right to keep himself steady. It was agony to get the shield off his left arm: unfastening the straps so that he could slip it off caused shocks of pain to course through his shoulder. He had dislocated joints before in combat, but this was something different. He knew he needed to find a place to rest and bind his wounds soon, or he would find himself in the Halls of the Death Goddess within hours.

The stones beneath his hand were smooth to the touch. He took a step and felt something crack under his boot. He knelt in the gloom and saw a pile of ancient torches. Praying that whatever oil in them would still light, he fumbled in his belt pouch for his flint. He moved one torch to his feet, put down the flint, pulled a dagger from his belt, and positioned it between his boots. It was awkward striking flint and steel this way, but he had no other option. Sparks flew about haphazardly, but one large one struck the torch and it began to smolder. Ignoring the agony in his shoulder and chest, Braden leaned forward and blew on the ember. It grew red-hot, then sprang into flame. He quickly picked up the torch and turned it, spreading the flames across the entire head, and then looked around. The torches at his feet were the only thing he could see within the circle of light his small flame cast. He raised the torch high and saw he was near a wall that stretched off into the gloom. He could barely make out the opposite wall. The tunnel was wide here and slanting downward. With only one hand he had no means of holding spare torches, so he prayed silently to Tith-Onanka, the God of War, that this light would last long enough for him to survive.

He moved down the hall.

Braden eventually staggered into a larger chamber. He could feel the weight of ages washing over him as if a tide of history had been unleashed. This room was so immense the illumination from his torch left corners darkened. What he saw moved him nearly to tears.

Deep within the heart of this hill, far below the surface, some ancient ruler had hidden his treasure. In piles rested items of beauty and precious craftsmanship, goblets studded with gems, chains of ebon and gold, piles of fine silks now fragile with age. One handful of fine gold chains piled near the entrance would have made Braden richer than any man he knew. Dryly he considered that he would die wealthy.

His arm was still numb, and his shoulder was in agony. He knew he was nearly giddy from loss of blood, and this was as good a place to stop as he had found. Finding a place to put his now-sputtering torch—a vase of costly chalcedony-set porcelain—he began to tend his wounds.

As best he could, he used his good right hand to unfasten the simple frog and loops along his shoulder and when he pulled the padded jack away from his skin, the dried blood stuck and pulled at his wounds. Pain shot through him and revived him a moment, and he forced his damaged arm out of the left sleeve.

Picking up a narrow bolt of silk, he pulled it, causing it to unravel in a torrent of pale blue. Cutting the silk with one hand was tedious, requiring him to put his left knee on a wooden chest, trying to pull the silk taut with his right foot, then cutting with his dagger. The strips were ragged and uneven, but they'd serve.

He bound his wounds as best he could and considered his next task; he had no idea how patient the tiger-men would be, but he doubted they'd give up their vigil outside the entrance any time soon. But then again, he didn't think they'd come in. The sputtering torch regained his attention, and he slowly reached out to retrieve it. Even the simple act of bending over to pluck it from the vase caused his head to swim.

How was he going to survive in here? He needed water, and something to eat. He was a townsboy: he knew nothing about foraging the way Chibota had. Chibota had been a hunter in some distant hot land, and he knew which plants were edible. Braden remembered Chibota saying some mushrooms were as nourishing as meat. But he had no idea what they looked like or how to find them.

His mind was wandering. There was no water, and no mushroom here. This vault was dry.

But in the flickering light he saw a throne against the rear wall, and arrayed at the base of the throne was armor.

He staggered over and touched it and felt something tingle on the tips of his fingers. He blinked and felt slightly revived. The armor was of a quality unlike any he had ever seen before, and he had thought he had seen every kind of armor known in this world; and if he considered some of the ancient Tsurani gear still around, from another world as well. A tunic, trousers, tabard, and even smallclothes were neatly folded in a pile. Next to these was arrayed a full set of matching armor: breastplate, spaulders, leggings, gauntlets, boots, belt, shield, and sword. Touching the massive black belt, he again felt a strong surge of energy up through his fingertips.

Without thought he set down the torch and doffed his clothing: first his boots, then his trousers, and the rest, until he stood nude in the guttering torchlight.

Carefully he picked up a garment of black. It felt like linen but finer somehow: silk, perhaps? He stepped into it for it was obviously smallclothes, and its touch on his skin was balm. He sighed as his thirst faded. For a moment he stood transfixed, his thoughts reeling as if he had visited one of the smoke parlors behind the brothel of the Sisters of Kindness in Maharta. The effect was intoxicating, and he felt his mind detach itself from his pain, a fey distancing as if he was starting to watch another person instead of himself. His body was still in agony, but the pain was muted now, distanced; and from his groin, where the black cloth touched him, he felt a flow of power into his body.

Workmanlike, he donned each piece of clothing and then the armor. A black breastplate with a crouching tiger on it. A girdle and skirt of black cloth. A pair of greaves, boots, bracers, and at last a helm.

He staggered, then sat down heavily on the throne.

He felt a change begin. His life was ebbing away, yet he was not fearful. Braden felt the armor speak to him, a faint voice in his mind.

He would sit here, quietly, and let the magic in this armor heal him, for he knew it would. As the torch burned lower, he found his vision dimming, but that was fine. He knew he would be here for a while, for much needed to change before he left the safety of this chamber.

He needed to be ready, for there were enemies to face. Not the tiger-men, for he knew instantly that when he reappeared they would be waiting and would bend their knee to him. He would command them and they would be only the first to serve him.

Images came to him unbidden, of ancient struggles and flying the skies. Out there was a massive black dragon waiting for his call. And into his mind came a name.

Draken-Korin.